P9-CEC-143

THE ARRIVAL

GENE RODDENBERRY'S EARTH: FINAL CONFLICT
Books from Tor Books

The Arrival
by Fred Saberhagen

The First Protector
by James White
(forthcoming)

Requiem for Boone
by Debra Doyle and James D. Macdonald
(forthcoming)

Visit the *Earth: Final Conflict* Web site at
www.efc.com

GENE RODDENBERRY'S

EARTH
FINAL CONFLICT™

THE ARRIVAL

FRED SABERHAGEN

TOR®

A TOM DOHERTY ASSOCIATES BOOK
NEW YORK

This is a work of fiction. All the characters and events portrayed in this novel are either fictitious or are used fictitiously.

GENE RODDENBERRY'S EARTH: FINAL CONFLICT—THE ARRIVAL

©1999 Tribune Entertainment Company and Alliance Atlantis Communications Inc.

"GENE RODDENBERRY'S EARTH: FINAL CONFLICT" and all associated names, likenesses and designs are trademarks of Norway Corporation. All rights reserved.

"ALLIANCE ATLANTIS" with the stylized "A" design is a registered trademark of Alliance Atlantis Communications Inc. All rights reserved.

"TRIBUNE ENTERTAINMENT" is a registered trademark of Tribune Entertainment Company. All rights reserved.

All rights reserved, including the right to reproduce this book, or portions thereof, in any form.

This book is printed on acid-free paper.

Edited by James Frenkel.

A Tor Book
Published by Tom Doherty Associates, LLC
175 Fifth Avenue
New York, NY 10010

www.tor.com

Tor® is a registered trademark of Tom Doherty Associates, LLC.

Design by Lisa Pifher

ISBN 0-312-87302-6

First Edition: December 1999

Printed in the United States of America

0 9 8 7 6 5 4 3 2 1

For Joan

THE ARRIVAL

ONE

Midnight had come, and the day that was now beginning would be unlike any that the human race had ever known, in the many thousands of years of its existence. A great invisible boundary was being crossed between the old world and the new. Jonathan Doors met the tremendous transformation standing on the flagstoned rear patio of his mansion in the hills of central California, with his wife beside him reclining in her wheelchair. For the past hour their two sets of eyes had been searching the starry sky for some sign of the eagerly awaited new arrivals, the unknown and mysterious entities who called themselves Taelon, or the Companions.

For nearly a year now, Taelon messages had filled the media around the world, but their senders were still virtually unknown to the native inhabitants of planet Earth.

When first received, those incoming radio and television signals, the soft voices speaking in flawless English and half a dozen of the most widely spoken other earthly tongues, had been almost universally assumed to be some kind of elaborate prank. But not for long. In a matter of days, scientific observers, using Earth's finest radio telescopes, had proven with mathematical certainty that the sources of those signals were in the outer reaches of the solar system. They were out there on the fringe of truly interstellar space, but they were moving very swiftly in the direction of the inner, minor planets, at diminishing velocities calculated to match the speed and location of the moving Earth. And that correspondence was calculated to take place on the very day that the soft voices themselves predicted their arrival.

And the messages promised many wondrous things.

Their authors proclaimed that they were coming across the immense gulfs of space in peace and brotherhood, and that they intended from now on to be Companions to the people of Earth.

They asked no permission for their planned landings. They ignored the warnings and threats beamed out to them by the militant leaders of some smaller nations. They simply spelled out the symbolic pattern in which they intended to alight upon our world. The first Companion ships were to touch down just west of the International Date Line, and just past the hour of local midnight. From there the pattern would march on west around the Earth, so that the new day and the Taelon presence would arrive together in every city and every nation.

As Doors and his wife intently scanned the skies, looking for the first sign of a Companion presence in California, television and radio reported that Vladivostok and Tokyo were already engaged in a mild verbal feud as to which of them had been first to welcome the newcomers.

It seemed there were going to be between fifty and a hundred landings altogether. Australia and Asia, Africa and Europe, had entirely entered the new world, and the front of transformation had now swept completely across the Americas, except for Alaska. Now, at midnight in California, the great event was about three-fourths accomplished.

Doors, a stocky, powerfully built man in his mid-fifties, stood leaning his thick, well-kept hands on the stone balustrade of his enormous house. He was conservatively, casually dressed, in a turtleneck pullover and dark slacks. His beloved wife Amanda, her brown hair neatly styled, was almost fully reclined in her motorized wheelchair, wearing warm slippers and a quilted dressing gown against the coolness of the night. She was dying slowly, of cystic fibrosis, and at the moment a nasal tube was feeding bottled oxygen into her ravaged lungs. Most people would have thought her a few years older than her husband, though in fact he was ten years her senior.

Here at the dawn of the Third Millennium, earthly medicine could do very little for her beyond making her somewhat more comfortable.

Beginning with their very first messages, the Taelons had been promising that the wonderful gifts they were bringing Earth included very powerful help in humanity's endless war against disease and death. Doors, like everyone else on earth with a loved one blind, or crippled, or visibly in danger of death, had known a sudden fierce pang of new hope.

A chill breeze, born over the Pacific miles away, wandered over the patio, and Doors reached to pull up a blanket around Amanda's shoulders. Her eyes opened in her pain-worn face.

Doors said to her gently, "I thought you'd fallen asleep on me, lover."

"Who can sleep at a time like this?" Once Amanda had been widely considered a great beauty; now perhaps there was only one man left on earth who would have judged her so. She showed her husband a wan ghost of a smile.

"Want a pill?" he asked, concern showing in his voice.

"No, not yet. Not just now. I want to keep my mind clear for a little longer."

"I understand. Let me know when you're ready."

Light from the bright interior of the house shone out through the open French doors, onto the flagstone pavement of the dark patio. A babble of excited voices spilled out too. A small crew of Doors's most trusted aides, his close business assistants and associates, were in there, keeping watch on the elaborate communications gear that never slept, connecting the far-flung components of his multibillion dollar empire. A few minutes ago, Doors himself had suddenly felt tired of looking at familiar screens and the new holographic presentations, and had stepped out of doors to take a look at the universe for himself.

Now the dark silhouette of a young man, one of his employees, appeared in the lighted doorway. "We should start seeing landings in our longitude any time now, chief," the man said.

"Thanks." Except to glance now and then at his wife, Doors could hardly tear his eyes from the clear sky. A great fever of excitement had been gradually growing in him for weeks, and over the past few hours the fever had risen toward climactic intensity.

As if by reflex, Doors unhooked his personal communicator from his belt and checked its tiny screen. Now, for half a day and half a night, the news reports from around the world had concentrated entirely on a story unprecedented in human history. They were chronicling an event that could never be repeated, even if the human race endured for another million years.

As the Companions' ships approached the inner reaches of the solar system—such radar measurements as could be taken put them all now within the Moon's orbit—the dominant mood of humanity in most of the nations of the earth had been one of celebration, though some people and a few governments were preparing as for a hostile invasion. Scientists observing the ships' progress from the destination world could only speculate as to what kind of propulsion could produce the kind of flight that they were watching.

In the Middle East, still ravaged, still literally smoking in places from the latest war, one or two ground-to-air missiles had been launched, with no discernible effect on the darting, blue-white ships that served as the vehicles of the Arrival. If any manned interceptor aircraft had left their runways, no one was talking about it in open communications. Nowhere, so far, were there any reports of armed conflict, once the Taelons and humans had actually come face to face. Once on the ground, the peaceful visitors were everywhere being greeted peacefully, most often actively welcomed, if usually not without some suspicion.

Doors had his own cynical doubts about the public picture thus presented. Surely, among Earth's uncountable madmen, at least a good handful must already have launched themselves, or ordered their fanatical supporters, in one violent effort or another at this target more tempting than any president or monarch could ever be. But any such attempts that might have been made so far had evidently been suppressed by other humans, with quiet and possibly ruthless efficiency.

"Is it going to work, Johnny?" Amanda asked. She made a feeble attempt to take her husband's hand.

He reached out and squeezed hers as firmly as he dared. After thirty years, he had no need to ask what she meant. "It damn well better work. One or two more wars like the last one, and . . ." He let the sentence trail off. The latest computer simulations indicated that nuclear winter, the fatal blocking of sunlight by explosion-raised dust clouds, would not be as hard to achieve as had been thought.

"Yes, it had better," Amanda added softly. "For Joshua. And for those grandkids you and I look forward to being able to spoil some day."

Doors nodded his agreement. Months ago, he had gone public with his personal opinion regarding the Companions, had expressed his own cautious optimism about the whole tremendous happening. He dared to hope it possible that at least some of the glorious Taelon promises to humanity might be fulfilled in real accomplishment.

"Is there a risk in taking these aliens' promises at face value?" he had asked rhetorically, in a famous interview only a few days ago. "Sure, there's a risk. But there's a damn sight greater risk in turning this into a hostile confrontation. We're already pretty good at making war, and what we need to learn above all is how to make peace. Our new millennium has become a new era of nuclear war. Humanity on this planet may not be given many more chances to survive."

Meanwhile, Jonathan Doors had no shortage of practical matters to occupy his attention. In effect, a new world was being born, and every facet of his worldwide enterprises was going to have to be rethought. The room just indoors from the patio was filled with communications gear that allowed the owner to keep in touch with governments, workers, and customers everywhere around the planet.

Listening now to the bursts of excited babble from inside, he gathered that his helpers had established some kind of betting pool among themselves as to how close the nearest Taelon landing would be to this house.

"Johnny." Amanda's voice was low and stressed. "Maybe you should get me a pill."

"Sure, lover." He quickly located the little box. Extracting a single tablet, he brought it to his wife with a glass of fruit juice. It was a medicine that eased the working of the lungs, but it could not be repeated often, and the effects were temporary.

"There's got to be one in ell-ay," said a voice of one of the workers inside the house, in the tone of someone recapitulating a series of accepted facts.

"San Francisco, for sure," a coworker replied, in the same mode.

Then the first voice again, in a sudden query, in a tone that had abruptly turned to current business. "What's coming in now, Bess?"

Bess was the radar operator currently on duty at the nearby small private landing strip, owned and operated by Doors International, and her latest communication to the boss was an eye-opener. Suddenly her voice was on the speakerphone, and she was saying: "Chief, it looks like there's gonna be one a whole hell of a lot closer than ell-ay."

Doors turned, moved toward the lighted doorway. "What do you mean? Where?"

Bess's answer filled the space around him. "I think your house is sitting just about on ground zero."

Doors turned away from the light and automatically looked up. By luck he was just in time to see it coming, a darting, blue-white presence in the sky, an insectoid shape, openly, gaudily bright with its own interior lights. To Doors it seemed to be saying: *Here I am, Earth-folk. Take a shot at me if you choose, if you want to waste your energy that way.* The Taelons, it seemed, had nothing to hide, and no need to be afraid of anything the warlike folk of the third planet from the Sun might try to do to them.

Not knowing the size of the visiting spacecraft made it hard to be sure, but as nearly as Doors could judge the ship was coming down within a hundred yards of his house, just below the orchard whose leafy treetops formed an irregular surface at eye level when he looked out from his patio. The approach was swift, smooth, and startlingly, almost frighteningly silent.

Bending beside the wheelchair, he murmured, "Mandy, I think we've got visitors."

"Oh, Johnny. We may get to see them, talk to them."

To be thus singled out for alien attention was of course surprising. But Jonathan Doors was not utterly astonished; in the back of his mind he had been half-expecting something of the kind. He was, after all, one of the most influential people on the planet, and it was not to be wondered at that the newcomers, well-educated in our ways, should choose to approach him soon after their arrival.

The trees in the small orchard below the broad stone patio displayed spring blossoms. Doors was already moving, going down to meet the visitors to his property halfway.

Amanda called something after him just as he was leaving the patio, but in his single-minded haste he had not tried to understand her, or respond.

Moving quickly and decisively as usual, he descended so

rapidly to ground level that none of his employees were able to catch up in time to accompany him; and so he was alone under the flowering trees of his small apple orchard when he came face to face with two visitors from beyond the stars.

How beautiful, was his first thought, when he got his first good look at the two bipedal beings who came walking gracefully toward him. Not far behind them their ship sat, looming, glowing. They themselves were not that much different from human beings, but he knew with his first glimpse of the visitors that he would never mistake one species for the other. And that first thought was followed quickly by another: *How appropriate, this time and place for this meeting.*

The two were considerably taller than Doors, both, he judged, well over six feet. Doors thought the Taelons were a good match for the pictures of themselves they had been transmitting for almost a year now. Their heads, uncovered and practically hairless, looked slightly larger than any human heads he could remember seeing. What he was able to observe of their skin was pale in the uncertain light, their faces handsome. Their limbs, inside close-fitting blue costumes, were willowy without appearing weak, and the way they carried themselves suggested models, or monarchs. One of them seemed to be wearing a kind of backpack, while the other was unburdened by any baggage or equipment.

In an open space between rows of trees, facing the star travelers from fifteen feet away, the human stopped.

He said, "I am Jonathan Doors, and I bid you welcome to our world." As he spoke, he extended both arms in an open gesture. This tentative offer of an embrace, or a handshake, was graciously declined.

The Taelons stopped where they were. One spoke, introducing first himself and then his companion. His voice was almost seductive, of great unthreatening tenderness. He gave his name as Va'lon, and introduced his companion, who was wearing the backpack, as Namor. As some of the recent radio messages had suggested, single names were apparently the rule, at least when visiting alien worlds.

"We are grateful, Mr. Doors, for your hospitable reaction to our intrusion," Va'lon said. "Most of our landings have not been on private property, but in your case there were important reasons why we did not choose to wait through all the intricacies of diplomacy."

Moving back a step, Doors gestured with a wide sweep of one arm. "Come into my house." When they were walking, the three of them more or less together, he added, "I suppose your 'important reasons' have something to do with economics? In my experience, most important reasons do."

"Something, indeed, Mr. Doors. There will be many matters of trade to be discussed. But that is not the over-riding reason for our presence here at your house tonight."

As Doors and his visitors approached the house, two or three of his employees were hurrying to meet them, down the stairs that led from patio to orchard. The humans began a babble of questions as soon as they caught sight of their chief, but instantly fell into awed silence when their eyes fell on the two who walked just behind him.

No sooner had the two Companions walked onto the patio than they discovered Amanda in her chair, and immediately approached her. Everyone else was temporarily ignored. Before anyone had time to make a speech—not that anyone seemed eager to do so—Va'lon and Namor were bowing graciously over the lady of the house and introducing themselves. Almost in the same breath, or so it seemed, they began to press her with solicitous questions about the reason for her being incapacitated, and her prospects for recovery.

"You must not suppose that our curiosity is idle," Va'lon hastily assured her when she seemed bewildered. Moments later, when Amanda only closed her eyes and nodded faintly, the Companion turned to her husband. "No, Jonathan—may I call you Jonathan—?"

"You may."

"—I believe it quite possible that your wife's health can be fully restored."

Doors, feeling suddenly light-headed, looked around for some patio furniture, spotted the nearest chair, went to it and sat down. For just a moment, the great events affecting the whole population of the earth would have to wait.

"Do I understand you correctly?" he got out at last. Looking halfway across the flagstoned space, he met Amanda's dark eyes with his own. "You think she can be cured?"

Namor's head moved immediately in a small, tilting nod, obviously a sign of agreement. It would seem he had been practicing earthly gestures as well as speech.

The Companion said, "Of course I will be able to speak with greater authority when I have conducted a thorough examination. The case appears somewhat difficult at first sight, but I think we may safely promise that at least a great improvement in her condition is attainable."

"If you could do that . . ." Doors got to his feet again.

"We can do many things that you will find surprising," Va'lon assured him.

One of Amanda's regular nurses had come out onto the patio, and more introductions were in order.

At that point Amanda said that she was feeling tired, and wanted to be taken inside. While that was being managed, Va'lon managed to steer his host away from the French doors and to one side of the darkened patio, where for the moment the two of them were quite alone. But there the Taelon seemed content for the moment to gaze at the stars, leaving it up to the human to decide what to do with this first real chance for private conversation.

Jonathan cleared his throat. "So, Namor is a physician. It seems that may be very fortunate for Amanda and me."

"Yes." Again the gesture of agreement.

"And you?" Doors asked. The Taelon had not been shy about asking blunt questions, so he thought he too might as well be direct. "A space pilot, perhaps?"

Va'lon turned to him with the same gentle smile. "No, my real profession—to use the nearest term for it that I can find in your language—is something else entirely."

He paused for a moment, as if considering the best way to approach his subject. "It is generally considered, among our people, that one of the surest indicators of an advanced civilization is its willingness, even eagerness, to seek out intellectual engagement with other—perhaps, though not necessarily—lesser cultures. By such engagement I mean not only direct contact, but an involvement through collection, preservation, study."

Jonathan took a moment to think that over. "Ah, I see. Or I think perhaps I do. You mean you are something like a museum curator?"

"That is very close to what I have in mind." And once more Va'lon performed the modest, almost self-effacing bow.

Doors wasn't sure what he would have predicted as an opening topic of conversation, had someone asked him yesterday, but it would not have been this. But then, he supposed there was no reason to expect minds from beyond the stars to be predictable.

"Well, if museums are your chief interest," he said at last, "you've come to the right planet. Here on earth, as your thorough preliminary studies have doubtless informed you, we have a great many such institutions, and some of them are very good. One variety specializes in what we call natural history. Others are devoted to anthropology, or to specific kinds of technology. . . ."

"I understand." The Taelon was giving him keen attention.

". . . while many more, I suppose a majority, concentrate on art, in one form or another."

Va'lon moved closer by half a step, and his face, his whole being, seemed to open up. "I have been on your world only a few minutes," he said, evidently well pleased. "And we have come already to a subject that I find truly fascinating."

"I'm very glad to hear it—though I must say I am a little surprised at the turn the conversation has taken."

The Taelon did not seem interested in his surprise. "I understand that you, Jonathan Doors, are the owner of one of the finest, the most catholic—you will understand that I use the word in the sense of 'universal'—collections of art, of antiques, of historical memorabilia of all kinds, on the entire planet."

Doors frowned at his guest. "I don't know who told you that. I'm no collector, never have been . . . but wait. Oh hell. Yes, of course I am now, in a sense. I've hardly even laid eyes on much of the stuff yet, but it's been legally mine for the last couple of months. You're talking about San Simeon, of course."

Va'lon gravely signed assent. His attention was now riveted on Doors even more closely than before.

TWO

Half an hour later, Doors and Va'lon were sitting indoors, at a small table on a kind of covered porch just off the room that had been dedicated to computers and communications. Somewhat to Doors's mystification, San Simeon was still the prime subject of discussion. As often as the human attempted diplomatically to turn the talk to some (as it seemed to him) more interesting subject, such as space travel, cosmology, or the prospects for the conquest of disease, his new Companion neatly turned it back again.

Meanwhile Amanda had retired to her own sitting room down the hall, accompanied by some of the people who handled her day-to-day care. She must be, her husband thought, pretty well worn out by a long day. Despite her tiredness she had given in to Namor's eager willingness to begin a thorough physical examination at once. That project was now getting under way, with the help and under the observation of the two human nurses and one physician who happened to be on hand.

When Doors turned his head to look in the opposite direction from Amanda's room, he could see that the French doors to the patio had been closed. The visitors from space had assured their host that there would be no more spacecraft arriving tonight in the skies of California. On that subject he had to assume that they knew what they were talking about.

Jonathan had of course offered his visitors refreshment, but they had graciously declined. He certainly wasn't going to press them, thinking, God knows what their ordinary food might be.

He himself, feeling excited but by no means too excited to eat, was enjoying a ham sandwich and a bottle of beer.

So far, only a few snippets of information had come out of the room in which Amanda was undergoing her latest medical exam. These were items repeated by a nurse, who had heard the Taelon physician utter them, and they were all cautiously favorable. Optimistic enough so that Jonathan Doors knew a steadily growing elation. This emotion he tried, with all the grim experience of late middle age, to keep under tight control.

If he was going to keep his mind from dwelling uselessly, prematurely, on his wife's prospects for a near-miraculous cure, he had to think actively of something else. And this effort to refocus his attention was enormously helped by the fact, incredible yet undeniable, that a true interstellar alien was at this moment sitting only an arm's length from him. Jonathan Doors had been granted the opportunity of a lifetime to engage in a preliminary exploration of a mind, a keen intelligence, that had to be vastly different from his own.

So far, from the intellectual point of view there seemed to be only one flaw, and that perhaps a minor one, in this situation: it *was* something of a disappointment that Va'lon kept relentlessly turning the talk back to the subject of the San Simeon estate. More particularly the Companion seemed interested in the mind-boggling trove of treasure, arts and antiques in every form, accumulated on those grounds by William Randolph Hearst, the famous newspaper publisher who had now been dead for something like half a century.

Doors decided that since he seemed doomed to spend his first hour of conversation with an extraterrestrial on the subject of the late Mr. Hearst and his treasures, he might as well make sure the Taelon had his facts straight.

"Within the last few years," Jonathan began, "the state of California, finding itself in some financial trouble, went on a big privatization kick. They started selling off buildings, lands, and monuments left and right. It seemed likely that the Hearst estate, which had been a state monument for years, would be sold off, including over a hundred acres surrounding the buildings. The real-estate developers were ready to move in. Now I see nothing intrinsically wrong with developing real estate. But—it just seemed to me a very special place. Some people call it the enchanted hill. Besides, I thought I owed the people of California something. My business here has been very successful."

Va'lon, who had an incredible air of seeming perfectly at ease in what to him must be utterly alien surroundings, had made a graceful tent out of his long fingers.

"And your expression of gratitude was indeed vigorous," he observed. "The purchase price, I understand, was something more than two billion dollars."

"That's about right," said Jonathan. And added simply. "I could afford it."

"But the estate had never been owned by any member of your family before."

"No-o!" Doors emphatically shook his head. "My folks have been well-to-do, as the saying is, for the last few generations. But they were never in that league, financially."

"Indeed, Jonathan," the exotic visitor pressed on, "I can scarcely restrain my eagerness to examine the collection there. I trust it is being well cared for."

"I think I have the right people there to do a pretty good job of caretaking—if I ever grow lax about that, and I won't, the insurance companies would keep me in line."

"And your ultimate plans for the estate—?"

"That's still to be decided, except that I want to preserve it pretty much as it is, for people to visit and enjoy. It's closed to the public right now, but I'll be glad to give you a tour anytime."

"Possibly this very morning?" And the Companion shifted in his chair, gracefully conveying the idea of impatience. It was as if he had rushed halfway across the Galaxy, or for some comparable distance, with no more urgent or profound goal in mind than visiting San Simeon.

Jonathan blinked at him, and took a moment to remind himself yet again that when visitors dropped in from beyond the stars, there was really no reason to expect them to come equipped with a familiar and predictable psychology. Still, he thought he himself had a well-developed sense of when people, including extraterrestrials, were serious and when they were not. And Va'lon was as serious about this as anyone could be, without giving the impression of fanaticism that crossed over into mental illness.

"We could go right now, if you're that eager," Doors offered. "Be there in maybe half an hour. There's a landing strip near the house at San Simeon, and my plane's available here. Of course I'd really enjoy a joyride in that ship of yours."

"I would prefer not to use either the aircraft or the spaceship." Va'lon's reply came without hesitation, smoothly but firmly. "Surely it cannot be a very long journey from here by surface vehicle?"

Doors tilted his head back and stared at the ceiling, considering. "About three hours on the highway. Maybe less. Traffic will be light now in the middle of the night—even *this* night, by God, I'll bet. Everyone will be home watching on television as your people arrive."

But of course everyone would not, really, be doing that. Jonathan Doors was thoroughly aware of how tenaciously the world went on its way, big changes usually coming only with glacial slowness. Millions would have slept through midnight's transformation, either because they misunderstood, or they simply did not care whether interstellar visitors dropped in or not, or perhaps just because they were tired. Billions around the world had been and would be getting up and going to their jobs as usual, not fully understanding that the world they labored in today was not at all the same as yesterday's. That whatever happened from now on, the world would never be the same again.

"Are you personally willing to make the journey with me?" Somehow the Companion's manner suggested that he was issuing an invitation to a momentous adventure.

Doors got to his feet. "If that's really how you want to spend your first morning on the earth, yes, I am. Let's go." There flashed through his mind the idea of possibly calling the governor, getting an escort. But no, no, that would mean hours of delay, and the drive would be made in the company of a thousand swarming media people. He and his new house guests would have to face that all too soon in any case.

But of course, no matter how much wealth and power a man might have, or maybe just because he had so much, few things could ever be accomplished quite as quickly and simply as he would like them to be. Right now there was, as usual, a lot of Doors International business to be taken care of around the world, and the midnight shift in California was a bit short-handed. Doors called together the helpers he had on hand, gave a few people some final instructions, and considered that things were pretty well under control.

When business was taken care of, for the moment, the last thing Jonathan Doors did before leaving—and he had saved it for the last deliberately—was to go into Amanda's sitting room, to let her know what he was doing.

"How's she doing, Dr. Kimura?" he inquired.

"I want her to get some rest." The human physician, a generation younger than her patient, was, like everyone else in the room, staring helplessly at the two Companions. "But it can wait until . . ." The words trailed off.

Amanda, still clothed in robe and slippers, reclined now in a comfortable armchair, looking sleepy, but no sleepier than an invalid on supplemental oxygen ought to look when kept awake until well after midnight. Namor made no objection to her husband's sudden entrance, so Doors brusquely inter-rupted the proceedings to kiss his wife goodbye, and murmur something reassuring.

The room was fully lighted, and there was an atmosphere

of calm. The human doctor and nurses were looking on in utter absorption, now and then asking a question phrased in medical jargon, to which the Taelon physician replied calmly. Doors noted that several items of exotic hardware, evidently drawn from an extensive medical kit that Namor had been packing on his back, had now been deployed around the patient. Tubes of various colors looped around her limbs, and her head wore something like a small skullcap, so some phase of the medical exam was evidently still in progress—each piece of extraterrestrial medical gear, on any ordinary day, would have drawn Doors's attention for a good chunk of time.

Namor pleasantly assured Doors that all was going well so far, and said he would soon be preparing his preliminary report on Amanda's case.

"I'll drive myself," Doors informed Va'lon briskly, a minute later, as the two of them headed downstairs through the big house to the garage. He was thinking that the whole place was a little short-handed tonight, and anyway he liked the idea of having the alien all to himself for a time—talk about exclusive interviews. Beside him, Va'lon easily kept pace, sometimes taking two stairs at a time with his long, unhurried, graceful stride.

His stride . . . or *hers?* Doors, who had been taking a certain matter for granted until now, was suddenly uncertain.

"Sitting and watching is all right," he went on. "And sometimes it's the only thing to do. And talk is good. A talk like the one we've just had is very good. But then the time comes when it's necessary to *do* something." He studied his recently acquired Companion with frank curiosity. "I suppose you know what I mean?"

"Our philosophical tradition regarding the need for action and its consequences is an ancient one, and rather complex." Va'lon accompanied the words with a self-deprecating smile, as if to say: *I know this is not the direct answer, either confirmation or argument, that you were looking for. But it is perhaps too soon to give you that.*

Lights came on automatically in the garage under the house as soon as they passed through the door, striding into a domain of white paint and smooth, gray concrete. Yellow lines defined a dozen parking spaces, of which only two were occupied at the moment.

Doors hesitated only momentarily, then chose the available SUV over the Jaguar. He wasn't sure just how much headroom his tall guest was going to need for comfort, and anyway he himself when driving preferred to look out over the world from a slightly higher platform than that provided by any regular sedan. In a matter of seconds Va'lon was installed in the front passenger seat, where Doors saw to it that his seatbelt was properly fastened. This vehicle provided ample room for the passenger's high cranium. A few seconds more, and Doors had the engine started and was backing out of the parking space, taking just a moment as he did so to scan the diagnostics on the instrument panel. The fuel tank was almost full, and all systems were in the green.

The big garage door rolled itself up at the vehicle's approach, and closed swiftly again behind it as they went roaring up the ramp outside. The gravel driveway curved away from the big house, quickly leaving behind all the lighted windows. Doors got a passing look at the alien shuttle—if that was the right word for the conveyance in which the visitors had arrived—still sitting where it had landed, not on but near the landing strip. Its shape put Doors in mind of some monstrous predatory insect. The strange form, still faintly glowing blue and white as it had in flight, was partially obscured by the trunks of his orchard's trees. Under these conditions it was hard to judge the shuttle's size.

Now a tall gate, formed of thick steel bars in ornamental curves, opened on its electronic cue to allow the SUV to pass out of the private drive. And a minute after that they were cruising on the highway. Jonathan's prediction about traffic was proven correct; at the moment there were no other headlights or tail-lights to be seen in the California night.

"So," said Doors, after half a minute of peaceful silence in the snug cabin of the SUV. "What's it like out there among the stars?"

"It is very beautiful, and sometimes it is very dangerous. But you need not ask me that, Jonathan. Your world here is as much 'among the stars' as any other."

"I suppose it is," said Doors after a thoughtful pause. "But now I'd like to hear about your world, Va'lon. Tell me about it, if you will. I want to hear everything that you can say to me about your people, and what they do there."

And Doors glanced sideways to study the enigmatic Companion countenance beside him, washed in the faint glow of the instrument panel, and the reflected white of the SUV's own headlights coming in through the windshield.

"I am truly sorry, Jonathan." And indeed the pale alien face now turned his way did look unhappy. "But that I may not do as yet. There are vitally important reasons for my reticence, that you will come to understand in time. For now, I must ask you to accept what I *can* give you, as a token of our good will."

Doors shook his head, his vision once more concentrated on the narrow, winding highway. "More than a token, believe me. If you can give me what you suggested back there—if you can restore Amanda to health—that will mean more to me than I can express. You will never have to give me anything else."

"I am glad that we can be of some assistance to your wife. Perhaps there will come a time when you can—I believe the phrase is 'return the favor'?"

"That is the phrase, yes."

Time passed while thick tires hummed swiftly on the smooth, two-lane pavement. The clock on the panel said it was a little after two in the morning, Pacific Time. That meant dawn was still hours away. The sky, where it was not bleached by headlight glare, or by the glow of distant cities, was still black as midnight and jeweled with twinkling stars. Doors had to assume that the incredible wave of Arrival was rolling on westward, past Alaska and Hawaii and Samoa. And that when—it would be very soon now—the wave came full circle, back to the Date Line where it had started, there would be Taelons scattered over the entire surface of the Earth.

Now that he was once more moving toward the destination he so yearned to see, Va'lon seemed quite relaxed, willing to be peacefully silent. How many of their ships had come down altogether, and how many of their people? Somewhere Doors had heard that there were supposed to be seventy-one Companions landing. Had he been alone in the vehicle he would certainly be, for once, listening to the radio, trying to absorb any real news that filtered through.

Now they had reached the place where the highway began a thorough imitation of a roller-coaster, up and down, up and down, with now and then a sharp turn left or right. This was cattle country and wine country mixed together, mostly pastures and vineyards, with scattered dwellings, mostly belonging to prosperous landowners, some of them showing lights despite the lateness of the hour. Here and there the SUV's headlights illuminated the fringe of some neat hillside cultivation of vines.

"Well, if you can't tell me all about your world," Doors tried again, "maybe at least something about yourself."

"I hope I can do that. What would you like to know?"

"Well, Va'lon, are there . . . dammit, I don't want to step on any taboos. But I assume you have two sexes, the way we do?"

Now his companion was smiling a little more broadly than before. "It is a fair question, Jonathan, and not unexpected. It deserves an answer, of course—and in time one will be provided. But assumptions regarding us should be made sparingly. For now, it will be best if you and your fellow humans consider me—consider all of your new visitors, including me—as male.

Even if the term does not adequately express all aspects of Taelon physiology."

"I see. Well, I don't see, really. But I'll accept that answer for now, just as a matter of social—now what the hell is this?"

The barricade was made up of several vehicles, all with lights turned off, parked crosswise to effectively shut off traffic on the two-lane highway and its shoulders. The site of the roadblock, in a dip between hills, made it rather hard to see from any distance, so Doors roaring over the hill at a good highway speed had to come down hard on the brakes to keep from crashing into the obstacle, or running down one of the dimly seen figures that milled about brandishing firearms in the fitful light of red flares and lanterns.

The SUV had no sooner come to a stop than it was quickly surrounded, and a babble of men's voices went up. The beams of several powerful flashlights pierced the windows to spot the Taelon's hairless head.

A raucous shout went up. "There *is* one of 'em here!"

"We got one, boys!"

"Drag him outta there!"

Va'lon was sitting passively, looking straight ahead, while the standing vehicle bounced with the weight of men pulling and pushing, trying to climb onto it. Their eager hands tried to wrench open the locked door on the passenger side.

Doors already had his own seatbelt unfastened, and now he opened his own door, hard. Enough adrenaline was suddenly in his muscles to send a couple of would-be boarders reeling back.

He got halfway out of the SUV, standing erect with his left foot on the running board, a position that raised him high enough to look out over the heads of the small crowd. Faces, all of them male as far as he could tell, all of them white, were demonic in the flickering glare of red flares. Hands were starting to reach for him. Jonathan saw armbands with indecipherable symbols, saw one real steel helmet, US Army style, saw plenty of vests and bandoliers and camouflage clothing—but nothing anywhere that he would consider a real uniform.

"*Back off!!*" Doors roared, in a voice that stopped them in their tracks. "What the *hell* do you men think you're doing?"

"This is the New Free Coast Militia, mister, and we are defending our country against alien invasion." The man who spoke was threatening Doors with a weapon, a firearm in a strange contorted shape. Some kind of gun collector's special, Doors supposed, capable of a thousand rounds a minute—if any man could carry a thousand rounds of ammunition.

"Friggin' government won't do its job," the gun-pointer snarled at him. "So the people have the right!"

The wicked little black hole now aimed at Doors wasn't the first gun barrel he had ever seen from the wrong end. And he was angry enough right now to be able to ignore it. He kept the volume of his voice riding high. "Who's in charge of this show? Get him up here, now!"

The pause in activity was only momentary, and he had to roar the command again to get results.

"Where's the colonel?" someone in the crowd was shouting.

And another voice chimed in, "Get the colonel over here on this side. Tell him we got us a hostage. Maybe two."

From his elevated post of observation, Doors could now see that the highway had been doubly blocked, a second line of vehicles parked athwart it some thirty or forty yards west of the first blockade. Any eastbound traffic would have to stop at that western barrier.

A small group of men was now moving across the intervening space toward Doors standing on the running board of his SUV.

"Colonel Shelby, this way, sir!" some man called excitedly.

But not everyone in Jonathan's immediate vicinity was willing to wait for the colonel, whoever he might be. One of the men on the driver's side of the vehicle was trying to push the muzzle of his hunting shotgun in through the half-open door.

Whether the fellow was firmly bent on assassination or just trying to be menacing was impossible to tell, and Doors did not wait to find out. Without pausing to calculate the risk he grabbed the gun barrel nuzzling at his hip and forced it away from his own body and from the quiet form of his passenger. He was still gripping the barrel when the shotgun fired, perhaps by accident, blasting out the left rear side window of the SUV.

As if the shot had been a signal, hands grabbed at Doors, too many hands for him to fight free, and he was pulled down off the running board. Meanwhile other hands were immobilizing the man who had been holding the shotgun at the start of the wrestling match.

Things could have gotten worse in a hurry, and they probably would have, except now the man who was evidently Colonel Shelby, a lean fellow of forty years or so, with a handlebar mustache, and a cap bearing the logo of some veterans' organization, was on the scene. Shelby was shouting louder than anybody except Doors himself, and in a minute some semblance of order was restored.

Jonathan shot a quick glance into the vehicle, saw Va'lon still sitting in the same position, apparently unhurt.

He shook free of the last clinging hand, and climbed up on his running board again.

"I wasn't expecting to find a roadblock here, Colonel," he announced, staring at the handlebar mustache, raising his voice enough for everyone to hear. "Though I felt confident that this would be patriots' territory." Now he had gained a moment of near-silence, a window of attention and opportunity, and his mind skipped ahead, planning how to make the most of it.

With a gesture that most of those in the crowd could see he indicated his inert passenger inside the SUV. "My *friend* here is out of action right now," he announced, a little louder than before. His tone gave the word a special, contrary meaning. "I mean to keep him that way. But I also mean to *keep him in one piece*, until I get him to a place where he'll be of some value to our side."

Pausing for a moment, taking in the uncertain faces that surrounded him, he saw that he was making an impression, but realized that the issue still hung in the balance. He would have to gamble, not knowing whether what he was about to say would get him lynched by this crowd or gain him their respect and trust.

He took the plunge. "Some of you men must recognize me. I'm Jonathan Doors."

The impact on Colonel Shelby, at least, seemed to be favorable. "Mr. Doors," the mustached man acknowledged, and then hesitated.

"Colonel." Doors nodded respectfully in return. "I see your men here are ready for action. Now, I've got to get my passenger here to San Simeon, where there's a certain *effort* already in progress. I can't take the chance of spelling out all the details, but a minute ago, someone here spoke of having a hostage—well, let me assure you, hostages are worth a lot more in the hands of people who know just what to do with them."

"Ah," said Shelby. His was not the quickest mind Doors had ever encountered when it came to reassessing a situation, but at least he was now moving in the right direction. "We'll give you an escort."

"No. No, I'm afraid that won't do, Colonel." Jonathan thought rapidly. Tilting his head back, he scanned the stars, trying his best to look keen and competent. "A while back there were some helicopters out scanning the roads. I managed to avoid them. The feds, of course. But anything like a convoy of vehicles going up to the castle is out of the question. That would draw too much attention, from the Taelons and from their friends in our so-called government."

"I understand," said the colonel—who, Doors thought, had surely never been anywhere near a colonel in any greater force than this ragtag mob. And the man seemed on the point of adding "sir."

"Your job is here, Shelby." Jonathan gave another serious, approving nod, as if confirming the wisdom of his own decisions, his reliance on Shelby the outstanding patriot. "If anything like an organized pursuit comes after me on the ground—I want you to do all you can to delay them." Again Doors raised his voice a notch, and looked round at his audience. "Knowing the level of force that may be coming down this road in pursuit of me, I won't ask you men to stop them entirely. The army may be involved. But I know I can count on you to do all you can to slow them down."

As he spoke, Doors noted with satisfaction that with every word the murmuring enthusiasm of the surrounding mob seemed to be losing steam, falling away toward silence. Some of the hand-held lights were going out, and weapons were less in evidence.

"Yes, sir." This time Shelby's response was just a second late. But he actually did salute.

THREE

Doors was thinking that sunrise at San Simeon would probably always be a very special time—it certainly was very beautiful today. But then he supposed that all times were special in this place. Not that he really knew it very well at all. He had visited the high castle twice in his youth, as a mere tourist, and then twice more several months ago, while he was making up his mind to buy it. Four visits over a period of months, most of them lasting for only a few hours, and he hadn't yet seen half the rooms. The main impression he retained was that of a sultan's or emperor's palace. At least all the zoo animals and birds were decades gone, eliminating one set of problems for the new owner.

Once the roadblock was behind them, the remainder of the drive, up the winding coastal Route One from Cambria, had been gloriously uneventful. Fresh, bracing sea air circulated briskly through the shotgun-blasted holes in both rear windows, the left break considerably bigger than that on the right side. The rear seats, which had fortunately been unoccupied, were never going to be quite the same again. Nor would the lock and window mechanism of the right rear door, against which some of the pellets had expended their energy.

Va'lon had come through the incident without a scratch, and his nerves seemed quite solid enough for an interstellar adventurer. He had not moved or spoken until the SUV was a hundred yards from the opening made for it in the roadblock, and gaining more distance at a brisk rate of acceleration. Then he had turned his handsome head slightly toward the driver's seat and said, "My deepest gratitude, Jonathan Doors. You have managed to return the favor even before it could be fully granted. Thank you."

Doors grunted, checking out the red flares that were fading fast in his rearview mirror. "*Por nada*, as they say south of the border. I would've done as much for anyone. I don't take kindly to being practically kidnapped, having firearms stuck in my face."

"I begin to appreciate, Jonathan, that your reputation for leadership is well deserved." The Companion turned his head, slowly, gracefully of course, to look behind. Then he added, "I wonder if the unhappy Colonel Shelby and his men will continue to guard their barricade against invading aliens."

"We can hope they don't. I thought I'd kind of suggest that a couple of tanks were more than likely on the way. Unless the New Free Coast Militia is totally crazy that ought to bring them to their senses and send them home."

"I must say it once more. That was an almost incredible performance, Jonathan Doors."

"Some people will tell you my whole life has been an incredible performance." Did that sound too much like bragging? Well, it was the truth.

There was only a relatively small crew of caretakers at San Simeon, a mere half-dozen people on the job tonight, but they were all awake and active. The owner's arrival with an alien being as his guest had not quite taken them entirely by surprise—Doors had radioed ahead when the SUV was only a few miles down the road. He had also managed to get a message to the Highway Patrol regarding the roadblock.

"Looks like you had some trouble, Chief," the man in the

guard booth remarked, wide-eyed, when the SUV pulled up at the entry port, and the high gate of steel bars was rolling open. Then the man's gaze landed on the passenger, and he fell silent, jaws gaping in astonishment.

"You might say that." Doors reached for his controls to drive on, but then delayed again. "Oh, and listen, Carson. Keep a sharp eye on this gate. There are some crazy people running around the roads and highways this morning. If anybody shows up calling themselves the new official militia, or the patriots' army or whatever, you are to be very firm that they don't get in. You can be confident about this glass in your booth. The State of California tells me it's really bulletproof."

"Yessir."

"If we do have any callers of an unwelcome type, alert the house right away and we'll call the cops from there."

"Yessir." Then Carson made a visible effort and pulled himself together. "By the way, Mr. Doors, I'm supposed to tell you right away there's an e-mail for you."

"An e-mail? What do you mean?" It was not unusual for several hundred such messages a day to be addressed to him, and to catch up with him at all hours of the day and night, wherever he happened to be.

"Yessir, this is a special one, I understand, from your father. They have it up at the house." And the guard pointed inland.

All that at more or less the crack of dawn. Then, the drive up the winding, narrow, partly unpaved road, from the entrance to the grounds to what some people called the Castle, and old Hearst had christened Casa Grande, six miles to make a climb of some eighteen hundred feet. Va'lon was looking round him now with interest, as well he might.

They had turned east, inland, coming off the coastal highway. Mostly behind them, to the west, the Pacific was coming out of its shroud of darkness, seemingly almost of nonexistence, into morning light; all around the gently curving hills clothed in brown grass whose color at this season always made Doors think of white bread toasted to perfection. Right now his thoughts were easily turned that way. Come to think of it, he hadn't had much to eat in recent hours, and he felt ready for a ravenous confrontation with some kind of breakfast.

And ahead, more than a hundred feet high and coming a little closer with each reversal of the winding road, the twin towers of the main house, Casa Grande. Arrayed within a few yards of its front door, but not visible until the traveler drew closer, were the three smaller guest houses, Casa del Mar, Casa del Sol, and Casa del Monte, each a minor palace in its own right. The whole place, considered as an extravaganza, went beyond anything the Rockefellers or du Ponts had ever thrown up in the eastern United States. People who had seen both edifices had been known to compare San Simeon to the royal palace at Versailles.

Half an hour after the new owner's arrival, the damaged SUV had been taken off to a garage to await repairs, and one of the caretakers was bringing Doors some breakfast on the terrace beside the outdoor swimming pool.

The Neptune Pool, he seemed to recall, was so named for its most prominent group of white marble statuary, showing the sea god with his usual guard of horses and tritons. It was one of the features of the place that old W. R. Hearst, something of an enthusiastic swimmer, had evidently prized the most. Three hundred and forty-five thousand gallons of heated water, Doors seemed to remember from some list of specifications, and he could see that it was over a hundred feet long. The indoor pool, of course, was comparable in size and elegance; but that was for rainy days.

One of his first acts on arrival had been to personally decode the message from his father. The result was reassuring in a way, but had done nothing to relieve his curiosity. It simply let him know that Jubal Doors was on his way to San Simeon, and wanted to see his son about a matter of some urgency as soon as he got there. Jubal might, of course, have called his son directly on his global communicator, but the old man tended to prefer the older methods.

And just what might be so urgent was something of a puzzler. Jubal was now getting well into his eighties, and had been substantially retired for a decade. Jonathan, who generally had a thousand other things to think about, tended to lose track of his father, sometimes for months at a time, and on occasion he felt guilty about it. But as far as he knew, the old man remained as healthy and active as his age would let him be, energetically pursuing his own interests, reading, writing, and gardening. Finances were certainly no problem.

Rather than eating more simply and practically in the kitchen of the main house, Doors had asked the worker doing temporary duty as cook to bring his breakfast out on the terrace, mainly because the Taelon had practically insisted on remaining outside, and he did not want to leave his guest alone.

It was the outdoor statuary that seemed to impress Va'lon most. And there was certainly a fair amount of work to be inspected, in marble and other stones. Single figures and carved groups were scattered plentifully about, on the esplanade that curved around the pool and branched to the three guest "cottages"—the smallest had ten rooms—and along the broad white stairs that went up to the plaza in front of Casa Grande.

Va'lon had politely declined offers of various kinds of food and drink. He had not yet consumed anything by mouth, not where Doors could see him anyway, but had made what seemed a limited concession to biology by visiting a bathroom shortly after their arrival. Now the Taelon was coming back from a quick walking tour around some of the buildings, on which he had been accompanied by one of the security people. Doors noted for the first time that the Companion was carrying a small device, probably some kind of camera.

"I can well believe that this establishment is unique among the constructions of your world," the Taelon commented on his return to stand beside the table where Doors was breakfasting.

Beside Jonathan's personal communicator, there was already a small stack of papers on the table, mostly print-outs from communications gear recently installed in the Casa Grande room that was going to be his temporary office; the need to make certain business decisions had inevitably caught up with the master of the house.

In response to a gesture of invitation, Va'lon pulled out a chair and sat down gracefully. "It is indeed impressive," he continued.

"Wait'll you get a look inside the main house." Doors nodded in the direction of those formidable walls of stone, the huge mass suggesting a Spanish church or fortress. "One visitor here some decades back—a man named George Bernard Shaw, maybe you've heard of him—said that this place shows what God could have accomplished, if only he'd had the money."

Va'lon inclined his head gracefully, in a way that seemed to indicate he had some awareness of the identities of both God and George Bernard Shaw. Whether he appreciated the point of the joke was a little harder to determine.

"As I believe I mentioned before, Jonathan, we consider the creation of fine museums among the highest esthetic achievements of advanced civilization. This estate that you now own is certainly a fine museum, whatever other values it may possess." Without a pause, or change in tone, the Companion added, "We would like to buy it from you, with all its contents and appurtenances."

Doors paused in the act of wiping some egg yolk from his plate with a piece of toast. "Excuse me, did you say 'buy it'?"

"I did indeed."

"I don't know if we're on the same wavelength here,

Va'lon. It wasn't long ago—remember?—that I paid the state of California more than two billion dollars for this property."

The Companion performed his gracious little bow, which he could do with perfect ease while seated. "We realize that, and we understand that you would be entitled to make some financial profit. Still, our offer is quite serious."

Va'lon looked around at palm trees and a hundred other kinds of vegetation, with four Mediterranean mansions of various sizes raising their red-tiled roofs in the background, and white marble scattered about in stark emphasis.

"In my personal opinion, this would be an ideal site for us—for the Companions—to establish our North American headquarters. Perhaps even our world headquarters. Your price would be paid in earthly currency, in dollars if you prefer, as soon as trade has enriched us to that extent—which I believe will not take an enormous length of time, considering what we have to offer. Or we could supply you with commodities of equal value."

Doors sipped his coffee, a necessary move to give himself a little time to think. He felt an impulse to accept the offer at once, and an even more generous impulse to deed the property over to the Taelons as a gift, in the cause of cementing human-Companion relations. But the same wary instinct that had enabled him to amass an enormous fortune now made him insist on having a little time to think the business over.

His need to answer was further postponed by the sound of a small aircraft, purposefully entering the airspace over the estate, at such low speed and altitude that the shape of its wings could be easily made out. Va'lon looked up sharply at the sound, and his face showed the first expression like real alarm that Doors had seen on it. But for the moment he said nothing.

Doors pushed aside the remains of his breakfast and stood up, stretching, and rubbing his eyes. "Looks like my dad is here," he announced. "This place has its own little airstrip, as I mentioned before." Then he stared.

The Companion, who a few hours ago had endured a near lynching with apparent calm, was now definitely showing signs of uneasiness. Va'lon asked, in a suddenly abrupt though still melodious voice, "I had not expected this. Is it possible to divert the aircraft elsewhere? To ask that your father complete his journey by land, as we did?"

Jonathan squinted into the steadily rising sun. "Might be possible, even at this late stage, but . . . no, I guess not even possible now. Looks like the pilot's already on his landing approach."

"It is going to land beyond that hill." And the Companion seemed relieved. "It will not fly any nearer—any nearer the house than that?"

"That's right. Our strip's over there. It's not a helicopter, or one of those VTOL craft some people have. Just a middle-sized fixed-wing jet. We're still somewhat old-fashioned here at San Simeon." Doors chuckled, but privately he had been given something to wonder about. Why should the interstellar explorer be nervous about the approach of an ordinary airplane? Even if Va'lon had been asked to ride in one, he must know that the safety records of human flying machines at the start of the twenty-first century were pretty good. But of course he hadn't been pressed to take a ride. And the plane that worried him hadn't even flown directly over his head . . .

Meanwhile Va'lon seemed quite his usual self again, calm and philosophical. "I look forward to meeting your father. Will you walk with me, Jonathan, while we await his arrival?"

Doors rubbed his face again. "Of course," he agreed, and tried to remember just how long he'd been awake. Well, as soon as he'd seen his father, he'd hit the sack for a few hours.

The Companion showed no hesitation or uncertainty about where he wanted to go on his little walk. He led his wondering host along one sun-drenched walkway after another, until they were standing in front of Sekhmet. Four similar, though not identical, black stone images of the same goddess of ancient Egypt, arranged around a fountain, now dry, and flanked on two sides by pink tile steps and half-encircled by a stone balustrade. Here Va'lon, his camera—if it was a camera—once more in hand, stopped to discuss his theories regarding archives and their curators.

It was all very interesting, or ought to have been, but Doors found himself having to struggle to repress a yawn.

In a little while the sound of tires crunching on gravel sounded from a lower level, and Doors glanced at his wristwatch. He announced, "I'd say that's my father now, having just got a lift over from the airstrip. I don't know if dad has any idea that you're here, but I'm sure he'll want to see you."

Va'lon responded with one of his courteous nods of agreement, and the two walked back in the general direction of the outdoor pool.

Jubal Doors was a smaller, leaner man than his only son. What little hair he had left had long since turned white. Bushy gray eyebrows, grown even bushier with age, gave him a formidable look. At about the time of his eightieth birthday he had taken to using a cane, but most people on meeting him would still have thought him ten or fifteen years younger than he was. Usually dapper, today he was tieless, wearing an old suit that his shirt and shoes made no pretense of matching, which suggested to his son that the old man had probably started on his journey to San Simeon in a hurry.

Jubal was ascending one of the countless short flights of white steps that led up to Casa Grande, using his cane to good advantage. The pilot who had just brought him here from Charleston, a balding young man with wrap-around sunglasses, climbed solicitously half a step behind the old man.

Jubal was halfway through a brisk greeting to his son, when his eye fell on the tall alien figure behind Jonathan. The old man fell silent at once, and his face became immobile.

Probably, Jonathan thought, that was not an uncommon reaction to one's first look at a Companion, and it was probably very much like his own response.

He performed the introduction, which went smoothly. Shortly thereafter, as if understanding that father and son might have urgent private matters to discuss, Va'lon considerately excused himself. A room in one of the guest houses had been got ready for him, and he now retired into it, though he did not specifically admit to being tired or needing sleep.

"Well, Dad," said Jonathan, as they watched the carved door of Casa del Mar close on their visitor. "I don't know what Taelon habits are. He may not be going to sleep, but I'm about to. Escorting aliens around is wearing. Have an uneventful flight?"

"Yeah, yeah." The old man, hobbling energetically with his cane, had turned away from Casa del Mar and was heading in the other direction. He still looked worried. Well, he would come out with his problem, or idea, whatever it might be, in his own good time. Jonathan, from a lifetime's experience, knew better than to try to push him.

They were out in the middle of the esplanade again when Jubal stopped to look around him. "I haven't set foot on these walks for decades," he said in a hushed voice. "Amazing how little things have changed in sixty-five years or so." He lifted his cane as a brisk pointer. "Those palm trees are a whole lot taller."

"That's right, I remember you telling me you were a weekend guest here once. When you were only sixteen. How about some breakfast, Dad?"

"Had some on the plane."

"Well, I'm going to sit down and have some more coffee. I guarantee it won't keep me awake. So, what did you think of your first Taelon?" Jonathan asked his father.

Jubal sat opposite him, and tried to prop his wooden cane on the smooth curving edge of the small table, from which position it promptly fell clattering to the pavement of imported tile. The old man ignored it, and his sharp brown eyes under the thick brows turned quickly on his son. "If you mean this fella here"—a nod toward the newly occupied guest house—"he's not."

Jonathan blinked. "Not the first Companion you've seen? There was a landing in Charleston, then? I hadn't heard about that one."

"No there wasn't. Charleston somehow got left out."

"No? Then what . . . ?"

"There was no official word about the one coming down in your back yard, either: just that there had seemed to be a Companion arrival, as they call it, somewhere in your neck of the woods. But I had a hunch, and called the house, and Amanda said there had been, and you had jumped in a car with one of 'em and were headed here."

"So—?"

"I'm trying to tell you, son. The first Taelon I ever saw was right here at San Simeon, but it wasn't this morning. No, it was a good long while before you were born. Back in 1936."

FOUR

When Jubal was sixteen, the Doors family had been financially successful but not enormously wealthy. In that respect they were doing a lot better than most Americans in the middle thirties. Maybe the country was really coming out of the depths of the Great Depression, as the politicians and the newspapers kept promising it would, but a lot of people would believe that times were good again only when they could get a steady job.

Jubal's father had never actually worked for William Randolph Hearst in any capacity, as far as Jubal had ever been able to make out. His dad had certainly never been an editor or publisher, and the Hearst empire was primarily one of newspapers. But Dad had known the editor of a certain Denver paper, one of the hundreds across the country that W. R. Hearst owned or controlled. That acquaintanceship had led the elder Doors into a meeting with Hearst in Chicago, and that in turn to some kind of projected business deal. Jubal's dad tended to play his cards close to his vest, and neither his son nor his wife had learned the precise details until later.

And in 1936 the acquaintance had also led to the family's being invited to a weekend at San Simeon. And whatever the exact business relationship Jubal's father and mother had been trying to establish with the multimillionaire, they were very keen on making a good impression.

His father had been as excited as Jubal had ever seen him.

"Even if it's not a matter of direct employment, or direct sales. The power that those hundreds of newspapers—literally, almost seven hundred!—can exert is awesome."

Jubal at sixteen was ready and willing to be impressed by great power in any form. "Dad? Is Mr. Hearst the wealthiest man in the world? Or in the country?"

His Dad had to give that query serious consideration. "I honestly don't know, son. There can't be more than a few who have more money. Maybe Carnegie, maybe Mellon, or du Pont. One or two other possibilities. I'd be willing to bet, though, that Mr. Hearst *spends* more money than any other individual in the world."

"What does he buy?"

"What does he buy? Anything he wants. Just about everything. You'll see."

Still, as the family eventually realized, the odds were pretty good that neither Jubal nor his father would ever have laid eyes on San Simeon had it not been for Esther Summerson.

Before the fateful weekend arrived, Jubal had managed to catch her recorded voice once or twice on the radio. At that point in her career Esther hadn't been one of the really famous singers, whom you could hear every day.

The word was that Hearst seldom or never went to parties at other people's houses, but he loved to entertain at his, where he could control the timing of events, the guest list, the menu, and the rules—including, to a great extent, the amount of alcohol dispensed.

Hollywood people made up a very large proportion of the usual weekend-guest contingent. Esther, an up-and-coming teenage singing and acting star, had been invited to the "Ranch" for a weekend—with her mother as chaperone, of course—and to one of Hearst's advisors it must have seemed a good idea for some other young people of her age to be invited, to keep her company. As a rule there were very few children among the many guests, and in fact Jubal was her only contemporary for the weekend.

No one on that fateful weekend realized the fact, of course, but 1936 was just a couple of years before the crash of Hearst's empire. "Crash" being a relative term. The empire would not decline into total ruin, no, far from it. But the crisis led to the ferocious cutting back that had been necessary to save him and his organization from complete disaster.

On the appointed Friday, the last leg of a long train journey delivered Jubal and his parents to the village of San Simeon, and a small fleet of Hearst limousines had been waiting at the station to bring them and several of their fellow passengers up the Hill.

The grass covering the surrounding hills still showed traces of green from the recent rainy season. The driver said the annual display of wildflowers was past its peak, but they were still impressive.

Later on in the weekend, Jubal counted twenty guests in all, which he gathered was not a particularly large number for a weekend. He had no idea who most of them were.

The ride along the winding, unpaved private road was notable for several things, among them the signs that seemed to show up every fifty yards or so:

ANIMALS HAVE THE RIGHT OF WAY

"The largest private zoo in the world," Jubal's dad informed his family, in an almost-reverent tone.

There were frequent stops while cattle gates were opened in front of the vehicles and closed after them, and once a delay of several minutes when a water buffalo appeared out of the mist and refused to yield the necessary width of road.

At last a final set of gates was passed, and the small caravan of limos pulled up at the foot of a span of white stairs, with the enormous bulk of Casa Grande looming mistily above them.

They were officially welcomed to the Enchanted Hill by a motherly looking woman who introduced herself as the head housekeeper, and began at once to speak of practical things like mealtimes, and the chances of a visitor's getting lost, an accident not necessarily limited to the out-of-doors; it appeared that the chances of losing one's way inside Casa Grande were not trivial.

While the housekeeper was still talking, there appeared a lean fellow of average size, wearing nondescript khakis, who looked to be somewhere in his late thirties. The housekeeper introduced him as Captain Murray, head of security. Captain Murray beamed on them all briefly, rather shyly Jubal thought, and took himself away. Then the housekeeper gently conveyed the fact that the enormous wealth of treasure with which the owner and his guests were now surrounded had to have a watchful eye kept on it, just on general principles. No one here would be so insulting as to suggest (horrid thought!) that any guest might have an overwhelming urge to appropriate a souvenir.

Among the bits of information conveyed in the welcome lecture was the fact that Mr. Hearst liked to refer to his castle on a hill and its surrounding territory as the Ranch. Naturally other people had taken to calling it that also, though most of them tended to smile when they used the term.

And indeed it turned out to be unlike any ranch that Jubal, newly arrived from Colorado, had ever seen, heard of, or dreamt about—he would have bet no one had ever imagined a place like this. Despite the fact that there *was* a real cattle ranch—altogether apart from the zoo of exotic animals, and the aviary of fifteen hundred birds—on the land surrounding the castle. Something like a hundred thousand acres altogether, if Jubal's Dad had got his numbers right.

Their bedrooms were adjoining, in Casa del Mar. Most of

the guests were put up in the main house, where there were almost forty bedrooms, so even a large party was unlikely to feel crowded.

All very interesting. But it didn't take Jubal long to decide that the most interesting aspect of the weekend was going to be Esther.

Actually Esther Summerson was only her screen name. The publicity handout Jubal had glanced at, when his father picked it up somewhere and brought it home, said the name was taken from some character in a Charles Dickens novel, when a rousing musical version of *Bleak House* was being planned. There was talk that Hearst might be going to finance the film, as he had so many others. Somehow the young girl's real name was never mentioned in the handout, or at their first meeting, and Jubal supposed that maybe it didn't matter any more.

Jubal, who sometimes tuned in on his parents when they whispered about the situation between themselves, gathered that Hearst had probably been hoping to get the big part in *Bleak House* for his long-time girlfriend Marion Davies. She was a well-known actress who had starred in half a dozen movies, and might have done very well in Hollywood even had the hundreds of Hearst newspapers not supported her and puffed her achievements outrageously at every opportunity. But at this stage in her career Miss Davies seemed reluctant to do a musical, and the old man had finally allowed himself to be convinced that she was now too grown-up for the part. "Grown-up" was his word for her situation. She herself was ready to admit that she was well past thirty, and forty was probably more like it.

She was a sweet lady, though, nice-looking though her shape was no longer quite that of a teenager, and with nothing the least bit stuffy about her. She'd made a special effort to put

young Jubal Doors at ease when he arrived with his parents on
Friday afternoon.

Marion Davies sized up young Jubal with a single glance and
moved to take him under her wing at once. At the first opportunity she got him off away from everyone else for a little private talk. When they were on the far side of the swimming
pool from everyone else, they might as well have been in
another county.

She spoke with an occasional stammer that had somehow
become an endearing help rather than a hindrance to her
career. "Look, kid, don't let these movie people awe you.
You'll see some faces here that you'll—you'll recognize
because you've seen 'em on a big screen, but so what? They
put on their pants one leg at a time just the way you and I do.
Remember, if someone took a c-camera and put your face on
the big screen, it would look just as big as theirs."

"You're a movie star too, Miss Davies," he'd said impul-
sively. He knew that, as everyone did, though he'd only actually seen one of her films, *Operator 13*, which had just come
out last year. That was only because comedies weren't really
the kind of show he liked.

Somehow in talking with this lady Jubal had already got
the feeling that he need not be on guard, that it would be all
right to just blurt out whatever came into his head. The fact
that she stuttered and stammered from time to time only made
her more approachable.

And Marion was delighted. "*There* you go! See? Sure, I-
I've been in a couple of movies, but that don't mean you have
to be scared of me. Here you are, talk—talking to me just like
anyone else."

"Thanks, Miss Davies."

"Call me Marion. Now where's this girl Esther Whatsher-
name? I hope you and her can get along. Sure you will."

* * *

Mr. Hearst himself was a big man, gray-haired and obviously getting well up in years, a lot older than Marion, with a long, straight nose and a piping voice so surprisingly tiny that some people almost burst out laughing when they first heard it coming from his huge frame. No one at San Simeon was laughing, though. Jubal had heard it whispered that this was the man who had actually started the Spanish-American War, back around the turn of the century, though how he might have done that Jubal had no idea.

Mr. Hearst kept his gaze fixed on Marion Davies whenever she was in sight. Not as if he were suspicious, or worried, but just in a kind of appreciation. Obviously there was a special relationship between them. He shook hands with Jubal as if welcoming some important business partner, giving him a full minute of undivided attention.

Despite the efforts made to put him at ease, Jubal had inevitably been somewhat awed by the first recognizable big-screen faces he encountered, those of Errol Flynn and the lesser-known David Niven. But thanks to the inoculation administered by Miss Davies, the feeling hadn't lasted long.

Jubal's disenchantment was helped along by the fact that he did not seem to exist at all in the eyes of Esther Summerson, when she finally showed up. Their train had been delayed, and of course there was nothing to be done about that. Her parents, even more nervous than Jubal's, seemed irritated by her attitude. Jubal wasn't the only one she tended to ignore. Esther's thoughts and feelings were obviously far away from San Simeon, but who knew where? She had already played midsized roles in a couple of pictures, but she wasn't a big star, and not very recognizable, but everyone at the Ranch that weekend seemed to take it for granted that she was going to be.

Esther in person was brittle and keen-looking, not like the image she generally projected on the screen.

Jubal and Esther were introduced on the evening of their respective arrivals, and after a few minutes' general conversation the girl and boy had been left more or less alone in Casa Grande's billiard room. The room itself was just about enough to leave you speechless; one of the housekeepers, probably trying to be entertaining, had been telling Jubal how all the visible surfaces in this and practically all the other chambers in the house had once been part of several different rooms in Europe.

For example, the carved, dark wood beams and panels of the billiard room's Gothic ceiling (whatever kind of ceiling *that* might be, thought Jubal; he had no clue) had been imported at tremendous expense from somewhere in Spain, and they were somewhere around five hundred years old. Jubal might have been tempted to believe that the housekeeper was making it all up, but what he had already seen of the rest of the house and its surroundings had him just about convinced that here at the Ranch anything was possible.

So Esther and Jubal were left pretty much to themselves in the billiard room to socialize, under the unobtrusive but persistent chaperoning eyes of some of the household help, most of whom seemed to be Filipinos. Meanwhile all the adult guests would be going through what sounded like a regular evening ritual of cocktails at 7:30 in the Assembly Hall. That was what the little printed notices called the room, which to Jubal made the whole place sound uncomfortably like yet another kind of school. Not that it looked in the least like any kind of school he had ever seen, or even imagined.

The advance scouting report received by Jubal's dad, from someone who knew someone who had been there, said the Assembly Hall covered twenty-five hundred square feet, an area bigger than the entire floor space of many houses. Its walls of imported stone, like those of many of the other rooms, were at least two stories high, and were hung with an emperor's ransom in ancient European tapestries. The silver and the furniture of the Assembly Hall would have been welcome additions to any museum on the planet.

Jubal's dad had also been warned that Hearst liked to get aboard his private elevator at some other level, and then enter the Assembly Hall through a concealed door to the left of the enormous fireplace—also imported, of course, though no one seemed to know from where—doing his playful best to startle guests who had been keeping an eye on the regular entrance in expectation of his arrival.

No, schools of any kind were not Jubal's favorite places.

When he said something along that line, just trying to make conversation with Esther Summerson, she turned her eyes his way and seemed to look directly at him for the first time. It soon turned out that the two of them had at least a dislike of school in common, which was more than either of them had expected. Jubal had been somehow expecting to meet some kind of spoiled, impossible movie brat, and Esther . . . well, he didn't know exactly what she had been anticipating from him, but as they conversed in the billiard room she began to seem a bit relieved, if not pleasantly surprised.

Jubal of course had been made to put on a coat and tie for the occasion, and Miss Summerson, as old W.R. himself had called her when they were introduced, had on what Jubal supposed should be classified as an evening gown. They were expected to amuse themselves for an hour or so, and then they would be notified when the time came to join the adults for dinner.

There weren't too many places to sit down in the billiard room. Esther hitched one leg up, putting a strain on her fancy dress, and perched sidesaddle on the edge of the billiard table, indifferently giving Jubal a glimpse of leg up to about the knee. Her legs weren't bad, in his opinion, but nothing spectacular. She selected one of the ivory balls and began to roll it back and forth on the firm green surface, bouncing it gently first off two cushions, then off three, trying to get it to come back to her waiting hand.

Jubal noted that the massive table at the north end of the billiard room was really for pool, while that on the south, lacking pockets at the sides and corners, was for billiards. When he mentioned the fact, the distinction was lost on Esther. Jubal's education was fairly advanced in some ways—but games of any kind had never seemed very important to him.

"What do you do in Colorado?" Esther finally asked, after she had managed to get the bouncing ball to return obediently.

"My Dad owns some mines there. And some cattle. I go to school."

"You ever work on the ranch? Or in the mines?"

He almost had to laugh out loud at the last suggestion. "Wouldn't work in the mines, nohow. I've seen how that goes. Last summer I worked for a while on our ranch."

Next they talked about horseback riding. Esther had tried it twice before discovering that she was seriously allergic to horses. That was going to be a problem in some movie roles, and the possibility of having to ride was already costing her some sleepless nights.

Conversation soon turned to animals in general—both liked dogs, but neither owned one—and from that to the particular specimens in old Hearst's zoo.

Esther and Jubal had each caught glimpses of different exotic species, from their respective cars, when they arrived. Each vehicle had been forced to stop and wait for a minute or two, until some creature decided to get out of its way.

"The lions and bears are locked up, in cages out behind the main house somewhere, but sometimes you can hear 'em roaring. That's what they say, I haven't seen 'em yet."

"Let's go take a look."

Jubal looked at his wristwatch. "Maybe we better wait till after dinner. We can play hooky from the movie."

FIVE

At about nine o'clock on Friday evening, the well-fed company rose from the dinner table, amid a general murmur of social conversation, mostly in anticipation of the new movie they were about to see. Jubal and Esther, exchanging glances, avoided the general migration in the direction of the fifty-seat movie theater built into the lower level of Casa Grande. Tonight's feature film, according to the neatly printed little schedule distributed earlier in the day, was going to be *Charge of the Light Brigade*, starring Errol Flynn and featuring, among others, David Niven.

The picture sounded pretty good to Jubal, but Esther wasn't into war movies, and he would rather spend time with her than with Errol Flynn. Now, while their host and his other guests were going to the show, Esther and Jubal slipped out of the house. A minute later, they had left the more brightly lighted area of the walks and patios to take another look at the beasts. Esther seemed fascinated by animals in general. Jubal could take them or leave them.

There was no problem getting around the grounds at night, at least in the areas that guests were generally expected to inhabit, and which were as well-lighted as any downtown streets that Jubal had ever seen. The lamps, on pillars, weren't simply glass, but glowing globes of alabaster.

One of the caretakers at the zoo had already told Jubal that there were about three hundred animals altogether, not counting the fifteen hundred or so birds, who of course had their own enclosures. Of the four-legged beasts, the great majority were grazers—elephants, antelope, several kinds of goats, you name it—that were pretty much allowed to run free, inside vast fenced areas.

Currently there were only a few meat-eaters on hand—one lion, a few bobcats, one cheetah, one leopard, and a bear—and all of these were behind secure barriers of one kind or another. The whole zoo area was brightly lighted, like the rest of the walks and patios.

Halfway between the lion's cage and the leopard's, Jubal stopped and tilted his head to listen. "Sounds like another plane coming in."

"Will they land at night?" Esther wondered.

"I bet they've got lights at the strip. Sure, at a place like this they must have."

And that, as Jubal Doors was to tell his son more than six decades later, that was where the experience began that was to change his life forever.

First came the *sound*, echoing in Jubal's brain. Putting his fingers in his ears did not muffle it at all, suggested it was being created somehow inside his head—anyway, surely no animal that had ever walked on earth could make a noise like that. Not that it was actually that *loud*, but . . .

And the noise was only the beginning, it was only the least important part.

Nothing seemed to have changed objectively in Jubal's surroundings. But it was as if the whole world had suddenly become a strange, forbidding, and unnatural place.

None of the outlines or colors of the objects that he could see had been changed, but everything had somehow been transformed. The trees had extra branches, and their leaves were strange; palm fronds looked sawtoothed like dandelions. He saw a flower opening its mouth, and there were teeth inside. Whether these disturbing alterations were taking place only in Jubal's mind, or somewhere in the foundations of the surrounding world, he couldn't tell. But he endured a momentary, unpleasant suspicion that he was dreaming, followed quickly by an illogical regret that he was not. He was wide awake, and could not seriously imagine otherwise.

At the same time, Esther gave a nervous start and looked around.

"What is it?" he demanded of her sharply. *He had the feeling that if he once acknowledged the strangeness, the sickness, in his own mind, it would only become more powerful.*

"I don't know." The tone of her voice was hard to interpret.

Doing his best to be casual, Jubal said, "No need to be jumpy. No one minds if we stand here looking at the animals."

And he thought the animals seemed to have been affected too. The leopard backed into a corner of its cage, and the lion began to cough out a series of odd sounds, almost like the beating of a drum. Almost, but not quite.

Esther was saying, "It's not that. You heard it too?"

"I heard something."

"It's just that—well, I thought I heard something like that earlier today. And I saw some strange sights, too."

"Strange sights like what?"

"Oh, never mind."

They started strolling again, leaving the suddenly noisy lion behind them, and leaving the zoo by a different footpath than the one that brought them there. But the new way only led them back in a great loop, to the upper-level esplanade, close to all the mansions, great and small.

"Here I am again," said Esther in a faintly puzzled voice, coming to a stop.

"What?"

"Nothing. Just that somehow I seem to keep coming back to this place, and I find myself looking at these stupid statues."

Jubal hadn't really taken much notice of this particular group before. Compared to the dozens of life-sized figures in white marble that were scattered around the grounds, these were very crude. But now the more he looked at them the stranger they appeared.

Water from a small pipe-fountain trickled into a little pond that was more or less surrounded by the four dark, staring, leonine faces carved of stone. Two of the four statues were little more than heads, the other two included slender, human-looking bodies, tall though portrayed in a sitting position. These two were marked as female by rounded breasts, carved under light stone draperies. Their arms were bent at the elbow so their hands lay flat on their skirted thighs.

"What are they supposed to be?" Jubal wondered. "They all four look alike."

"I asked my father, and he found out. It's an Egyptian goddess called Sekhmet."

"Huh." He couldn't find anything more intelligent to say.

Just as the young people were about to turn away again, Jubal thought he heard a kind of heavy, grating sound that seemed to issue from one of the versions of Sekhmet, he couldn't tell which.

"What was that?" he demanded. Now he wondered if someone was playing jokes.

"That squealing sound? I heard it too. It's not the lion or the leopard."

"No. And I wouldn't call it squealing, exactly."

It turned out that their two sets of ears had heard two quite different sounds.

All the faces of Sekhmet looked as strange as ever, but no stranger than they had looked before.

One of the statues had full womanly breasts, represented by two spherical stone bulges of unattractive regularity, half-covered by stylized rolls of hair, or mane, or head-dress—Jubal could not be sure which. The lower half of the body was clad in a long, carved skirt or kilt, below which thick leonine ankles showed, and bare human feet. The wrists and forearms were heavy too. If the stone body was ambiguous, of some uncertain and imaginary species, the head was all inhuman predator, and he had no doubt that it was meant to represent a lion.

Walking back and forth before the trickling fountain, Jubal sized up the statues first from one angle and then from another. Something about them bothered him . . . but he couldn't say what. But the something was connected with his odd feeling of a few minutes ago. It wasn't the real lion that had brought the feeling on. No, it emanated from these stone figures here.

"Jubal. Let's move on." Esther had her arms folded now, as if she could be cold in the mild late evening. "Really, I don't like this."

"In a minute." There was a kind of fascination, and the more he looked, the more it grew.

"I'm moving on," Esther said in a softly frightened voice.

He could hear her high heels tapping on the walk. And a moment later, he had finally wrenched himself away from Sekhmet and joined her. He wasn't sure how much of his own odd feeling was just something that he'd caught from his companion.

Whatever it had been was over now, the world around them sane and stable once again.

Esther, sounding worried, said, "You must think I'm very timid. Actually I'm not like that at all."

"I guess you couldn't be, and be an actress. I know I get stage fright, if I have to stand up and do anything in front of folks."

Hearing that admission from Jubal seemed to make her feel better. "Different people are bothered by different things," she told him soothingly.

And then somehow, before they knew it, their aimless stroll had brought them back *again*, standing before the black statues, listening to the trickling fountain.

This, Jubal thought to himself, *is getting ridiculous.*

A couple of minutes ago there had been four Sekhmets here—but now there were only three. One of the carved stone chairs, standing slightly above and to the rear of the other figures, was empty, the image that had occupied it gone. Earlier Jubal had assumed that each figure and its support were carved in one piece, but obviously that was not so.

Esther had stopped beside him, evidently coming to the same conclusion.

"Weren't there four of them here only a couple of minutes ago?"

Jubal tried to adjust his memory to fit with what he saw before him now. The effort was complicated by the unpleasant feelings the place had aroused in him earlier.

"I thought so—but I don't see how there could have been," he said at last. "One of those things must weigh a ton, it couldn't have got up and walked away."

The young couple were just ready to move on when they heard strange noises out in the cool night fog—the "high fog" that he heard Californians talking about, when Jubal would have called it simply clouds.

"There it goes again—what was that?"

They had just seen that all the predatory animals were secure in their cages. Anyway, the sound wasn't a roar—it was more like the whining mewing that a housecat could sometimes let out, if you could imagine a full-grown lion trying to imitate the noise.

"Mountain lion?" Jubal hazarded. "Is there anything like that around here?"

And again.

"I don't know. But *that* didn't even sound like an animal. I don't know what it sounded like."

They listened some more, but now there was only silence.

"Wish we had a flashlight," Jubal said. The alabaster spheres that served as streetlights provided a lot of illumination, but between them now there seemed vats and reservoirs of darkness.

"This place is weird," said Esther, more in admiration than in fear. Then she had another thought. "You know what? Maybe it was bagpipes. I've heard people at the studio playing bagpipes."

Jubal was still thinking of mountain lions; he had heard wild ones make some pretty screechy sounds. If he had lived all his life in the flatland back east, where he had spent his early childhood, he would have been willing to accept these rolling hills as mountains. But the fact was that he had spent his last couple of years growing up in the Rockies, and so his attitude was somewhat different. He would not have felt too ill-at-ease prowling around these hills by night or day. A mountain lion wasn't normally going to attack a human; though of course it was not impossible.

Jubal left Esther at the door of the guest house in which she and her parents were housed. "See you for a swim in the morning?"

"That sounds like a good idea."

"Maybe take another walk tomorrow night?"

Jubal was walking around early Saturday, sizing the place up on the first morning of his weekend visit, when his attention was caught by a group of workers who had surrounded something on a grassy slope, about a hundred feet from the walk where the Sekhmet statues stood, and slightly downhill.

Somehow he thought he already knew what the men were looking at, before he got close enough to see it.

And when he got close enough, he saw that he was right. The workers were trying to get the statue of Sekhmet back where it belonged.

Something is really wrong here, Jubal told himself. *But I don't know what.* He thought it would take more than two men to drag the thing back up the grassy slope where it had somehow, unaccountably, come tumbling down. And somehow it had been hoisted over the stone balustrade that stood between.

The men who seemed to have been charged with restoring the statue to its place could only look at it and scratch their heads. Jubal couldn't blame them.

Finally one of the workers asked the others, "Are we going to tell the Chief?"

The man who seemed to be in charge was shaking his head. "I don't want to bother him unless we have to. Let me ask Murray first." The worker sounded genuinely concerned about the old man. Jubal had heard that Hearst paid well, as a rule, sometimes very well indeed, and he could be spectacularly generous with his employees when he learned about some special problem, such as illness in a worker's family. The other side of his attitude was that he was not at all slow to fire people when he thought they failed to measure up.

At last one of the men said, "If we could lever it up on a cart somehow we could haul it, but you'll need some kind of a crane, a block and tackle, to get it back up on the pedestal."

Another was frowning, walking around, estimating the width of the gaps of open grass between plantings. "I think we'll have to get a truck in here."

Saturday morning on the Hill was sunny and pleasant, free of peculiar sounds and feelings. The guests got up whenever they felt like getting up, and went to the refectory for breakfast whenever they felt like it. Then there was that enormous swimming pool, inviting as a great calm ocean. Calm and *warm;* all that water was heated to a comfortable temperature, and you could have put a hundred people in it without crowding, but in fact there were seldom more than a small handful at any time.

Everyone said that Mr. Hearst really liked to swim, but he never got up until after noon. When the night's private movie show had been concluded, around midnight, and most of the guests were retiring to their rooms, he would head up to his library on one of the upper floors of Casa Grande and there amuse himself by some energetic hours of work, studying stacks of his newspapers that had been flown in from all over the country, and preparing comments for their editors. The comments were always couched in gracious language, but they were not always favorable. Sometimes an unfortunate press lord in Chicago or New York would be roused by a phone call from the Chief at two a.m. California time, and be given a politely phrased suggestion about some necessary improvement in his paper.

As the morning went on, more and more people kept showing up at poolside, but they were still all in separate groups, widely separated around the shores of this artificial lake.

When Esther appeared, wearing a yellow suit, she joined Jubal where he was sitting on the edge.

A moment later he touched her on the arm. "Here comes Flynn," Jubal remarked. Last year Jubal had seen him in *Captain Blood*, which had been a big hit, raising Errol Flynn to the status of major star. And of course the new one, *Charge of the Light Brigade*, on the bill at San Simeon last night. If anyone asked Jubal how he'd liked that show, he would have to admit that he had missed it.

Esther threw a quick glance across the pool and looked away again. "That's him." She was apparently not impressed.

No doubt about it, here came Captain Blood himself, six feet two and leanly muscular, white trunks contrasting with his dark hair and tan, entering the pool with an expert dive, to go splashing athletically across its width, then pull himself out

again on another remote shore. From across the gulf of water
he treated Esther to a dazzling grin with his capped teeth,
which Jubal thought were white as billiard balls.

"And there's David Niven." Niven, about the same size
and shape, with slightly wavy light brown hair, was not nearly
as big a star as Flynn had suddenly become, not yet anyway.
But the two actors seemed to be on the best of terms, waving
to each other across the water, and after Niven had swum
across finally settling down in adjoining wicker chairs with
dark glasses over their eyes.

Esther seemed to be even slightly going out of her way not to
be impressed. She had her back turned to the actors now, and
actually they didn't seem to be paying her much attention
either.

"Want to help me put on some lotion?" she inquired of
Jubal. "I don't want to get too tan, I might have a test coming up."

"Sure."

And Jubal was assigned the pleasant task of rubbing some
white cream on Esther's back and shoulders, above the top of
her yellow one-piece swim suit. *Look at me*, he thought to himself suddenly. *I wonder if I'm making Errol Flynn jealous.*

He had a great and sudden impulse to lean forward and kiss
the back of her neck; only the certainty that at least one or two
of the security men were watching kept him from doing so.

Down a few more flights of white steps from the houses
there were two tennis courts, actually occupying the enormous
flat roof of the low separate building that contained the vast
indoor pool. And there was horseback riding. Jubal would have
considered trying that, although despite the time he'd spent
on the ranch he had never really got used to it and didn't do it
very well, at least compared with the cowboys. But Esther of
course, being allergic to horses, was not riding today, and he

chose to keep her company. It wasn't at all a difficult decision.

"You can go riding if you like," Esther assured him. "You don't have to hang around here on my account." But she didn't sound eager to be rid of him.

"I can see horses any time," Jubal cheerfully allowed.

Jubal's parents, on the comparatively rare occasions during the weekend when he saw them, kept fiercely urging him to be polite to the girl and keep her company—that was, after all, as they had begun to realize, the main reason the family had been invited here.

"Yes, I know," he responded patiently. "I will."

By this time, being polite was not a problem. He was actually looking forward to spending some more time with Esther.

As far as the Hearst collections were concerned, the paintings and statues and rugs and who-knew-what, that many of the visitors kept oohing and aahing at, Jubal was impressed by them and even awed a little. Not that he knew anything about art, he didn't, and so far had never had reason to care about it. He was impressed by the artifacts because they too represented a kind of power, power over minds and bank accounts of some very important people. All he could be sure of was that all the *stuff* with which these tables were piled, and these walls were hung, made the place a lot different than any other house he had ever been in, though some of those other houses were pretty fancy too.

And, talking about power, what about the power of Sekhmet? Scary stuff, or it could be, but so far Jubal felt more challenged than afraid. And Esther seemed even more ready for adventure than he was.

It occurred to Jubal that if he was going to be taking

Esther on any more strolls after dark, the flashlight he had wanted to probe the mystery of Sekhmet might be a very valuable thing to have along. So he watched for his opportunity, and after quietly checking out the contents of three utility closets, two in Casa Grande and one in Casa del Mar, managed to find the very thing he wanted on a shelf, just waiting for some needy person like himself to come along and borrow it.

On Saturday afternoon, Jubal decided to conduct a solo scouting trip, sidestepped a meeting with his parents, and set out by himself.

Earlier that day Esther had promised to come out and meet him, if she could. So far it looked like she couldn't—but maybe she'd be able to join him later.

For an hour or so, as he waited in his ridiculously exotic room, occasionally testing his borrowed flashlight, he had entertained an entrancing daydream of slipping out of his room at night, meeting Esther who had also slipped out of hers, and finding her willing to look for a private spot and engage in some activity more interesting than billiards. But it seemed that an hour or so was about as long as any dream like that could last, in these conditions.

For one thing, real privacy of any kind was hard to come by, anywhere outside of your assigned bedroom and bath. The walks and patios, and the area around the outdoor pool especially, stayed brightly lighted all night long, by what amounted to fancy streetlamps. Pure white light, filtered through glowing globes of alabaster.

The servants and security people were almost never intrusive, and as a rule kept their distance from the guests as much as possible. But they were rarely entirely out of sight for longer than a minute at a stretch. And for another, Esther seemed to have her worries on some other subject, maybe her career, so continually on her mind that it was hard to imagine her putting them aside for five minutes.

Late Saturday afternoon, when Jubal left his room intending to scout the grounds before dinner, he listened briefly at the door of his parents' room. All was quiet, and he thought they had probably already reported for the evening social in the Assembly Hall.

In a way he was beginning by now to feel almost at home at San Simeon. Locked doors seemed to be the exception, and he never had the feeling of being closely watched. Of course the servants and maintenance workers were generally around somewhere, and sometimes the security people. They all tended to keep their distance from the guests, unless they had some immediate business to take care of. But Jubal was willing to bet that if in the middle of the night someone dived into the pool with a big splash, there'd be three or four guards on the scene inside a minute. And that whenever anyone slipped in for a quiet swim, no matter what hour of the day or night, someone would have the assigned job of keeping a casual eye on the swimmer from a distance. The pool stayed brightly lighted dusk to dawn. There were going to be no accidental drownings here, and no midnight orgies or drunken parties, either.

Not while Mr. W. R. Hearst was in charge of things on his estate, as he most definitely was. Jubal's mother had been vaguely worried about taking her baby into a Hollywood atmosphere, when she'd heard who they were likely to encounter at the Ranch, but Jubal's dad had done his best to reassure her. Old W.R., as everyone seemed to call him, might be in a long-term sinful relationship with a movie star thirty years his junior, but he had no taste or even tolerance for wild parties or even dirty jokes.

And W.R. was reportedly proud of his cellar of fine wine,

as part of what seemed to be his lifelong private campaign to own the world's best of everything. But Jubal's parents had been diplomatically cautioned against expecting to enjoy more than one drink before dinner.

Jubal had not been exploring the grounds for very long before he was joined by Esther.

They strolled along chatting for a little while, discussed the way the sunset was shaping up, and then heard someone crashing through the bushes.

Jubal immediately assumed that the racket was being made by some drunken guest, and this assumption was quickly justified when the unmistakably handsome features of Errol Flynn appeared. His youthful face was somewhat mottled and puffy, and he swayed slightly on his feet, being somewhat the worse for drink.

"Greetings, children. I am in search of the Northwest Frontier of India. Does it lie somewhere in this vicinity?"

Esther only sniffed and moved on. Jubal, still somewhat awestruck despite himself by the living presence of Captain Blood, murmured something, the words sounding so stupid in his own ears that he immediately tried to forget what he had said.

The bushes rustled again, and presently the face of David Niven appeared, calling after Flynn in urgent whispers that somehow conveyed his British accent.

"Errol? Where the bloody hell have you got to? Errol?"

"What is it, sport?"

Niven was not quite as handsome as Flynn but at the moment considerably more sober. He, too, had the little penciled mustache cultivated to perfection. Leaving Flynn and Niven whispering, giving off the sounds of some feverish unsober plot, Jubal hurried to catch up with Esther, and they walked on together.

After they'd gone a few steps she said, "I guess we know now who was making all the strange noises."

"I guess we do," Jubal agreed. He didn't want to argue, but in fact he was not convinced. What he'd heard earlier had not sounded like any kind of a Hollywood sound, or even a human sound. Whether Errol Flynn was acting or just raising hell, he could not have made a noise like that.

SIX

ater in the afternoon, Esther had retreated to her room, saying she wanted to change from sports clothes to an evening dress for dinner. Jubal would be expected to change also, but it wouldn't take him long. He decided to continue for a few minutes in his attempt to scout out the grounds.

He was being as methodical as he could about a very uncertain plan, still nursing his vague and so far utterly vain hopes of locating some spot where he and Esther might manage to be alone and unobserved for half an hour—even just ten minutes would be something. Not that Esther had yet given him any reason to think that she would really go very far with him, especially with her career being somewhat on the line. And not that he, with his father's business future hanging in the balance, had as yet actually tried to persuade her to do anything of the kind. But, all the same—just suppose.

Right now the plan was no more than a half-serious game in the back of Jubal's mind. He told himself that as soon as he had demonstrated the idea's utter impossibility to his own satisfaction, he'd be able to relax and forget about it.

This time around, as Jubal passed the place where the black stone images of Sekhmet stood clustered round their fountain pool, he noted with slight interest that one statue was still missing from its carved stone chair. It looked like the workers might have decided to wait until the weekend was over and the guests had all gone home, before beginning any disruptive project. And he wondered how in hell the thing had ever got down where they had found it. Someone playing jokes. But only in a movie could anyone, even Errol Flynn, drag around a chunk of rock that size.

Looking past nearby vegetation as best he could, down over the adjoining hillsides, he observed that Casa Grande and its cluster of associated buildings were enclosed not merely by one fence but by several, in a widespread, irregular, concentric array. The outer defenses were hundreds of yards distant, and most of them were fairly inconspicuous. How effective they might be was hard to say. Some of the Hearst security people were no doubt out there, patrolling at some distance from the house, but others were always nearby. With a little ingenuity it ought to be possible to figure out where those watchdogs were concentrating their attention at the moment. And then to look around for interesting territory to explore in another direction, somewhere off the brightly lighted walkways . . .

Now. A quick glance around assured Jubal that at the moment he was almost certainly unobserved. If, the next time he went walking with Esther, they just left the regular walk right about *here*, and then went stepping carefully through this flower bed, taking care not to break or crush anything more than was absolutely necessary . . . then it should be possible, on reaching *this* point on the far side of the flower bed, to slide between *these* bushes. . . .

Having penetrated the screen of bushes on this trial run, Jubal stopped to look around again. He had now attained a position where he was almost screened from anyone who might happen to be passing on the nearby walk, or looking this way from any of the houses. But almost wasn't going to be good enough. He would have to move on, a little farther from the houses.

Another point to keep in mind was that at night it was probably going to be pitch black in here among this vegetation: good thing he had borrowed the flashlight.

He moved on, enjoying his exploration. The thing to do was to look the place over carefully, now while he still had daylight.

The next screen of bushes proved not to be as thick as it had looked at first glance. On its far side, a slope of California's long, golden-toasty coastal grass went down fairly steeply, folding with other slopes into a snug ravine containing still more bushes and a small grove of trees. Beyond that, again, were large but unspectacular outbuildings: probably the stables, Jubal thought, and there must be workers' housing somewhere, besides dog kennels and whatever buildings were needed for the private zoo.

But when he came to the place where the men had been struggling with the stone weight under morning sunshine, the men were gone and so was the wandering image of Sekhmet. Maybe it had been hauled away somewhere, to be repaired or refinished, or—

What was *that?*

What it was, was the damnedest sound he'd ever heard. Something like the noise he'd earlier heard with Esther, but different now, and louder.

Jubal first heard a rustling, then saw, beyond some bushes, a strange figure, a sight so unexpected that it stopped him in his tracks. It was that of a tall, bald man clad all in blue, moving in an odd way, as if he were running in place. Then the man in blue abruptly disappeared.

Moments later there followed unearthly groans, and another moment after that the boy saw, practically overhead, what looked like a huge splash of something liquid flying through the air. It scintillated like fine particles of ice. But unlike any liquid that Jubal had ever seen before, this stuff evaporated before it fell. It looked so realistic that he dodged back to get out from under it, but then stood gaping as the vision vanished.

... for a moment it seemed that the ground was shaking beneath his feet, and he felt again the indescribable sensations that had earlier possessed him when he entered the vicinity of the black statue. But what really set the hair rising on the back of his neck this time was a soft yet trilling kind of cry, the kind of sound he could imagine coming from the throat of Esther Summerson in deep distress. Not that *she* was out here now, of course; but . . .

. . . he was leaning forward, bracing his hands on his knees to try to give his body some stability. Though it wasn't really his body that needed to be stabilized, it was his mind. The sound of the groans again called up a mental image of a woman or girl, in some kind of horrible trouble. Without stopping to think, he turned and moved forward again, away from the big house.

The world around him had regained equilibrium, but all was not well. There in the long grass lay *something*. . . .

Jubal's heart gave a lurch, and a moment later his stomach followed suit. He needed to take three or four deep breaths before he was able to get himself under control.

The body of a man lay sprawled, face down and arms out-flung, just where the slope became gentle and almost leveled out. Surrounding bushes, at a little distance, concealed the spot almost entirely. The man was hatless, wearing a black leather jacket, head covered with thick, fair hair cut short. Both hands were gloved in what appeared to be black leather.

There were no obvious signs of violence.

Gingerly Jubal knelt beside the motionless form, and tentatively put out a hand to touch one arm. A moment later he snatched back his fingers and recoiled. The body was warm, but incredibly, inhumanly stiff, as hard to the touch as any Egyptian statue that had ever been carved. Jubal's tentative tug meant to roll the man over created only a slight rocking motion of the entire figure.

No matter what he thought he had seen a little earlier, the one creature immediately in sight was a human being, obviously not the bald man dressed in blue. And just as obviously dead.

The face, halfway turned in Jubal's direction, was undamaged, but at the same time it was about the deadest face that Jubal had ever seen. The open eyes were blue glass. And it was not a face that he had ever seen before.

Slowly he got to his feet, and backed away, one step and then another, without taking his eyes away from the horror in front of him. The man wasn't dressed like one of the groundskeepers, or security guards, and he certainly wasn't one of the waiters, who were mostly Filipino. Some kind of intruder, then, who had simply sneaked onto the grounds? Maybe he was a burglar, or would-be kidnapper? Someone who thought he had a grudge against Hearst?

Only when Jubal's thoughts had moved in that direction did he spot the pistol, lying almost concealed by tall grass, near the man's rigid right hand. It was so close to Jubal that he almost stepped on the weapon before he noticed it.

The pistol seemed to dispose of an alternate possibility that had just crossed Jubal's mind: that the corpse before him was that of some poor drifter who had just wandered onto the estate looking for a handout. One of those Okies who kept on migrating west to California, their Oklahoma farms having virtually blown away in the great drought of the Dust Bowl. But from what Jubal knew of Okies, they weren't likely to be wearing leather gloves; most of them would be lucky if they had shoes. And they probably didn't carry pistols. Whoever this man was, he looked well-fed, well-groomed, and was not actually that poorly dressed.

But figuring out what exactly had happened here wasn't Jubal's problem, nor was the identity of the victim. His immediate problem was that he had to find someone, tell someone, at once.

Back on his feet, he had taken no more than four or five

strides, running up the nearest grassy slope when he met Captain Murray, the chief of security, flashlight in hand as if anticipating the approach of dusk, and his own pistol holstered on his hip.

Murray's lean body was moving quickly, and his hawk-nosed face was set in a grim expression. Trotting along beside him was one of his men who Jubal had not seen before, also in khakis, which seemed to be the usual garb, practically a uniform, of Hearst's security people on the estate.

"Some kind of a problem?" the captain snapped out. Jubal got the impression that a moment earlier Murray had been on the point of asking a guest politely how he had managed to stray this far away from the usual walkways. But the look on Jubal's face must have made him shelve that query in favor of one more practical.

"Over there," Jubal told them succinctly, pointing downhill. The two men hurried past him to bend over what was lying in the grass. A moment later the captain turned and beckoned for Jubal to join them.

Jubal did so. As he came up, he gestured awkwardly. "I was just walking around, and I heard . . . something. . . ."

"Yeah, we heard it too," said the assistant. Unlike his boss, he was wearing no holster on his belt. "Funny noises. Seemed to come from over this way."

Captain Murray was now discovering for himself something Jubal could have told him about if asked, the terrific stiffness of the body. Rigor mortis had obviously set in. When Murray pulled on one arm, the whole body moved as a unit, like some dummy from a store window. Awkwardly the captain turned the corpse over, a grotesque process. Jubal got the eerie impression that even the blond hair seemed disinclined to move, except all in one piece, like the bronze hair on a statue. Then he inspected the figure of the late stranger for holes in the clothing, or blood. He found none.

"There's a gun," Jubal pointed out helpfully.

Both men looked at the weapon where it lay on the

ground. "Didn't hear any shots," observed Murray's assistant. "Did you?"

"No," said Jubal.

Murray had gone down on all fours in the grass, to sniff at the revolver without touching it. "Hasn't been fired any time recently," he commented.

The assistant was shaking his head. "Never saw anyone get as stiff as this feller. Must have been here a few hours."

"Maybe. But it can happen real fast, sometimes," his boss assured him. "I seen it in the war, Oscar. Cadaveric spasm, the medics called it."

"I'll be damned," said Oscar, duly impressed.

"Quite likely you will," said Murray in an abstracted voice. Meanwhile he had turned back to Jubal and was gazing at him thoughtfully.

Oscar was now taking his turn at examining the body, which meant poking gingerly at it with two fingers. "Not a mark on him, huh? That's good, means we don't have to go lookin' if all the big cats and bears are in their cages."

"No," said the captain, still abstracted. He was still staring at the only available witness. "They're in their cages all right. You're Jubal Doors, right?"

"Right."

"Know this fella, Jubal?"

Jubal shook his head. "Never seen him before. No idea who he is. I was just kind of exploring around . . . and there he was."

"Should I call some of the boys over here, Captain?" asked Oscar helpfully. "Search around before it gets dark?"

"No, not yet. Search for what?" Then the security chief made a vague gesture, as if shooing his aide away. "Lemme think a minute first. Got to find the right way to handle this."

Murray didn't have to think long before he looked up sharply and asked Jubal if he'd seen anyone else around who looked like he didn't belong on the property.

"No," Jubal answered promptly. His earlier half-glimpse

of a tall, blue-clad figure in the bushes had been so brief, so vague, and so outrageously disconnected from everything else in his surroundings, that he still wasn't sure if he'd really seen it there or not.

The afternoon was very quiet now, ready to go shading into evening twilight. The westering sun had disappeared behind a bank of clouds low out over the ocean.

Oscar had been quiet long enough. "Cap'n, you know how the Chief is, on certain subjects. He will blow his top when he hears about this. Or he'll just curl up and die, I don't know which."

"Yeah."

In the short time Jubal had been at San Simeon, he had already heard several casual references to Mr. Hearst's strong aversion to death, even as a topic of conversation.

"And we'll get the blame. This happened on our shift." The helper sounded genuinely worried.

"Shut up a minute, I said, let me think."

Jubal was having trouble picturing Mr. Hearst curling up and dying for any reason, let alone over any simple piece of news, no matter how unpleasant.

But the chief of security knew his boss a lot better than Jubal did, and evidently had a different view of the situation. At last Murray said, "You're right, Oscar, seeing or hearing about anything dead really gets to him. Remember when his last dog died? Little dachshund."

"Yeah." Oscar was nodding solemnly. "And we even had to paint that dead palm tree green, until we could get a replacement in."

"Yeah." Murray was wearing a tin whistle, hung on a cord around his neck, and now he fished the whistle out from where it had been tucked inside his shirt, and held it in his hand and looked at it. But he didn't look like he was going to blow it.

Jubal sat down in the grass at last. His knees had gone a little shaky for a minute there, but he thought they would be steady when he stood up again.

At last, looking at Jubal again, Captain Murray said, "I'd say this fellow came on the grounds intending no good."

His helper had now had time to get a suggestion ready. "How 'bout this, Captain? Say there were two burglars, kidnappers, or whatever. They sneaked on the grounds, and got this close to the house, and then had a dust-up about something. One killed the other, then gave up on doing whatever job they'd intended, and just ran for it."

"Killed him how?"

"Hit him over the head, maybe? Or maybe this character just had a heart attack."

"Maybe." Murray was still thinking. "Though he don't look like he's been hit over the head. And he's young for a heart attack, can't be much over thirty."

With a sigh of dissatisfaction, the security chief bent over the victim again, and gingerly began going through his pockets. Whoever he was, he had not been carrying a whole lot with him. Jubal hovered, shifting his position so he could watch closely. The search turned up nothing at all that gave a clue as to who the man might be. A couple of keys, a pocket knife. No billfold or driver's license. No loose change, but a surprising amount of paper money, fives, tens, and twenties in a money clip. Jubal estimated between fifty and a hundred dollars.

It seemed an awful lot of dough for a casual burglar to be carrying, especially before he'd even got near enough to the houses to burgle anything. Murray didn't even count the bills, but rubbed them between his fingers for a moment, and then, regretfully but decisively, tucked them back where they had come from.

Oscar let out a faint sigh as the money disappeared again.

With an air of having made a decision, Murray slapped his hands on his thighs and stood up straight. He said, "This is almost sure to get reported sooner or later. But I'd feel happier about it if he wasn't found on the grounds."

Then the senior security man seemed to be struck by a

sudden thought. He looked at Jubal sharply. "You tell anyone else about this, kid?"

"No." Jubal shook his head. "How could I? There wasn't time. I just saw him lying here, and went and touched him and saw that he was dead, and turned around and met you guys."

Murray, looking as if he was growing to like his sudden thought, was nodding slowly. Jubal thought he could guess what course of action the man was considering. It would be a hard decision—a security guard would have to be reluctant to stake his own job, his own future, on the idea that a mere kid like Jubal could be trusted to keep his mouth permanently shut about a thing like this. But then, on the other hand, when Jubal stopped to think about it, maybe the risk to Murray and Oscar wouldn't really be that great. Jubal was willing to bet that any of Hearst's employees, at least any one the old man was willing to go to bat for, would have to do something pretty terrible, worse than just moving a dead body, before he would be in danger of arrest by any of the local cops.

The security captain was still looking at Jubal, even more meditatively now. Murray said to him conversationally, "First time you see this kind of thing, it tends to make you sick."

Jubal shook his head. "Not the first time for me. I've seen worse than this. There was a mining accident last year, and I was helping with some of the men when they brought them out. I'm not going to be sick over this."

"Oh," said Murray. Both men gave him a look of reappraisal. Then Oscar the helper put in, "I'd say that if you're a guest here, you're no miner's kid."

But the captain still looked uncertain. "With old W.R.," he said, "you never know for sure who he's going to invite."

"I'm not a miner's kid," said Jubal calmly. "My dad owns a couple." He jerked his head in the uphill direction, toward Casa Grande. "He's in there socializing now. Maybe by now they're sitting down to dinner. He's trying to arrange some kind of a business deal."

"I see," said Murray. "So how about your father?"

"How about him what?"

"I mean, are you going to tell him about this? Maybe you feel you have to tell him?" Security's tone said he could understand that. Jubal telling his father would be perfectly natural, and perfectly all right with him.

But Jubal was shaking his head. Now that he'd had a couple of minutes to recover from the first shock and think the situation over, it was pretty obvious where his duty lay. He turned his gaze toward the bulk of Casa Grande, where soon, at dusk, the floodlights would be coming on to light up the huge white walls. The walls of the enormous house looked old, much older than their inner construction really was, and in places it seemed they might almost be ready to crumble. But that wasn't about to happen. Jubal had heard that underneath a sprinkling and scattering of imported stones taken from ancient buildings they were all modern reinforced concrete, designed and built to resist fierce California earthquakes.

He said, "My father wouldn't want to be interrupted while he's trying to score points with Mr. Hearst. Last thing in the world Dad would want would be for someone to come busting in on them, maybe make Mr. Hearst stop one of his favorite movies in the middle, to deliver this kind of news." Especially, thought Jubal, if it turned out that I was the one who made the discovery. It wouldn't be good if the police were to show up here in the middle of dinner or the nightly movie, or maybe early tomorrow, and spend all day talking to Dad's only son.

Murray sighed. "I been sort of thinking along similar lines myself, Jubal. Why should we bother your dad and the rest when they've got important business? Now this fella lying on the ground here is dead, and nothing we do is going to help him in the least."

"That's true," the boy agreed.

"Sure, it's got to be reported, and it will be. By somebody. But I don't see why it has to be reported as having happened at San Simeon."

Jubal nodded thoughtfully. "I don't see that either," he assented.

Oscar the faithful assistant chimed in with, "Bringing the Chief news like this would be about the last thing in the world that he'd want us to do."

Murray nodded soberly. He seemed about three-quarters decided that Jubal could be trusted. But it seemed he still hadn't absolutely, finally, made up his mind.

Jubal, who had now solidly made up his own mind, pressed for a favorable decision. "If anyone asks me what I've been doing tonight, well, I've got nothing to tell. I wasn't even out here tonight, away from the paved walks. And as far as I know, you weren't either. In fact I haven't seen either of you guys anywhere this evening."

He turned his head to bestow a sideways glance at the terrible thing that lay on the ground. Now the sky had grown dark enough that Murray's flashlight when he switched it on made a noticeable circle of brightness enclosing the dead face.

"Never seen him anywhere, dead or alive," Jubal reiterated.

Now it seemed that the real decision had already been made, somehow, and the two security men concentrated on technical details. They could do the hushing-up fairly readily; there seemed no chance that the victim had been any kind of a celebrity. But whoever he really was . . .

"We can't just bury him like a dead dog," said Oscar the helper, as if feeling last minute qualms.

The captain shook his head. "I'm not thinking we'll bury him at all. I think it wouldn't do him any harm to be found beside a highway somewhere, a good long ways from San Simeon."

Oscar began to nod. Explain to him what the job was, and he could do it. "We'll get an old piece of canvas to wrap him in."

Jubal thought that wrapping-up would be a job, with the man's arms sticking out stiff the way they were. But such details weren't Jubal's problem.

Meanwhile the captain was going on with his plan. "Then

we'll back a truck around down there below these bushes." He made vague circular gestures, aiming downhill. "Load him in the cab, take him down to the highway, go well past the village. Drop him off somewhere, far enough away so there's nothing to connect him with San Simeon. He's got his money still in his pocket, and the cops won't be looking for any robbers. Accidental death."

"What about his revolver, Chief? Looks like a Smith & Wesson, don't it?"

"No, I don't care what it is. I don't want it on me, or on you. I don't want it found anywhere near San Simeon. Everything that's his goes with him."

"Okay, boss," said the helper.

"Even his money, hear?"

"Okay."

Pulling out a clean and neatly folded handkerchief, Murray used it carefully to pick the gun out of the long grass and tuck it away in one of the side pockets of the dead man's leather jacket.

Presently Jubal returned to his elegant room in the guest house called Casa del Mar, leaving the stiffened corpse in what seemed Security's capable hands. After washing up a bit, he went to Casa Grande, managing to enter the refectory almost unnoticed, though he was somewhat late. Since dinner tonight, like most meals, was served buffet style, his tardiness was less conspicuous than it might have been.

Jubal saw his parents at dinner, but as usual conducted most of his conversation with Esther, who sat beside him. After dessert tonight, the two young people along with most of the other guests went to the movie. *The Last Outpost*, starring Cary Grant.

Later, Jubal heard that Flynn and Niven had missed the show.

*   *   *

His parents had the bedroom next to his, which in the daytime afforded them unsurpassed views of the sea, beyond a mile or so of declining slopes.

When the movie was over, and people were generally turning in for the night, Jubal tapped on their door to say good night before heading for his own bed.

"Have fun today, Jube?" his mother asked.

"Sure, it was all right."

Speaking simultaneously, they both asked him what he had thought of the movie.

"It was all right."

His father, taking off his reading glasses to wipe them, grumbled, "I understood it a lot better than last night's show. For some reason, they moved the whole Charge of the Light Brigade from the Crimea all the way to India. Hollywood!"

Jubal's mother had just about zero interest in the Light Brigade or where they ought to charge. She asked, "How are you getting along with that Summerson girl? You seemed to be talking to her nicely at dinner."

"Okay. We were swimming early this morning. Then this evening we shot pool and walked over to look at the animals again."

"What kind of suit did she wear?" asked Jubal's mother, yawning in her dressing gown, putting down her magazine.

"Suit?"

"When you were swimming."

Jubal's dad put in, "I guess if Jube didn't notice her suit, there must have been enough of it." His mother half-seriously swatted at her husband with the magazine.

"Her suit was yellow," Jubal said. "It looked kind of old-fashioned."

"Good." Mother was reassured. "Everyone knows old W.R's a little prudish, but that's not a bad attitude to take, these days."

Father put in, "He has these parties almost every weekend,

well, half the time anyway, and I'm sure he's determined there are going to be no scandals coming out of them."

Jubal nodded as he listened, putting on his face the look that said he was earnestly absorbing information. Privately he was trying to picture to himself what Mrs. Hearst looked like, and what she was doing in New York. She and W.R. were said to have five grown sons. And Jubal was wondering to himself just how big a scandal it would be if prudish old W.R.'s wife walked in on one of his famous prudish weekends and found him with his mistress. But it wasn't hard to figure out that that just wasn't going to happen.

When Jubal turned out the light in his room, he was vaguely worried about bad dreams, but his sleep turned out to be sound and uninterrupted. The remainder of Saturday night passed without any general alarm being sounded because of a dead body. Certainly the Enchanted Hill got no visit from the police.

After breakfast on Sunday morning, hours after Captain Murray had presumably disposed of the mysterious dead man, Jubal looked around for a newspaper every chance he got, and tried for a while turning off the piped music in the billiard room so he could listen to the radio. There was nothing in the news about the discovery of any mysterious corpse. When Jubal had thought about it for a while he decided that mysterious corpses were probably a dime a dozen out there in the real world, where miners died in cave-ins. Hardly a day passed, probably, without a nameless corpse being found beside a highway somewhere.

So on Sunday morning it looked to him like the excitement, such as it had been, was over. Someday maybe, maybe years and years from now, he'd be able to tell his dad how he'd saved his important meeting for him. The only problem would be in getting Dad to believe such a wild story.

*   *   *

Many times during the years to come, when Jubal as a man looked back on how concerned he'd been about not spoiling Dad's important meeting, he would shake his head and marvel silently: it was funny, it was really hilarious, how important that meeting had seemed to the men involved in it, and also to the sixteen-year-old and the security chief who had tried to protect their business deals.

But of course at that point not one of those people had had even the ghost of the faintest idea of what was really going on at San Simeon that summer weekend.

And in fact Jubal never did relate the wild story to his Dad. Instead he kept quiet about it for six and a half decades, and then, gripped by a trembling old man's fear, he poured out to his son every detail he could remember.

SEVEN

On Sunday morning, Jubal saw nothing at all of Oscar, and got only one brief look at Captain Murray. That was at a distance, when Jubal happened to be floating on his back in calm water out near the middle of the Neptune Pool, under a sky that promised another flawless day of California summer. The khaki-clad man, no longer wearing a pistol on his hip, stood gazing in Jubal's direction for perhaps a full ten seconds, and Jubal looked back. But they were too far apart to exchange any subtle signals, and neither of them was going to wave. Feeling somewhat reassured by the captain's silent presence, Jubal turned over in the steam-warmed water and pulled in a long crawl stroke for the far end of the pool, where Neptune drove his energetic team of marble horses.

Jubal's parents were not regular churchgoers, and they saw no need to change their habits here. Hearst did not go to church, and few or none of the Hollywood crowd seemed interested; it looked to Jubal like few of them even got up before noon, except he heard one of the maids saying that Marion Davies sometimes rode a limousine into the village of San Simeon to attend Mass in the small Catholic church there, taking with her any other guests who were similarly interested.

All through the early hours of Sunday, Esther stayed in her room. Jubal caught only a glimpse of her in passing, during breakfast in the refectory. Word passed from her parents (Jubal thought they didn't like him, though he didn't know why) was that some new Hollywood project had come up, and she had to study a new script, in preparation for a screen test that she soon might or might not have to take. So Jubal was thrown back on his own devices for most of the day.

Built into a wall panel of each and every guest bedroom at San Simeon was a cloth circle concealing behind it a radio speaker, and just below each speaker were controls with which the guest, if he or she chose, could tune in a steady diet of music from a record player somewhere in the main house. Alternately, it was possible to listen to any of six regular radio stations, three in Los Angeles and three in San Francisco. Jubal tried each station several times in the course of the day, but still failed to hear any news regarding the discovery of any mysterious body.

Also he checked out both the L.A. and San Francisco papers, when he had the chance; the ones delivered to the Ranch were all Hearst papers, of course, and they tended to have the same comics in them, whatever city they came from. Another thing they had in common was a total lack of news about the discovery of any mysterious dead man, anywhere in the state of California. That at least was a relief.

Jubal figured that Esther would have to come out of her room for lunch, and that proved to be the case. At the Ranch there was no room service, no way that anyone was going to eat lunch, or any other meal, anywhere but in the regular dining room—another of old W.R.'s little quirks. If you wanted as much as a cup of coffee, that was where you had to go. And when Esther came out of her room for lunch there was a short interval of time when she and Jubal had the big refectory table practically to themselves, and he had a chance to talk to her.

Today's lunch, like every other San Simeon meal that Jubal had partaken of so far, was being served buffet style. One vast sideboard held a big silver dish of something that Jubal guessed was probably lobster, and another dish of eggs that seemed too small to have been laid by any ordinary chickens. Jubal sniffed at these and passed them by; he helped himself to some clam chowder, and then a plate of little sausages and a kind of fancy mashed potatoes, not so much transformed that he couldn't tell what they were. Pouring into a fragile cup from a big china pot, he got himself a drink of something that turned out to be tea.

There was a bewildering array of fancy silver urns and trays and utensils on the single long refectory table, as well as on the two enormous sideboards, which also held plates and cups of some kind of antique china—but then, deployed at intervals along the table, were plain ordinary jars of yellow mustard that you could buy in any grocery store, and plain, cheap glass bottles of Heinz Tomato Ketchup, along with ten-cent boxes of paper napkins. This, obviously, was the way that W.R. wanted his dining room arranged. No one seemed to know why.

Esther, casually dressed as if for croquet or a picnic, showed up when Jubal was about halfway through his solitary lunch, and he tossed aside the latest newspaper, in which he had most recently been searching without result for some word of a dead stranger.

"Hi."

"Hi."

At first, Esther was not in much of a mood to talk. Then she explained that she had been having trouble with her parents.

"I argue with mine quite a bit," he assured her.

That seemed to make her feel a little better. But other things were bothering her too. Like, for instance, the wandering statue. "I had kind of an ugly dream about that, last night," she informed him.

And the moment Esther said that, something stirred in Jubal's memory: some kind of lurching horror that had disturbed him in the night too, but which his memory had somehow managed to bury again. Until now. But of course he had had more than stone statues to give him nightmares.

"I was dreaming too," he told his companion.

But Esther was still focused on her own bad dreams. "If we take another walk, I don't want to go that way."

"Okay. Sure. We don't have to. There's plenty of other stuff to see." But Jubal suddenly knew an irrational fear that they were going to stumble over another dead body.

The half-dozen or so guests who had gone out horseback riding early in the morning were back by lunchtime. Some of them looked cheerful, and some looked bored, but it was pretty obvious that none of them had stumbled over any dead bodies along the trail.

Prowlers on the grounds, and unexplained dead bodies, seemed like good reasons for him to stay in his room at night, and to make sure that anyone he cared about did the same.

Fortunately that wasn't a problem as far as Mom and Dad were concerned. Dad took his exercise in the early morning, when he took any at all, and Mom much preferred sitting and gossiping.

Esther of course was another matter. Jubal felt certain that she could have heard nothing about his unpleasant discovery. Because she was now hinting strongly that she could be talked into coming out late at night for another stroll around the grounds; Jubal thought there was even a suggestion that the two of them might somehow find a private spot, where they could feel free to get to know each other really well. It crossed his mind to wonder if she was really fighting with her parents now, and whether she might be ready to put her own career in danger just to spite them.

He had no intention of wrecking anyone's career, but it just wasn't in the cards for him to turn down an invitation like that. It wasn't that he had some special need to try to score with a movie star. Actually it wasn't even that Esther was all that good looking; Jubal didn't have any trouble coming up in his own mind with the names of a couple of girls he knew in Colorado who were considerably prettier. But Esther sure did have— something. Something that must come through when pictures of her were put on film. A certain liveliness or electricity, a kind of appeal possessed by no other girl that he had ever met.

And anyway, even if she'd been plain as a mud fence, he wouldn't have felt right, knowing what he knew, if he let her go walking around the grounds by herself, especially at night. Even leaving aside all worries about strange rigid corpses and moving statues, there were more ordinary matters to be considered, such as the fact that someone like Errol Flynn was quite likely to come along, and this time Flynn might be sober enough to be dangerous to any young woman's virtue. If the movie star's reputation rested on any real basis of truth at all, the fact that Esther was only sixteen wasn't going to offer her much protection.

It was on the third night of the long weekend that the real crisis came.

On Sunday night Jubal was hoping and expecting that Esther would be able to come out of her room and walk with him again; he thought, and devoutly hoped, that she still had not the faintest idea what had happened on the grounds on Saturday night.

Every Sunday afternoon at five o'clock, Pacific time, about half the people in America had to stop what they were doing to listen on the radio to Edgar Bergen the ventriloquist, and Charlie McCarthy his wooden dummy, who most of the time seemed a lot livelier than Bergen. The dwellers in Casa Grande, and the outlying guest houses, were no exception.

Dinner was behind them, and the night's movie had been watched and then rewound into cans of film. So when the appointed time, eleven thirty, came round, Jubal turned off the lights in his room, put on his sportcoat against the coolness of the night, omitting the necktie that he'd worn to dinner, patted his pocket to make sure he had his little borrowed flashlight, and quietly went out as he had planned.

A minute later, he met Esther, as if by accident, and the two of them went strolling.

"You keep looking around tonight," she commented, when they had gone only a few yards. "Getting nervous like me?"

"You're not really nervous, are you? Or you wouldn't have come out walking."

"Sure I would," Esther said. "You can't let things get you. If something really bothers you, you've got to do it."

Jubal had heard cowboys talk like that, about overcoming fear when your job involved riding dangerous horses. "Reason I'm looking around," he said, "is that I'm just wondering who else might be out walking."

"If there is anyone else, it's probably just the security people. They'll see to it that you go back in your house when we finish our walk, and I go back in mine. And that's the way it's going to be. People get thrown out of here, sent down the Hill, for any kind of hanky panky."

"What a way to go," said Jubal. On an impulse he casually pulled out of his side coat pocket the flashlight he had borrowed, tossed it up and caught it in his hand.

"What's that for?" Esther asked, evidently intrigued.

"Well, you never know. Suppose there was a power failure, and all the lights went out."

"Huh." Esther didn't seem to think a power failure likely.

"Or, suppose we saw something mysterious that was a little bit off the trail, and we wanted to go and look it over?" Jubal flicked the bright beam briefly out into the nearby grass and flower beds, then quickly turned it off, not wanting to draw the attention of any curious security folk who happened to be around.

Esther seemed taken by the idea of exploration. "What kind of a thing would that be?"

"Oh, something mysterious. The kind of thing that you can't tell what it might be until you get a good look at it."

"That sounds mysterious, all right."

"When our walk is over, you'll go back in your house and I'll go back in mine. But security might not be watching us every minute of the time while we're out walking. Especially if we were just a little way off the walk somewhere, looking at something mysterious."

And then, to Jubal's surprise, it was actually Esther who very casually took his hand as they were walking. So he suddenly wondered if security was actually looking at them at this very minute, and suppose he were to make a move to kiss her, right now . . .

He was on the brink of stopping, with some such intention in mind, but Esther at the crucial moment kept on moving, her hand still in his, tugging him along.

Jubal thought he had been doing fine until now, talking with this movie actress, but awkwardness suddenly took hold. He wanted to tell her something that would let her know how he was starting to feel about her; and he knew that as soon as he was alone again, he would be able to think of a dozen things he should have said. . . .

And he had carefully planned for this moment to arrive when they were somewhere else, so what were they doing *here*, again? Jubal was perfectly certain that they *had* turned off the walk at a different place, hardly ten seconds ago. But here they were, somehow back in the mystic, troubling spot beside the Sekhmet statues.

And once again reality was beginning to grow uncertain.

Now, paradoxically, as if time or space or both had suddenly gone wobbly, Jubal and Esther were also very near the place where he had found the dead man—yesterday? Had it really been only yesterday?

In spite of all Jubal's careful effort to choose paths leading somewhere else, they were still—here. Like there was no way you could possibly get away from it.

Esther's voice seemed to reach him from a considerable distance. "Jubal, what's wrong? I thought I saw . . ."

"What?"

She didn't answer. What spooked her couldn't have been another dead man, though; she wasn't looking at the ground, which was the logical place to discover corpses, but past Jubal's shoulder, into some tall growth.

And now he had lost sight of his companion altogether. As if some tremendous—fog—could be covering the whole estate. Or covering his eyes and mind . . .

Jubal used the flashlight boldly at last. Being noticed by security was suddenly the least of his worries. In the sharp beam he could see Esther's face. But there was a new problem now: she was first drifting away, then coming closer again, as if the status of the hill beneath their feet was unreliable, though neither of them was really moving.

And now he saw there had to be something wrong with the flashlight in his hand, for there seemed to be multiple beams projecting from its glassy eye. First about a dozen shafts of light, then a hundred, as if Jubal with the electric torch in his hand were struggling in a universe of mirrors.

Earthquake?

No, whatever force was trying to twist and turn the world was too silent for that. And it seemed to be reaching even deeper than the center of the earth.

"Esther? *Esther?*" The second time it came out as a scream. "Jubal!"

The two of them were hardly more than an arm's length apart, and moving toward each other, but still it was impossible for their outstretched hands to touch.

After screaming his name Esther fell to making little sobbing noises, and from the look on her face he was afraid that she was going to faint. He himself wasn't doing too well either.

But suddenly they were close together once again, and now he reached to take her in his arms.

Now the immense bulk of Casa Grande, seeming to loom almost over their heads, had four towers instead of two. Two of them were bathed in red floodlights, and none of the four were exactly alike. Near at hand, Jubal could see two bushes where a moment ago there had been only one. And then he was looking at a bush of bushes, all of them waving insubstantial leaves and branches, no two of them quite precisely alike. First heated air, then cold, blew in his face. Odors that he had never smelled before assailed him. In his ears there sounded a drumming and a babbling, and a screaming of immense bagpipes. There were two dark statues looming, and one of them reached out for him with rocklike hands.

Sekhmet. It seemed to Jubal that a whole chorus of discordant voices chanted out the name.

Esther was suddenly gone, had been snatched off somewhere out of his sight. And all Jubal knew for certain was that the world had gone crazy around him, and he too was being somehow dragged away, into a blue-white vortex. . . .

EIGHT

Jubal had to fight his way through a rapid succession of ugly dreams, each more frightening than the one before. In some of them he was being pursued by tall, black figures that moved with the stiffness of stone statues. In other visions the world seemed to be changing beneath his feet, in such a way that he knew that he was damned to hell and lost forever. But Jubal's mind tore free of all bad dreams in the process of waking up. And by the time he was completely awake, their terror and loneliness were all but totally forgotten.

He was awake now, no longer terrified. But as soon as he began to look around him fear was replaced by almost total bewilderment. He had awakened lying flat on his back on a narrow, flat, firm kind of bunk or couch, which stood in the middle of a small room formed by curving overhead and walls. The room contained no other furniture besides the bunk, and it was like no other place that Jubal had ever seen.

The windowless walls were composed of broad triangular panels or tiles, most of them blue in an assortment of shades. A few of these triangular segments were glowing white, and these provided light at a comfortable level. The walls went up straight to a height of about eight feet, then curved gently into a smoothly rounded ceiling of the same materials and design, so no sharp edges or corners were visible. At the far end of the room, only a little beyond the foot of Jubal's bunk, were two full-length, doorless openings, set directly across from each

other in opposite walls. Both doorways were at the wrong
angle for him to see much of anything through them as long as
he remained lying on the couch.

Sixteen-year-old Jubal Doors sat up with a jerky motion,
noticing confusedly as he did so that the narrow bed on which
he lay lacked any kind of sheet, blanket, or pillow, and was
entirely covered in a smooth brownish fabric something like
leather. More startling was the fact that he was still fully
clothed, even to his shoes and sportcoat.

He had not the remotest idea of how he had come to be
lying where he was.

Raising an arm, Jubal looked automatically at his wristwatch, which was still ticking away. But in his strange state of
mind, the position of the hands failed to register.

The room, the compartment—whatever the proper
name for the space he now inhabited—was quiet. And when
he swung his legs off the couch, the gray, smooth floor, or
deck, was steady beneath his feet. Still, Jubal delayed for a
moment before standing up. He wasn't dizzy. *Numb* was a
more accurate description of his state. And the numbness
was not of his body, but of his mind. Something was not
quite right.

It was at that point that he stumbled over an odd object on the
floor, something that tripped him so he almost fell. Looking
down, Jubal saw a reddish, rubbery-looking thing almost a
yard long and an inch thick, with several branches, like a snake
that had been hatched as Siamese triplets. One of the branches
ended in something that looked like a needle, and others in flat
disks with flat, smooth little panels set into them. Jubal had no
idea what it was, but it had an ugly look about it, and he kicked
it to one side of the room with an instinctive movement.

Then he recoiled from it momentarily; the thing was
writhing, as if it might be alive, or half-alive, like a beheaded
snake. Holding his breath, Jubal moved a step nearer and

peered at it closely. Now it looked as dead as rubber, and he couldn't see any head, or other organic parts.

There had been nightmares—
Forget the nightmares, and the rubbery snake as well, he had bigger problems to worry about. He was wide awake now, and he could still think. More or less. If he made an effort. What kind of hospital put its patients to bed without taking off their shoes? And he registered the fact that his small borrowed flashlight still rested in one pocket of his sportcoat.

Someone must have carried him or dragged him into this chamber, and put him on this bed. But who, and why? Could he have fainted, somewhere? But he had never in his life just passed out cold.

Trying out his memory, he had to reach back for what felt like a long way before he came to anything that felt like firm ground. There was a recent Friday that felt solid enough. That was the day when Jubal and his parents had arrived on a visit to the fascinating place that old W. R. Hearst called the Ranch. The day when Jubal had talked to Marion Davies, who'd assured him that everything would be all right . . .

But now he felt certain, without having to think about it, that his present surroundings had no connection whatever with San Simeon. He had seen a fair number of the rooms in Casa Grande, and in the smaller houses, and all of them were certainly strange. But they were strange in ways very different from this one.

Now, slowly, more pieces of memory were coming back. The days of the weekend, Saturday and Sunday. Swimming in the Neptune Pool, going for walks with Esther, rubbing lotion on her back. Chatting with Marion, saying hello to Errol Flynn. Eating unfamiliar food from almost priceless dishes. Statues of Sekhmet that would not stand still, strange sensations. The discovery of a dead man, listening to the radio for news . . .

There were still some gaps. But now Jubal remembered how, on Sunday night, he had met Esther according to their arrangement, and how the two of them had gone walking together in the grounds.

According to Jubal's plan, they had turned off the walk at what he'd *thought* was a nice, safe, convenient place . . . now he could recall all that pretty clearly. But everything that had happened after they left the walk had now faded into obscurity.

Sekhmet had been there, somehow. Jubal felt unreasonably sure of that. Every time he turned around, waking or dreaming, he seemed to run into Sekhmet. . . .

But then somehow, at some time, for some reason, someone had carried or dragged or wheeled him into this strange place, and laid him on this peculiar bed. Did it make sense to assume that there'd been some kind of accident, and he'd been taken to a hospital? All right, this didn't really look like a hospital. But what else could it be?

What bothered him most immediately was the fact that *here* was very strange.

He was surrounded by the silence, an almost eerie silence, the blue walls and ceiling, patterned with smooth white triangular panels that gave off a gentle, even light. And the two open doorways. Soon he was going to have to take a good look through them.

Coming to in a regular hospital after his tonsillectomy, years ago, Jubal had been sick, and he wasn't sick now. At least he wasn't nauseated. On the other hand, he was perfectly sure that he wasn't completely right.

The temperature of the air in this peculiar environment was comfortable, and its atmosphere held hints—but only hints— of strange, exotic odors. But the smells were not the never-to-be-forgotten hospital blend of sickness and disinfectants. These were even sharper, stranger things.

Where was Esther now? And where was he?

Once more Jubal looked around him, this time seeking actively for clues, trying seriously to take stock of the room. It hardly deserved to be called a room, being only an enclosed space no more than eight or nine feet wide. Looking over the foot of the bunk, he stood facing one of its blank walls, and it was next to that wall that a pair of door-sized apertures, one on the right side and one on the left, offered opportunities for exploration.

Still Jubal remained standing close beside his bunk. It ought to be perfectly easy to chose one of the doorways, move a couple of strides to his right or left, look through it, and very likely be able to find out where he was. But for some reason he felt frightened of what he might discover.

Instead of moving, he called out for Esther, trying her name several times, a little louder each time, with no result. And then he called out a sharp *Halloo* for anyone who might happen to be listening.

This second effort brought a response. It was a strange, wounded sound, making him think of injured girls and dying cats, though not, thank God, of any noise associated with moving statues. But Jubal couldn't tell whether it had reached him through the right doorway or the left.

Doing his best to move quietly, which was easy enough on this dull gray floor with its slightly yielding surface, Jubal went through the opening on his left, for no particular reason other than his impression that the light entering his chamber from that direction was slightly brighter than that coming through the other doorway.

He went through, and then immediately stopped, realizing that he must be aboard some kind of ship or aircraft. The compartment he had now entered was approximately the same size as that in which he had awakened, but here the shape was distinctly different. This one suggested to his inexperienced mind the cockpit or control cabin of a big airplane, though he saw no recognizable controls of any kind, no joystick or steering wheel or rudder pedals. A pair of seats, rather oddly shaped as

Jubal thought, were placed facing a broad glassy surface like a windshield, with below it another surface planed and angled like the dashboard of an automobile, the latter studded with lighted gauges or instruments, indicators of some kind that indicated nothing to Jubal.

Just outside the windshield—if that was the right name for the frontal glass in this kind of vehicle—was a small lump on the hull housing a bright light. The light was blinking in a regular pattern, red, green, blue, red, green, blue, sending intermittent flashes and beams of brilliance pulsing away into the darkness. Out in front of the ship there seemed at first glance to be nothing but endless gloom, speckled in the distance, directly ahead, by a very few faint blue stars.

There was no visual clue to suggest that the ship was moving, but he supposed it might be. He had heard of automatic pilots being used on airplanes, though he had no idea how such a device might work.

One of the items on the dashboard was like nothing that Jubal had ever seen before—perhaps it was some kind of a gauge. It bore a little glowing image that he would have sworn was a solid object, a rotating block or cube, and he moved closer, caught up in a momentary fascination. But when he tried to touch the spinning cube, his cautious finger went right through it. Snatching back his hand, he inspected it fearfully, but nothing had happened to his finger.

This was in its own small way a wonderful event, but still Jubal almost immediately forgot all about it. Because the broad, high, glassy screen or window above the instrument panel offered what he had to accept as a look at the outside world.

And the world it showed him, when he began to consider it seriously, was bizarre indeed.

For a few yards beyond the windshield, or window, the view was almost what a sharp lad from Earth might have expected, once he realized that he was getting his first ride in a spaceship. There was an indeterminate amount of, well, space, and just outside and below the windshield the suggestion of a bulge representing the ship's nose. But beyond that . . .

What Jubal saw when he tried to look into the distance in any direction was not a landscape of any kind. Nor was it a sky of any type that he could recognize, because it was neither blue, nor cloudy. The only stars in sight were the bluish handful dead ahead. He could not call the space immediately around them either bright or dark. Rather it was a kind of pure distortion, as if in that direction the entire universe turned, at some unfathomable distance, into cloudy glass. A distortion that tormented the eyes, not with physical pain but with a psychological discomfort, bred out of its uncertain depths and distances, and the seeming impossibility of bringing any part of it clearly into focus.

When Jubal tried to look steadily at this phenomenon for more than a few seconds, it hurt him, not in his eyes but somewhere in the space behind his eyes, and not physically so much as mentally. At certain places, that might have been farther away than others, the distortion gave the impression of wrinkling and unwrinkling, very slowly. . . .

Concentrating on objects inside the cabin was a little easier, even though he could not understand what he was looking at. But here, what bothered him most, even more than the lack of visible controls, was the total absence of any sense of speed, almost of movement of any kind.

So, just to stand in the snug cabin was something of a challenge. But what made Jubal retreat from it at last was not the psychic discomfort that it caused, but the sound of a feeble voice he did not recognize, somewhere behind him, persistently calling him by name.

He had a confused impression that several other voices were also clamoring softly for his attention. But they were not calling him by his name, and he managed to tune them out for the time being.

Turning his back on the chamber he now thought of as the control cabin, he passed through the room in which he had awakened, to find himself in another compartment that was almost identical.

In this chamber also the furniture consisted of a single couch, and it was occupied. Timidly Jubal approached to stand beside it. On closer inspection, this bunk was somewhat different from the one where Jubal had regained his senses, more closely resembling an ordinary hospital bed. This one had a rail on each side, rather like those on a baby's crib. And at a distance of about three feet from the head of the bed a projection from the curving blue wall held small panels, each displaying an intricate pattern of small, shifting lights, at an angle where they would be readily visible to the occupant of the couch. A number of strange devices, tubes and coils, came curling up out of the lower portion of the bunk to clasp and connect in several places with the body of the single occupant.

This was a bald, long-bodied but fine-boned man (after momentary hesitation Jubal rejected the possibility that it could be a woman) who would be tall when he stood up. Not that he seemed capable of standing at the moment. Most of his body was covered in what appeared to be a single, tight-fitting garment of shaded blue, and his pale and not-quite-human face was turned anxiously in Jubal's direction.

The eyes in that pale face were blue, and very human-looking, and at the moment they seemed to be struggling to stay open. The man's gaze was aimed not up at the panels, but directly at Jubal.

Jubal could only hold his breath.

Pale lips opened slowly in the pinched face.

Words came, slow and soft, in a voice that would have been musical had it not been filled with strain. "My name is Lekren, Jubal. Pronounce it if you can."

Jubal swallowed. His lips moved. "Lekren."

"That is correct. That is good." But oh, the words were

coming slowly now. "I am a Taelon, not an earthly human like yourself. But I would be your Companion."

The voice continued to be gentle, totally unfrightening. It spoke quietly and soothingly. At first Jubal had trouble understanding the words, but only because of the persistent shadows of dark dreams in his own mind. Then gradually they began to come clear.

"You know my name," Jubal got out at last.

"I know. Your name."

Now the one on the couch appeared to be having some difficulty breathing. He gave the impression that there were many things he wanted to say, and with considerable urgency, but it was as if he could get out only a few words at a time.

"I know. Some things. But not enough, it seems." Breathe in, breathe out.

"How did I get here?" Jubal asked, humbly.

The answer surprised him. "There has been. A terrible fight. And I. Have been hurt. I trust you have not, Jubal."

Jubal didn't feel hurt, not really. "I'm all right," he said. And he waited, hoping it was true.

This time Lekren needed an even longer pause for breath. Then at last he got out, "This ship will. Take us to a place. Where we will find. The necessary help."

And with that there came a distant roaring in the air, reminding Jubal of certain strange noises in the gardens of San Simeon. Not that, he didn't want any more of *that*, whatever it had been. No more of *that* just now, please God! He swayed on his feet, and to keep his balance had to cling to the rail on the side of the strange bed.

"How did I get here?" he asked again, still humbly.

"I brought you aboard. I was too badly hurt. To do more. All I could do. To get here to my own bunk." The occupant put out a hand to touch Jubal's where he held the rail. The contact had a warm and human feel.

"You must not fear me, Jubal. It was not I who hurt you. Nor did I hurt your friend." The bald head rolled a little, side to side, negating such ideas. The breathing was just a little easier now.

"My friend?"

"She is here too. I am doing my best. To save your lives. Along with my own."

"I'm not hurt," Jubal said. He moved his limbs gently, and blinked his eyes, testing himself. *My friend? What friend?* But of course, this strange man had to be talking about Esther. "I don't think I'm hurt." The waves of not-quite-dizziness, of numbness in the brain, were gradually receding.

"That is good."

Lekren talked to him a little longer, doling out words as best he could, a few at a time, all of them meant to be reassuring, none of them very informative. Jubal's head began to feel a little clearer now. He still had no idea of where he was, but another question seemed even more urgently in need of an answer.

He said to the figure lying before him, "I saw something . . . when I was still there at San Simeon. . . ."

"Go on. Tell me. Take your time."

The gentle encouragement of the voice helped him to relax a little more. "Back there I thought I saw . . . it looked to me like one of the statues had come to life."

"Sekhmet," said the being on the bunk, without the least surprise or hesitation.

Jubal closed his eyes; he knew he'd heard that name somewhere, but he had to think for a minute. "Yes," he said, and opened his eyes again. "They were statues of Sekhmet. Some Egyptian god."

"What you call Sekhmet. Is really our enemy. Yours and mine. A very powerful enemy."

"But statues."

The head of the supine figure on the bunk was shaking, ever so slightly, from side to side, signaling no. "Four figures standing. Around a pond. Three of them were really stone. But the one that you saw moving was not really a statue. It was never that." Pause. Now the breathing began to go considerably easier.

"A long story, Jubal. Of how Sekhmet came to be there, with the statues that resemble him. Great mistakes were made. Not by you. Or me. In a certain—museum. Very far from here."

"A museum?" Jubal wasn't sure he'd heard that right.

"The story is so long. I cannot tell it now."

Jubal murmured something. Briefly he wondered again if he might be going to faint.

"Jubal. You must listen. About Sekhmet. The one you call Sekhmet. Is an Urod. There are certain beings in the universe. Who, though intelligent, have forfeited those innate rights. That intelligence commonly confers."

"An Oo-rod."

"Yes."

"What's an Urod?"

Around them the strange spaceship, if that was really what it was, was silent. The man on the couch seemed unable to come up with any kind of quick explanation. Maybe that was because he again had to work hard at his breathing. Meanwhile Jubal drifted, gaping. The only being he was now able to talk to had just told him that there had been a terrible fight, of some kind, but everything might still be made to turn out right. Somehow the words Jubal was hearing stayed with him, so he was able to turn them over in his mind and try to extract their sense. So far there didn't seem to be a lot of sense to be extracted.

The wave of faintness was retreating. Time to go back to basics. "I'm sorry," he said to the man on the couch. "What did you say your name is?"

"I have said my name is Lekren. I am a Taelon. I would be your Companion, your faithful friend."

At that point Lekren had to pause again. Now the boy got the impression that the man was in considerable pain. "I'm sorry if you're hurt," Jubal said.

A slight nod of acknowledgement. "Do you understand me, Jubal?" the soft voice asked presently.

"I don't know. I don't know what I understand any more and what I don't. Let's start with where I am."

"You are on a ship." The voice remained patient despite its controlled pain. "Call it my ship. You will be returned. To your home. In good time."

"A ship."

"Not the kind of ship that sails the watery ocean." That all came out in one long breath.

Jubal shook his head. "I didn't think it was."

"So you are beginning to understand. That is good. You are a clever young man."

"I've been up forward already, looking out." He gestured with a nod. "There didn't seem to be any pilot."

"I am the pilot." Lekren's breathing was going a little easier now. "But this ship can steer itself. For a time. Listen to me, Jubal. Try to help me, and we will have nothing to worry about."

Jubal thought about that one for a while. "Help you do what?"

"We will come to that. Are you sure your body is not injured?" the pilot prodded.

Jubal shook his head, no. "I'm worried," he got out at last.

"Of course you are. It would be a sign of poor mental health if you were not worried, given the situation in which you find yourself." Breath was coming almost normally. "And what has already happened to you. A re-adaptation of reality can be a trying experience for the most psychologically secure of beings—"

"Re-adaptation."

"Yes—and you humans of Earth are hardly the most secure."

"Hardly," Jubal echoed. Again it seemed that he could feel himself drifting. It would be a great comfort to wake up and find that this was all a dream. But he knew that wasn't going to happen.

"Re-adaptation," he repeated vaguely. Then, with a new stirring of alarm, "I'm not dead, am I?"

"I assure you, you are certainly not dead. As I have already told you, I hope soon to be able to send you on your way home."

"And I'm not dead."

"Not in the least."

Indeed he seemed to be fully awake, but his condition was *strange*. Trying to think constructively about anything was like moving heavy weights of lead.

"Esther Summerson," said Jubal at last. Esther had to be the friend this man was talking about. "What happened to her?"

"You will see your friend presently. Nothing that you need concern yourself about has happened to Esther. As I have said, I am doing my best to preserve her safely, and you as well."

"But what's happened to her already?"

"Nothing serious," the gentle voice repeated. Then the speaker seemed to sense that more explanation would be required. "She is on this ship with us, and I expect you will see her soon. Much of her memory has already been altered. Her career as an entertainer will go on—or at least I see no reason why it should not. If you ever see her again, you will both hazily recall a certain weekend at San Simeon, but to neither of you will it seem especially memorable.

"People there will think you have been gone no more than a few hours, and you will not remember what happened during those hours. This ship will be entirely gone from your memory, and so will I. Your doctors will call the condition that you have amnesia. Those who care for you will be worried for a while, but there will be no more episodes of amnesia, and your life will go on much as it would have done, had you never met a Taelon or an Urod."

"If she's on this ship," said Jubal, "I want to see her."

"Of course. Presently. But first, have you any other questions?"

Jubal thought, then nodded. "Who was the dead man? The one I came across last night? Or, no, I think that was two nights ago. Everything is a little blurred."

Now, suddenly, the pilot's breathing difficulty was back, so he once more had to speak in jerky little phrases. "Our enemy. Has a way of doing that. Blurring minds as well as. Demolishing bodies." A painful pause, and then a wretched gasping groan.

"Our enemy the Urod," Jubal prompted, when the man on the bunk seemed to have recovered somewhat.

"Yes. Actually, Jubal. There was no dead man. The man you discovered did not move. Could not move. Because for him. Time had been slowed. In a very special way. The result was. That he appeared. Lifeless and rigid."

"But he wasn't dead?"

"Is not."

"Who is he, then? Where is he?" Jubal looked at the doorway he had not yet tried, that must lead on to other rooms.

"His name would mean nothing to you. I had hired him, recruited him, to help me. With a hazardous job. Which as we see. Proved to be more hazardous. Than even I . . ."

The words died off. The lids over the blue eyes sagged halfway shut.

"Lekren. Lekren?"

No response. Jubal wondered if he should try to shake this pilot—if he was really a pilot—awake, but decided against it. Lekren had said the ship could fly itself for a time. And so far, being able to talk to Lekren had actually not been very helpful.

Jubal looked at the colored lights on the little panels on the machine that nursed the prostrate pilot, but their occasional changes in brightness and position told him nothing. Except that change of any kind suggested continued life.

He turned away from the bunk and its unconscious burden, and decided he might as well go exploring further. But first his body was making some practical demands that would soon need to be dealt with—and if this was a dream it was getting awfully realistic. For one thing, his bladder was growing uncomfortably full, and before trying to accomplish anything else he wanted to discover some facilities where he could deal with that. On top of that, he was starting to feel an overpowering thirst. And he was hungry too, or had the feeling he would be as soon as his more urgent needs allowed him to concentrate on food.

Returning to his original compartment, he soon discovered that one end of the low bunk's top surface lifted easily, revealing beneath what appeared to be a kind of toilet, reminding Jubal of the type of plumbing he had encountered on train rides. Right now his need was such that he was willing to take a chance; when he had used the fixture, and lowered the lid again, he heard a reassuring, purring kind of flushing noise.

Having relieved one urgency, he was able to concentrate more thoughtfully on his surroundings. Now he noticed on one wall a kind of cupboard built inconspicuously into the blue paneling, which opened to reveal a fountain with a small basin, that seemed designed for both drinking and washing.

Packed neatly into pigeonholes above the basin were several dozen small white packages, unlabeled but giving off a faintly foodlike smell. Choosing a pack and tearing open its fragile wrapper, he found inside a cluster of biscuit-like objects, some pale and some dark. Now the aroma, somehow suggesting both fresh coffee and frying steak, was strong enough to make his mouth water.

A couple of minutes later he had slaked his thirst with a good drink, washed his hands and face, and was munching with satisfaction on a biscuit, having already stuffed several more into his pockets. Now ready to set out exploring, Jubal first looked in again on Lekren, and to his disappointment found the Taelon still unconscious. After pausing at the bedside for a few moments, Jubal moved on through the next doorway in the series.

He found himself in another similar compartment, containing yet another bunk, more like the one in which he had awakened than like Lekren's. And having come this far he was not enormously surprised to discover Esther lying at full length on this bed, her eyes closed, her slender body still clad in the fancy dress she had been wearing when they went for their last walk. The hem of her skirt was decently smoothed down over her knees, her small feet were still shod in party shoes.

Going to her side immediately, Jubal took her hand. "Esther. Esther, wake up."

There was no response, and her arm remained totally limp.

It was a relief to note the slight rise and fall of her breasts, and reassure himself that she was breathing. But it was frightening that her eyes stayed closed and she appeared to be unconscious.

Leaning a little closer, Jubal called her name, first softly and then louder. No good.

Taking a step back, he looked things over. Esther's situation was not exactly the same as his own had been when he woke up. A soft cuff of some material encircling the girl's right arm was connected by a flexible tube to the foundation of the bunk, and so was a pad of similar stuff that lay like a pillow beneath her head. But Esther's connections to the machinery were not nearly as intricate or numerous as those of Lekren in the next room.

Still, the thing wrapped round her arm looked somehow familiar. It took him another moment to recognize it as practically a duplicate of the Siamese snake he had tripped on and kicked aside when he got up. He wondered if this one too was somehow half-alive. Right now it seemed totally inert.

He could, of course, try to remove the strange thing from

her arm. But for all he knew it was serving some vital function, keeping Esther alive.

Jubal tried again, gently and tentatively, to awaken her, touching her arm away from the snake, and her shoulder, but still her eyes remained closed.

He started to leave, heading for the next doorway in the series, opposite the one by which he'd entered. But he turned back at the last moment.

"I'm going to look around a little more," he assured Esther's unresponsive form. "I'll be back soon."

Then he turned away to go exploring.

NINE

Lekren had told Jubal that the man was not dead, but had made no mention of his being aboard the ship. But there could be no mistake about this discovery. In the bunk of the fourth compartment in the row, after Jubal's chamber, Lekren's, and Esther's, lay the very man whose rigid corpse Jubal had once discovered stretched out in the long grass of San Simeon. Jubal could recognize the clothes, including the leather jacket and gloves, the same short blond hair. The only difference seemed to be that he was no longer a rigid corpse. The man's eyes were now closed, and his arms lay more or less normally at his sides. Jubal could not resist poking at one shoulder to see if the terrific rigor still persisted. It did not.

This bunk, like Esther's, was equipped with visible support systems, about the same number Esther had, connected to the occupant. And close inspection showed that the man was now breathing gently. Around his right arm, right over the sleeve of his black leather jacket, twined a rubbery Siamese snake.

For some time Jubal remained standing by the bunk, trying to manage something in the way of constructive thought. Captain Murray had said, plainly enough, that he and Oscar were going to haul this man's body away and dump it somewhere beside a highway. If Hearst's security agents had really done that, then the body, living or dead, must have been picked up again, somehow, by someone else, and brought aboard the ship. And cured of its rigor, and made to breathe.

Was it possible that Murray was somehow in league with Lekren? Had the security captain, instead of dumping the body somewhere at roadside, brought it directly here, aboard this ship?

Suddenly Jubal remembered the revolver, and Murray's demonstration of tucking the weapon back inside the stranger's pocket. It was still there; when Jubal gingerly pressed the leather over the jacket pocket, he could feel the hard metallic bulge.

And Jubal's memory of the numbness in his own mind was now taking a more definite form.

Suddenly he remembered the dark dream that had troubled his most recent sleep.

What had Lekren called it, the thing that brought on fear and nightmares, and threatened to change the world? Yes— the Urod. The memory had come back to him because now Jubal could once more feel its pressure on his mind.

Now Jubal's eyes turned, slowly, reluctantly, to the next doorway in the series of compartments. He didn't want to go through it and confront what lay beyond. But he knew that he really had no choice.

The light was somewhat dimmer in the fifth small room in the row, and Jubal hesitated in the doorway, waiting for his vision to adjust. This chamber also seemed to be the last one in the series—or at least this time there was no visible doorway in the rear wall. And this one contained, as Jubal discovered when his eyes had accommodated themselves, yet another variation on the basic bunk. This unit, occupied like all the others, was less like a bed, more like a slab-like table or machine, with a different constellation of readouts and controls emerging from the walls to connect to it.

There was another notable difference. Here, there was no sign of rubbery artificial snakes, and no connections of any kind seemed to have been made to the occupant. No doubt it would have been hard to do so, because the figure on the rectangular slab was obscured inside a similarly shaped block of—something.

Its appearance at first suggested to Jubal that it might be a huge chunk of ice. But a tentative touch with one finger indicated that it was much stranger stuff. Its interior looked as shadowy as fog, and seemed to contain drifting movement. But the surface was hard as rock, and much too warm to be ice. Something in the feel of it struck Jubal as so unnatural that he jerked his fingers away, as if from burning heat.

He could just make out that there was something else inside the shadowy solid. A figure, so heavily obscured that Jubal needed half a minute or so to be sure of its appearance. But once he got a good look there could be no doubt: he was looking at one of the tall statues of Sekhmet from the walkway beside Casa Grande.

He had already gone beyond surprise. And there seemed a kind of logic in the discovery, as there might have been in a dream.

Not a statue, said Lekren's remembered voice. *It was never that. A very powerful enemy.*

Now, gazing at the encapsulated shape, Jubal felt, or thought he felt, a faint stirring of the world, a variation in the reality around him. He thought he could see now that the black eyes had opened, stone statue or not, and that it was looking at him. Given the obscuring effect of the sealing material, it was hard to be sure, but somehow he could not really doubt the fact.

And in the next moment Jubal felt a telepathic touch, an approach to his mind by someone—or something—whose strangeness made the inhuman Taelon seem almost ordinary.

Jubal knew, without knowing how he knew, that this being, this presence, had no name, except such names as might have been given to it by its enemies, of whom there seemed to be a great many. So, at least, was Jubal's shadowy impression. The entity before him now had, in some sense, gone beyond names, as Jubal had gone beyond surprise. And he could see, could feel, that it was not really male or female either. In some way it had gone beyond sex and gender too.

Now he knew, beyond a doubt, the source of the strange dreams that had been troubling him.

"Urod," Jubal breathed. That was Lekren's name for this. And what Lekren had said to him came back: *There are certain beings in the universe. Who, though intelligent, have forfeited those innate rights. That intelligence commonly confers.*

And it was at that moment that the inhabitant of the fifth compartment managed, in his own voiceless and terrible way, to open communication with Jubal. Jubal had no choice in the matter—if someone in the same room shouts at you, you have no choice but to hear him.

Jubal had no doubt that he was now confronting the powerful enemy of which Lekren had spoken.

In the same shadowy, nonverbal way, Jubal also got the impression that the Urod, like Lekren, had been injured. But he also had an overriding sense that, even imprisoned as it was, it had not given up the struggle that it waged against the Taelon. It was bound and entangled, but not completely, paralyzed but not entirely. Its mind was still largely free, and it was still patiently, relentlessly, endeavoring to seize control of the Taelon vessel that had been sent to effect its removal from San Simeon and from the Earth.

Yes, Lekren had told Jubal there had been fighting. But whether the Taelon realized the fact or not, the fight was certainly not over yet.

And the Urod was, from the beginning, very firm in its

wordless insistence that Jubal should somehow enable it to get free. Currently confined in the crystalline mass, the Urod was time-frozen, bound in a condition out of phase with the rest of spacetime, and thereby restricted from exerting all but a fraction of his real power on his surroundings.

But already the Urod had somehow managed a mentally violent and almost-successful attempt to take over the ship. The wounded and enfeebled Taelon pilot had barely managed to beat back the attempt.

The only tool the Urod might now be able to use to achieve that end seemed to be Jubal himself.

It was hard to be sure, when the ideas communicated by the Urod lacked the hard form of words. But Jubal thought he could understand two things: first, that he was definitely being offered an alliance against the Taelon; second, that the Urod seemed to be making an effort to explain to him, as a potential ally, its own version of what was going on.

But the strangeness of alien thought and emotion was too much for Jubal just now. Turning his back on the Urod, he started to retrace his steps toward his own compartment, and was much relieved when the mental pressure suddenly disappeared.

Meanwhile his mundane hunger persisted. He had pulled another biscuit from his pocket and was beginning to chew on it. The dark ones and light ones had somewhat different flavors; they both tasted like nothing he could really identify, but both were good enough to keep him coming back for more.

He meant to confront the Taelon again, and get some straight answers as to what this situation was all about, and he also felt an instinctive compulsion to put as much distance as possible between himself and the Urod.

The nameless man had still not stirred when Jubal passed back through his compartment. Neither had Esther, when he reached hers.

Feeling tired, Jubal sat down briefly on the edge of Esther's bunk, put out a tentative hand and stroked her smooth forehead once, reverently, regretfully.

"Did I get you into this?" he murmured. "Was it something I did? I don't think so. But if it was, I'm sorry, girl, I'm sorry."

Being sorry, of course, wasn't going to help either one of them. But then, at the moment, Jubal couldn't see any way to do Esther any good, or himself either. It seemed pretty clear now that Urod and Taelon were engaged in some kind of long-term struggle, and that they had more or less fought each other to a standstill in this round.

And the truly frightening thing for Jubal was that he couldn't be sure that the dark urgings of the Urod were not more truthful than the crippled Companion's reasoned words. Obviously the Taelon had thought it necessary to bring Esther and Jubal aboard the ship, but Jubal was not entirely convinced that Lekren had their own safety in mind.

Returning to the room where the Companion lay, Jubal was slightly, unreasonably relieved to find Lekren once again awake and evidently anxious to talk.

Speaking was no easier for the Taelon than it had been before. "Jubal. What is happening?"

"I've been down that way," said Jubal, pointing. "I've seen the Urod."

The Companion on the bunk nodded, a slight motion. "You did not—talk?"

"No. How could we? That thing it's in—it's all sealed up."

"That is good."

Jubal raised both hands to his own head. "We didn't talk, but it was trying to get into my mind. Is that what you mean? I think it's been giving me nightmares. I can hear it—or feel it—now, if I try."

"Do not try. Understand that it has been—weakened.

Rendered comparatively weak. For the time being. Even now I. Am engaging what remains of its powers. With my mind. So it cannot really hurt you. As long as it remains confined."

"I wish I could keep it out of my head."

"You must try to do so. That is vitally important."

"Yes. I am trying. But—" Jubal raised both hands to his head, a helpless gesture. "How can I do that?"

"When we reach. Our destination. You will be given. Whatever help you need. Before you are returned to Earth. Your memory will be. Washed clean of nightmares, and of much else besides."

"Good," said Jubal. But he wasn't sure he meant the word wholeheartedly. It might not be good to lose all his memories of this incredible experience. If such things as Taelons and Urods really existed, and it seemed they did, then it was important to know about them.

But on the other hand, if he could just go home—he and Esther too, of course—he wasn't going to quibble about the details. As for the blond man—well, he'd been dead when Jubal first saw him. Any change from that state seemed like progress.

After a moment he asked Lekren, "What is our destination? Where are you taking the Urod?"

"To a place of encasement."

"You mean—confinement? A prison?"

"That is close to the reality."

"Is that the same place as the museum you were talking about before?"

"The two are together, yes."

Lekren had some kind of answer for everything. But it seemed to Jubal that the answers had really explained nothing yet. "But how did I get on this ship? And how did Esther?" Jubal wanted a clear explanation from the Taelon, some alternate version of the dark reality that had been painted for him by the Urod.

The Companion said, "It was necessary to bring you both.

For your own good. As I have told you. There was fighting. Great local re-adaptation of reality."

"Great what?"

The only answer was difficult breathing.

Jubal pursued, "And once we've reached this prison, or museum, or whatever it is, Esther and I can get the help we need?"

"Yes. All the help. Whatever may be needed."

"And then, as soon as all that's been taken care of, we can go home? You'll take us back to where we came from?"

"That is what I hope and plan."

And Lekren lapsed into unconsciousness again.

There was an interval in which Jubal tried to examine his surroundings more thoroughly. He really had to believe it now, the marvelous and crazy fact: He was riding aboard a spaceship. The word called up crude images from comic strips and sent them floating through his mind, pictures of rocket ships resembling armored naval vessels, rows of rivets showing in their sides. In his mind's eye he could call up page after page of newspaper comics, with Buck Rogers and Killer Kane blasting away at each other with their disintegrator guns. . . .

Not the kind of spaceship ride he had ever imagined, though. And Jubal could not rid himself of the suspicion that the Urod might have told him the truth, that it was really the Taelon who was his most dangerous enemy.

"Have you any other questions?" the bald one asked Jubal when the boy had come back to talk to him again.

Now that Jubal's mind felt like it was working again, he had so many that he didn't know where to start. "Yes. Who are you?"

"I have told you my name."

"I remember that, but—you said that you are a—Taelon?
Did I get that name right?"

A weak nod of assent, eyelids lowering.

"Sorry, I don't know what a Taelon is."

"The more you learn . . . the more you will be required to
forget. Before you return home."

"Then Esther and I are going home?"

"You need not. Ask so repeatedly. I am doing all I can. To
make that possible."

"Thank you."

Again the small nod of acknowledgement.

"I guess my real question is—well, I just don't understand
what's going on."

"There is much you cannot know as yet . . . even if I
explained . . . much of my explanation—would have no meaning to you. You may think of me as a shade, or a phantom, for
in a few hours I will be utterly forgotten. In the meantime, you
may think of me as your Companion."

"Why will you be forgotten?"

That question received no immediate answer. Jubal went
back to his own bunk, where he took off his shoes and coat, lay
down, and tried to think.

He was more tired than he realized, and before he even
knew he was near sleep, dark dreams had claimed him once
again.

TEN

This time the dreams were even more vivid than before. Through dim rooms and endless hallways that might have been those of Casa Grande, he was pursued and terrorized by a horde of dark stone statues. Even as he ran, Jubal knew that flight was useless, because all the world around him was being put through a wringer of hideous changes, and when it was over, the world would be unrecognizable and uninhabitable as well.

There came a moment when a monumental figure that was huge and black, but armed with gleaming white teeth very much like Errol Flynn's, had pursued Jubal into the Neptune Pool, where it was threatening to drown him. Meanwhile a woman he knew had to be Esther Summerson, all grown up, wearing a palm tree for a hat, sat at poolside taking notes. Jubal wanted to scream for help, but didn't dare because his father was in a meeting with important dead men in the great house, and at all costs must not be disturbed.

But then Jubal did scream anyway, at least he thought he did. And with the loud noise he came immediately awake.

He was sitting upright on the bare bunk, breathing heavily, almost on the brink of screaming again, and he knew a terrible disappointment that the whole business of Lekren and the spaceship seemed to be reality and not a dream. He could only wonder if his second awakening here was delivering him into a worse nightmare than the one he had escaped.

* * *

When Jubal sat up, his eyes had immediately turned to the doorway leading aft, to Lekren's room and Esther's. That was also the direction in which the Urod lay, radiating a power that had filled Jubal's mind with dreams of terror, visions of a black statue that might be going to walk in through that doorway any second now. Visions of a changed world, an altered reality in which any imaginable horror could become real . . .

But no one and nothing came through the doorway into Jubal's little room. He remained as alone as he had ever been. Gradually his breathing slowed to normal.

Overwhelmed by a sudden urge to know what time it was, to form some estimate of how long he had been in this mysterious place, he looked at his wristwatch. But to his shock and horror he discovered that the timepiece was no longer ticking. The hands indicated a quarter to five, but that was meaningless. It had run down and stopped—he had forgotten to wind it.

Getting to his feet, Jubal deliberately walked through the little chain of rooms again, pausing briefly in passing to look at the occupant of every bunk. Again he found every one of them unconscious: Lekren lay changing color faintly even as Jubal watched; Esther slept on, like the princess in some tale of magic; and the nameless blond man seemed to be enjoying his mysterious restoration to life. None of them were wearing wristwatches, though the two humans still had rubber Siamese snakes wrapped on their right arms.

Moving on boldly, not giving himself a chance to think about it, Jubal stepped into the last compartment. Once more he dared to look directly at the source of dark dreams, the Thing, the Urod. This time Jubal seriously considered whether he ought to be trying to find some way to kill it. Whether it might be able to detect his thought he could not tell. Anyway, he could imagine no way of getting at it, inside the thickness of its ice-hard armor.

Having inspected all his shipmates again and learned nothing new, Jubal returned to the compartment he was unhappily coming to think of as his own. There he once more stretched out on his bunk, and tried to relax, tried to come up with a constructive thought.

There was an awesome loneliness in his predicament, being the only conscious being, human or inhuman, aboard the ship. He had spent time at the bedside of each of his four fellow passengers and had tried talking to all of them. So far, only one, Lekren, had answered—two, if you counted the Urod's onslaught on his sanity as a reply.

The situation was immensely exhausting, and Jubal was actually dozing off again when something happened that jarred him wide awake. No mind-games this time, this was *real!* There had been a slight but definite change in his physical environment. A little bump, a jar, followed by a subtle alteration in the air around him.

Something in the sound and feel of the event sent Jubal's mind jumping to the conclusion that the ship had probably just landed somewhere. What had happened hadn't felt at all like the landing of a rocket ship on a planet, at least not the way Jubal's imagination, fueled by movies and comic strips, had pictured such an event. Somehow the coming together of two massive objects had been accomplished so gently that Jubal could not be sure that anything had really changed. There was a subtle change in air pressure, a slight difference in illumination, as if doors somewhere in the ship, but out of his line of sight, had been silently opened, giving access to a different environment, a brighter world.

And now, long moments after the original bump, the floor or deck beneath his feet vibrated slowly in a limited up and down motion, like an elevator starting and stopping. It went through one cycle, and that was that.

Jubal waited for the sound of more doors opening or closing, he braced himself for footsteps, and unfamiliar and probably inhuman voices. If no one got off a newly arrived ship, and he didn't see how anyone could have disembarked from this one, then people, or Taelons, or *someone* ought to be coming on board to investigate.

If the ship had really landed somewhere, then there ought to be bells, announcements, *something* . . .

But nothing further happened. There was only silence.

It occurred to Jubal that if the ship had reached its intended destination, maybe Esther would now be allowed to wake up. Lekren had said something about medical help being available when they landed, help for himself and for Esther if they needed it. The pilot, in his rambling discourse with Jubal, had also raised the idea of an interstellar museum, but Jubal thought that might have been only delirium, due to Lekren's mysterious injuries.

Finally Jubal's anxiety to learn what was happening overcame his reluctance to move. If they had landed, if any doors had really opened, he had to find out where. Jumping to his feet, he hurried forward to the control cabin. This time he threw himself into one of the seats, to get the best view possible out of the forward window. The small light was still blinking rhythmically, red, green, blue, but otherwise the view had altered drastically. Now on the right side there appeared a curving, blurry-looking bulk, very near, that of some unidentifiable dark mass against which the ship had evidently come to rest. This object was so featureless that Jubal could not immediately tell whether it was another ship, a building, or part of a planet.

Now that the ship seemed to have come to rest somewhere, Jubal kept hoping from one moment to the next that Lekren the Taelon would call out, summoning Jubal back to his bedside so he could tell him or show him what to do next. Failing that, he expected that someone (another Taelon probably) from the facility where they had landed would come aboard and somehow set matters right.

But nothing happened. If the ship had indeed landed somewhere, it seemed that no one knew or cared.

Returning once more to the Taelon's bedside, Jubal made a serious attempt to awaken him. The effort took some time and involved considerable difficulty, including repeated shakings. But at last he managed to partially rouse the Companion. By that time Jubal had received the chilling impression that Lekren's condition seemed to be worsening instead of getting better.

The blue eyes were squinting at him now, as if the pilot were trying to get a clear view of Jubal from a great distance.

Jubal tried to speak loudly and distinctly. "Lekren? I think we've arrived. Somewhere."

"Jubal. What—?"

"I say, I think we've landed."

Only gradually did the Taelon seem to become fully aware of what was going on around him.

Still making an effort to protect his control over his ship, the pilot was able to concentrate intermittently on the little panels extending from the wall display above his head.

He lay for some time making strange gestures at his instruments, and squinting at them as if he had never seen them before. After a while he spoke again, with as much difficulty as before. "Yes. It seems we have arrived. But our problems. Are not over."

"What's wrong now?"

"Understand, Jubal. We must be in the midst. Of a great and. Prolonged conflict."

"What kind of conflict? You mean a war?"

The Taelon ignored the questions. "But there is no help for it," Lekren enjoined his human passenger. "We must go forward."

It took Jubal a moment to understand that Lekren was not talking about mere physical movement inside the ship. "Forward where?"

"You must help me with the Urod, Jubal. Take it—to where it must be taken. And you must carry Esther off the ship as well." Lekren wanted to say more but he had to rest.

Another spell of gasping overtook him. The color of his face, the very texture of his skin, was varying strangely. But eventually the changes went away, leaving him with his original appearance.

"But you want to take the Urod off the ship first?" Jubal wondered.

A small nod signed agreement. "Dealing with. The Urod. Will be difficult. And even dangerous. But we must. Do it. Every precaution. Must be taken. To make sure. That he does not escape."

"How can he escape? He's in that block of—of stuff like ice."

No answer, except hard breathing.

"And if he did, how could I stop him?"

The blue eyes seemed to be gazing from a great distance.

"What do you want me to do now?" Jubal demanded at last, feeling himself near despair.

Again the pilot turned his attention to his private display, the little panels of shimmering lights, and studied them in silence for a time. Then he raised one arm and let it fall again, in a graceful gesture of near-despair. Jubal had the sudden impression that the arm in its blue sleeve now was thinner than it had been, looking wasted, even though the blue sleeve seemed to fit as well as ever.

The Taelon's lips were moving again. "If only I can speak to the Synod. Everything will be all right."

"I didn't get that. If you can speak to the what?"

Lekren was great at ignoring questions. "We have landed, have we not?"

"As far as I can tell, we have. I went up forward and looked out, but . . ." He fell silent; the Taelon wasn't looking at Jubal and didn't seem to be listening.

Suddenly Lekren burst out with a relatively long speech, in a strange, fluting language that reminded Jubal of birdsong.

Once again Jubal had the ugly feeling that Lekren's mind, the mind of the only being with whom he could now communicate, was wandering. Only his awareness that Esther was lying, utterly helpless, just down the corridor, kept Jubal from cracking under the strain.

There were moments when he knew he was on the verge of running wildly, screaming, stampeding up and down in an effort to find a way off this ship and hide somewhere. But Esther *was* on board, and he, Jubal Doors, was her only hope. He couldn't just abandon her, whatever else might happen.

Perhaps the Taelon sensed some of what the human was thinking. Lekren's delirium, if that was what it was, had passed. "Jubal, you must help me. And help your fellow human."

"Yeah, I know, I can see that. Why is she asleep? Or is she knocked out? Can't you wake her up?"

"Not now."

"Then when? I don't know what's going on, but I know we need help, and I'll do my best. But you've got to tell me what to do!" By the time Jubal finished speaking, he was raising his voice in desperation. But of course it didn't help.

"It is time. Jubal. Now it is time to convey the Urod off the ship. Then after that—then we must effect. The removal of Esther from the ship as well."

"But how? Tell me how!" In Esther's case, Jubal thought he could probably pick her up and carry her, but that wasn't going to work with what was effectively a big stone statue, especially when it was encased in the equivalent of a ton of ice. "How am I supposed to manage the Urod?"

But Lekren's lids were sagging shut again. He lapsed into unconsciousness without saying anything else.

The pilot's eyes were closed. Jubal couldn't see if he was breathing or not, but could just distinguish a pulse in the temple on one side of the hairless head.

Leaning over the rail on the side of the bunk, Jubal laid his hand on the Taelon's forehead, which felt slightly cool and very human to his touch. But the man did not respond in any way.

* * *

Jubal considered. Assuming he could find some way of even lifting the Urod, moving that monstrous creature anywhere without help was out of the question—even if he knew where the Urod was supposed to go. Lekren might as well have told him to haul away the Washington Monument.

Of course, getting Esther off the ship might be within the realm of possibility. But before trying anything like that, it was necessary to make sure that the ship had really landed, and that some kind of help was actually available. So far no one in the world outside the Taelon ship seemed to be taking the slightest interest in its arrival.

Moving slowly back into Esther's compartment, Jubal stood gazing down at her unconscious form. A sense of utter helplessness had been growing in him for some time, and now he was becoming more and more afraid. Now Jubal thought that Esther's pretty little hands—unlike those of his run-down watch—had changed their positions slightly since the last time he'd walked by; otherwise he would be wondering again if she was still alive.

Yes. Yes. Her breasts were still rising and falling under the party dress. The movement was very light and slow, but it was there, and Esther was alive.

Well, he could only try. Jubal drew a deep breath and with a considerable effort pulled himself together. Something had to be done, and he seemed to be the only one aboard ship who was able to do anything.

Moving closer to Esther's bunk, Jubal picked up her left hand, which was totally limp, squeezed it, then rubbed it briskly.

"Esther? Jeez, come on, girl. You can't just leave me to struggle with all this all by myself. You can't, I tell you!"

But oh yes she could. No sound came from her lips, no change of expression crossed her sleeping face.

Once more he tried to wake her, first shaking her lightly

by the arm and then slapping her cheeks lightly. But such gentle methods had no effect. He had been rougher with the Taelon, but here he was afraid to try anything more strenuous.

Sick, panicked fear kept trying to take him over, and there were moments when the dark terror came near winning. She might be dying, for all he knew. She obviously needed help, and by now Jubal was pretty well convinced that she wasn't going to get it here on the ship. Jubal already had some misgivings about simply following the pilot's orders, but on the other hand he didn't want to sit here and watch Esther sleep her life away. She was going to starve to death if nothing else.

He decided that the only thing to do was to get off the ship and look around. It was a good measure of his helplessness that he didn't even know how to do that.

ELEVEN

The Urod must have been aware of Jubal's decision to seek some way of getting off the ship. Because no sooner had the young human started his search for some suitable hatch or door than he was again assaulted by that other voice, the wordless, frightening one that had come to bother him so fiendishly in his dreams. Now it terrified him by breaking in on his thoughts even while he was awake.

All of a sudden a wordless jumble of orders, of compulsions, came trampling through his brain, like an alien army on the march. Now he received the exact opposite of the warning given him by Lekren. *He was not to listen to the Taelon's lying words. If he did, he too would become a victim, another in the long series of those abused and slain by the so-called Companions. Soon he, Jubal, would also find himself shut up in a breathless, lightless void, buried beneath an infinity of smothering mud and rock. . . .*

And behind the power of the message, Jubal caught glimpses of the ruthless, domineering one who sent it. It was the portrait of a mind and not a body. Of a dominion of awesome power, consumed by ravenous hunger, and able to twist the foundations of reality in quest of satisfaction. No mere human could understand the limits of what this hunger wanted, how it might possibly be satisfied. It was a craving such as he, a feeble child of earth, could not even come close to understanding, such as he had never even imagined. . . .

Lekren the Taelon had urged Jubal to close his mind to

such intrusions, and now he could understand why. But closing one's mind was easier said than done. Although, thank
God, he was not compelled to do anything that the intruder
commanded.

After a pause of less than a minute, the Urod's soundless,
wordless voice was back in Jubal's skull again. Now it was urging, commanding him to do violence to the Taelon. It issued
orders with great authority, but still Jubal was not absolutely
compelled to obey.

He might refuse to obey the voice, but he could not escape
it. Now it was thrusting vivid images before him, reminding
him of the availability of the revolver, whose function the
Urod evidently understood very well. Jubal saw, as in a dream,
the gun in his own hand, aiming point-blank at the bald and
helpless head of Lekren on his couch. . . .

And then suddenly, as swiftly as it had burst upon him, the
vision was gone, and so was the Urod's stream of wordless
commands. Cut off, blocked out, muffled to a point where
Jubal would have had to strain to hear it in his mind.

It came to him that Lekren must somehow be aware of
what was happening, and he, Jubal, must be getting Taelon
help.

For a minute he stood leaning against the side of his bunk,
eyes closed, both hands clasped over his ears. He was going to
have to take some kind of action soon, it would be impossible
to endure this situation as it was much longer.

Locating a way out of the ship turned out to be no trouble at
all, once Jubal started to look for it in earnest. There was what
certainly appeared to be a door, the very door he wanted, easily visible in the right sidewall as you stood in the control
cabin, facing forward. Jubal hadn't noticed a door on any of
his previous visits to the cabin, but then his mind had been
much occupied with other matters. And the door was easy
enough to overlook, being mottled in shades of blue just like

the wall around it. Anyway, it was certainly there now, a tall, wide, rectangular panel, situated just where, as he thought, the ship's side must lie against the mysterious dark object, whose enormous bulk was still partially visible through the forward window.

No obvious knob or latch was visible, only a diamond-shaped boss in the center of the otherwise plain panel. As soon as Jubal touched that spot, the door went sliding silently aside. Now Jubal stood looking through what must be a matching hatchway, also conveniently open, in the side of the mysterious dark object, straight down a narrow corridor some ten or twelve yards long. The corridor was lighted well enough to show its discoverer a number of surprising things.

Involuntarily Jubal gasped. Whatever vague expectations regarding this landing place had been forming in his mind went dissolving back into chaos. The walls and floor and overhead of the short hallway before him were of some dull beige material. And their surfaces would have been almost featureless, except that they were pocked and cratered and scorched, as if a crew of brawny, eager workers had gone over them with a set of heavy hammers and a blowtorch. Here and there a jagged edge, a fringe of frayed material, showed where a hole had been punched or blasted. And in the same moment there wafted in through the newly open doorway the smell of death, of rotting flesh.

Some thirty feet from where Jubal was standing, the corridor split into two branches, diverging at right angles. Just at the intersection Jubal could see lying on the deck what looked like a couple of bundles of old clothes, each bundle partially concealed within one branching of the passage.

A moment passed before his perception suddenly shifted, and he realized that he was looking at two fallen bodies. One, on the left, he assumed to be that of a Taelon, mainly because it was clad in blue like Lekren. The other, for all that Jubal was able to distinguish from this distance and angle, might well have been human. Dark wavy hair was barely visible, beyond a mound of clothing of bright, discordant colors.

Jubal's first impulse was to jump back into the ship and slam the door on the horror he had just discovered. But he would learn nothing by doing that, and he desperately needed knowledge. Instead, he took a firm grip on his nerves and slowly advanced.

Keeping his gaze fixed on the bodies as he moved ahead, he saw to his amazement that the nearer he came to them, the harder they were to see. Each was gradually engulfed by a field of shimmering transparency, suggesting to Jubal that he was looking at some kind of an illusion. By the time he reached the intersection, both corpses had entirely disappeared. In dull bewilderment he stared down at an empty floor.

Bending over, he found that he could pass his hand freely through the space where he had clearly seen two dead bodies lying. Amazingly, the smell had disappeared as well.

Straightening again, he turned his gaze down the left branch of the split corridor, which ran straight for many yards. Here the walls and ceiling were of neutral gray, and featureless except for being marked here and there by damage. The light was adequately bright, and as far as Jubal could tell, it sprang out from nothing but the walls themselves. In the distance, as far away as the remote end of a football field, he thought there might be more bodies lying on the floor, but they were so far away that he could not be sure. At about the same distance, the corridor seemed to turn into a kind of vaulted arcade. From that direction there also came faint noises, a whining that might have been produced by strange machinery, or possibly from living throats. In the circumstances the sound was intimidating.

Nothing Jubal could see or hear gave him any encouragement for seeking help in that direction. He supposed that the distant corpses might also disappear when he came near them, but he felt no urgency about finding out.

Turning his gaze down the corridor's right branch, he

observed that at a distance of thirty or forty yards it opened into a high, broad, cavernous room, more brightly lighted than the hall, but only partially visible through the narrow doorway at the hallway's end. Jubal could see parts of several large pieces of furniture, including tables, some brightly colored. Next to one table stood what looked like a wheeled cart, or hospital gurney, whose designed purpose might very well be the transport of live patients or dead bodies. Here was at least the faint suggestion of a hospital, implying some possible availability of medical help. Whether or not Esther really needed help, Lekren surely did. The furnished room would definitely have to be checked out.

Jubal started down the right branch, but slowed to a stop after only a few steps. He was receiving too many warning signals, not from the Urod now but from his own senses. The visible signs of destruction were everywhere in this place, along with the occasional smell of death. The evidence seemed overwhelming that a kind of gun battle, perhaps a war, had indeed been fought through these corridors and rooms, weapons of some strange type scorching and breaking the walls, pocking them as if by the blows of massive hammers. And it seemed more and more ominous that no living person came to meet him, no one even knew that he was here.

The boy thought of calling out, trying to summon help, but the words stuck in his throat. After all, he wasn't completely sure whether Esther urgently needed medical help or not. And he could not escape the feeling that in this weird place, littered with ghostly dead, a loud call for assistance might bring disaster down on him instead.

After a few moments of hesitation Jubal decisively turned his back on the distant room and started to return to the ship. Just as he stepped through the double hatchway into the control cabin, he gave one more glance back over his shoulder. The fallen bodies at the intersection were once more clearly visible, just as he had first seen them.

*   *   *

Shuddering faintly, Jubal touched the center of the exit door again, and to his great relief it immediately slid closed, sealing itself with a solid sound. He slumped against it, breathing more freely, only to jump to attention a moment later, when it occurred to him to wonder if the door could be opened from the outside. He looked for some way to double-lock it, but could find none.

For a full minute Jubal remained leaning against the door, trying to rest and think. Then moved out of the control cabin and walked partway aft through the series of small rooms. It was strange to realize that compared to the place he had just visited, this ship was beginning to seem like home.

Entering Lekren's compartment, Jubal was disappointed but not surprised to find the Taelon still unconscious.

Moving on again, he observed in passing that Esther had turned her head a little more to one side, but she still gave every appearance of sleeping peacefully.

Jubal supposed that she must have been brought on board at about the same time he was, but he had awakened spontaneously and she had not.

Why?

The only answer he could immediately come up with was that he had had no odd Taelon device, no rubbery Siamese snake, attached to his arm.

Proceeding aft into the compartment of the unnamed man, Jubal found him still as thoroughly knocked out as everybody else. The blond man's right arm, like Esther's, still bore a coiled artificial snake.

Contemplating the final doorway in the series, Jubal braced himself for another mental assault from the Urod. But this time he did not enter the Urod's room, and he was left in peace. The last onslaught, though, had reminded him of something that might prove to be a useful asset in his situation: the existence of the revolver that ought to be still available in the side pocket of the blond man's jacket.

The man on the bunk did not stir when Jubal relieved him of his weapon.

Last summer on the Colorado ranch, the boy had done a little shooting, with his father's approval, and under the supervision of one of the hands who had a reputation and a way with firearms. Jubal had not shown much natural talent as a marksman, but he had gained enough familiarity with this type of weapon to be able now to swing out the cylinder and count the five blunt-nosed, brass-jacketed cartridges that lay in their chambers ready to go to work. One chamber out of the six was empty.

Being armed did not banish fear completely—far from it. But the weight now in the side pocket of his own coat did make him feel at least six inches taller. He had the feeling that he was going to need all the advantages he could scrape up, if he had to go exploring in that eerie place where the dead vanished but the stink remained.

Moving forward through the ship again, chewing on one of the dark, flavored biscuits and trying to get up his nerve for another expedition into the strange place where the ship had landed, Jubal was pleasantly surprised to discover that Lekren was awake—more or less. The blue eyes regarded Jubal groggily as he came in.

Stepping up close to the Taelon's bunk, Jubal said without preamble, "I've been off the ship."

The pilot took a slow breath or two before responding; indeed he appeared to be only half awake. At last he said, "You have entered the station?"

—and somewhere in the mental background, the struggle between Taelon and Urod was still in progress—

"If that's what you call the thing, yes. I've entered the

place that the ship is now connected to. Or that we've landed on. Whatever you want to call it, I've been there."

Lekren's high forehead creased in a frown, as if this information presented him with some new problem. "Did no one meet you—in the station?"

"No one met me. Because there was no one there. No one alive, that is. I think some of the people who are supposed to be there have probably been killed."

Jubal had to repeat the essence of his story several times, and describe the fallen bodies in as much detail as he could remember, before the meaning seemed to come through to the exhausted Taelon. Over and over, using simple words, Jubal tried to convey something of the sights and sounds and smells that had surrounded him during his scouting trip and made him cut it short.

And even as he stumbled through the simple narrative, he kept trying to understand: Where had he really been, when he went into what Lekren called the station? If the station was on a planet, attached to something like the earth, the Taelon had made no mention of that. But where else could it be, unless it was just drifting in space? It could be a bigger spaceship, of course—monstrously bigger, to judge by the length of the visible corridors aboard. Unless that too had been some kind of an illusion.

The Companion seemed vaguely shocked and certainly surprised by Jubal's tale, but it took him a long time to respond to it. He was silent for so long that Jubal wondered if he had been rendered speechless.

Finally, desperate for solid knowledge, Jubal prodded his only conscious shipmate. "What were those bodies? The ones that vanished when I got close to them?"

"Re-adaptation," Lekren got out at last. At least that was the word that Jubal thought he heard.

"Listen, sir. Lekren. I'm asking if you can tell me anything about those bodies."

"Re-adaptation."

Jubal also thought that he had heard the Taelon use the same word before, but it was no more helpful now than it had been the first time around.

"What do I do now?" he pressed again. He wasn't totally sure that it would be wise, or even safe, for him to simply follow this stranger's orders, but it might help to at least know what the orders were.

After pondering Jubal's unwelcome information for a while longer, Lekren got out a few more words. "The station. Has been damaged."

"Yep. I'd say that's for sure."

Lekren gasped suddenly. His eyes went wide, and his body arced up on the bunk, startling Jubal so the boy took a step back.

". . . the Urod!" the Taelon choked out at last. "It contends with me . . . again . . . in my own mind. . . ."

"What should I do?"

There was no immediate answer.

Presently Lekren, struggling visibly, managed to get himself under control. "There is nothing," he managed finally. "Nothing you can do—about that."

"Then what?"

"We must unload the Urod," the Taelon suddenly commanded, summoning as much strength as he could into his voice. When Jubal would have pressed him with another question, he managed to raise an imperious arm, cutting him off. "Carry it . . . into the station."

"Carry it how?"

"I will tell you how. The Urod must be. Our top priority."

"All right, I'll try to help with that. But what about Esther?" Jubal wasn't going to let that question be forgotten. "She's still unconscious. Has she been hurt or hasn't she? Didn't you say she needed help?"

Gradually the Taelon seemed to be regaining full control over his own mind and body. But he was obviously still very weak.

"Yes," he got out at last. "Esther. You must convey her into the station too. But first—the Urod. For that you need to obtain. The means of transport."

"And how do I do that?"

"It may be. Difficult, Jubal. At places aboard the station, the pull of gravity may be—different."

"The pull of gravity." Jubal wondered if the pilot was delirious.

"Yes." After a pause for gasping breath, Lekren's body suddenly surged again, but this time the movement was entirely voluntary. He was making a great effort to sit up, and on the verge of succeeding.

Jubal, taken by surprise, stood frozen for a moment, then stepped forward and tried to help. But the Taelon's body was heavier than it looked. The blue-clad frame went limp, and Lekren was soon forced to abandon his effort and let himself fall back, groaning and literally changing color.

For a time those groans were the only sound in the silent ship, while Jubal stared amazed at the panoply of visual transformation. Bright shades of red and green were coming and going rapidly, as if Jubal were looking into a kaleidoscope.

"You must go, Jubal," the Companion whispered at last, in a voice even weaker than before. He had now returned to his original appearance, or very nearly. "Must go back aboard the station. Only you can do what must be done. We must neutralize. The Urod. At all costs."

"But what should I *do?*"

"I will tell you."

Lekren did his best to give instructions. It cost him a lot of effort, spread over many minutes. But at last Jubal had the outline of a plan in mind.

TWELVE

A few minutes later, Jubal was back aboard the station, trudging once more through the battered corridors. In his mind he kept doggedly going over and over the orders Lekren had just given him. This, he hoped, would keep him from forgetting too many of the intricate details of what he was supposed to do, and also free his mind from useless worrying. At the same time he was trying hard, though with only moderate success, to convince himself that the weight of metal in the right-hand side pocket of his sportcoat really made him feel safer.

In an odd way it was almost reassuring to see the phantom corpses lying as before, as if they were waiting for him, at the first intersection. Again it gave Jubal an eerie sensation to walk through the empty spaces from which those fallen bodies magically disappeared at his approach. He had told Lekren about them, and the Taelon had seemed shocked, but had not doubted Jubal's story.

After a single glance down the left-hand passage, at those other, distant bodies lying mounded there, Jubal turned his back on them, and strode determinedly down the right-hand branch, concentrating fiercely on the job at hand. According to his mentor, all the objects he had to find and the things he had to do lay in this direction.

Moments later Jubal had entered the large, furnished room. It was a chamber as big as an indoor gymnasium, with a pale, vaulted ceiling two or three stories above the floor, plenty high enough for basketball. But what Jubal saw when he looked around drove any images of sport out of his mind. Here the destruction had been even more savage than in the hallway. From inside the big room he could see that the very structure of the station was badly wrecked. Several cavities had been blasted in the deck, each one easily big enough for a man to fall through. Large jagged holes in the walls revealed their impressive thickness, and through the lowest of these gaps Jubal could catch glimpses of other rooms beyond, strangely lighted and eerily designed.

Everywhere he looked, something strange invited exploration, and at the same time sent signals urging caution. But his only chance of getting out of here seemed to lie in going forward. Detouring warily around the big holes in the floor, Jubal stared down into uncertain darkness. He thought of using his little flashlight to probe those depths, but decided he'd better save the batteries for some time when he really needed light. Besides, he wasn't sure he wanted to see what lay hidden by the darkness below. Bad smells were coming up. And there were other places where the floor, or deck, felt unsafe. Once the surface under his feet vibrated sharply when he stepped on a certain spot, sending him briefly staggering.

Large portions of the walls of the big room were relatively undamaged, only scarred and pitted here and there, and these bore functioning displays. Electric symbols in languages he had never seen before were flashing on and off in different colors, eerily reminding Jubal of neon advertising signs. None of the symbols meant anything at all to him, but in his current mental state, their very shapes seemed to convey a kind of menace.

For all that Jubal could tell, the only real function of the room he was now exploring was as a storage place for furniture. There were tables and cabinets, chairs and benches—and certain other objects that might have served as chairs and benches, except that their users would require an anatomy considerably different from human or Taelon.

Besides the passage by which Jubal had entered the big room, four or five other corridors of different sizes led into the chamber at floor level. Jubal carefully made the rounds of the room's perimeter, avoiding the several pits in the floor, taking a good look down each passageway. A couple of them, unfortunately including the one Lekren's instructions required him to use, were almost totally blocked by wreckage. All were littered with debris, scarred and burned. And Jubal could see, scattered down two or three of those mysterious hallways, more of the ghostly dead.

Choosing the nearest open corridor, he explored it to a distance of thirty or forty paces. At that point it took a sharp curve, in what seemed the wrong direction, if he was going to reach the destination Lekren had assigned. Some of the bodies of the slain were clearly visible ahead when Jubal entered the tunnel-like passage, but as before they disappeared like desert mirages when he drew near.

There were never any Urods among these spectral casualties, as far as he could tell—certainly he had spotted nothing that looked like a statue of Sekhmet. Some of them, he was sure, were blue-clad Taelons. Others looked like earthly humans, dressed in a variety of ways but not in uniforms. And there were other shapes and forms that he did not know how to classify.

Jubal's only knowledge of warfare came from books and films. But it seemed to him only logical that if there were many slain, there ought to have been some wounded too. So far he had seen no survivors of the carnage, and he could only suppose vaguely that they must have been taken away somewhere by the victors in the battle—whoever they had been.

Returning to the big room, he turned his attention to examining its contents. He noted with some satisfaction that what had looked from a distance like a cart or gurney proved to be just that. It was basically a metal frame about waist high, with a flat, smooth top and four black wheels—there were several other units like it scattered among the other furniture, and their simple, comprehensible shapes made them seem about the least-alien artifacts that he had seen since waking up aboard the spaceship.

Eyeing the width of one of these rolling tables, Jubal thought it would fit easily through the hatchway to the ship, which was relatively broad, and might just squeak through the narrower doorways between compartments aboard.

But, he supposed, even if the cart proved too wide, he could pick Esther up and carry her out of the ship in his arms—assuming he could harmlessly detach the several pieces of equipment that were now connected to her.

But such details could be worked out. Jubal had bigger problems. What Lekren seemed to be saying, and what Jubal had gone along with until now, was that Esther really stood in serious need of medical help; it had occurred to Jubal that it might be only the device wrapped around her arm that kept her in an enforced state of sleep, and if it were disconnected she might wake up spontaneously, just as he had.

And there seemed another reason to be wary: whatever help Esther might need at this point, it seemed very doubtful that she could find it anywhere in this ruin. The place was looking less and less like a hospital, or even a first-aid station, with every minute that Jubal spent inside it. Nor had he actually seen anything yet that seriously suggested a museum. A prison? Possibly, though the explorer had not yet come to any cells or prisoners.

When it came to carrying people off the ship, Jubal supposed he might be able to manage the Taelon pilot too, though he didn't look forward to making that attempt. But Lekren was focused on moving the Urod as the most important objective, and that would be quite another matter. If Jubal really had to attempt that, he was going to need serious help.

Leaving the gurney behind for now, Jubal set out to try to find the site where Lekren was so determined to deliver the encapsulated image of Sekhmet. The direct route being blocked, he would have to try to find a way around.

*   *   *

Walking, then climbing over wreckage, he made some head-
way down the next passage he attempted, which was only partially blocked. When he was stopped, he made some further
advance by burrowing, shifting some of the fallen debris—
there were mounds of powder that he could scrape aside like
sand, in double handfuls. There were chunks of what might
have been stone or concrete, some much too heavy for him to
lift, and there were long springy rods or stems, also very hard
to move, of some material he could not identify. Jubal worked
for several minutes without being able to advance more than a
few feet. Another couple of minutes were enough to convince
him that this was the wrong approach; he might succumb to
old age before he cleared the way.

He would have to try one of the other corridors.

He was trying to decide which passage to try next when he was
startled by a loud, disturbing noise. A distant, reverberating
crash, as if something enormously heavy, like a whole level of a
building, had collapsed. The deck shuddered violently beneath
Jubal's feet, and for a moment blind panic rose up threatening
to overwhelm him.

Instinctively he began to retrace his steps in the direction
of the ship. But before he had gone more than a few paces, the
distant rumbling died away, and the world around him seemed
as stable as it had ever been. When things had remained quiet
and seemingly secure for another minute, he resumed his
exploration.

While in the midst of probing another half-blocked passageway, Jubal suddenly experienced an urgent if illogical need to
know what hour of the day it was, and of what day. He didn't
know how long he had been asleep aboard the ship, but cer-

tainly days had passed since their strange departure from San
Simeon. It might be Tuesday by now, or even Wednesday.
Whatever else was happening, by now the people gathered on
the Enchanted Hill must have launched a search for him and
Esther. They must be trying desperately to guess whether the
two kids had run off together or had been kidnapped. And if
the influence and resources of William Randolph Hearst were
behind the effort, it would be one tremendous search indeed.

If (no, when!) he and Esther got home, no one was going
to believe the story he had to tell. But right now Jubal would
gladly swap his current crop of problems for that one.

Jubal's watch could not tell him how long he and Esther
had been Lekren's guests—or prisoners. But he had rewound
the timepiece and set it running, and it could at least let him
know how much time he had now spent aboard the station.
His original plan had been to use no more than an hour in this
scouting attempt before he headed back to the ship.

Again he worked hard for a few minutes at trying to clear
wreckage from the latest passage he had entered, and again he
made just enough progress to bring him in sight of even
greater piles of rubble ahead, huge enough to convince him
that trying to get through this way would be a hopeless task.

Lekren had told him of a certain symbol—a blue blade, or
wedge, carving a sphere of black—that marked the door of the
room to which they must convey the Urod, and Jubal was constantly on the lookout for it. As soon as he had located the
door bearing such a sign, he was to open it, enter the room
behind, and inspect the machinery that it contained. If none of
the equipment appeared badly damaged, he would report the
fact to Lekren, and then the two of them would somehow convey the Urod there.

The instructions Jubal had been given were simple, easy
enough to remember, despite the fact that he kept being confused and distracted by his surroundings. This place was truly,

utterly, and wildly strange, so alien that he didn't see how he'd ever be able to get used to it, if he were to live here for a year.

That thought was enough to make him shudder. But it wasn't going to happen. He, with Lekren's advice and help, was going to do the job the Taelon wanted done, and then they were heading back to earth. Lekren had promised, or as good as promised, that as soon as they had the Urod disposed of, Jubal and Esther would be on their way home.

Yes, his instructions were simple enough. The only problem was that they were so far proving impossible to carry out. Jubal was stopped by blocked passageways, and he saw no blue wedges or black spheres. In several places he peered through walls of colored glass into other rooms, most of which were very notably the wrong shape for any human activity that Jubal could imagine—except maybe some of them would do as giant playground slides, or rooms in a funhouse in a highly challenging amusement park.

Once, coming to a closed door marked with a highly intriguing neon symbol, very nearly a regular American dollar sign, he took a chance and fooled around with the door until he found a way to open it, only to slam it shut again a moment later, just in time to shut out an advancing swirl of what looked like blowing yellow dust. Beyond the dust there had been a suggestion of green foliage in the background. It was an intriguing sight, but not, he thought, worth risking the yellow whirlwind for.

There was yet another chamber of a most peculiar shape, long and bent, crooked as the drawing of a lightning bolt, and filled almost from wall to wall by an object that reminded Jubal of nothing so much as an enormous banquet table, and therefore put him vaguely in mind of the refectory in Casa Grande.

On earth, among objects as familiar as trees and buildings, clouds and stars, Jubal generally found his sense of direction quite reliable. But before his newly rewound watch had ticked off an hour in this environment he began to worry about being able to find his way back to the ship, never mind locating the place Lekren insisted they must reach. Still he pressed on. He thought that if he could find a ball of string, he would unwind it as he progressed. In some ways this reminded him of the funhouse in a big amusement park; and of course nothing so prosaic as a ball of string was anywhere in sight.

Sometimes it seemed to him that each step forward brought a fresh surprise. Jubal didn't see how he could ever regard this place as homelike, but he gradually began to feel a little less insecure, to lose his fear that *something* deadly or horrible was going to jump out at him from around the next corner.

Jubal had another problem that worried him more than the chance of getting lost: He still couldn't decide whether he should trust the Taelon wholeheartedly or not. If he decided not to co-operate with Lekren, then what about Esther? There would seem no point in bringing her off the ship at all.

But what would happen to her then?

No, he wasn't ready yet to declare open rebellion, he had to learn more about the situation first. Lekren gave the impression of being a man—or a Taelon—badly hurt but struggling to do his duty. And Lekren, after all, seemed to have some idea of what this was all about, and Jubal simply did not.

Before collecting the hospital gurney and wheeling it back to the ship, Jubal made one last effort to locate the place to which Lekren was so fanatically determined to deliver, at all costs, the encased and time-frozen body of the Urod.

So far, wherever Jubal had moved aboard the station, the pull of gravity had felt perfectly normal to him, just as it had on the ship. He had never thought about it, any more than he would have when walking in Colorado or California. Probably it would never have crossed his mind that conditions might be other than they were, had not Lekren mentioned the fact in one of his rambling statements. But something else about the orientation of the spaces that Jubal was now exploring had been subconsciously bothering him, and eventually he figured out why.

"Down" here inside the station had started out being identical with "down" aboard the ship. But that did not hold for everywhere he went.

Eventually Jubal took note of a distant landmark, a tall column standing in a high room, whose top apparently tilted more and more away from him as he moved farther and farther away from it. Other distant features behaved in a similar way.

The truth, as he finally realized, was that "down" was gradually shifting. He was moving about through the outer layers of a huge sphere, and down was always toward the center of the sphere, just as it was on the earth. But this world was so enormously smaller than the earth that its curvature was readily visible.

But even that was not the strangest thing in this environment.

For a while it seemed to the explorer that he was climbing uphill, and then that he was going down again; and yet again he was sure that the floor of a room was steadily increasing its slant beneath his feet as he advanced across it. Hastily he scrambled in retreat, before the slope became too steep for him to cling to it at all.

Jubal experienced the most obvious example of this peculiarity when he reached a kind of observation deck.

Now he had finally reached a portion of the station where there were no visible signs of battle damage. If he was going to discover a living survivor anywhere, he thought, it ought to be here.

Poking around nearby, he discovered more toilets, of the

same general kind as that on the ship. There was a water fountain, too, but unfortunately no food. Not even any place where
it seemed possible that food might be stored. He was getting
sick of the taste of those damned biscuits, that at first had been
so appetizing. But he was going to need something to eat.

The deck was a large space, well-lighted and big enough
for a softball game, and furnished with an assortment of
objects some of which looked like chairs, and more things that
might have been chairs, if their users had bodies that folded in
the wrong places when they sat down. This broad area was
walled on three sides by a smooth curve of glass offering a
panoramic view of the outside.

From this broad window the outer surface of the Station
sloped down and away for several hundred yards, then
dropped off abruptly into a gulf of space and distant stars. For
some reason the view of space from here was much clearer
than the only one he'd been able to get from inside the ship,
and what Jubal saw now bore a much more convincing resemblance to the night sky of earth.

But he spent only a little time gazing at the stars, because
what he could see in the middle distance was more interesting.
The distant rim of the long slope was divided into dozens,
scores, of smooth notches, like so many spaces waiting to be
occupied—that was the purpose that immediately suggested
itself to Jubal, because one of the huge notches—and only
one—was filled already. A smooth, almost cylindrical object,
which had to be large although at the distance it looked quite
small.

Somehow Jubal felt certain at first glance that the smooth
cylinder was the spaceship in which he had arrived. Because a
small tight beam of light, stabbing out from the ship at intervals, occasionally swept across the observation window. In the
intermittent flashes Jubal recognized the same pattern of dots
and dashes as he had noted from inside the ship's cabin. Red,
green, blue, red, green, blue. He had come on a long, twisted
walk, and he was now looking back at the little ship where

Esther was sleeping helplessly, in the company of strange monsters.

Jubal remained on the observation deck for what felt like a long time, looking out. Seeing part of the outer surface of the station, seeing the tiny ship in which he had traveled, all against the incredible backdrop of unfamiliar stars. All of it true, all of it real. He was gripped by a sense of wonder that was strong enough to ease his fears.

He was on his way back to the ship when at last, almost by accident, he did manage to locate the place that his Companion had been so eager for him to find.

"This has got to be it," he murmured to himself aloud.

Large and plain and unmistakable on the door was the symbol Lekren had told him to look for—it did indeed resemble a blue blade, or wedge, carving a sphere of black. The sign looked three-dimensional when Jubal first saw it from a distance of twenty yards or so, but had flattened out into a mere decorated plane when he looked up at it from almost directly underneath.

The size of the door and its impressive decoration suggested that something of great importance lay beyond. Jubal had an odd feeling that he had seen this entrance somewhere before, and then suddenly realized that it reminded him of the great iron-barred portal that served as the front door of Casa Grande.

No knob or lock was visible, but when he pushed gently on the huge grill it swung back smoothly to let him in.

The room behind the door was cavernous, and Jubal's spirits rose when his first glance around showed him very little damage. But as he examined the room's equipment more closely he felt let down.

"The House of Tomorrow," he muttered to himself.

Occupying a central position, and dominating the chamber with its bulk, was an object that reminded Jubal of nothing so much as one of the experimental television sets he'd seen in the House of Tomorrow, a few years back. That had been at the Chicago World's Fair, that he'd visited with his parents back in 1933. Except that the mysterious device before him now was much bigger than the television. It was round and enormous, with a glassy door in front, easily large enough to accommodate the Urod in his capsule—or to hold a small elephant, for that matter.

Turning away, he soon discovered a door in the rear of the room giving into another long corridor, a kind of tunnel, and when he had followed that to its other end it opened up into a vaster space, as big in itself as any museum he'd ever seen or imagined. Here were cases and cases of specimens. Various animals, and a great assortment of what appeared to be exotic vegetables, displayed in various stages of growth and development, on stages and worktables. Wandering into this area and looking around, Jubal discovered more of them, and still more, all neatly available for easy inspection.

There were dozens of display cases in all—no, he decided, probably there were hundreds. They were all constructed, for the most part, out of some hard glassy stuff, but smoother and clearer than that encasing the Urod on the ship. Here you could walk around each separate exhibit, and look at the specimen that it contained from every angle.

The visitor stood for a long time, awestruck, before one case, whose occupant was utterly reptilian in appearance, with scales and claws and pointed teeth, yet stood on two legs and held out a pair of fingered hands of very human shape.

He could detect no system, no plan, in the order in which the specimens were arranged and displayed. If there was any pattern, it was one that made no sense to Jubal. Rather the assortment seemed completely random.

He was about to turn and leave, when an image more shocking than any he had seen yet caught the corner of his eye.

It took Jubal a moment to realize that what had grabbed his attention was the visual impact of a shock of red human hair.

Approaching that particular case to examine it closely, he discovered one very human young woman, posed in a lifelike manner. Her body was completely nude, like all the other specimens, and under different conditions she would have been more than a little attractive. Her blue-green eyes were open, staring straight in front of her over Jubal's head, and he could see no sign of breath or pulse.

Her skin was pale, though not too pale for life, and freckled somewhat on arms and hands and face. Her long hair, hanging loose, was a natural-looking red.

As was also the case with most of the other specimens, an outfit of clothing was shown in the case beside the woman's body. There was a summer dress in a floral print, high-heeled shoes, sheer silk stockings, and a small collection of undergarments. Yes, and there was a hat, and a black leather purse. Had she been wearing those clothes, she would not have looked out of place walking down any street in any American city of Jubal's memory.

Putting a hand against the flat glass of the case, he made a startling discovery. The touch must have activated some kind of a control, for at once the body inside (or the image of a body, if that was all it was) began to move with a dancer's grace, smoothly adopting different attitudes, sitting, bending, lying down. Suddenly some of the clothing that had been exhibited separately was on the body. Now she was carrying her purse under one arm. Another movement of Jubal's hand near the touchless external controls sent the purse jumping magically back to its original position.

When he moved back a step, all motion stopped, the woman resuming the pose she had had at the beginning.

Eventually Jubal turned away, beginning a slow retreat with many backward glances. But then he turned his back on the woman and resolved not to think of her until he could talk to Lekren again. Right now he needed no more amazing things to contemplate, no more terrible mysteries. He had a job to do, Esther's life as well as his own to save.

THIRTEEN

His mission had been fundamentally successful, at least from the Taelon point of view. Now Jubal, unable to think of any better course of action, supposed that he had better return to the ship and report to Lekren. Then, before he did anything else, he would demand an explanation of why the young woman was in the glass case.

Besides, he was very tired. He was going to have to lie down somewhere, sometime soon, and get some sleep.

Jubal decided to collect the gurney and bring it with him on his way back to the ship—on his way home. Of course the road to his real home lay through the ship, but over the last few hours the ship had actually taken on a positively homelike aura, in comparison with his present surroundings.

As Jubal moved through the alien rooms and corridors, on his way to claim the cart he needed, he kept looking over his shoulder, ever fearful of being attacked by some unearthly enemy. In his mind was the image of the woman in the display case, and he was afraid of whoever or whatever had put her there. It was the same power, he supposed, that had stocked all the other cases too.

But meanwhile, despite his fears, another part of his mind kept seeking desperately, hoping hungrily, to meet *someone*, practically anyone besides the dazed, half-human Lekren. He hoped it would be some reasonable authority, who could tell him what he ought to be doing next. And he really hoped it would be a human being. But he was ready to welcome almost anyone or anything that talked.

It could be another Taelon. Jubal was almost—but not quite—ready to seek companionship even with another Urod. Hell, it could be a goddamned talking jellyfish, if it would take some of the responsibility off his shoulders and give him good advice. But so far no luck. Everything he saw and heard indicated that he himself was the only living thing currently aboard the station.

So, he would go back now and report to Lekren, and between the two of them they would somehow dispose of the Urod, and it would cease to raise its frightening echoes in his mind. Then Lekren would show Jubal how to obtain from the station whatever help it might be able to offer Esther. And maybe there was something here that would do the blond man some good— though he actually seemed in relatively good shape now, for one who had been frozen stone dead—and *then* they would all get back aboard the ship, and Lekren would set a course that would deliver his human clients back to earth, to San Simeon where they belonged. Then, presumably, the Taelon could go back to his own home, wherever that might be.

All very fine. But meanwhile, Jubal's feet were dragging, his head was spinning with weariness, and he had eaten his last biscuit—how many hours had passed since he had walked out of the ship to run Lekren's errands? It was impossible to tell. He could no longer remember the position of his watch's hands when he had last reset it. Maybe his mind was going, failing, with the strangeness all around him and the Urod's wordless gibbering.

Well, he wasn't going to let it fail. He would concentrate on the next job to be done, and then on the next after that.

Briefly Jubal worried about his ability to find his way back, even as far as the big room. But there proved to be no difficulty. On the outward leg of his journey he had done his best to keep a series of landmarks in mind; there was no trouble, on the station, in finding objects of distinctive appearance.

Nothing had changed in the big room since last he saw it. Once Jubal laid hold of the gurney with intent to use it, he discovered with considerable satisfaction that it needed only a touch from his hand to start moving, turn right or left, or stop again. It propelled itself, as surely and tirelessly as if it had a motor aboard, though there was nothing of the kind that Jubal could see, only a platform and frame and wheels. And the cart displayed another eerie capability: whenever it came to one of the many holes in the deck, it automatically detoured around the gap. Jubal found it heartening to discover that something aboard the station still worked.

And the gurney indeed proved easily narrow enough to fit in through the hatch, and after that slid through the ship's doorways, one after another, with about an inch to spare on either side. Jubal moved quickly, almost triumphantly through the rooms, guiding the empty cart ahead of him. He found the Taelon pilot still lying on his bunk, awake now and apparently expecting him.

The Taelon's eyes lit up faintly when he saw that Jubal had brought the cart, and he did not appear to be discouraged by his helper's brief, pessimistic report.

When Jubal had concluded his recital, Lekren's lips parted, looking very thin and dry. The Taelon said, "You have done well."

"Thank you."

"Now." A pause, as if to gather strength. The inflexible purpose was still there. "The Urod . . . we must . . ."

"You want him brought into the station. To that room where the processing or whatever is done."

"Yes."

Jubal fidgeted a little, then came out with what was bothering him. "Is that really the most important thing we have to do?"

"It is." The answer was immediate and emphatic; Lekren had no doubt at all of the overriding importance of the Urod, whatever the fate of anyone or anything else might be.

"What about the woman I saw in the glass case?"

"An image, Jubal. Like the other specimens you saw. One type of intelligent life. A picture, only."

The boy hesitated, finally disagreed. "I don't think so, she looked real solid."

"We can make. Solid pictures."

Jubal might have automatically rejected such a claim as unimaginable, except that Jubal had already seen an example. The image of the solid-looking little cube on the instrument panel was still sharp in his memory.

But other points still bothered him. He demanded: "You're hurt, what about getting you some medical care? What about getting Esther care, if she needs it?"

Lekren was shaking his head gently, side to side. "My condition will improve. When the Urod is finally subdued. And then I can give Esther. Truly effective help."

Jubal shrugged mentally, deciding that for the moment he would continue to go along—mainly because he couldn't see that he had any real choice. "All right. But I don't see how I can move the Urod by myself. He looks like stone, is he as heavy as stone? Not even counting that stuff he's sealed up in. Besides, I'm tired out, I have to get some rest."

"Yes. Indeed. Very heavy."

"Yeah, that's what I thought. So, I'm going to need a lot of help."

Lekren fell silent, nodding to himself. Then, making what appeared to be a superhuman effort, he lowered the bar on the side of his couch nearest to Jubal. Then he got to his feet.

For a moment Jubal could only stare in amazement at the Taelon pilot, who was now supporting himself by leaning on the bed with one hand and on the cart with the other, with changes in coloring shimmering across his face. The Companion's limbs were willowy without appearing weak, and when he managed to hold himself upright he carried himself in a way that suggested some beautiful actor or fashion model, and at the same time great authority.

Standing straight, Lekren towered over Jubal, but the Taelon could not hold that pose for long, and was still too weak to walk normally. He could make progress only by leaning on the cart, or on the walls, furniture, or on Jubal.

"Want to ride on the gurney?" Jubal suggested.

"No." With the effort of standing and moving, the melodious voice had dwindled to a tormented whisper. "I must not. Lie down again. I might be unable. To get up."

They pushed on aft, into the Urod's room.

Moving steadily, the Taelon approached the bed on which his enemy lay physically confined. Lekren passed his hands rapidly over the wall beside the bunk, and then over the bed itself. His hand movements were smooth, and precisely directed. Jubal, though watching closely, knew he could not have duplicated them accurately, even supposing that the machinery would respond to him at all. Then he thought that probably it would; he had been able to make the red-haired woman dance inside her glassy tomb. Now he shuddered at the memory; it had been like watching a corpse perform on puppet strings.

In response to Lekren's latest commands, the same apparatus that been keeping the Urod bound and sealed now delivered him onto the cart, which received the massive weight without collapsing.

"And now—?" the human apprentice asked.

"Now we must. Convey this creature immediately. Aboard the station." The normal colors of Lekren's face had gone flat with fatigue and injury, and he did not appear to relish the job before him. Jubal, watching warily, wondered if he could catch the pilot when he started to fall.

*　*　*

But the Companion seemed driven by a steely will, and presently the two of them, Taelon and human, had left the ship, and were moving through the scarred corridors that Jubal, despite their strangeness, was beginning to find familiar.

Lekren went first, moving only at a snail's pace, undoubtedly the best that he could manage.

Jubal had charge of the gurney, and kept guiding it with the whole weight of the encapsulated Urod balanced on it, rather insecurely as it seemed to him. He could not remember ever feeling this tired before. Fortunately almost no energy was required to direct the self-powered cart and its strange, shimmering, almost crystalline burden.

Jubal thought he could have found his way back to the place alone, relying on his learned landmarks.

But Lekren was obviously determined to come along. When his energy flagged, he enlisted Jubal's help in climbing onto the gurney, where he rode first sitting, then lying sprawled atop the body of his almost helpless enemy.

Exactly how long the journey was Jubal could not have said. On his first trip he had thought of counting steps, but then had given up the idea, having too many other things to think about.

This time neither Jubal nor the Companion had much to say during the long walk. When Lekren did talk, he seemed to be speaking mostly to himself, in the fluting birdsong language. Though sometimes he uttered words in English, bemoaning the fact that there ought to have been a much better way to accomplish this task. And so there must have been, Jubal thought, under ordinary circumstances. But the station had been so badly shot up that the only really puzzling thing to Jubal was how anything at all could be expected to work.

On they moved, hauling the encapsulated Urod through the strange hallways and indescribable rooms.

Despite the fact that Jubal had warned him what to expect, Lekren seemed shocked and saddened by the destruction through which they passed.

When at last, after many necessary detours, they had passed through the door marked by a blue wedge, Lekren slid down from his resting place atop the Urod and spent a minute or two gathering his strength.

Then he directed Jubal to position the cart directly in front of the machine which resembled a giant experimental television. When that was done, Lekren tugged Jubal back, away from the equipment, while the machine itself unloaded the Urod from the cart, using a mechanism much like that which had transferred the burden to the gurney in the first place.

Then, for a time, nothing happened.

"What do we do now?" Jubal had to ask the question twice, for it appeared that the Companion was closer than ever to complete collapse.

The stiff, stonelike body of the Urod, still fixed with seeming permanence in a sitting position, was resting on a kind of worktable. Something happened that caused the glassy packaging to start to glow.

Then smoothly working mechanical arms emerged from somewhere to gently peel that crystal encasement loose. It had felt as hard as rock, but the machine had whatever key was needed to make it soften and disappear, leaving not a trace behind. In only a few moments the black statue stood totally exposed.

But, having proceeded smoothly to that point, the process seemed to stall.

Twice Lekren approached the great machine, and tried with futile gestures to activate some machinery. But the only result of this latest effort seemed to be another wave of mental fog unleashed by the Urod. Jubal felt the effects, but he knew the assault was not directed at him. Several times the Taelon stumbled as he moved about the central platform that held his nemesis.

Now it was becoming mentally painful just for Jubal to watch. He had to fight back an impulse to jump up and run away. A background hum of mental noise made it difficult for him to see straight or think straight.

He thought of calling out to Lekren, but what would he say? Jubal put his fingers in his ears, and squinted his eyes shut, but it didn't help against the torrent of hate and violent images. The main effect the onslaught was having on him was to convince him the Taelon was right in wanting to dispose of the damned creature.

Lekren continued fanatically intent on processing his captive Urod into this system; his attitude seemed to say that he would get this done if it killed him, and his appearance suggested that it might well do so.

At last he summoned Jubal to him with a weary gesture, and put his hand on Jubal's arm, in what seemed the gesture of one about to plead for his life.

"You must return to the ship." It seemed both a plea and a command.

"Yes?"

"Then you must put Esther on the cart and bring her here. You can do that. Without my help. She is not heavy. Or dangerous."

Jubal felt a wary impulse to withdraw. "No, she isn't. But I don't see how bringing her here is going to help anything."

As Jubal pulled away, Lekren's hand fell weakly back to his side. "If you wish her to regain her senses. If you wish her to recover. You must bring her here."

"Why?"

The Taelon drew a deep breath. He shook his head gently, as if to clear it. "It may be possible. To use the Urod. To help Esther."

"Oh. I'll go get her, then." Jubal's doubts rose up and his shoulders slumped. But what else could he do? "You're staying here?"

"I must remain. On guard." Lekren gestured at the Urod,

and Jubal got the impression the Taelon was afraid to let his enemy out of his sight for even a moment. Or possibly the Taelon was simply too weak to move. But just as Jubal was about to leave, Lekren called him back and gave him a special warning. "Esther is wearing a *sken*. On her arm. You must not try to disconnect it."

"The thing that looks like a black rubber snake. A *sken*."

"That is correct."

"What does it do?"

"Later. All will be explained."

Jubal started off with the cart, but as he was about to leave the room whose door was marked with the blue wedge, he paused and looked back, as if he could force the truth out of Lekren just by staring. So far, nothing seemed to be happening to the Urod, while on the other hand both human and Taelon were being treated to another blast of mental interference.

Having made his way back to the ship without incident, he positioned the gurney close to Esther's bed, just leaving room for himself to stand between. She still slept on—not a thing in the world to worry about. Not even the rubbery snake that clasped and bound her arm. The *sken*—he thought that was what Lekren had called it.

"All right, girl. Here we go."

But before he actually tried to move her, Jubal paused, assailed by suddenly growing doubts. What was he doing? Following the orders of some inhuman alien who might, for all Jubal knew, be some kind of maniac . . . but if he rebelled against Lekren's orders, what else was he going to do?

Getting Esther out of her bunk and onto the cart was physically a much easier job than moving the massive Urod. But the longer Jubal contemplated the implications of the move, the stronger grew his instinctive reluctance.

He had to fight back an instinctive urge to unwind the Siamese snake from Esther's arm, throw it on the deck and kick it, as he had the similar device he'd found near his own bunk. But the Taelon had specifically warned him against doing that.

Picking her up was made easier by the fact that the bunk held her body high, almost at the level of his waist. Also she was small and light, and though Jubal was not big he had wiry strength. One arm under her shoulders and one under her knees, and up she came, just as neatly as some movie hero's girlfriend who fainted when the bad guys were closing in. Maybe Errol Flynn could do it better, but then again maybe not.

Pushing the cart with Esther on it back through the station, Jubal found himself again and again taking a wrong turn. His eyes would close, and he would start to doze off while he was walking. There came a point where he knew he had to lie down to rest, or he was going to fall over in exhaustion. Maybe if he got just a little nap, he would be able to think straight, to decide what to do. Only a few minutes. Even if he only rested his eyes . . .

Stretched out on the deck beside the wheels of the cart, he dreamed, a comparatively normal dream this time. He was in the museum, but as a specimen and not a spectator. He was on exhibit, sharing a display platform with the naked woman with red hair. When Jubal looked at her closely, the head of a rubber snake came out of her mouth and started for him. Struggling to hold his own jaws shut against the serpent's penetration . . .

In a sudden shift he was dreaming that he slept and dreamed, and in this inner dream he woke up to find the damned thing fastened to his right arm, put there by some inanimate machine. Then he realized that no, it was the pilot,

Lekren, who had fastened it to Jubal's body. And how was he ever going to get it off? He struggled with it for a few dream-hours, and then suddenly he was back in the ship and the ship was moving again, and in the next moment the *sken* had fallen off all by itself.

He was going to take Esther in his arms and kiss her, and suddenly her *sken* had bound itself to him as well, tying Esther and Jubal indissolubly together.

. . . and Jubal woke up gasping, on the verge of screaming his head off.

When he looked at Esther again, her condition was unchanged, except that one of her shoes had fallen off some-where. He felt irrationally worried about the loss.

A little later, pushing the cart again in the direction of the processing room where Lekren presumably still waited, Jubal realized what it was that had made him keep imagining, for a little while, and despite all the evidence to the contrary, that he was in a hospital. Whatever the true purpose of the station might be, it was, like a hospital, in some sense a people-processing place. They both tended to have some kind of pushcarts on which people could be moved around. The machine that the Urod could not quite be forced to enter might have been a fancy X-ray or fluoroscope.

No, he couldn't remember the pilot ever telling him in so many words that the station could provide ailing humans with whatever medical treatment they might need. But he had said, over and over, that help would be available here, and Jubal had somehow assumed that medical help was what Esther, not to mention the Taelon himself, seemed to need.

When at last Jubal pushed the cart back into the blue-wedge room, he expected the Companion to bawl him out for being late—how many minutes or hours late, Jubal could not have said. But he had needed sleep so desperately that he was ready to put up an indignant defense.

But the boy need not have worried. When Jubal pushed the cart into the blue-wedge room again, he found Lekren collapsed, right on the deck. Going to him, Jubal saw that he was not dead. But the Taelon was now almost delirious.

The Companion was stretched out almost at the Urod's feet, so that the antique Egyptian god, sitting there motionless as if on a great throne, looked like the conqueror and the Taelon like his slave. He kept moaning and complaining that he was unable to make proper contact with his Synod.

"Lekren? Lekren!" It took Jubal a while to get him up.

Lekren, his face and body turning colors, dragged himself to his feet and laid hands on the cart, pulling it closer to the central machine and the Urod. Then he tried to lift Esther from the cart, but he was too weak.

"Jubal. Help me."

"You want me to put her into the same machine with that thing? Why?"

"Jubal. I am too ill. To argue." Lekren gestured feebly. "Come. Do what I say."

"Maybe you're too ill to think straight." And then he was afraid that he shouldn't have said that. Talk about thinking straight, he couldn't do it either, not with the Urod continually hammering at his mind.

Only now did Jubal notice that two large objects had somehow been brought into the room since his last visit. These were two empty museum cases, their two glass doors standing open, which now had been moved into place beside the central machine.

"One of these is for the Urod?" Jubal asked.

"That is correct."

"And the other?"

Lekren did not answer.

*   *   *

The Urod bombarded Jubal with images of himself, Jubal, and Esther, dead-eyed and naked in their separate cases, two mindless bodies slowly dancing on display.

"No!"

The feeling of being trapped in an impossible situation, the images his imagination presented regarding what was about to happen next, were suddenly too much for Jubal. It was all more than he could take.

He grabbed the taller Taelon roughly by the front of his upper garment, and shook the almost unresisting body. "Why do we have to put her right in there with that thing?" Jubal yelled at him. "What good is that going to do her?"

When Lekren did not answer, Jubal shoved the weary Taelon away by main force. The willowy blue-clad body staggered, and seemed at every moment about to collapse. But it did not.

Jubal bellowed out his fear and rage. "You lied to me, didn't you? About the woman in the display case. She's no image, she's real!"

Still, Lekren did not appear to have heard him. His blue eyes were fixed on Esther where she lay helpless, and now, ignoring Jubal, he was tottering back to her side.

Jubal thrust himself between them. "She's real! As real and solid as you or me. And so is Esther. Is that what you want for her? You can't have her!"

Crazy pictures were forcing their way into Jubal's mind, and he couldn't be sure if they were being broadcast to him from the Urod, or were only his own fantasy, born in a mind inflamed with uncertainty and fear.

The Taelon might have been carved out of blue-white stone. "We must." If he had been feeble moments ago, now he was immovable.

"I'm asking *why*. What good is it going to do?"

Now he was being bombarded with a new set of images from the Urod, in which the concepts chiefly conveyed were a hungry craving, a desperate need for freedom. The intensity of the barrage was such that he missed whatever Lekren might have said.

And when Jubal could stand it no longer, he grabbed the cart with Esther on it, wrenched it away from Lekren, and shoved it out of the processing room, driving it at a dead run down the first side corridor he saw.

He feared that he could find no safety anywhere. But he would have to do the best he could.

FOURTEEN

Jubal ran, in fear, pushing ahead of him the gurney with Esther bouncing on it. He could not have given a logical reason why he had to run so fast from a man who could barely walk, but instinct lashed him on. He feared that Lekren was something more than a man, and that even in his weakened state the Taelon could call on powers that were more than human.

The Urod's hunger, the Urod's fear, were raging like a forest fire in Jubal's mind. But at bottom it was Jubal's own will, something deep in himself that made the decision for him. Instinct urged him to turn against the Taelon pilot, and logic argued that the only way to do that was to give the surviving Urod some kind of help.

And at the same time Jubal was bitterly aware that neither he or Esther could long survive the Urod's hunger, if it was ever allowed to have its way with them.

He was chasing the cart down a battered corridor, as fast as he could run, entering a part of the station where he had not been before. Esther's body bounced a little as the cartwheels stumbled on the damaged deck, but the sweet dreamer's smile stayed on her face, just as the rubber snake stayed on her arm.

Ready now to try anything to foil Lekren's plan, Jubal played with the idea of getting the Urod out of the machine, and if necessary back to the spaceship. *If it could control the ship, if it could fly them back to earth* . . . He thought the Taelon might well be too weak to stop him.

But the Urod would have to wait. Right now getting Esther away to some temporary hiding place was Jubal's only immediate thought.

When Jubal stopped running at last, he was out of breath and his pulse was hammering in his ears. Around him, the station was as strange as it had ever been, strange as it always would be, no two rooms of it alike.

When the tumult in his own body had died down a little, he moved to Esther's side and looked closely at the device attached to her bare arm, just below the short sleeve of her summery dress.

Right now the mental turmoil emanating from Urod had faded into the background again. But Jubal was sure it would return. He knew that he had better get as much thinking as possible done while he had the chance, now, while his mind was relatively clear.

If only Esther could walk! If only she could think for herself, see and hear, listen to what Jubal had to tell her, and talk to him!

Maybe she would wake up if he could rid her of the Siamese snake. He debated with himself whether he ought to try to tear Esther free from the Taelon device by force.

Gritting his teeth, he clamped the rubbery snake in his left hand and the girl's arm in his right. He thought he felt the snake, the *sken*, squirm with some volition of its own, as he tried, first hard, then harder, to force them apart. But the only result was that Esther's forehead creased in a faint frown, and a moan escaped her lips. Jubal groaned louder, in sympathy, and ceased his effort.

If he couldn't free her from the snake, it was all the more important that he do everything else possible for her protection.

And Jubal, guiding and gently pushing the gurney with its

helpless burden, realized that he was now trying to find his way back to the station's observation deck.

He was possessed by the half-formed idea that another ship—some ship, any ship—might suddenly appear in one of the many formerly empty docking spaces, and that he would be able to signal to it from the broad window. Not that he had any reason to expect any such arrival.

Jubal had another half-formed reason for seeking out the observation deck—and this one, he had to admit to himself, was even crazier. It was just the kind of place where, if it were on Earth, he would expect to find a public telephone.

But somehow he had taken a wrong turn, and the observation deck eluded him.

In the course of his wanderings with Esther on the cart, he entered a room that seemed no stranger than most of the other rooms aboard the station—but it turned out to be a place where gravity was becoming dangerously intense. On entering that room there was a feeling like that of being on a rapidly whirling merry-go-round, but somehow reversed, so that the all-but-irresistible force tried to pull you to the center instead of throwing you away. And at the center of the room, there was only a blur, something so hard to see that his eyes at first refused to read it as a warning.

Almost too late, he recalled what Lekren had once babbled to him regarding treacherous variations in gravity.

Suddenly the gurney, only three feet closer to the center than Jubal himself, feeling as if it weighed a ton, was impossible to hold back. All Jubal could do was snatch Esther from it before it was swallowed up in blurry nothingness.

Staggering in retreat, he entered one new room after another. Always something new to see and hear, and now at every step he feared he would encounter some new danger. Carrying

Esther in his arms like a baby was okay for about a minute, but the strain soon began to tell, and Jubal could discover no convenient place to put her down. Meanwhile she remained a dead weight, frighteningly inert. If only he could simply tear that damned thing off her arm . . . almost he made the effort, but again he shuddered inwardly at the possible consequences, and held back.

Soon he had to stop and put Esther and her rubber snake down on the deck for a minute, to rest his muscles and catch his breath. When Jubal picked her up again, he wound up draping her over his shoulders in a fireman's carry, which was a lot easier.

Twice he stopped, realizing that he had been walking with eyes shut, and had gone astray from the right path.

That was all they needed now, for the two of them to fall into a hole.

He pushed on at random, and suddenly it seemed his luck had turned: He had found his way back to the observation deck.

Jubal wondered if there was any point in taking Esther back to the ship. Of course the two of them would have to get aboard eventually, if they were ever going to get home. But it was all too easy to picture himself carrying her into the control cabin only to find that Lekren was there too, and in full command. And even if it should turn out that Jubal and Esther had the vessel all to themselves, was he prepared to try to fly it?

Jubal didn't think so, not yet anyway. He was not quite that desperate. He had to try to find some other way.

Possibly there could be, somewhere on the station, another spaceship that would be easier to operate? But when he had looked out through the window of the observation deck, he had seen that all the docking spaces save one were vacant.

Laboriously he carried his limp burden back to the great window, to look again. There was still only one small flashing light in all that outer darkness.

At last, with his own weariness about to overcome him, he found what looked like a good place to put Esther down, where he at least could feel that she was relatively safe and partially hidden. It was a kind of high-backed couch, offering a broad bed, soft to the touch. Any searcher would have to approach her closely, and from the right direction, to see her.

Sitting beside her, Jubal tried to rest. If only he could work out some kind of deal with the Urod—but Jubal's repeated contact with its mind had led him to doubt that was possible. How could you work out an arrangement with an entity that used no words? Worse than that, how could you make a deal with something that hungered to eat your mind, squeezing the psychic essence from the brain like juice from an orange . . . by contrast, Lekren seemed eminently reasonable, and a whole lot closer to being human.

Once more Jubal was having to fight to keep his eyelids open. Once more he lay down and slept, exhausted, this time on the broad couch beside the girl he was trying to save.

When he woke up, mind relatively clear and rested after what had felt like a nap of perhaps an hour, Esther was still asleep. Probably her snake was too—at least it wasn't twitching. Jubal stroked her forehead, tenderly, and decided to leave her where she was for the time being. He had awakened with a decision ready: The only way out of this would be for him to reach some final settlement with Lekren. But first he, Jubal, would go back to the ship and try to gather more food. He was getting very tired of Taelon biscuits, but he didn't want to fall over with weakness either.

This time Jubal had no trouble finding his way. He was back in his original compartment aboard ship, and had discovered a different cabinet that he was now ransacking in search of some different kind of provender, when he heard rapid sounds, and caught a glimpse of a moving body in a doorway. Moving much too quickly and efficiently for it to be Lekren.

The figure in the doorway was not a Taelon, but still it was disturbingly familiar. A tall blond man in a black leather jacket, the former case of rigor mortis, now looking totally recovered. He was standing between Jubal and the control cabin, blocking the only way out. The man's cool blue eyes were fixed on Jubal, but he was talking to someone else, and Jubal could hear only half the conversation.

The man had something in his right hand, and for a moment Jubal feared it was a weapon. But then he realized, from the way the man was holding it, that it must be some kind of telephone, in use.

"He's here, Lekren," the newcomer was saying into the device. "Right. Yes. Yes sir. We'll join you at the processor in a little while."

"You!" Jubal gasped.

The man in the dark jacket clipped his telephone—if that was the right word for the device—onto his belt. He seemed faintly puzzled by Jubal's recognition.

"Seen me before, kid?" His voice, the first human voice other than his own that Jubal had heard in several days, sounded straight American, gravelly and competent.

"Yes. The first time I saw you was at San Simeon. I thought you were dead." Jubal let go the lid of the cabinet he had been holding open, and the door promptly slid shut.

The other received the information calmly. "Oh, that's it. No, not quite dead. I tangled with a Urod there, and got a touch of time-freezing. But Lekren pulled me out of it."

Only now did Jubal notice that the man was no longer wearing his rubber snake. The leather gloves were gone too, revealing large, pale, capable-looking hands.

"My name's Lobo, by the way. Lekren gave the ship a call,

told it to wake me up. So here I am." He smiled as if he were aware how wild that statement must sound.

Jubal nodded. "Lobo."

Lobo gave Jubal a look, sizing him up, and Jubal was reminded of Captain Murray, though in fact the two men did not look much alike. "Lekren tells me your name's Jubal. Jubal Doors."

"That's right."

"Lobo means 'wolf' in Spanish, in case you're wondering."

"Okay." It crossed Jubal's mind that the blond man did not look at all Spanish.

Lobo leaned in the doorway, seeming perfectly at ease. He said, "Lekren tells me also that there's some things you don't seem to understand." Now it seemed to Jubal that he was speaking with just a trace of some accent that Jubal could not identify.

"What is it I don't understand?"

"How important it is to help the Taelons." Lobo sounded like a preacher, teaching an elementary lesson in how important it is to pray.

"Why?"

Lobo ignored the question. "See, the thing is, Jubal, the Companion thought you were going to be a real help to him when he got here—that's why he brought you along in the first place."

That didn't seem to make sense. "But Lekren wasn't expecting this place to be all shot up like this. Was he?"

"No. No." And Lobo frowned and shook his head, as if at the suggestion of something horrible.

"So, what kind of help did he think he would need from Esther or me?"

Lobo stared at him, not angry, just puzzled, as if the idea of argument was something he hadn't encountered before, and so he wasn't quite prepared for it. After thinking it over for a little while, he said: "What Lekren has to do here, the business with the Urod, is very important. You can't imagine how important that really is."

"All right, maybe so. Lekren's doing a great job. But I still don't get it. Why *did* he have to bring me and Esther? What was going on at San Simeon?"

Lobo, leaning in the doorway with folded arms, seemed to be pondering how best to begin a lengthy story. "How much has he told you about the Urod?"

"Not much. Only that it's very dangerous. And for some reason it has to be run through a certain machine, here on the station."

Lobo nodded reasonably, as if to say yes, yes, he knew all that. "Like I say, Lekren originally thought you'd be a big help. But then he began to realize that you just didn't understand—that *you* needed help. I guess the shock and all had been too much for you. So he woke me up. I've been here before."

Jubal could feel his body starting, trying, to relax. Here at last was a human voice, two open human eyes. Reasonable, so far unthreatening. Someone he could communicate with. "Why didn't he just wake you up in the first place, instead of me?"

"Mainly because he wasn't sure how healthy I'd be—like I said, I had a little run-in with the Urod too." Turning and beckoning, Lobo led Jubal forward, into the place Jubal thought of as the control cabin. When they were both in there Lobo gestured at the right-hand seat. "Here, kid. Sit down."

"You're going to take off? Not without Esther!"

Lobo was faintly amused. "No, we're not going anywhere. Sit."

Taking the left seat himself, Lobo began to get busy.

First he did something—Jubal could not quite see what— that turned off the bright flashing outside light. Then he began making gestures over the instrument panel, not quite touching it at any point. The displays all changed as he tinkered with them, still not touching. Jubal realized, with a creepy feeling in his scalp, that the whole panel could be set to give readings in human language, setting out letters and numbers that Jubal found familiar.

One of the dashboard readouts looked like a little stage, and on it a tiny glowing image danced. Jubal couldn't tell what the object was, but it looked as three-dimensional as a chair.

Lobo waved his hand over the panel in a certain way, almost the movement of a musician's fingers, and suddenly the content of all the displays shifted. Now there were colored numbers in many places, and for example Jubal could read in one place a little label that said, in plain English, "miles per hour." At the moment the number in that square was zero, which he supposed made sense, because the ship wasn't going anywhere.

Lobo seemed proud of his knowledge, glad of the chance to show it off, like a kid with a new toy. "Ever seen anything like this?"

"Not hardly. Never," Jubal murmured absently, taking in the wonders. What he mainly noticed was that there was no way he could fly this thing—it would be like jumping into the cockpit of an airplane and trying to take off, where you'd be almost guaranteed to kill yourself. Except that this would probably be a hundred times worse. Only as a last, really desperate resort.

"Lekren knows what he's doing, kid."

"I guess maybe he does," Jubal admitted. He couldn't argue with the fact of his own ignorance. "I wish he'd tell me."

Lobo leaned back in his pilot's seat and paused. When he spoke again it was in a new tone, as if he had decided it was finally time to get down to business.

"Lekren tells me you've got a girl hidden somewhere."

"What I've been trying to tell you. Her name is Esther Summerson, and she's got a rubber snake on her arm just like you had. She can't wake up, and she needs help. Help from her fellow human beings."

Lobo did not react to the name. Well, Esther was hardly a famous movie star as yet. "Where is she?" he inquired patiently.

"I put her where she'll be safe. How is she going to get the help she needs?"

The blond man continued to be mildly reasonable. "She can't get any kind of help if you keep her stashed away."

"Seems like she can't get any if I bring her out. Lekren was planning to—do something to her, and I didn't know what. I don't trust Lekren," Jubal burst out. Then his pent-up need for information broke loose. "Do you know where we are?" he demanded. "What is this place?"

Lobo's smile was a little crooked, showing moderately bad teeth. He seemed pained by Jubal's confessed lack of trust. "Sure. Maybe not the exact astronomical details, but in a way, I know where we are. We're way up in the sky, sonny boy. Way, way up in the sky."

"I figured that much."

"You did, huh?" Lobo shot out an arm and almost touched something on the panel, and a screen appeared, an unexpected window in the solid surface. The window lit up, and began to present a series of pictures, that Jubal could recognize as various views of rooms and corridors inside the station. The jagged holes and blasted places showed up clearly.

Lobo studied the pictures with his eyes squinted almost shut, as if he found it painful just to look at such extensive damage.

Jubal got the impression that the man's earlier attitude of confidence was gradually being replaced by desperation.

Lobo muttered: "I've been here before, but the place wasn't wrecked then. I remember my first visit. That was the trip of a lifetime." The man seemed perfectly serious, and again the tone of reverence crept back into his voice. "All the stuff on the station was working then."

That was interesting, but Jubal had different matters on his mind. He said, "So you just work for Lekren. You do whatever he tells you." Jubal could feel the weight of the pistol in his side pocket, but he didn't put his hand in there. Not yet. If he was going to force Lobo to fly the ship away, he had to first get Esther back on board.

The man smiled, a superior look. "Listen to the kid. Yeah, in a way. You could put it like that, I just work for him. I was once a private detective, had an office in ell-ay. Then one day I got hired for a certain job—and it turned out to be a helluva lot more than just a job."

Jubal harked back to something he'd said earlier. "When I saw you at San Simeon I thought you were dead."

"Yeah, Lekren's told me about that. He and I went up against the Urod there; that was basically the job he'd hired me for. I got time-frozen for a little while; but—"

"Time-frozen, like the Urod?"

"Sort of. I just got a little touch, like I said. That was nothing."

"Nothing?"

"Nothing. Lekren took care of it, found me, carried me aboard the ship, started the treatment to bring me out of it." The man's face creased suddenly, and it seemed he might be about to weep. "But then *he* got hurt, going up against the Urod without any help. He says it wasn't my fault, but I . . ."

Lobo had to break off there. His voice was threatening to crack, as if he was unable to endure the thought that he had failed to save his Taelon master from injury.

The man took a moment to pull himself together. Then he got up from the pilot's seat, and stretched. "Come on, kid. We're going to find that girl you stashed away."

One thing Lobo was certainly being truthful about: the man had indeed been aboard the station before. It showed in Lobo's familiarity with this exotic environment, in the control that he could exercise over at least some of its machinery.

Jubal, thinking furiously, battling confusion as best he

could, decided that he had to show Lobo where the girl was hidden. How else was he ever going to get Esther back on board the ship? It was either persuade the man beside him to help his fellow humans, or pull out the gun and try to shoot him. Jubal wasn't sure he could do that in cold blood—but if he ever thought he had to, to protect himself and Esther, he would give it a good try.

Right now pulling a gun didn't seem like a good idea at all. Lobo was his most likely potential ally, the only other person here who could talk reasonably. And without Lobo there would be no one but Lekren able to control the ship. And Jubal was sure it would be no use trying, even at gunpoint, to get the Taelon to take them home.

Lobo was upset on first entering the station and getting a direct look at the damage. "My God, there must have been a real battle." Lekren had told him about it, and he had seen some of it on the screens in the control cabin, but it hadn't really sunk in until now.

"It looks like there was," said Jubal. Then, still starving for information, he asked, "Who was doing the fighting here, Lobo? Was it Taelons against Urods, or someone else?"

At first Lobo would only shake his head. "I'd just be guessing," he said at last.

"I saw a specimen of some other kind of race, back there in the muscum, that looked like a reptile. But it had clothes and everything with it."

Lobo only shook his head, as if to say how about that. He did not seem surprised to hear mention of a museum.

Jubal was growing almost frantic for solid information. They passed some scattered corpses, only distantly visible. He pointed toward them. "Are these dead bodies real or not?"

Lobo tossed a glance in that direction. He was not really surprised. "You'd better believe they're really dead."

"But—are they really *there* or not?"

He didn't get a straight answer. It looked like there were some things that Lobo understood no better than Jubal.

The communicator at Lobo's belt began to buzz, and a moment later Lekren had joined them, in the form of a wavering image on the small screen of what Lobo said was his global communicator. This time Jubal was standing where he could see the unit better. No doubt about it, it was more than a wireless telephone, it was an amazingly small two-way combination radio and television.

Jubal was perfectly ready to carry on his argument with two people at once. Directing his question at the little picture, he demanded, "What good is it going to do Esther, if we carry her back there again?"

Lobo held the little screen turned toward Jubal. From it came Lekren's voice, trying to be musical but wheezing with infirmity. "Jubal. Do you wish to assume command?"

"I—no, but I—"

"Then your only alternative in this emergency is to follow orders. Is that not correct? To help your fellow humans and to help me."

"I guess it is." But the more time Jubal spent aboard the station, the more he talked to Lekren, the more he shivered in the mental presence of the Urod, the more he contemplated the memory of Esther's gentle, helpless face, totally dependent on him, the more rebellious he felt.

Lekren and Lobo exchanged worried comments about the possible presence aboard the station of something or someone they called a Jaridian.

"What's that?" Jubal asked. Nobody bothered to answer him.

"Where'd you put her, kid?" Lobo, hanging the communicator back on his belt again, continued to sound patient and sympathetic.

"I'll show you." But Jubal had had a sudden idea. There was something else he wanted to show Lobo first.

"We're heading toward the processing room," Lobo remarked a minute later, as they trudged along.

"I know." Then Jubal lifted his head, listening. There were times when he wondered if there could be some other dangerous entity roaming about the station. Now and then strange, distant sounds came drifting to his ears, and sometimes he seemed to catch a dart of movement from the corner of his eye. And several times the thunderous crash that had so alarmed him was repeated. But all that might be explained by the fact that decks and bulkheads were progressively collapsing.

Obviously Lobo was worried too. "Doesn't sound good," was his comment on the latest distant uproar. His gaze darted this way and that. "Doesn't look good in here. I mean the whole damn station. We'd better get this job done and get out."

Jubal's heart leaped up at the suggestion. "Good idea," he agreed. They walked on a few more paces in silence while he tried to decide how to phrase his next question. At last he said, "You have a kind of special feeling about Lekren, huh? I mean you worry about him."

"Oh yeah." Lobo was casual. "I feel that way about all Taelons."

"You do? Why?"

"Told you I was here on the station once before, when everything was working. Well, that time they gave me a type of brain implant." He jerked a thumb casually over his shoulder. "Back there's the room where they operated on me."

At first Jubal wasn't sure that he'd heard right. "Operated? What for?"

"To make me better."

Jeez, was the man crazy? "I meant, what was wrong with you?"

"It wasn't so much that anything was wrong. Just that I didn't have the right ideas about certain things." Lobo humorously tapped his own forehead, smiling. "But that got taken care of."

"They put something in your *head?*"

"Sure."

"You let them?"

"Yes. It helps me think clearer. I have a better life."

"What is it?"

"They call it a cyber-viral implant. It's an experimental model."

"A what?"

Lobo shrugged. "CVI for short."

"Something that makes you want to work for them."

"Right. Working for them, feeling better, that amounts to the same thing."

"Huh," said Jubal, not knowing what else to say.

Lobo smiled at him. "They had to do mine twice before it took properly. But the second time was a big success." Lobo paused, gazing into the distance. "Big success," he repeated.

"Huh." Jubal was staring at Lobo's head, looking for some evidence of the surgery, but all he could see was a thick growth of hair, no trace of any scar.

"They don't want to waste me," Lobo said. "They've got a big investment in me, and I've probably only got a couple of years."

"A couple of years to what?"

"The CVI shortens my life to some extent—"

"You call that better?"

"—but it's well worth it. I may only have a couple of years to go, but I can get a lot done in that time." He registered Jubal's look of horror, and tried to reassure him. "They'll find better ways to do it, soon enough. Ways to extend the life-span with a CVI."

Jubal couldn't find anything to say.

Lobo gave him a knowing look. "Time will come when everybody on earth will have one."

"What—? How—?"

"Yours will probably be a lot better than mine, less side effects. They'll have perfected the business by then. So in a way, Jubal, you shouldn't envy me. In fact I could almost envy you."

FIFTEEN

Their conversation was interrupted by a heavy vibration in the deck beneath their feet, followed quickly by a loud noise that raised in Jubal's mind the image of a series of gigantic doors, slamming one after another. He raised his head and listened to more of the same, with variations. The sounds he was hearing now had nothing directly to do with Urods.

"What is it?" he demanded.

But for once Lobo was, if anything, more surprised than Jubal. "Don't know," the man said. "Something else must be breaking down."

Pulling out his communicator, he hastily put in a call to Lekren, to make sure the Taelon was all right, down at the other end of the long corridor from the museum.

The two of them held a conference. This time Lobo held his phone turned away from Jubal, so the boy could see nothing on the screen, and hear only one end of the conversation.

Meanwhile there were more and more sounds of disaster, suggesting walls and floors and whole buildings collapsing. It seemed to Jubal that the spans between episodes of noise were growing shorter and shorter. First the gaps had been measured in hours, and now only in minutes.

A faint cloud of dust came drifting toward them, through an array of openings in a nearby wall.

Jubal started to look around for some place to take shelter, but then decided that if the whole station was going to collapse in the next few minutes, there was no point.

"Jubal, Lekren wants to talk to you."

And the Taelon, his voice drifting over the communicator, his face small on its little screen, said something to the effect that they must get the Urod taken care of before utter destruction overtook them. "Otherwise all our efforts will have been in vain."

Jubal muttered something that might have been an agreement. Eventually things quieted down. Slowly he forced himself to let go of the stanchion he had been gripping; it looked like the station was going to hang together for a while yet.

He had to get on with what must be done.

He and Lobo resumed their walk, which was supposedly taking them to Esther. And Lobo was able to tell Jubal more, on the subject of how wonderful it was to have a CVI.

"Don't bother," Jubal said. "I promise I won't envy you for having a Taelon thing stuck in your head. Just help Esther and me to get home. And while we're waiting to do that, tell me what this place is."

The other shrugged. "Just think of it as the station—we don't have to know any more than that."

"That's what Lekren called it. Like a railroad station?"

"Something like that. It's a place where meetings happen. Connections are made, and things and people get moved around. But also where certain things are stored."

"What kind of things?"

"Things like museums have. Specimens, like the ones you saw. Not only people, but animals, vegetables, flowers. Some of them are rare, some are dangerous."

"Like the Urod."

Lobo nodded. "Like Urods, for example. Nobody wants to keep a Urod in his own back yard, but people can come and look at them here, when necessary for scientific reasons."

" 'People'?"

"Companions." Lobo's look said that Jubal ought to have understood that without being told.

"I see. Go on."

"Not much more to tell. But, Jubal."

"Yeah."

Lobo had an earnest, worried look. "I love the Companions. It's only right and just for all of us to love them. You should too."

"Great," Jubal said.

"They're so much better than we are." The man sounded perfectly sober and sincere.

"Great. Sure." Now Jubal was really beginning to believe what Lobo was telling him about the implant. Still, he couldn't be a 100 percent sure. Jubal supposed that being temporarily dead, or time-frozen if you wanted to call it that, might be enough to scramble anybody's brain.

Jubal wasn't at all sure about how he felt about taking orders from a dead man.

They were approaching the museum area now, from a direction opposite to that of the processor room. The vast array of display cases would be only a short distance ahead.

Then suddenly Lobo started pressing the fingers of both hands to his temples.

"What's wrong?"

The blond man shook his head. "My CVI."

"What?"

"The thing they put in my head. Sometimes it hurts a little."

Seizing the moment when it seemed that Lobo might be a little distracted and uncertain, Jubal made a last try at argument. "Do you know how to fly the spaceship?"

"Fly it? Yeah, Lekren's taught me quite a lot. Makes me more useful. I could fly it if I had to." With a contented little smile, Lobo spread his large, pale hands, made rapid motions with his fingers, putting Jubal in mind of a piano player warming up.

Jubal tried to make his voice as casual and reasonable as he could. "Then I think we'd better climb back aboard the ship right away and get out of here. No, wait, listen to me! I know what Lekren says he wants, but he's sick, or hurt, his mind is wandering most of the time."

Lobo was shaking his head.

Jubal pressed on. "I don't think he knows what he's doing, Lobo. He can stay here with the Urod if he wants to. But Esther needs help, and you and I need help too. You'd better fly the three of us back to earth. We're not going to get what we need here."

Jubal had started out forcefully, but his words trailed away. Lobo looked normal again, but he wasn't even taking Jubal seriously enough to be annoyed.

"Jubal, I think you're the one whose mind is wandering. The Urod's the first thing we have to worry about. Lekren needs us to help him."

"All right, so maybe he's in worse shape than any of us. But he can't get what he needs here, the whole place is a ruin. If you love him as much as you say, you'd better get him back to earth and into a hospital."

Lobo almost chuckled. "Fat lot of help they'd give him." Then the man turned grim again. "I know he's hurting bad, and it worries me; but once the Urod goes, he'll be better."

And for all Jubal knew, that might be true. Lekren himself had once told him the same thing.

"I bet the spaceship has an automatic pilot."

"I bet it does." Lobo was perfectly ready to admit all kinds of things.

"And you know how to use it."

"So?"

"Then send us back, me and Esther," Jubal pleaded.

"No. Can't be done."

Jubal itched to draw the gun, and give orders with Lobo looking down the muzzle. But suppose the man was so crazy that he still refused? Or suppose he agreed to set the controls of the ship, how would Jubal know how he was really setting them?

"Can't be done," Lobo repeated. "She has to be at the processing center."

"But *why?*"

Lobo shook his head. His face had the expression of a man forced to listen to stupid questions from a kid. "'Why?' I'll tell you. Ever see how a man handles an alligator, kid?"

"An *alligator?*"

"At one of those 'gator farms they have in the South. Say you've got one of moderate size, not too big to lift, but big enough to chew your arm off. And you want to carry it from one pond to another."

"No, I never saw a 'gator farm. What have 'gator farms got to do with anything?"

"More than you think. I'm trying to explain. The only way to handle a Urod, kid, is to give it something to *bite* on. With gators they use chickens. While a 'gator has a nice, juicy chicken in its jaws, it's not gonna bother with your arm. Only an Urod don't have teeth, so you have to give its *mind* something to bite on—something nice and big and juicy, like an earth-human mind. Could be Esther's, or yours, or mine." Lobo's calm voice made what he was saying all the more horrible.

Jubal had to fight down a sudden urge to vomit Taelon biscuits. The last ones he'd eaten seemed to by lying in his stomach in an undigested lump. "I vote for yours," he said, and let his right hand hang near the side pocket of his coat, and wondered if he could make himself use the gun.

But Lobo was not offended, and if he noticed what Jubal's right hand was doing, he didn't seem to care.

"That's because you don't understand, kid. I'm too useful to Lekren in other ways."

Jubal supposed that maybe Lobo's implant rendered him a little careless when it came to dealing with other human beings. Jubal said, "Tell me about it so I understand."

"Okay. Right now, the Urod might be trying to push your

girlfriend, little Essie, away from him, because he knows she's bait. But get her close enough, and he'll snap her up. He won't be able to resist her nice human mind. Urods are like that, it's their weakness. And when he snaps *her* up, the big trap snaps *him*. Lekren's really got him."

"What happens to Esther?"

"What happens to the chicken? But that doesn't really matter, does it?"

"Doesn't *matter?*"

"Not if we can save Taelon lives. Don't you see the difference?" It was as if Lobo really thought that chickens and humans were practically on a level. "Look, it could have been you or me instead of her. But I'm too useful. And Lekren must have something else in mind for you too."

Jubal's right wrist brushed the bulge in his side coat pocket. He supposed that when Lobo was revived, the man must have noticed that his revolver was gone, but simply assumed it had been lost in the skirmish at San Simeon. So far Lobo should have no particular reason to think that Jubal had taken it. And so far he had not said anything to Jubal about the missing weapon.

Meanwhile the Taelon had said nothing about the pistol either—maybe it had never occurred to him, in his befuddled state, to pay any attention to earthly weapons.

"I want you to see something," the man said, and held out the communicator for Jubal to take. As soon as the boy reached with his right hand, Lobo grabbed him by the wrist and spun him into an embrace.

The man's arms felt incredibly strong, and he was as skillful at this as he had been at working the instrument panel; in a moment Jubal's balance was broken, and he came down on the hard deck with a crash that knocked out most of his wind.

Lobo's wiry weight was on top of him, completing his paralysis. In the next moment Lobo's hand was skillfully extracting the pistol from the side pocket of Jubal's coat.

Then the man was on his feet again, picking up the dropped communicator as an afterthought, and Jubal was free to try to get up, if he could. For the moment all he could think of was that now he was going to be shot dead while he lay helpless. But no one was shot. Lobo had the gun now, but he wasn't bothering to aim it. Instead he just dropped it in his jacket pocket and reached out to give Jubal a hand getting up; no hard feelings.

But Jubal didn't try to jump him—as soon as he was on his feet with a good lungful of air he darted away, rounding a corner into the museum, taking a winding path among the display cases.

With Lobo's feet pounding only a few strides behind him, Jubal led him to where the young human woman was on display. There Jubal stopped, gasping. He couldn't think of anything else to do, anywhere else to run.

Lobo seemed startled when his gaze fell on the naked woman in her glass case. Not really totally surprised; to Jubal he looked like a man suddenly reminded of someone of something he might not want to be reminded of, that he had long forgotten.

For the moment Jubal was ignored. Moving a little closer to the case, Lobo whispered a name to the woman inside.

"Rosie?" And for just a moment, amazingly, the man seemed about to weep. He stood in front of the display, gazing at her. Once he started to put his hand on the glass, but the figure inside twitched and stirred, ready to go into the first movement of her programmed demonstration, only to quiet at once when Lobo jerked both hands behind him. Evidently he knew what the performance would be like, and he didn't want to see it.

Meanwhile Jubal edged a step closer to him. "You know her?" Not that there was really any need to ask the question.

It took Lobo a long time to answer, but at last the words came readily enough. "Knew her pretty well at one time." He had fought down the urge to cry, it seemed, and his voice was tired and dull, fit for that of an old man talking about some event in his distant childhood.

"How did she get put in this case here, Lobo?"

Again there was a pause. "Last year," Lobo said at last. "Lekren was hunting another Urod, I was helping." Then he added, "Rosie worked for me in my office."

"Your private detective's office."

"Yeah."

"And Rosie was helping you—hunt?"

Lobo nodded.

Jubal pushed him, prodded him. "But the way it worked out, she was just what Lekren thought he needed—a chicken. Someone to put in the 'gator's jaws."

Again, Lobo nodded.

"And when her mind got—chewed up—in the process, her body got put in here, behind the glass."

Lobo's eyes swung around to focus on Jubal. The man was saddened by Rosie's fate, but he wasn't crushed. "I told you. There was another Urod. That was my first job for Lekren." An answer that was supposed to trump everything else.

Jubal decided he had got all the benefit from Rosie that he was going to get. He took the other by the arm. "Lobo, help me get Esther on the ship. She's still alive, she's still got a mind, we've got to get her away."

But it was useless. Lobo might shed a tear over the horrors in his own past, but he was shaking his head, and he could not be swayed.

Lobo's communicator buzzed again, and Jubal took advantage of the opportunity to slip away.

Hastily he made his way back to the place he thought of as the observation deck, where he had left Esther. Now, he could see only one faint hope left, and it would last only as long as Lekren and Lobo were away from the ship.

As Jubal ran, in the distance somewhere there came another rumble of collapse.

Esther had not moved on her couch, and Jubal braced himself to hoist her once more onto his back. But before he did that, he decided to get rid of the damned rubbery Siamese snake, the Taelon machine still coiled tightly round the girl's right arm. It was beginning to look like Esther was soon going to be dead anyway, one way or another, and maybe this way she would at least have some chance to think and act for herself before that happened.

The way the snake felt now in Jubal's hand, the way it twitched when his grip came on it, reinforced Jubal's earlier impression that the strange artifact was somehow half-alive.

Tearing it loose was a horrific business, but to Jubal's great relief it did not seem to do Esther any harm. No sign remained on her arm but a small red pressure mark, and that soon faded away entirely.

As soon as Jubal had ripped the snake away from her, Esther started to moan and stir a little in her sleep, though her eyes remained closed. She responded faintly when Jubal called her name, but though her eyelids quivered they did not really open.

Jubal picked her up in the fireman's carry again, and headed for the ship at the best pace he could manage. Every time he lugged his burden around a corner, he feared to see Lobo standing there, waiting for him. At some corners he was *sure* that either Lobo or Lekren would be there . . . or someone, something even worse, like a dark Egyptian statue . . . but he saw no one, only an occasional example of the station's ghostly dead.

To complicate his situation further, Jubal was getting more mental messages from the Urod. This time it was almost like having his own private television, except that he couldn't tell if what he saw was really happening, or if it was just something the Urod wanted him to believe

Jubal ran for the ship, desperate to get aboard before the station was utterly destroyed, and he was running as fast as he could, which was not very fast under Esther's bouncing weight.

Desperately he pounded down the last short corridor, and with a gasp of relief carried Esther into the ship, pausing long enough to close the hatch behind them. Then he slung her body hastily into the control room's right-hand seat. She moaned faintly—*she was still alive, then, still alive!*

Screens on the control panel in front of him showed scenes from the interior of the station, and one screen was focused on the processing room.

Jubal fell into the left seat, and raised his hands like some desperate sorcerer's apprentice, hoping that the ship somehow could be triggered into motion, made to carry them back to Earth—or at least free of the collapsing station. Right now he could see on screen that Lekren and Lobo were together in the processing room—and there was the Urod too. What came to Jubal from the Urod's mind melded with what was on the screen, so he knew the human and the Taelon were trying with all their strength to somehow finish the Urod off.

Behind them, above them, around them, total destruction threatened—it looked and sounded like the whole station was on the verge of exploding or melting down.

Jubal reached out his hands toward the panel, determined to do something, though he had no idea of what it ought to be. . . .

The little screen-figure of Lobo moved, and Jubal very clearly heard him say, "I will be happy to take her place, Lekren."

"I understand, Lobo," said the musical Taelon voice. "But I still hope to avoid that necessity. You can be of service. In so many other ways."

Then Lekren's body suddenly stiffened, and he turned to confront the basalt statue looming over them both on its new futuristic throne. The Taelon shrilled something in his birdsong tongue, first words then tailing off into a kind of scream—

Lobo was starting to draw his gun—

Jubal thrust his raised hands forward. He didn't know how to fly, he didn't know the first damn thing about it, but if you could get the engine running and the prop spinning, then you might be able to get her off the ground, and then—

Something happened, a kind of tiny lurch or jump, and in a moment he was certain that the ship was moving. He had really done it! He had certainly done something, because they had lurched free of the station. He felt no pressure of acceleration, but his eyes told him they had already gained terrific speed. Just in time, too, because there it went, the whole thing gone, in the biggest damned explosion he had ever seen or imagined. But quiet, shockingly quiet, still as a silent movie. Lobo gone, Lekren gone. Jubal could feel their deaths.

The Urod—?

The glare of the fireball was almost dazzling, even coming through the protective glass. And all in an eerie silence.

Control of the spaceship was in Jubal's hands. But what should he do next? Experiment. If he moved just one finger, just a little bit, like this—

This time there was no sensation of movement, of travel, of the passage of any time at all. This time there was only the void. . . .

Blackness. And then a hideous shock. His whole body engulfed, by something that felt like cold water . . .

It *was* cold water. Jubal opened his eyes, expecting, if he expected anything, to see the front window of the control cabin. But instead he was looking up at the floodlit twin towers of Casa Grande. He was sitting on the flat bottom of a shallow pool, with Esther practically in his lap, the two of them surrounded by four black basalt statues.

And in the foreground, poking out from between dense lilac bushes only a few feet away, a human face he recognized at once, that of a wide-eyed Errol Flynn. Beside Flynn's face another, some young woman Jubal had never seen before.

The movie star and his girlfriend were laughing merrily, calling out some drunken words. But Jubal hardly noticed them, except to register the fact that they were both fully human, and wore no rubber snakes. There were no Taelons anywhere in sight, no men in leather jackets. And there was nothing like a ship.

Esther's eyes were open now. The shock of the cold water. She squirmed around in Jubal's arms, and he said a great silent prayer of thanksgiving, and gave her an enormous kiss.

She threw her arms around his neck, and kissed him back.

SIXTEEN

The old man had fallen silent, staring into space.

"So," Jonathan Doors prompted his father, "the ship brought you right back to San Simeon?"

Their long conversation had been several times interrupted, as various urgent business matters were brought to Jonathan's attention. He also had to make some routine decisions regarding the upkeep of the estate. Also the two men had moved several times, Jonathan constantly looking to minimize the chance of being overheard by casual workers or curious Companions.

At the moment they were sitting in Jubal's room in Casa Grande.

Jubal's gaze returned to his son. "Not exactly, Johnny. That's not quite what I said, is it?"

"What do you mean?"

"We were returned to San Simeon, all right. But I don't think the spaceship brought us."

"You're losing me."

"One minute Esther and I were in the control cabin, like I told you. Next thing I knew, we were both sitting in the fountain, getting soaking wet—"

"You were right back in the pool by the statues, where it all started."

"That's what I'm saying."

"And you said you saw four stone statues?"

"If you want to be technical, which is a good thing to be in this case, I was looking at three statues and one Urod. That was back on its original pedestal."

A silence fell.

"So what happened to the Taelon ship?" Jonathan asked his father, after a lengthy pause.

"What ship?" The old man could indeed be irritating sometimes.

"The one that must have brought you back to earth. And was the return made on autopilot, or what? How?"

The old man sighed. "You're not listening, son. I didn't say the ship brought us back, or that it even came with us. Either the ship was destroyed along with the station, or its autopilot fired it away in some other direction entirely. It might be goin' yet. Esther and I were translated back to earth by some other means."

Jonathan stared at his father. "Such as what?"

"A re-adaptation of reality."

"You mean the Urod brought you back." Jonathan was beginning to feel something of a severe letdown. Until they had come to this business of the impossible return, he had been almost convinced. Now, if he hadn't known his father as well as he did, he'd be ready to suggest that the old man had dreamed it all. "Somehow it survived that big blast you described, and it brought you back."

Jubal nodded. "I don't see any other way. Probably we two humans were transported just by accident, not out of the goodness of the heart a Urod doesn't have. I been thinking about it for damn near two-thirds of a century, and that's the best I can come up with. The Urod won its wrestling match with Lekren, in the end, and Esther and I were dragged along by accident, just because we were physically so close to it." The old man slowly shook his head. "But I'm not sure. Maybe, having come so near to devouring Esther, it didn't want to let her go. Maybe . . ."

"And you're saying Urods can do things like that. Space travel without a ship."

"How do you figure it got here in the first place?"

Jonathan's head was whirling, and he needed a distraction. Getting up from his chair, he wandered out into the hallway, and then into another room. His father followed, floor-tapping with his cane. This chamber, like most of the rest of the house, was obviously long vacant, such furniture as remained in it covered with sheetlike white cloth. Doors could faintly smell the mothballs and other preservatives that had been applied at some time in the fairly distant past.

Jonathan could hear his global ticking at his belt, and restlessly he tore off the latest geemail print-out and looked at it. The narrow strip urged him to do something quickly about his electronic stocks, and it bore the return address of Thomas Tonga, one of his chief investment consultants. No doubt about it, he had been letting his business slide for a couple of days; but he wasn't going to concern himself with numbers just now. It was just going to have to keep on sliding a little longer.

His father was too restless to sit down in the new room. Jubal said, "Don't know when I've done this much talking. I could use a glass of whisky, son."

"I think I know where we could find a bottle of beer at least." And Jonathan once more pulled his global from his belt, made contact with a face from the kitchen and asked whoever had a free moment down there to please bring a couple of beers upstairs. Judging from the reaction of the face, the only person in the kitchen at the moment happened to be very busy.

"That's all right. Never mind, we'll come down." The Doors men descended into the huge kitchen of Casa Grande to look for their own beer. On the way they passed a couple of painters touching up the interior trim, who had been chatting idly, but instantly began to look very busy, only a beat too late, when the boss hove into sight. Jonathan observed that the new owner's reputation was already well established among the help.

Beer bottles in hand, father and son wandered out into the plaza and sat on a handy bench. Jonathan noted that his father had chosen a place from which the statues of Sekhmet were not quite visible.

Jonathan Doors had arrived at San Simeon with Va'lon early in the morning of Day One, as the news media all around the earth had begun to call the first day of Taelon presence on the planet; and it was now late morning, Pacific time, of Day Two. Both men had had a chance to grab a few hours' sleep, between story-telling sessions. Va'lon too had evidently enjoyed a period of rest, for the Taelon had remained in his assigned cottage for some hours.

When Va'lon had emerged, he told Jonathan that three more Taelons would soon be arriving at the castle. One of them would be Da'an, Companion liaison to North America, and Va'lon somehow conveyed that this would be an important visit.

Doors hadn't been aware that the Companion had any communications equipment with him, but he didn't question the announcement.

"They'll be welcome," Jonathan had replied. And they would be, too, if only for the reason that he hoped to learn from them something about themselves, about the Taelon race in general. If they were really big shots of some kind in the Taelon organization, so much the better. What they said and did might help Jonathan Doors decide, one way or the other, what attitude he, and the rest of humanity, really ought to take regarding their alien presence on the earth.

Until the near-miraculous explanation of Jubal's and Esther's return home, Jonathan had been on the point of accepting his father's story unconditionally, but his mind boggled at the idea of human bodies being safely transported across some interstellar distance without benefit of spaceship. The point was still on his mind when he replied to Va'lon.

"How will they be traveling?" Jonathan asked. "In one of your shuttles? Or on the ground?"

Uncharacteristically, Va'lon hesitated and seemed uncertain. "We will see. Is their mode of transportation a matter of importance to you?"

"No. No, I suppose not." *Except it has some unexpected importance to you.*

Around the middle of Day Two the sky had started to cloud over, a heavy grayness rolling in slowly, almost majestically, from over the sea. Now whatever power controlled such things was trying to make up its mind whether or not today would see serious rainfall on this section of the California coast. Watching the continual pelting of large, fat drops that kept threatening to turn into a downpour but never did, Jonathan could not help wondering whether North America was still getting any measurable fallout from the recent nuclear exchanges in the Middle East. Most of the regular forecasts had stopped giving routine hourly and daily readings. Complicating their predictions was the fact that experts were divided as to whether the world's long-range weather patterns were in a transitional stage, and, if so, why.

Father and son had each finished their beer, and the bottles were resting at the foot of their bench.

Jubal roused himself from a brief reverie. "Just thinking about your mother," he announced, in response to a silent question from his son.

"She was quite a lady. Not that I can remember her very well."

"That she was, son. That she was. But in all our years

together, this was one story I never told her." Jubal sighed and seemed to pull himself together. "Sorry. What were you asking me a minute ago?"

"I'm still curious about that spaceship, Dad. You rode a Taelon ship out to the mysterious 'station' where all the really strange stuff happened. But I'm still not quite clear as to exactly how you and Esther got back. You say you were *on* the spaceship when the thing happened that brought you back."

"Right."

"So, what happened to the ship?"

Jubal sighed, looked for his beer again, and realized that it was gone. "As soon as I realized we were back home, I assumed the ship had brought us. But when I thought to look around for it, about ten seconds after I'd pulled Esther out of the pool, it wasn't there. I checked again later, and there was no trace of any ship. Not even a mark in the grass. If the ship *did* bring us back—and I told you, I don't believe it did—it just went away, the same way it came.

"There was never a word about strange sightings in the sky that night—at least I never heard any—so apparently no one on the ground ever noticed any spaceship. Which in itself proves nothing. Back then there was no radar guarding our airspace. Hell, I don't even know if our radar today can pick them up, if they don't want to be seen."

Jonathan nodded slowly. "So, answer one more question for me: Why is it, do you suppose, that even today our Companions have been very hesitant about approaching this place by air? I suggested to Va'lon that we fly over here from my house, and he'd have none of it. And I asked him just now if his associates were coming by air or on the ground, and he sounded even vaguer than usual."

"Huh. That's easy. The approach of any kind of machine by air is one of the things that can trigger a revival episode in the Urod."

"Really?" Jonathan stared at his father. "How do you

know that? Did your Taelon tell you? You said his name was—'Lekren'?"

"He was not my Taelon. But, matter of fact, he did give me some information on that point, when he was in one of his more lucid intervals. 'Course in his condition it was hard to be sure when he was lucid and when he wasn't. That's what he got for tangling minds with a Urod."

"But he didn't seem to care if he told you all the Taelon secrets. Things you'd be free to talk about when you got home."

"Son, I don't believe that son of a bitch ever thought I'd really be going home, or Esther either. Sure, he told me we would, but either he was just babbling, or he was lying to keep me happy. Only reason he brought either of us along was so we'd be available as bait for the 'gator's jaws."

"And he attached a special kind of machine to Esther," Jonathan mused, "so that she remained asleep. But he let you wake up. How come?"

"I think he meant to fit me with the same thing. He just didn't get around to it. Didn't I mention the funny-looking thing I stumbled over, the first time I woke up on the ship? I thought it looked like a Siamese snake?"

"Yeah, I got a clear mental picture of what that must have looked like."

Jubal nodded, mumbled something forceful.

"But then," said Jonathan, "once Lekren saw you were awake, he decided the easiest thing was to try to use you as an active helper. Because, for one thing, he wasn't sure if Lobo could be revived successfully, or how much he could rely on him."

"Not much, as it turned out." Jubal nodded. "Anyway, one of the things Lekren did tell me was that whatever shred of consciousness a Urod retains while time-frozen is always on the alert for the approach of a Taelon shuttle."

Jonathan filed that bit of information with everything else

his father had been telling him, and tried to think about it all. To call Jubal's narrative fantastic would be the understatement of the new millennium. Yet, for all Jonathan knew, it could be true, as true as the fantastic Taelon presence on the earth. Or some of it could be factual. To think that any part of it was bona fide was frightening. And the father he had known for half a century had never been given to flights of fancy.

Eventually he said, "That's quite a story, Dad."

"You going to tell me you don't believe it?"

Jonathan started a chuckle that got nowhere. "Wouldn't dare tell you I doubted your word, though I wish I could. Know what I mean? Even if the alternative seems to be to think that you've gone crazy."

The old man nodded, understanding. "I'd find that comforting myself. The idea that I was going nuts, I mean. Just by comparison. If I could just relax, and talk myself into thinking I'd just imagined it all. But if I could do that, I would've done it years ago."

Jonathan went on, "Especially I wish I didn't have to believe in Urods, but I don't seem to have any choice. So, tell me, what did you and Esther do next? You climbed out of the fountain, I suppose, and then what?"

"Well. At first I just kind of stood there, supporting her," Jubal said. He made a hoop of his arms, holding them out to illustrate. "Holding her up, for I don't know how long. But it couldn't have been very long, for she was at last starting to come out of her mental fog by then, thank God, and we commenced slowly hobbling along the walk. Meanwhile, Flynn still whooping with laughter in the background.

"Next thing I knew, the beam of a flashlight was in my eyes. I don't know what we would have done, if Captain Murray hadn't shown up when he did. With all the strange things going on, he'd decided to work the night shift himself Sunday night. And he'd noticed—something—that drew him back to the spot.

"He gave me a hell of a dirty look when he got a good look

at us. There I was, holding Esther so she wouldn't topple over, and she seemingly passed out. We were both disheveled, and I was in quite an emotional state, as you might imagine.

"Murray was working alone that night, and he came running up and grabbed me by the arm. He was angry as hell. Said he didn't know what the two of us had been up to, and didn't want to hear about it. That was fine with me. I know what he thought, naturally, but he was about as far wrong as it would be possible to get.

"We'd been on the wildest joyride that any two teenagers ever took, and all I got out of it, in that sense, was the one lousy kiss."

The old man came to a sudden stop, considering. "No, I take that back. That kiss was anything but lousy. But by the time Murray saw us, Esther, thank God, was coming out of her daze. And Murray was just so mightily relieved to see that neither of us seemed to be badly hurt, or passed-out drunk, or totally shot full of dope . . . we just took Esther to her room. Murray had a key of course. We took her shoes off, and then her dress, and a couple of other things—given our mental states, Murray's and mine, by that time we were as impersonal and trustworthy as two nursing nuns—wrapped her in a robe and laid her out on the bed. We tiptoed out and closed the door. Then Murray came back to my room with me, helped me deal with my wet clothes. Made sure I had no more adventures planned."

"But he never said anything to your father, or to Hearst, about—"

Jubal was shaking his head. "See, the good captain was kind of afraid to blow the whistle on me, being worried that if he did, then stories about hiding dead bodies would start to come out."

"I can understand that. Murray, you said his name was."

"Yep."

"I wonder if he's still alive. Couple of things I'd like to ask him."

"I've been wondering about that too, but it's not likely. He'd be at least a hundred."

"And the man named Oscar? The other security guard?"

"He'd be about ninety, I suppose. Never heard his full name. Anyway, he wasn't on hand that night when Esther and I came back from our big trip."

"And Errol Flynn's long dead," affirmed Jonathan. He was something of an old movie buff in his spare time—when he had any spare time, which was rare. "And the girl he was with that night—"

"Would be older than me, I suppose, and I never knew her name. She and Flynn saw Murray and me kind of carrying Esther along, and they waved in our direction and called out something jovial that I was too tired to hear. And if Flynn or his girlfriend saw a spaceship, or a Urod walking, they probably put it down to an attack of the DTs."

Jonathan grunted something.

His father nodded, and went on, "Now I really think that a whole lot of what Lekren told me aboard ship was probably the truth. You can well imagine that as a dumb kid back in the Thirties, when I came back from our joyride I didn't have any idea what to think. The only explanations I could come up with had a lot to do with dreams, and with myself going crazy. And it didn't help that the vehicle I'd been space-traveling in didn't look or act anything like the rocket ships I saw in Buck Rogers, or in the movies. Somehow that made the reality seem less real."

"Dad, one thing it occurs to me to wonder about is this: Why did the Sekhmet statue, the Urod, pick that particular weekend to act up? The way you describe it, weekends at the Ranch must have been pretty much alike—usually some kind of sedate party going on.

"And maybe there were more than the usual number of aerial approaches—I suppose there'd be more people coming and going at the landing strip on weekends?"

"I've been thinking about that too, son, and I have an

answer. It might not have been the number of planes landing and taking off that woke it up. On that particular weekend a certain other event took place, something I don't think had ever happened at San Simeon before."

"What?"

"Pretty obvious, I'd say. The Taelons arrived in one of their fancy spaceships, intending to take the Urod away. In that case not caring if they triggered a revival episode or not, because they were right on the scene to handle it, and because they were underestimating by a mile how tough the job was going to be."

"Okay. Okay, let me think." Jonathan paced, feeling a flow of nervous energy. "You've had sixty-five years to mull this over, and it seems I'll be lucky if I get that many minutes. But yes, perhaps that would fit. You just happened to be there on the weekend when this Lekren—and some other Taelons with him—?"

"Never heard about them, if there were."

"—came to collect the runaway Urod. Only it turned out to be a much tougher job than they'd anticipated."

"You can say that again."

Jonathan said, after taking thought, "All right, that moves my question back a notch. Why did the Taelons pick that particular time, that day, that weekend, to come after the Urod?"

"I can think of one good reason, son, why they came in the summer of '36."

"Tell me."

"They could have been worried about the possibility that ownership of the estate was soon going to change hands. Did I mention that the Hearst empire was on the brink of a financial crisis at the time?"

"I think you did say something about that."

"Well, obviously our dear Companions were already listening to our radio broadcasts, and paying careful attention. So they were well aware of our Great Depression. And if they knew anything of Hearst's spending habits they would have seen his problems coming. New ownership of San Simeon could mean that some unsuspecting humans would soon be hauling all the statues away—or trying to. So the Synod that my wounded pilot kept talking about might have given him orders to act pronto."

Jonathan, pacing again, was silent for half a minute. Finally he said, "I'll say this for your story, Dad—so far I've only been able to spot one big, glaring inconsistency in it."

Jubal snorted. Damned if he was going to ask what that might be.

The younger man paced some more, and stopped. "And during all these hours or days you were with Lekren, he was never able to communicate with this Synod that was so important to him?"

"Right. And I think there were two reasons for that. One, Lekren was injured, partially crippled in mind and body. Two, our captive Urod knew this, and kept him tied up in some kind of mental mud-wrestling match, so he couldn't reach his Synod in the usual way—whatever way that might have been." The old man paused there. "Anything else you'd like to know? What's your inconsistency?"

"It's in the times, Dad, as I'm sure you realize. First, this Taelon spaceship takes you zooming away to some place light-years distant. Then you say you were there for several days. . . ."

"Son, have you read up on the theories scientists have come up with in the last few years? The real stuff is getting wilder than Buck Rogers ever was, or Flash Gordon either. Faster-than-light travel, even time travel, all theoretical possibilities. There was no miracle involved in what happened to Esther and me. Not when Taelons and Urods are concerned. The Taelon ship was destroyed, but the Urod came back here the same way it got here in the first place."

"A re-adaptation of reality."

"Maybe. That was the magic word that Lekren kept dropping on me whenever my questions got especially awkward.

The Urod did what it could, and I was lucky enough to be dragged along with it, and so was Esther."

"So the pair of you were safely home again, and all the scary aliens were gone."

"All of them but one," Jubal amended, looking in the direction where the four black basalt statues were not quite visible. He fell silent for a moment. "And that one's still waiting. Maybe it just likes it here. I've been scared of it for a long time, scared I'd hear it was up to some new deviltry here. When I got here from Charleston I was scared to go near it at first, but I finally figured what the hell, I'm over eighty years old now and what am I worried about. I walked right up close to it, and I thought I could feel it in my mind, with just a little effort. It's still waiting for another Taelon shuttle to show up."

"Yes, okay. And you never saw a Taelon again, or heard from them, until—?"

"Until yesterday morning, when you introduced me to your friend Va'lon."

"I was almost ready to turn over the estate to him, Urod and all," Jonathan admitted with a sigh. "But now I'm damned if I know whether he's anybody's friend or not."

"I don't want him for mine," said the old man shortly. "I've had one Taelon friend in my life, and he almost finished me off."

"Hum."

"Yep. I've been thinking, Johnny. In 1936 they made a big effort to get the Urod out of here. They might have been successful, though at a heavy cost to themselves—if it hadn't been for the fact that there'd been some kind of battle at their deep-space station. Who knows who was fighting who, but it put a crimp in all their plans. After that fiasco, they had other things to worry about, and gave up on visiting earth for a while, gave up for the time being on trying to remove old Sekhmet."

"That all seems to hang together." Jonathan nodded slowly. "They postponed their efforts, until they could figure out some new method of Urod removal. And they had time to make whatever preparations they thought they needed, before they tried again. But the fact that Sekhmet was still squatting here has worried them all along—and it still does.

"Now, sixty-five years later, when they've decided to come openly to Earth—who knows why they've suddenly done that?—they see the Urod as a world-class problem, one of the very first things they have to deal with, as soon as they arrive. It's like they don't even dare to concentrate on anything else, like diplomacy and trade, until they're sure he's been taken care of.

"They've been studying us for a long time. Probably at least since we began sending radio messages into space, back around 1900. What if they've had a base here in our solar system for decades? Maybe for centuries?

"However that may be, they somehow know a hell of a lot about us earthlings before they arrive. Among other things, they even know that I've just become the owner of San Simeon. They're so eager to get Sekhmet out of the way, maybe so worried about what might happen if they don't, that they send one of their shuttles to land in my back yard. They arrange matters so that Va'lon is on the scene, right here"—he thumped with his hand on the armrest of the bench—"within a few hours of his landing."

"But taking care to make sure that he arrives in a ground vehicle."

"Yep."

"And they knew about Amanda too; I mean even about her illness."

"We've tried to minimize publicity about that, as you know, but it's certainly been no secret. There were news items on television from time to time."

"And the Taelons absorbed them all, gathered every scrap of information about you that they could. Because they had to have access to the estate as soon as possible, had to be able to set up some kind of elaborate Urod-snatching operation as quickly as they could, if possible without a media circus watching everything they did. Because they had to disable the remaining Urod before it really came out of its time-freeze for more than a couple of minutes, and did something to them that they couldn't stand—maybe yanked this whole solar system right out of their control."

The old man's voice was trembling now, and he emphasized his words with little jabs of a shaking finger. "Because the Taelons need us for *something*, son, or they need our world, this little chunk of dirt and rock and water. Don't ask me why, or for what, because I haven't got a clue. But our dear Companions need us like the breath of life!"

"Jesus," said Jonathan Doors, softly. He wasn't a profane man, as a rule, and this time he wasn't sure if he meant the word as an oath or as a prayer.

The rain, which had drummed down fiercely for a few minutes, was letting up again, and patches of blue had reappeared. Soon the sky would be as sunny as if it had never happened. Crazy weather patterns.

Meanwhile. Jonathan's father was still talking. "They went to great lengths to make sure they had you on their side. Landed one of their ships right in your back yard, and what was the very first thing they did when you met them? Sounds like they couldn't wait to get one of their own physicians started, testing and treating her."

"They've helped Amanda a lot already." But as soon as Jonathan said that, he wondered if it was mainly wishful thinking. He had talked to his wife by global within the past few hours, and she had seemed well satisfied with the new treatments, but there were no miracles as yet.

"Have they?" The old man didn't sound convinced.

"She'll be joining us here in a little while," said Jonathan, and felt a chill. What if the so-called Companions had some private reason, not so noble, for wanting to examine Amanda and provide her medical care?

"Driving over, or flying?"

Jonathan glanced at his watch. "She said they were going to drive. Ought to be getting here shortly."

SEVENTEEN

The van that had brought Amanda and her crew of medical support was parked at the foot of the broad tile steps just below the esplanade, and she was coming up the steps in her new motorized wheelchair. It was equipped with some handy accessories that largely solved the problem of stairs for someone who could barely breathe.

The smile froze on Jonathan's face when he looked down and saw her. The last time Doors had seen his wife, back at their own home, several Taelon medical devices had been attached to her. Most of those were gone now. But today there was a new addition, coiled round her right arm. This particular Taelon machine matched with terrifying closeness the image called up by Jubal's words, describing a rubber Siamese snake.

The thing on Amanda's arm, whatever it might be, touched Jonathan as he bent to embrace her, and he could feel his own left arm instinctively trying to pull back from the contact. Maybe it was only his imagination, but the rubbery texture suggested something half-alive.

"I'm very thoroughly wired up," Amanda observed in a weak voice. At the moment a nasal tube was feeding bottled oxygen into her ravaged lungs.

"I see that." It cost Jonathan a great effort to keep his voice light.

"Are there more stairs? No? Then let me walk with you," Amanda said, and got up out of her chair.

Amanda was having a relatively good day, up out of her chair and walking, leaning on a cane. She paused frequently to catch her breath, but was not gasping as much as Jonathan had heard her doing in the past.

This time Doors was on her left, and her left arm was in continuous contact with him. Every time he glanced at the snake on her right arm it gave him the cold chills; because what he saw matched so exactly his father's description of the device that had been attached to Esther Summerson.

He braced himself for his father's reaction, when Jubal got his first look at the thing on Amanda's arm. In the nature of things, that was going to happen very soon.

Still trying to keep his tone easy, even cheerful, Doors asked, "What's this new gadget?"

"It monitors my vital signs, and half a dozen other things, or so my new physician tells me. He didn't actually promise that it would make breathing easier, but there are moments when I think it's helping."

Jonathan frowned. He was all too familiar with the unpredictable variation of good days and bad days that cystic fibrosis inflicted on its victims and their families. "Does it have needles actually stuck into your arm, or what?"

Amanda raised her right arm slightly, and showed him how she could flex the elbow without much interference. "Do you know, I'm not certain? It doesn't hurt a bit, not even as much as a normal IV, so I don't believe so."

"Namor didn't say?"

She shook her head. "Doc Namor may be great, I suppose he probably is. But he's not the most forthcoming physician I have ever dealt with."

"No? I'll have a go at him when I see him again."

"Be my guest."

* * *

Even now, as Jonathan Doors looked out across an expanse of fancy foliage, punctuated by tile walks and white marble statues, he could see some of his workers in a distant flowerbed, doing something very industrious. A lot of the other flowerbeds were really getting rundown, now that he looked at them closely. It came to him that the place really needed a bigger maintenance and security staff, whatever else might happen in the next few days.

Amanda was getting her first look at San Simeon today, and she was suitably impressed, as was practically everyone who saw the place.

"As long as I'm here, I'd like to do a complete tour."

"So would I," her husband agreed. "I don't suppose I've seen a tenth of the rooms yet. We'll check it all out together one of these days, when I have time."

One of the bedrooms in Casa Grande had been made ready for Amanda's arrival, and her baggage had already been installed in it, while her human caretakers were assigned rooms nearby. Namor, the Companion physician, was out in one of the satellite mansions with his fellow Taelons.

Her human physician, Dr. Kimura, appeared loaded with a backpack and two large handbags. Doors supposed that some of the contents were medical equipment. Dr. Kimura only nodded and smiled in passing; Doors made a mental note to ask her whether the Taelon treatments were really helping.

"Looks like there ought to be enough room for us all," Amanda commented, getting her first close look at Casa Grande. "This is like standing in front of a cathedral."

"With thirty-eight bedrooms in the main house alone, we're not exactly pinched for space," Jonathan observed.

"Which one is mine?"

"You know what? You're in luck—there happens to be a vacancy right next to my own room. Nice views. I think the bed was once slept in by Cardinal Richelieu—or maybe his bed's in another room down the hall."

"I trust the cardinal is not still in it."

"I think he got up and left about four hundred years ago."

"Oh, goody. I'm going to like this place. So many rooms, so many beds. Have you tried them all out?"

"Not yet. That would be a big job."

"Could you use some assistance in the project?"

"Absolutely. It might take us years to complete, but we ought to at least make a start."

And Jonathan fell silent, because he had just seen Jubal emerge, cane in hand, from the main front door of Casa Grande, and start toward them with his usual briskness. But the old man stopped suddenly when he was still fifteen feet from Amanda, and his son saw him turn pale. Jubal's eyes under their bushy brows were riveted on the snake.

The old man's cane wobbled in his grip, and he made his way to a nearby bench, murmuring that he guessed he ought to sit down.

Amanda was concerned. "You all right, Jubal?"

"Yeah, yeah. Good to see you, Mandy. Go on in, talk to you later."

"See you soon, Dad." And father and son exchanged a knowing look.

Jonathan and his wife entered Casa Grande through the same portal Jubal had come out of, an enormous iron-grilled doorway that Doors had heard was once part of a Spanish convent. This entrance was set squarely in the middle of a massive white stone front, about four stories high, between a pair of hundred-foot steeple-topped towers.

Jonathan jabbed a finger skyward. "They tell me our water supply is up there."

"Where? In the sky?"

"Not the California sky. No, our water's pumped from a spring about a mile away. What I meant was, there's a big storage tank concealed inside each tower, just below the belfry."

"Ah. And I suppose the belfries are hung with real bells— let's hope they don't ring too loud."

"They don't. They better not, I've given some orders about that."

"How about real bats?"

"I don't remember any livestock being mentioned in the inventory."

Moments later the couple had entered Casa Grande by the front door, and were crossing a dimly lighted entrance hall, Amanda's cane tapping lightly on fantastic tile. Now they confronted a narrow, ancient grillwork door with a dark space behind it.

"This elevator looks like an antique," she observed. "Are you sure it works?"

"It probably is. But it has, for me, so far. Though usually I use the stairs, just for exercise. Gee, that would be awful—the two of us trapped in a little elevator like this."

Presently they were settled in the suite, and one of the workers was bringing up Amanda's baggage. There were many things that Jonathan wanted to tell his wife, but his fears of being overheard had not abated. He had to assume that Taelons possessed superb eavesdropping technology, if they wanted to use it.

When Jonathan asked Amanda for more details regarding her experience with the Taelon treatment, she gave him a mixed report. But on the whole he got the impression that she felt that her condition was improving. The treatment itself caused no discomfort of any kind. It bothered her somewhat that Namor was remarkably reticent about the details of the therapy, how it was actually supposed to work. Maybe the human medics would learn an enormous amount from him some day, but so far that hadn't happened.

Then Mandy had a question of her own. "Heard anything from Joshua? Is our son all right?"

Jonathan thought back over the past few days. "No, to the first query, probably yes to the second. I wouldn't worry about

Josh. Successful and ambitious lawyers probably don't have
time to take notice of little things like mass alien landings."

"I suppose you're right, but I wish he'd call." Amanda hesitated. "The two of you aren't fighting again, are you?"

"Not that I know of."

"Oh, Johnny. You and Josh are so much alike. I suppose
that may be the problem." Amanda sighed and seemed to consider going into the subject at some length, but then decided
against it. "So, tell me, what are our new Companions like?
What do you think of them?"

"Right now my main concern is how much or how little
they're helping you."

"For the moment I'm tired of talking about that. There
must be other things about them worthy of attention."

"They may be egotistical, but they certainly don't talk
much about themselves. You may have learned more about
them than I have."

Amanda said, "Outside of medical matters, about the only
thing they want to talk about is the San Simeon art collection.
I gather they have a special interest in some Egyptian statues
standing out on the grounds. Didn't I hobble past something
like that just a few minutes ago?"

"Yes, they're interested. No accounting for taste."
Jonathan wanted to change the subject. "What's the news of
the world? I haven't been keeping up."

"Mostly a lot of craziness, about what you'd expect."
Amanda went on to mention some recent events occurring in
conjunction with various local arrivals around the world: the
proclamation of a holy war by an Islamic splinter group ("So
far, thank God, they're not getting much support"); the wave
of suicides in Panama and in Malaysia. A cult leader claimed
that the Taelons had commanded those; the Companions
denied that forcefully, and seemed genuinely horrified at the
idea.

Most of the items she mentioned were indeed news to
Jonathan, whose attention had been forcefully distracted for

the last day or so. There had been scattered incidents of violence or attempted violence, directed at the visitors and those who welcomed them. But so far it was thought that no Taelons had been injured, and they had faced nothing like an organized military attack from any nation.

Jonathan absorbed the details, mentally discarding most of them as irrelevant to his concerns. Now and then he commented on some point, and asked a few questions. Nothing that he heard suggested to him the presence of other Urods anywhere else on the planet.

His attention was caught when Amanda observed, "You personally are getting rather more coverage than usual."

"How's that?"

"What did you expect? Media people have been taking note from a distance, of the goings-on at San Simeon, and they keep speculating about the possible significance."

Meanwhile, in the privacy of his own thoughts, Jonathan had been going over and over his father's story, looking for some way to test at least some of its outrageous claims and statements. If any substantial part of the whole was true—incredible thought!—a drastic change would be required in the whole attitude of humanity toward the Companions.

Simple faith in their good will would no longer do. Wary coexistence would have to become the watchword, even while people continued to make warm-hearted speeches about growing trust and friendship. The best that could be hoped for would probably be an armed truce, while humanity kept secret the amazing knowledge of Taelon duplicity held by a few of its members, and watched and waited for its chance to strike back at the subtle invaders. Above all, humanity must *learn*. . . .

The Taelons had brought to the earth an overwhelming technology that afforded them power and authority. But humanity did have some advantages. Sheer numbers, for one thing, billions against a handful.

For another thing, secret knowledge.

Supposing, Jonathan thought to himself, just for the sake of argument, that Dad has been telling me the exact sober truth about his wild adventure back in the Thirties. The way the story wound up, there was no reason to think that the Taelons of the twenty-first century had any record of those events. Lekren could hardly have survived the final catastrophe at the space station. Nor had the Taelon pilot ever been able to communicate with his Synod during the time he was in contact with Jubal. So, Va'lon and his twenty-first–century contemporaries ought not to have the faintest suspicion that Jonathan's father knew more than any human had a right to know about their ships and deep-space installations.

And about the uses they could occasionally find for human beings.

Jonathan remarked on this to Jubal when they were once more alone together, adding, "What the Taelons don't know won't hurt us."

Now Jubal was holding his heavy wooden cane in his two hands as if he might be going to unscrew the pommel at the top. "That's my thought exactly, son. My whole adventure with 'em was so improbable—maybe just the presence of the Urod brought on improbabilities."

"Could the Urod—can this particular Urod—do that?"

"I've told you what happened, as best as I can remember it. Having seen what I saw, and felt what I felt when I was out there, I don't want to put any limits on what a Urod can do."

Jonathan felt himself being forced more and more firmly into the position that the old man's story was essentially true. But, granted that was the case, how to use the knowledge? To talk of an immediate holy war was nonsense at this point. That would probably produce plenty of martyrs if it began now, but hardly a victory.

*   *   *

About a year ago, when the Taelons had begun transmitting pictures of themselves to earth, Jubal had been shocked to recognize, in their bald heads, pale skins, and slender bodies, that they were of the same race as the strange being he remembered as Lekren the pilot. Strong evidence that, after all, the whole experience had *not* been some kind of delusion, as he had almost managed to convince himself it was—

Then the more nightmarish aspects of his long-ago trip to Taelon-land had begun to bother him again.

Jubal knew he would have to face something he had so far avoided thinking about: All evidence pointed to the fact that the powerful, inscrutable Urod still waited at San Simeon. Why at this particular spot on the surface of the earth? The answer to that question seemed well beyond the current state of human knowledge. Maybe San Simeon was about as far as the Urod could get from its enemies, and if those enemies were still determined to turn the Urod into a museum specimen, they were going to have to come after it here, where perhaps, for some reason unknown to humanity, it felt best able to put up a defense.

"Why didn't you tell me sooner, Dad?"

"Bah. What would you have done? What could you have done? You would have thought for sure that I was crazy. You'd probably have sent a team of high-priced soothing headshrinkers around to see me."

"No. I wouldn't have done that."

"Maybe not. But you'd have been worried that the old man was cracking up, and you'd have consulted somebody. And then, sure as shooting, the story I've just told you would be out, or garbled versions of it would be, on TV and radio."

"No. I'd make sure it wouldn't."

His father ignored the contradiction. "And *they'd* have picked it up, while their fleet was still months away from earth. By the time they arrived, they'd have pretty well figured out whatever they didn't already know about the events of '36, and my part in 'em.

"And soon after their arrival they'd have it arranged for me to die in some nice, natural accident—don't shake your head, son, I know what I'm talking about.

"Or else they'd come up with some way to prove me crazy, so no one would believe any story I might have to tell. Whereas, if I never said a word to you or anyone else about Taelons or Urods, I had every reason to hope that I could live out the rest of my days in peace. Now, what're you going to do, son?"

"I don't know."

Esther Summerson had gone on to be a famous actress, then died, still young, of an overdose. One of those supremely admired and successful folk whom millions envied.

"And in any case, she was unconscious practically the whole time you were away from earth. I suppose, even if she were alive, she'd have no memories of the whole alien-abduction episode."

Old Jubal winced. "I wish you wouldn't call it that."

"Sorry. Of course, I haven't seen or heard anything from Va'lon and Namor so far, to make me think they knew anything about you before they met you yesterday. Or that, even if they knew about 1936, they'd be especially likely to hold a grudge."

"Course you haven't, son. You're fairly smart, but you've been talking to some of the best con men in the universe. You can't see anything wrong with them, but what do you *know?* What do you know about 'em, really?"

The answer to that was so obvious that Jonathan didn't bother to give it. Instead he asked his father, "So, you say Murray tucked the two of you back into your respective rooms. What happened after that?"

"Not much. I told you my watch had stopped. But I *knew* we must have been gone several days, and I started trying to think up some story that people might buy to explain that length of absence. Fat chance! But it turned out Murray didn't want to hear any explanations. He wasn't interested, because he simply didn't think we'd been gone that long.

"So, before I said goodnight to the captain I came right out and asked him what day it was. He wasn't too surprised at the question—it must have fit right in with his assumption that I'd had too much to drink—and he gave me a straight answer: It was three o'clock Monday morning, and Esther and I couldn't have been gone more than about four hours.

"That made no sense to me at the time, but I couldn't think about it, and just accepted it gratefully. I was totally exhausted, as you may well imagine, and when I woke up in my bed in my room in Casa del Mar, it was just after noon on Monday, and my parents were knocking cheerfully on my door. I think Murray had even reset my watch for me before he tucked me in. I was starved, and I think I ate two breakfasts. Couldn't get the taste of those damned Taelon biscuits out of my mouth.

"My Dad was in a good mood that Monday, ready to go home, thinking he'd got some kind of business deal going. I don't remember what the deal was, but he counted our weekend as quite a success. We were due to leave San Simeon Monday afternoon, and my folks were chuckling and teasing me about how hard it was to wake me up."

"And Esther?"

"She overslept a little too, as her parents delicately put it. I saw her for just a little while on Monday, and we talked. She said she was missing her shoes somewhere, and her dress was ruined. But none of that seemed to be a big deal, and it was just perfectly obvious that she had no memory, none at all, of what we'd both been through. We said a friendly goodbye, and it was a long time before I saw her again. . . ."

"It would have been the easiest thing in the world for me to convince myself that it had all been a dream. Except for a couple of facts. One, I was stiff and sore in some unusual places. My back ached, and my arms ached from carrying Esther—but I was sixteen, and I snapped back fast. My clothes were pretty much a mess, but that could have happened anywhere. Another clue was something that happened when I looked in the mirror, in my bathroom in my room in Casa del Mar, when I finally got out of bed the next day.

"At that age I had started shaving—patchy little whiskers sprouting on my face here and there—and I swear my whiskers had grown a couple of days longer.

"Orson Welles did his *War of the Worlds* radio broadcast in October of 1938. Reporting an invasion from Mars scared the hell out of half the country, just a couple years after my own scare. I think it was his idea of a Halloween stunt.

"It was one of his regular radio dramas, but much of it had the sound of a special news program, and people who tuned in in the middle got confused. Panic broke out in places. There were even a handful of people, scattered here and there across the country, who were getting out their guns, ready to defend their families. Or actually to kill 'em, to keep 'em from being taken prisoner by bug-eyed monsters."

"I didn't know that."

"If you think I'm exaggerating, you could look it up. It was sheer luck that no one got killed or seriously hurt. If you created that kind of an uproar now, there'd be lawsuits from here to the moon and back."

The old man paused. "But can you imagine how *I* felt, listening to that broadcast?" Jubal paused again. "And I knew from the start that what Orson Welles put on the radio was only a play. If I hadn't known that . . ."

Jonathan Doors thanked his father for his warning, and assured the old man that he would deal successfully with the Taelons somehow, and that in the course of that dealing, however it went, he would let slip to them no hint of his father's adventures on a Taelon vessel a couple of human generations in the past.

Jubal indeed seemed to need reassurance, for he was growing increasingly worried.

He said, "They're back here now, and sooner or later they'll have another go at that black thing that's still sitting there. Have they said anything to you about it yet?"

"Not a word about that specifically, though they talk about the collection sometimes. And I have noticed Va'lon—well, looking at it."

"I'll bet you have. Bet your life he and his pals intend to do something about it, too. I'm worried that when they do, they'll find out what really happened back in '36, and they'll tie it to me somehow."

"How could they do that?"

"Who knows? Some of the things they can do are practically magic."

"Would you feel safer going back to Charleston, Dad?"

"Go back there and do what? Just sit around waiting for news reports? Nope. Actually I feel better staying here. At least I can keep an eye on you and Amanda this way, and maybe I can do you some good, answer a question for you or something."

Doors gripped his father by the hand.

EIGHTEEN

In the middle of the afternoon of Day Two, Jubal, pleading weariness and a lack of sleep over the last few days, had announced that he was retreating to his bedroom for a nap.

An hour or so later Jonathan tapped gently at the door on the third floor of Casa Grande, not wanting to disturb his father if he was asleep, then eased it open. He looked in at the old man, sound asleep in one of the house's many elaborately carved, royal beds. Bushy eyebrows gave his familiar face the stern, intelligent expression of a Renaissance prince at rest. His son felt a burst of irrational envy, of one who had passed on the basic responsibilities of life to someone else. But the feeling was only momentary. Jonathan had long ago convinced himself that envy of any kind was foolishness.

What he had wanted to say to his father this time could wait. Easing the door shut again, Jonathan made a quiet but determined effort to get away by himself somewhere, for a little while, and give his problems some intensely concentrated thought.

He unhooked his global from his belt and turned it all the way off, then snapped the unit back in place. For a little while, any emergencies would have to be managed without his help.

Had there been any horses in the old stables, he would probably have taken one out for a ride. But in recent years the property that old William Randolph Hearst had called the Ranch had been devoid of any kind of livestock.

Jonathan made a deliberate effort to keep from walking anywhere near the black statues.

He supposed there was still a slim possibility that his father was totally crazy, or at least that the old man had built up an elaborate set of false memories or delusions about the events of 1936.

Of course that would be an unwelcome and unpleasant situation, difficult to deal with. But it would be better than the only alternative. The more Jonathan thought about *that*, the worse it looked. It would mean that the Taelons, or some of their leadership at least, were very far from being the benevolent peacemakers and healers they represented themselves to be. They were instead major-league liars, capable of murderous violence. Highly intelligent, advanced beings, quite willing to install mind-altering implants in human brains, for no other reason than to make humans into more useful tools. Such healing and helping as the Companions might actually accomplish upon the earth would probably be done with the sole purpose of brightening their image in human eyes, thus ultimately creating billions of willing . . . allies? Servants?

To judge by Jubal's narrative, the relationship preferred by the Taelons would more likely be that of masters and slaves.

Another way to put the matter was to say that Companions could be as bad as humans at their worst. Jonathan seemed to remember that Jubal had put it that way once.

And when it came right down to it, Jonathan didn't, he couldn't, believe that his father was deranged. Or that, for some unfathomable reason, he was deliberately making the whole story up.

Jonathan thought to himself: *All right, let us assume that my father is telling the truth, that all or most of the fantastic things he describes really happened to him. What does the human race do now? In particular, what do I do? To be an effective leader, I must have some kind of plan.*

Even if the self-proclaimed Companions were as two-faced and treacherous as Jubal said they were, Jonathan could not simply turn his back on them. For if Jubal's story was true, then humanity was also confronted by Sekhmet. The Urod was a survivor of every attempt at its destruction that Taelon technology had been able to manage. On the other hand, there was no reason to think it had any friendship for humanity. It represented a peril even greater and more immediate than the Taelons, and one that had to be dealt with first.

And yet: *The enemy of my enemy is my friend.*

Jubal's story had several times hinted at the possibility of at least a temporary human/Urod alliance.

Fortunately, Jonathan thought he could see one way to determine, with reasonable certainty, whether his father's story was true or not. Jonathan thought: *If Va'lon gives me any evidence, any evidence at all, to support what Dad told me about the Urod—then I'm going to have to accept even the strangest parts of Dad's story as essentially true.*

Jonathan turned his global on again, and directed his steps back toward Casa Grande. He hadn't gone far in that direction when the unit buzzed. The smiling face of Va'lon looked out from the small screen to propose a meeting.

The two met, a couple of minutes later, in the old library, where Hearst in his years of wealth and power had amassed some five thousand volumes, many of great value as collectors' items. Almost all of the books had been gone for years, and empty shelves were gathering dust, though a few odd remnant volumes still remained.

When Va'lon suggested they take a walk, the two of them set out strolling on the esplanade—and Va'lon with subtle skill guided their steps so they wound up right in front of the statues. Jonathan had allowed himself to be guided, but now he stood with his back to the tall black figure, resisting an urge to turn and stare at it.

"Shall we sit here, Jonathan, and talk?"

"Why not?"

Companion and human occupied two wicker chairs, antique Hearst lawn furniture recently resurrected from some catacomb of storage. Jonathan thought he could feel his scalp creeping with a premonitory warning. It didn't help that for once the Taelon seemed almost at a loss as to how to begin. Several times Doors saw hints of the emotional color change begin on the surface of the Companion's body and then swiftly die out again.

"You said there was a matter of great importance," Jonathan prompted at last.

Va'lon nodded slowly. He seemed very calm, but Jonathan thought he could detect vibrations of considerable stress.

At last the Taelon said, "I have spoken with the Synod."

Jonathan was careful to show no strong reaction to the name, the same name that Jubal's Taelon had used for his council of directors or advisors, sixty-five years in the past. But it was only natural that he should ask the obvious question.

"The Synod? What's that?"

"I am borrowing a word from your language. For us, as for you, a synod is an important council."

"You had no problem about making arrangements to consult with such a council?"

"Problem?" Va'lon seemed distantly puzzled. "No. Why should there be a problem?"

"Never mind. Go on." With a sense of doom, of fatalistic calm, Doors set himself to listen. "And what have you and your Synod decided today?"

"My associates and I have agreed that a certain matter must be revealed to you. It is for your ears alone. For a time we had intended that it should be kept entirely secret—but now I feel confident that you can be trusted."

Having got that far, the Taelon uncharacteristically seemed not to know how best to continue. Again there were hints of what humans had started to call the blush.

Doors spoke into the silence. "Oh? I am always wary of being told other people's secrets."

Va'lon raised an almost invisible eyebrow, as if he were impressed. "That is commendable wisdom—or would be, in most cases. But when you hear this secret, Jonathan, you will understand why I reveal it to you. And why it must be kept from the rest of your people, at least for the time being."

Doors drew a deep breath, a man preparing himself. "In that case, I think you'd better tell me now."

The Taelon turned his gaze toward the dried-up fountain. "You of course know something of the history of the four statues here beside us, representations of the Egyptian god Sekhmet."

"I've been told a little about them." Doors felt a cold fist suddenly clenching in his midsection. And he realized that until this moment, despite the *sken*, despite everything, he had not believed in his gut that his father's story was true. It cost him an effort to keep his voice even, but he managed it. "They're supposed to be the oldest things in the whole collection."

"No doubt they are. But the most important point is that one of them is not a statue."

"Ah?" He did his best to look bewildered.

The story came out, calmly and efficiently presented, in only a few minutes of the Taelon's usual smooth prose. There were moments in the course of the telling when Jonathan had the feeling of being caught up in a bad dream.

One by one, essential portions of Jubal's secret narrative were solidly confirmed, including something of the Urod's nature. (Though, as Jonathan noted carefully, Va'lon had not referred to that strange being by name.) The Companion emphasized the threat that this enemy posed to life of all kinds, even to the very stability of reality throughout a sizable volume of spacetime.

But so far Va'lon had said nothing of any abortive Taelon attempt to remove the Urod in 1936, or at any other time.

The Companion concluded his revelation with a firm declaration, "This thing, this creature, must be removed from your world."

Doors while listening had turned on the bench to face the statue. And, without being consciously aware of the movement, he had slid a little farther away from it. He said, "I quite see that—if all that you've told me about it is true."

"When time allows, Jonathan, we will be able to provide you with further evidence. You appear shocked."

"I am."

"I quite understand."

"Do you?"

"Certainly. You must consider my assertions quite fantastic and almost incredible."

Doors nodded slowly. He didn't doubt for a moment that he looked shocked. *But actually, my dear Companion, the reason is just about the exact opposite from what you think. It's that I have no trouble believing what you've just told me.*

Aloud, Jonathan asked, "So, how do you go about removing it?"

"The safety of everyone concerned, human and Taelon, must be our first consideration."

"Of course. By the way, what name do you give these—dangerous creatures?"

"They have no name for themselves; indeed it is almost true that they have no language of their own. But we generally call them Urod."

"Oo-rod."

"Yes. Jonathan, I see that my revelations are having a strong effect upon you. I regret that I must cause you distress; but what I am telling you is the truth."

Doors nodded. "Yes, go on, tell me. Whatever it is. I want to know. I must know the whole truth."

Va'lon made one of his graceful gestures. "But that is the extent of the disclosure."

Oh, is it, now? "I see."

"Now you basically know the worst."

"Yes."

"Jonathan, our offer to purchase San Simeon is—how do you put it?—still on the table. I hope you will now promptly accept."

Doors shook his head slowly. His mind was racing. "I don't see how your buying the place would solve our basic problem, getting rid of this Urod. So I regret that my answer must be no."

"If it is a matter of money—?"

"No. It isn't that."

"What, then?"

"When I bought this property I had in mind preserving it for the people to visit and enjoy. I wouldn't feel right about selling it to be used for any other purpose."

"We would do our best to respect your wishes in that regard. Once the Urod has been removed, probably within a few days afterward, we would be able to open the site for public viewing once again."

But Doors was already shaking his head again. "Sorry, but the answer is still no. I'm not selling now. Maybe at some future time."

Va'lon studied him for a few moments in silence. Then the Taelon excused himself, saying he had to engage in another consultation.

Doors turned around on the bench and sat quietly for a minute, regarding the statue, which was, as always, as immobile and seemingly dead as any other piece of rock. Then he got to his feet and walked tiredly after his guest.

When Va'lon met Doors again, only a few minutes later, he said he had just been communicating with his Synod.

Va'lon smiled. "We are now ready to propose a slightly different course of action."

"Go ahead."

"If you decline our offer to purchase the estate, will you still allow us to occupy it, in effect take it over, for the next few days? To continue to exclude the media and the public, while we move in substantial amounts of equipment, and conduct a difficult operation?"

"I can do that, if you will allow myself and the people I have here now to remain. Perhaps I will even want to bring in a few more workers for one thing or another. Routine maintenance and security. Will this 'difficult operation' also be hazardous?"

"I cannot deny that there will be some degree of danger. But the long-term risk will only be greater if we do nothing."

"Then what do we do?"

To effect the safest possible removal, the Companions wanted to be able to restrict all human presence from the immediate vicinity, and then to surround the hazard with their own people, their own machinery of some unimaginable kind—even so, Va'lon was conspicuously unwilling to promise that all risks were eliminated.

Jonathan said, "You mentioned before that there is some immediate danger involved in this process. Even when, as you say, you are taking all possible precautions."

"I regret that is unavoidably the case."

"I see. And what exactly is the scale of this menace we're talking about? I mean, should we be evacuating everyone for ten miles around? Or are we putting half the state of California in jeopardy?"

"The menace already exists, Jonathan. What we are doing now is preparing to remove it."

"That wasn't my question."

Va'lon still evaded giving a straight answer.

Doors looked at the statue and shook his head. "A perfect resemblance to natural black stone."

"Indeed."

* * *

Jonathan Doors was sitting in his wicker chair, as if collapsed, rubbing his face with one hand. Around him the California sunlight was bright and cheerful, and a lot of flowers were trying their best to bloom.

The Taelon sounded sympathetic. "I am sorry, Jonathan, that the truth is so upsetting. But it is better that you understand."

"Of course. Actually it is essential that I understand. Yes. I see. All right, I suppose you will have to move in whatever gear you need to deal with the problem. I'll see to it that my people all stay out of your way."

"I was confident that when you knew the facts, you would give us your full cooperation."

Jonathan got up out of his chair and paced the walkway for a time, casting grim looks at the Urod. Then he turned to confront the Companion.

"All right, I'll go along with that. But, damn it, Va'lon, it's still hard to believe. How could something like this Urod that you describe have possibly have wound up *here?* I mean, the thing has to have been sitting here for—for decades."

"Oh, it has. As you are well aware, the man who ordered all this built"—Va'lon gestured gracefully, including all the buildings and what they contained—"was concerned to gather treasures from all past and present civilizations upon this planet. He did business with many dealers in antiquities. From one such dealer he purchased, in good faith, a set of ancient Egyptian statues, one of which was not at all what it seemed to be—"

"Just a moment. What about the other three?"

"It seems virtually certain that the genuine statues were carved with the Urod as model."

"Carved by ancient Egyptians."

"Yes."

"But how could such creatures as the originals, such monsters, have come to Earth in the first place?"

"The skies of your world have always been open and unguarded, Jonathan."

Jonathan looked up at heaven's sunny vault. "Yes, I suppose that's true."

Va'lon went on, "The powers commanded by the Urod are sometimes hard to believe, hard to accept, until one has seen them in operation—only a few do that, and some of those do not survive the experience. Sometimes members of that race achieve with seeming ease what we Taelons manage only with considerable effort and difficulty—and what humans may have trouble even imagining. Such as crossing the great intervals of time and space between the stars."

"But you told me that this Urod was—time-frozen, you said. Somehow confined, encapsulated, in an almost helpless state."

"Comparatively helpless—as it still is. But still capable, under the right conditions, of transporting itself over the great intervals."

"Do you mean—are you saying—they can transport themselves through space—even between the stars—without a ship?"

Va'lon inclined his head in a graceful nod. "This one was attempting to escape absolute confinement. It fled to a vast distance, but it fled in vain."

"I see," said Jonathan. "All right, then. I—I see." He refrained from asking whether any people who happened to be nearby when such a jaunt occurred might be accidentally swept along with it. His skepticism knew when it was licked. "A confinement, to which you now intend to return the Urod."

"That is correct."

"In a kind of—prison, somewhere?"

"The facility I am thinking of might be more accurately described as a hospital."

Or a museum? But Jonathan resisted the temptation to ask that question aloud. He also refrained from inquiring whether there had been some kind of a violent battle, fierce fighting at the prison-hospital, more than sixty years ago.

In the course of their discussion, Va'lon at last did mention to Jonathan, almost offhandedly, that there had been a Taelon visit, or expedition, to San Simeon in the 1930s, an attempt to remove the Urod.

"It was of course a secret attempt as far as humanity was concerned, carried out without any general awareness on the part of your people."

"Of course. And with what result?"

"That attempt encountered great difficulties, and I must confess that it ended in failure."

"Is that so."

Va'lon smiled ruefully and nodded. "We still do not fully understand the details of what went wrong. But the effort we now propose will of course be undertaken only after much more thorough preparation, and with a fuller understanding of the difficulties."

Jonathan Doors thought about it. Then he said, "So there may be, there may have been already, recurring episodes of strange phenomena here on earth, specifically in this immediate area, brought about by this Urod, struggling to get free."

"That is so."

"But it has never been able to free itself completely."

"We intend to do all we can to make sure that it never does so."

Jonathan Doors stood up and walked around and looked at the Urod again. "It has a very convincing resemblance to a stone statue. But it's not dead, actually alive. Just somehow—frozen in time."

"That is the best explanation I can give, to one at your level of scientific sophistication."

Putting it politely, Doors thought. *If somewhat condescendingly. To one at my level of ignorance, you mean.* "Still hard to believe," he said aloud.

"Indeed. But if you will walk with me, a little closer to the specimen we are studying, I will try to arrange a small demonstration."

Jonathan Doors and Va'lon walked out along the esplanade, pacing a kind of loop up onto the plaza right in front of Casa Grande and back again. On the lower walk they stopped once more to gaze at the four images of Sekhmet, all but one of them dark stone, and that one indistinguishable from stone as far as human senses were concerned.

Doors deliberately walked near. "Which one is it? I can't see any real difference in them."

"Over the centuries it has made itself look more like the statues, and also caused the statues to become more like itself."

"It can do that."

"It can do many things. There are, as I have said, distinct alterations in reality. The Urod is the tallest of the four." And Va'lon raised a willowy arm and pointed.

Jonathan Doors moved closer to it by another step, and from the corner of his eye saw his Taelon guide begin to raise a hand, as if to restrain him from some rash act. His human senses told him that this was surely only a statue, nothing more. Now the whole idea once more seemed utterly fantastic. Jonathan said, "It looks like stone. I can even see a—a vein, a layer, of slightly different colored stone, running diagonally across the legs, the base."

"An illusion," said Va'lon calmly.

"What if I took a hammer and chisel, and . . ."

"That would be inadvisable. Oh, probably you would experience nothing worse than another illusion, to the effect that you were actually chipping stone. But possibly you would not survive at all. Allow me to offer you a closer look at reality." Producing a small device, the Taelon initiated a small demonstration.

When it was over, Jonathan wiped his forehead. He had seen a version of himself with a crocodile's head, and one of Amanda as a rubber snake. "I can see that we must get rid of it, yes. How soon can you get started?"

It seemed that preparations had evidently been going on for some time, for Va'lon had said earlier that more of his compatriots were arriving. But very soon there was evidence that some kind of massive effort was truly getting under way.

Doors thought the Companion shuttles bringing the equipment must have been waiting in near-readiness, not far away. They did not land anywhere on the hundred-plus acres of the former state monument, but at a distance of almost a mile.

Jonathan Doors decided that as soon as he had the opportunity, he would sit down with his wife and tell Amanda everything that Va'lon had told him.

Later, with the sun about to go down, he sat looking out from the window of his bedroom on the third floor of Casa Grande. He could see them clustered on ranch land, beside a small hill that would shield them against casual observation from the coastal highway.

Talking to Amanda at his side, Doors passed on what Va'lon had told him about the process. From the landing place, the necessary gear would be transported carefully up the slopes of the Enchanted Hill. Now, even as Jonathan watched, three sleek blue machines, self-propelled, the size of large pickup trucks, were being carefully guided up the slopes.

"Be nice if we had some binoculars handy," Amanda wished.

"I'll try to remember, next batch of aliens we get."

Each Taelon machine had a long projection in front, like the neck and head of a brontosaurus. Each had one of the Companions walking beside it, or sometimes mounting on its back and sitting in a cab rather like one of the howdahs in which folk of the nineteenth century had ridden their tame elephants. And each machine, when necessary, eased its way somehow, with the care of a stalking cat, over fences and other obstacles.

Gradually Doors could discern the pattern in how the Taelons were disposing of their engines. He had not asked Va'lon for any such details, but he was curious. When this stage of their deployment was complete, they formed a rough triangle, surrounding the group of figures at a distance of between fifty and a hundred feet. The machines' nozzles were all focused on the same central point.

NINETEEN

As soon as Jonathan Doors had the opportunity, he sat down with his wife, in the small but luxurious sitting room that connected their two bedrooms, for a long talk about their situation. He had decided that if the Companions were really determined to eavesdrop on his conversations in the house, there was probably nothing he could do about it, given the technological disparity. He would have to rely on their not being interested enough to make the effort, particularly with the Urod keeping them as busy as they were.

The chairs and the little table were certainly antique, and probably worth a small fortune. Glancing through the open door of Mandy's room at Cardinal Richelieu's supposed bed, oxygen tanks standing beside it, he wondered idly how many houses of European wealth and/or nobility had contributed to the furnishing of this one small suite of rooms in the fantasies of an American newspaper publisher.

But at the moment neither of the human occupants were much interested in the problems of interior decoration.

"All right, Johnny, let me have it," Amanda told her husband. "And it better be good."

"Oh, it is."

In a low voice, Doors tersely laid out the essentials of what Va'lon had told him about the Urod. The Companion had practically sworn him to silence, but surely the Taelons, who had studied him so intensely, would know that he shared almost everything with Amanda. They would expect him to do so now.

And, if they objected, to hell with them.

"Do you believe what Va'lon tells you?" Mandy asked when she had heard the story. She had connected herself to an oxygen bottle again, and at the moment a thin plastic nasal tube was feeding the bottled stuff of life into her ravaged lungs.

"In this case I do." Earlier, one of the household workers had come upstairs unbidden with an armful of wood and kindling, and had considerately started a fire on the medieval hearth. Doors poked at the wood fire now; later, he thought, it would feel good against the damp coolness of the evening. "I have my reasons."

His wife sounded consideringly neutral. "It sounds somewhat fantastic to me."

"Mandy, did I ever tell you you have a gift for understatement? His claims are indeed fantastic. But then, so is everything about the Taelons. And yet here they are, as real as you and me."

Amanda was briefly silent. Then she asked, "What does your father think of them?"

"Dad doesn't like 'em much." Certainly the time would come when Jonathan repeated Jubal's story to his wife; but he was not ready to pass it on to anyone just yet.

There followed another small, uncomfortable silence, broken only by the crackle of the fire. Then Amanda asked, "Would it be very ungrateful of me to say that I don't either?"

"You should say what you really feel."

"Then I'll say this: I get the feeling there's something you haven't told me, Johnny."

He rubbed his face. "Only things I'm not totally sure about." *And things it might even be dangerous to say aloud.*

After thinking about it for a moment, Jonathan rummaged about on shelves and in drawers until he found a scrap of paper. Pulling a pencil from his pocket, he wrote out that last unspoken phrase and handed it over to Amanda to read. When she looked up at him, wondering, with newly haunted eyes, he gently reclaimed the paper from her hand and threw it into the fire.

For some hours now Doors had been privately, silently pondering the possibility of quickly putting Amanda and his father on a plane and having them flown away. One problem that would first have to be solved was what to do with her rubber snake, the Taelon machine to which she was now attached, but Jubal's story suggested that, despite Namor's warnings, the device could be removed without doing Mandy serious harm.

Whether he sent his wife and father away from San Simeon or not, Doors himself would be staying on. He couldn't cut out on his loyal workers. That would be a dirty trick, leaving them to confront as best they could a deadly Urod whose very existence they did not suspect, as well as a crew of Taelons who were probably just as dangerous.

Of course he might, alternatively, assign Amanda and Jubal a driver and a car and send them off by road in the direction of Maine, or of Alaska—provided he could persuade them to leave at all. By all reports the roads were now safe enough. The New Free Coastal Militia, as well as several similar groups of lunatics, had by now been forced to abandon their effort to block highways and disrupt society. News reports kept reassuring listeners that they had been arrested, dispersed, chased back up into the hills.

Amanda's thoughts seemed to be running roughly in the same track. "When are we going home, Johnny?" she asked after a minute's silence."If there is danger from this Urod, as you say, but only the Taelons are capable of dealing with it— well, is there any reason for you, and me, and your father, to stay here and confront it?"

"I don't want to leave the Ranch right now. Some of my people are going to have to stay here, and I'm staying with them. I want to be here while our friends from outer space are handling the Urod. In case it becomes necessary to—mobilize some kind of human help."

Amanda considered, then asked, "Is that likely?"

"I don't know. There's an awful lot I don't know, Mandy, about what's going on." He shook his head. "But my feeling is that the immediate danger from the Urod is not that great. Besides, I'm not sure we could travel far enough to avoid any problems that do develop."

"Then I'll stay as long as you do. What about your father?"

"I asked dad what he wants to do. He's signed on for the duration too."

She was studying him closely now. She reached out a feeble hand to hold one of his.

Amanda said, "And Va'lon has not suggested that we leave San Simeon, or proposed that all humans be evacuated from the area. Has he?"

"No."

"I didn't think so. Actually, it was Namor's suggestion that I join you here."

Jonathan blinked at her. "I didn't realize that. What do you mean?"

"Just what I say. Namor did raise the point with me, when I was still at home. It was that I might want to join you here. I was about to tell him I wanted to do so, since you didn't seem in any hurry to come home, when he beat me to it. I think perhaps he just wanted to come here and see what was going on, and bring his new patient along with him."

"Interesting," Doors grunted. In fact he had no idea what to make of it.

Distantly he could hear a couple of his current indoor staff, somewhere downstairs in the big house, calling back and forth in cheerful Spanish. Well, if any of them thought that would keep the Anglo boss from understanding them, they were going to be surprised some day.

* * *

Amanda retired into her bedroom to get some rest. Left alone again, Jonathan regretted that his wife had ever come to San Simeon. But there wasn't much to be done about it now.

If only he dared to really talk to her! Sooner or later he must find a way to unburden himself of Jubal's terrifying story! That would have eased his own mind enormously. But Jonathan still held back, not wanting to risk having any of his father's secrets overheard. There were at least five Taelons at San Simeon now. Maybe eavesdropping was one of the functions of the Taelon machine that was supposedly recording Amanda's vital signs. *Sheer paranoia, Doors?* Maybe. There were situations in which only the paranoid survived.

And when Amanda came out of her room following her nap, and Jonathan got a close look at her again, he had to admit to himself that she really did not seem to have benefited much from Taelon treatment.

And the continued presence of the rubbery Siamese snake on her right arm did nothing for her husband's peace of mind.

"Did Namor tell you anything new about this?" He touched it with one finger, and shuddered inwardly at the sense he got that the thing was partially alive.

"Oh, one thing. I was given a calm but very clear warning that its connection to me must never be broken by clumsy earthborn human hands."

"Those were his exact words?"

"Not really. To that effect. Something about the thing bothers you, doesn't it?"

"Do you feel any better, really? Since Namor's been treating you?"

"Johnny, I honestly don't know. Sometimes I think I do, sometimes I have doubts." Amanda paused, then added, "They're not magicians, Johnny. Not really miracle workers, though they can do some things that look miraculous to us. And they did warn us my treatment might take time."

"That's true." *And that was perhaps the worst of all: that the hopes of a cure had been raised again, only to be dashed.*

"I'm still looking at your rubber snake." He tried to keep his voice light and easy.

"Yes, I can see that. Your dad was staring at it too. My new doctor says that all his regular Taelon patients routinely get one to wear. Just as we put wristbands on people when they go to the hospital."

"Do they have a name for it?"

"If they do I haven't heard it."

Sken, that was the name according to Jubal. Doors casually tested his wife's *sken* with his fingers. He didn't get the feeling that it would be easily torn off, though of course he wasn't try-ing to do that yet.

"Looks like they fastened it on pretty solidly," he observed.

"I suppose that's good. Isn't it?"

He would have given much to be able to deny the horrible fact, but he could not. His beloved Amanda had now been fit-ted with the same equipment worn by Esther Summerson, when Esther was tagged as an intended human sacrifice back in 1936.

In silent desperation, Jonathan clung to the one slender advantage he could still realistically hope that he possessed: simply that Va'lon and his compatriots did not suspect how much he knew about them: their secret installation, part museum, part surgery, part God knew what, somewhere in deep space; and their historical dealings with the race of Urods. Nor could they suspect that he realized just what the rubber snake might mean.

Suddenly he wondered if, when the human mind had been chewed up and destroyed, the body, perhaps undamaged, would be exhibited as a specimen in one of those fantastically remote display cases.

At least, he thought with some relief, they hadn't yet suggested that she be pushed into the same machine with the damned monster.

"Anything wrong?" Mandy was asking him.

"No. Just tired." But he realized that he was now beginning to get mental signals from the Urod, even as Jubal had got them long ago.

And something, some image that came to him with the latest touch of the Urod's mind, gave Jonathan something new to worry about: Did the Urod recognize in the aged Jubal the young human who it had dealt with in some fashion in 1936? And if so, what would be the consequences?

Jonathan, who had been watching his father's reactions closely, got the old man aside before Jubal burst out with something that would alert the Taelons.

Neither man said much about the tag to Amanda. But Jubal whispered his recognition to his son.

"I know. I remembered your description."

"What're you going to do, son?" For once Jubal sounded almost humble.

"I don't know. Might try to get her away, of course. But there are Taelons everywhere, scattered all over the surface of the earth—and isn't it possible they can trace her as long as she's wearing the snake?"

"I don't think it worked that way with Esther, when I was trying to hide her aboard the station. But maybe this is an improved model. You might just yank it off her arm."

"Have to give them a reason if I do that. I'm not ready yet for a real fight."

Jubal nodded, sighed.

Jonathan went on, "So, we'll just politely decline any offer of hospital treatment that they might make. Unless, maybe, they want to set up a hospital here on earth, after the Urod's gone." And he nodded in the direction of the Urod and the triangle of blue machines. "Any suggestions, Dad?"

"I'm retired from making suggestions." The old man moved a hand in the direction of the Taelon activity on the plaza. "Are they doing what I think they're doing down there?"

"They tell me we've got a Urod, and they're going to get rid of it for us."

The next time Jonathan saw Namor, he asked the Taelon again about the snake, and got the same answer Amanda said she had been given, "It is part of the routine procedure. Just as the patients in your hospitals routinely wear wristbands."

And then the Companion calmly but very directly repeated the warning directly to Jonathan, that the connections between Amanda and her Taelon machine must not be broken by clumsy earth-human hands. What might happen if that was done was left unspecified, but it would certainly be terrible.

"I see." For the time being he had to let it go at that.

Jonathan Doors had a feeling that the world was closing in on him. He didn't know yet what he would do. But he was going to have to do something.

When he slept, briefly and unsatisfactorily, his rest was marred by evil dreams that he could easily attribute to the Urod.

Immediately after Amanda's current session of treatment, Namor asked to sit down with the couple for a serious talk. Jubal was standing in the doorway, and Jonathan gave him a look. "Come in, Dad."

Namor's slight smile was absent this time, his voice less musical than usual. "Amanda, Jonathan, I have been reviewing the latest information from Amanda's monitoring unit."

"What's up?"

Namor went on to explain that unless she could be treated in a Taelon hospital, it was highly unlikely that her recovery would proceed successfully.

Some folk who had long acquaintance with Jonathan Doors said he was at his best, his most dangerous, when his worst fears were confirmed. But his voice held no hint of panic, only natural, intelligent concern. "Isn't there some other way you could continue with the treatment here on earth—?"

Namor said in gentle tones, "If I am to be responsible for my patient's welfare, I must insist." Then the Companion's eyes turned compassionately to Jubal. "Are you ill, sir?"

Jubal shook his head energetically. "Just old, son, just old."

When the old man had hobbled away, Namor also offered to examine Jubal, and Jonathan Doors stalled him off.

"Frankly, I don't think my father would appreciate that. He has his own doctors, in whom he puts a lot of faith."

"That is understandable. Especially in one who has entered his advanced stage of life." The Companion made a gesture that seemed to push the matter decisively to one side.

Every indication that Doors could read, in the look or the behavior of his wife of thirty years, every sign conveyed by her gestures and in the tones of her voice, told him that she was sick unto death of this ghastly existence.

What he saw also reinforced his strong new suspicion that the Companions had now given up on trying to heal her—he wondered now if that had ever really been their goal—or were they in fact intent on preparing her to face the same fate that had been intended for Esther Summerson.

The doctor (if Namor really was a doctor—once you knew

they were absolute liars, you doubted everything they told you!) said they would take her to a place where her case could be "studied and treated."

Once more, Namor smoothly repeated his advice that Amanda had better be transferred to a Taelon hospital for study and treatment. This time Namor's manner as he made the suggestion was brightly upbeat. He was rubbing the palms of his hands together in a slow circular motion. He said, "We are fortunate in that transportation is immediately available."

"Immediately?"

"Within a few hours."

Doors kept his own voice neutral. "You mean, on the same ship that will transport the Urod?"

The Taelon physician was confidence personified. "Yes; the journey will be perfectly safe. We are taking every precaution."

"Of course. And just where is this hospital?"

"It is hard for me to describe the location, in terms that would be familiar to you."

Jonathan looked at Amanda, who at the moment seemed too busy trying to breathe to pay much attention to the talk going on around her. But her eyes were alert, and she and Jonathan held a brief silent conversation, in the way that is possible with couples who have been married for thirty years.

Amanda: *You've been warning me about offers like this, and I don't intend to accept.*

Jonathan: *I agree 100 percent.*

Turning back to the Taelon, he did his best to give an impression of a man struggling to make a difficult decision. "How long would she be at this hospital of yours? Would I be able to visit her?"

"Even with the best of care, it is impossible to know in advance what length of treatment may be necessary. I regret that visits would not be possible."

"Oh? Why not?"

Namor raised his eyes toward heaven, momentarily giving the impression that he prayed: *God of the Taelons, deliver me from this stubborn earthman.* But all he said was, "There would be—difficulties."

"What sort of difficulties? If the journey is really as safe as you say?"

To soothe him, and insure his willing co-operation, Namor appeared to be granting a considerable concession. "Perhaps, after all, some way could be worked out."

Doors nodded thoughtfully. "I'll talk it over with my wife. We'll have to think about it."

The Taelon bowed gracefully. "I feel sure that you will reach the right conclusion. But remember, a decision must be reached soon."

Jonathan nodded yet again, and favored the Companion with a tired but friendly smile.

TWENTY

No one got to be a billionaire without accumulating a number of energetic and dangerous enemies. Years of experience had taught Jonathan Doors that it was vital to learn as much as possible about your opponents, as quickly as possible. That was the first step in trying to come to grips with them. Therefore he yearned to get a good close look at the three newly arrived Companions, who were currently in the process of jockeying their three large blue machines closer to the big house at San Simeon. But his chance of being able to study them in any detail seemed remote. At a distance Jonathan found the trio of newcomers, all tall, slender, and blue-clad, indistinguishable from the Taelons he had already met.

He was soon absorbed in observing the three massive units of newly arrived equipment—the three blue dinosaurs he had earlier observed making their patient way cross-country from the landing site, the lowering sun casting their long shadows across the golden California grass. Watching them in action, Jonathan was reminded of three huge, self-propelled earth-movers, except that instead of shovels or scraper blades, these machines sprouted enormous nozzles, putting him vaguely in mind of the heads of long-necked machines. Doors wondered whether they intended to spray the Urod with something when they got close to it.

The machines had been moving along divergent paths as they advanced, like units on a battlefield expecting to come under heavy fire. Now they suggested to Jonathan's imagination a trio of huge robotic infantry, crawling on hands and knees. One of the units had to make a laborious passage clear around Casa Grande and its encircling plazas and gardens, to reach its assigned position. Meanwhile the other two waited in place, marking time until the first was almost in position, before they moved forward again.

When the three machines were finally deployed, their positions defined a triangle, at the center of which stood the Urod and its small cluster of accompanying statuary.

Once the three sleek blue machines had reached their assigned positions, all was quiet for a while. Each had its nozzle extended toward the central target, but nothing was being projected, as far as Jonathan could see.

After a minute or two during which nothing seemed to happen, the cab of one machine swung open, and the Taelon who had been inside came out and climbed down to the ground. He started toward the house but disappeared momentarily behind a clump of foliage.

A moment later Jonathan, observing as carefully as he could from a high window of Casa Grande, saw this Taelon approaching the main house on foot. When he was halfway across the plaza, just in front of the main entrance, Va'lon came out of the front door to meet him.

Immediately the two Companions began an animated discussion, in their own trilling, flowing language. Jonathan was so distant that only an occasional sound reached him, faintly. He decided he ought to find out what was going on, and after a word to Amanda started downstairs. He had just reached the ground floor when he met Va'lon and the newcomer, entering the house.

Va'lon looked up and called to him cheerfully, "Jonathan, my friend, we were coming to find you. This is Da'an, Companion liaison to North America, and he has expressed a desire to meet you before we proceed any further with our current operation."

The name meant nothing to Doors, but the title sounded important, and Va'lon's manner reinforced the suggestion.

"Pleased to meet you too," Jonathan responded. Having observed on several occasions that Companions preferred to avoid shaking hands, at least with mere earthlings, he did not attempt to do so this time, but only nodded.

Da'an in return performed the slight Taelon bow, accompanied by a simultaneous graceful lowering of eyelids, even more elegantly than Doors had expected. Every time a Companion did that it was hard to escape the impression that he really was expressing his respect.

The newcomer's voice was even more melodious than Va'lon's. "I heartily commend you, Jonathan Doors, for your co-operation with us in this matter of the Urod."

"Thank you." Jonathan could be gracious too. "It seemed the only thing to do. I hope the matter can be settled, quickly and safely."

"I am confident that it will be. We are currently delayed for technical reasons, but in a few minutes will be able to resume our progress."

"I'm glad to hear it," Doors assured him.

"Allow me," said Va'lon, "to take this opportunity to emphasize once more the importance of all humans keeping their distance from our machines and their operations. It may appear that nothing is now happening there, but appearances are deceptive."

Jonathan nodded agreeably. "That is often the case, isn't it?" He looked out over the portion of the esplanade where the innocent-looking black statues in their fountain formed the center of the triangle formed by the siting of the three large Taelon machines.

He added, "I will speak again to all my people here. By the way—Da'an—I also want to thank you and your colleagues—perhaps I should say your Synod?—for your special assistance to my wife."

Again the gracious bow. "You are quite welcome."

"Am I going to be introduced to your two newly arrived colleagues at some point?" Doors jerked his head in the direction of the front door. Beyond that barrier all was silent, but he felt sure that nevertheless some kind of a struggle had already begun.

"Later there will be time and opportunity. For a little while now we are all going to be extremely busy. But I wanted to meet you before doing anything else."

"I am honored." And Doors made his own attempt at something like a Taelon bow.

Now that the introduction Da'an had wanted was out of the way, it became obvious that the three most recent arrivals had not come to San Simeon to socialize. Da'an soon rejoined his compatriots in their confrontation with the Urod, and the trio of large machines became unceasingly, untiringly busy. The black statues at the focus of attention of the blue dinosaurs looked utterly insignificant by comparison. Otherwise, there was not much for earthly eyes to see in what the Taelons were now doing, nor for human minds to comprehend.

Dusk was now beginning to engulf the low-lying areas of the estate, shadows filling the sharply cut ravines, and lengthening on the east side of buildings and clumps of trees. Bright Taelon lights stabbed out from each of the big machines, bathing the figure of Sekhmet in glaring illumination from several directions.

Not until several hours after the three machines had settled into their chosen positions on the ground, did Jonathan at last see a Taelon shuttle land directly on the estate. The sun had set in modest glory, and all the outdoor lights were on. The newest visitor was a comparatively small ship, and it came seemingly out of nowhere to descend slowly onto a broad walkway, only a few yards from the statue that was really not supposed to be a statue. Jonathan did not see anyone get out of the shuttle, but it opened a large cargo hatch, a huge black vacancy in the middle of its belly, from which a sloped ramp extended itself to rest on the walk.

Va'lon meanwhile had come to seek out Doors, the owner of the property, and apologized to him for damage inadvertently done to several flower beds.

Jonathan abstractedly told the Companion not to worry about it. He was still looking at the huge open hatch of the latest Taelon arrival. He thought this vessel looked very much like—and perhaps was the very same—as the craft that had descended with Va'lon and Namor aboard, bringing them right down into the Doors backyard, only a few days ago. Somehow that already seemed a long time in the past.

Obviously the silent struggle between Taelon and Urod was still going on, though as far as the earthly observers could tell, nothing much was happening.

"Do you need more lights?" Doors asked the nearest Taelon—who happened to be the physician, the only Companion now in the house.

"That will not be necessary," Namor replied at once. Evidently he had no need to consult with any of his colleagues on the matter.

"Are your people almost ready to take our friend away?" Doors asked.

" 'Friend,' Jonathan?"

"The Urod."

"Ah. Yes, we are almost ready."

Presently Va'lon was called out of the house, a message conveyed to him by some means that had escaped Jonathan's observation.

Then Da'an appeared once more, to confer with the Taelon physician in the plaza outside the enormous front door of Casa Grande. Doors got the impression that the removal of the Urod wasn't going as well as the Taelon engineers had hoped. Presently Va'lon came back to the house, the Companion liaison to North America climbed back into his blue machine, and the silent struggle with the Urod went on. The mental tumult that it engendered seemed now to be continually in the air, like the noise of some vast, distant construction project. But so far Doors, and most other people he assumed, were managing pretty successfully to tune it out.

Now, whenever Doors did manage to catch sight of a Taelon face the look on it was grim.

Time dragged on. But no one on the Enchanted Hill thought of retiring for the night.

The next time Amanda was alone with her husband, she took the opportunity to whisper to him. "Johnny. I don't want them to take me away from you."

"I don't want you to go with them, Mandy. In fact I'm not going to let you go." And at last he had to admit to himself that he would soon have to tell her more, pass on some of the frightening information about Jubal's story and the events that tended to confirm it. "I've learned some things—about them." His tone made it clear that the knowledge gained was not favorable.

"Learned what? And how?" Amanda squeezed her husband's hand as hard as she was able, but she did not seem utterly surprised.

"Long story. I'll tell you about it later. I want to tell it exactly right, and I'm afraid I can't if I try to condense it into a couple of dozen words."

She sighed in exasperation. "This is one of those times when you have to do it all alone?" There had been a very few such occasions over the past three decades.

"I'm afraid it is, Mandy. For a little longer, anyway."

Down there on the encircling walk, only a little distance beyond the plaza in front of Casa Grande, two races from beyond the stars were contending, in ways that no human could fully understand, and few even begin to grasp. If Doors could not begin to understand the struggle, he could sense it in the back of his mind. It would certainly seem that this time the Taelons ought to have the advantage; they had known what they would be facing here, and they had come prepared, armed with tremendous weapons. And yet, the contest did not seem to be all one-sided.

If we cannot understand them, well, so be it. They will never be able to comprehend us fully either. To Taelons and Urod, we will forever be beings who live out beyond the stars.

And Jonathan tried to think what reason he might give the Companions, to explain his wife's refusal, backed up by his own, to be transported away from the earth to receive the best in Taelon medical care.

What was the best reason he could give, without arousing their suspicions?

TWENTY-ONE

Hours ago, Doors had assembled his local staff—about half of them in person, the others electronically—and had given them a partial explanation of what was going on tonight. The general idea he wanted to convey was that the Taelons would be engaged in a difficult and possibly dangerous operation, involving some of the statuary, and it was important for everyone to stay off the plaza and walks in front of Casa Grande, out of their way.

"Any questions?"

Mostly he got blank looks, but he thought he could read their minds. Statuary? Didn't all that stuff belong to the boss since he bought the place? And so, couldn't the Taelons ship some of it away if he had given them permission?

Jonathan sighed. He wanted these people to be concentrating on their jobs, and he wasn't going to hit them now with any more of the truth than he deemed absolutely necessary.

He raised his voice a little. "I'm telling you this because there may be some element of danger involved for anyone who stays on the grounds while this is going on, and any of you who want to leave can do so now. Come back in the morning and I won't hold it against you. I don't think it's a very big risk—you'll notice I'm still here, and so is my wife, and so is my father—but you deserve to know."

One of the security people raised a hand. "Excuse me,

boss, what kind of danger are we talking about? Taking care of some of the tough stuff is what you're paying us for, after all."

"Thanks, Frank." Doors nodded his appreciation. "The problem has been presented to me in extremely vague terms, and all I can do is pass it on to you that way. Any other questions?"

There were only a couple, which he dealt with fairly successfully. In the end, no one left. At first, Doors was rather startled by the fact that none of his workers even seemed to discuss the possibility of leaving; but when he thought about it, he was not really surprised. He tended to hire people with an adventurous streak in them.

. . . and the struggle between the Companions and their uncanny enemy went on, the creature's dark thoughts rolling like thunderclouds across the background of Jonathan's consciousness. It was called the Urod, by the Taelons who feared it mortally, but the dark thing gave itself no name. It had no words, or it chose to use none, when it tried to communicate with Jonathan Doors, but only offered him glimpses of terror and power.

Jonathan dismissed his workers and went to look for his father.

"Dad." Jonathan raised a tentative hand to his own head. "I'm feeling a kind of . . ."

He didn't have to finish what he was trying to say. Jubal had already recognized the problem.

"I know, I'm getting it too. Like some damn nightmare, that keeps coming back, and back again."

"But I never felt anything like this."

"That's Mr. Urod calling, son. The fella who lives time-frozen in that black stone body." Jubal was trying to keep a light tone, but he looked and sounded a little sick. "Not nearly as bad as it hit me in the Thirties. Maybe it realizes that I don't make the decisions anymore."

"What the hell does 'time-frozen' mean, anyway?"

"Dunno. I've looked in scientific dictionaries now and then over the years, but never found it. Judging by what happened to Lobo, one thing it can mean is being paralyzed, unable to move physically. Fortunately or unfortunately, that kind of paralysis doesn't slow down a Urod much. I've never seen this one in any other mode."

"Dad, does the Urod—do you think it knows you, recognizes you from way back when?"

Jubal nodded. "The idea scares me, but I kind of think it does. It knows me, but it just doesn't care."

It was about ten o'clock of a dark and moonless night, when Da'an, evidently taking advantage of some kind of recess in the ongoing struggle, approached the house again, calling ahead on his communicator to say he wished to talk with Jonathan Doors.

Jonathan met him on the ground floor. "Are you making satisfactory progress?" Doors inquired mildly.

"There is progress indeed, though not entirely satisfactory. We have now moved the Urod several yards, and prevented any significant re-adaptation." Da'an did not appear perturbed, exactly—perhaps a little worn. His coloring was stable.

He said to Jonathan, "The business will perhaps require more time than we expected. I have come now to warn you that there will be a risk of occasional bad dreams tonight. This applies to anyone sleeping in the great house, and to a lesser extent, in any of the three smaller mansions, which are at a slightly greater distance from the center of activity."

Doors observed that the only ones who had been assigned quarters in the smaller houses were the Taelons themselves.

The gracious gesture, the small bow. "Then, as we do not intend to sleep, it is necessary to consider only those humans residing in Casa Grande."

"I will pass along the warning. But I doubt that anyone in the house will be getting much sleep tonight anyway."

"They may attend, from a distance, if they wish. But there will not be much for them to see."

"Maybe not, but we're all interested."

Da'an asked if any of his family members, or workers, were feeling any ill effects so far.

"I haven't been told of anything," Doors reported.

Actually the handful of humans now in residence could all have been not only accommodated but lost in the big house. The workers, excluding medics but including maintenance people, were all currently housed in the part of Casa Grande that used to be known as the servants' quarters. Only Jonathan Doors, his wife and father, and Amanda's human physician, Dr. Kimura, were installed in the guest bedrooms.

"But, excuse me, Da'an, wait a moment—are bad dreams the worst possibility we have to worry about? Does that mean this Urod represents no real, material danger?" Jonathan, still straining for crumbs of useful information, wanted to get the Taelon to talk about its enemy as much as possible.

"Unfortunately there are other risks, and they are very real. Though perhaps they present no material danger, in the strict philosophical sense. Reality itself is not precisely material."

Jonathan thought that one over, or tried to. Then he considered that he might have been better off just trying to get a good night's sleep. Philosophy had never been his strongest suit.

"Could you amplify that a little?" he asked the Taelon. "I mean, is there danger of a—great explosion? Or a meltdown? Something on that order?"

The Companion said, "An event of physical violence on the scale that you suggest is highly unlikely. I am told you personally have now experienced something of the powers that the Urod is capable of exerting. It is possible, that in its last desperate bid for freedom, it might be able to induce a substantial re-adaptation of reality."

"A 're-adaptation'?"

"What now appears as a stone statue might possibly acquire some other aspect. The contours of your great house, or some other object, might be slightly changed."

"Well. That doesn't sound too bad."

Da'an said nothing.

"I'm not sure I understand just what . . ."

"This is one of those cases in which verbal translation must be always difficult. Perhaps we could find a better word, but I hope there is no need. In its mildest form the reaction I am describing might bring on unpleasant dreams in any human mind nearby."

"Implying that we might also anticipate some other forms, that would not be so mild?"

"If all goes well, we will not have to worry about those."

"And if all does not go well?"

The Taelon raised almost-invisible eyebrows. "Patience, Jonathan. If there is any serious cause for alarm, I will let you know in time to take appropriate measures."

"What sort of measures?"

But one of the other Taelons, whose name Doors had never learned, had come into the house, some urgency apparent in the speed with which he moved. Da'an had already turned away to confer with his compatriot, and answered Jonathan only with a gentle wave.

Jonathan went back into the house, not certain that the latest conference had taught him anything at all.

Doors pulled his global from his belt, flipped it on and passed along to his crew the latest warning from the Companions. "I'm told that anyone who falls asleep in this building tonight may experience bad dreams. Take it for what it's worth."

By about eleven o'clock, Jonathan and Amanda were once again alone together in their third-floor suite of rooms. They had opened one of the windows, which afforded them an excellent view of what was happening below, on the plaza and in the nearby areas that were not obscured by trees or bushes.

Just beyond the plaza and to the left, on a slightly lower level, they had a good view of the statue (despite everything, as often as not Doors still thought of it that way: as a stone image carved by human hands), still bathed in bright light. It seemed to be resting now on some kind of low platform, equipped with rollers, and it was very slowly being inched along a broad walkway, toward a sloping ramp that led up into the interior of the waiting Taelon shuttle. Inside that exotic cave a haze of blue lights now awaited the Urod's arrival. People, or objects, indistinctly seen, were moving around in there.

Gradually Jonathan's expectations were being realized: Almost every other human on the Enchanted Hill seemed to be watching too. Just about all the windows on the west face of Casa Grande that turned most directly toward the broad plaza and adjoining walkways, were occupied by heads. None of the local employees of Doors International needed to rest, it seemed. It looked to Doors like no one had gone to sleep. Maybe, he thought, I just don't work them hard enough. Or maybe they were all really afraid of nightmares.

The chief effect of Jonathan's latest warning seemed to have been to reinforce the curiosity engendered by the first. Now, apart from a couple of workers who were unable to leave their posts of duty—one at the front gate, one at the improvised communications center—the whole staff wanted to see what kind of a fantastic enterprise the Taelons were up to. Heads were visible in several windows in the big house, and men and women had found various other places from which to watch, outside the crudely marked-out triangle of Taelon power.

That power, like the other alien force it was opposing, trying to contain and seal away, seemed to be operating essentially beyond the range of human senses: Jonathan could not see, or hear, or feel, that the Companions' three mechanical dinosaurs were doing anything at all. Only the intense concentration of their operators, whose pale faces and slender bodies were partially visible inside the glassy cabs of their machines, testified that something very important was going on.

"It's very strange, Mandy." *Oh, if only I dared to tell you just how strange it really is. Maybe I had better take the chance and tell you now. If anything were to happen to me, and Dad, no other human being on earth would know. . . .*

"It sure is, Johnny. Look!"

It seemed to the observers that the difficult process of loading the Urod had now been partially accomplished. The black object on its transporter was halfway up the ramp. But evidently the struggle was not yet over. Something, some last-ditch resistance on the part of the confuser of reality, prevented the loading from being completed.

It seemed to Jonathan, though he could not be sure, that some kind of crystalline encrustation had now begun to take shape around the Urod. There were glimpses of an almost ghostly framework, coming and going. In a way it reminded him of the Taelon blush, but this phenomenon was taking place outside the Urod's body, not on its surface.

With a feeling of inevitability, he recalled the encapsulation his father had seen on the Urod's body, while they were both inside the Taelon spaceship of 1936.

Beside him, Amanda whispered that she could see it too.

There'll never be a better time to talk to her than now, he thought. *Now, when they're all distracted.* Jonathan cleared his throat, then whispered. "Listen, Mandy. I've got to tell you—"

A figure leaning from another window, only a few feet lower in the great white wall, raised an arm suddenly and pointed urgently outward. Not at the Urod and its opponents, but beyond them, into the California night, deep black beyond the circle of Taelon light and activity.

I can't see anything at all out there, thought Doors, staring at nothing to no avail. *Only sheer blackness. Now what—?*

And at the same moment, someone at yet another window was having the same thought.

"But what's that?" The voice carried plainly, conveying innocent curiosity.

The answer came, loud and terrible and shocking, in a barrage of bullets, gun flashes visible in the darkness out beyond the lighted plaza, rapid automatic fire, in a continuous blasting roar, all aimed toward the great house, pocking the front of Casa Grande. Moments later another weapon joined in, and then another.

TWENTY-TWO

The castle's surroundings were dimming rapidly, in sudden leaps of advancing darkness, as antique and precious alabaster globes of light were shot away. Now it sounded like the outbreak of World War III.

"Who the *hell*—?" But almost before Jonathan could formulate the question for himself, he knew the answer. Colonel Shelby, of course, or someone like him. Maybe one of Shelby's rivals, leader of some different band, perhaps a little better armed and organized.

Already Jonathan's mind was abstractedly critiquing the operation: *They should have waited until the hour before dawn. They're not going to catch anyone at San Simeon asleep at midnight—not tonight.*

Meanwhile his body was already in rapid motion, as if by instinct.

"Get down, Mandy! Get under the bed!"

She had moved, as quickly as her disability would let her, to one side of the window, but she was still hovering beside it. Her voice was clear and sharp. "You get under the bed if you want to, Jonathan Doors! I want to see what's going on!"

"At least keep away from the bloody window!" he bawled at his dear wife, and hauled her by main force into the maximum shelter that the walls of Casa Grande could provide.

Jonathan knew those walls were thick with layers of reinforced concrete inside the facing stones, and ought to offer at least some measure of safety. An oxygen bottle, connected to Mandy by a plastic tube, came banging behind her as he dragged her down. God help them both if a bullet should hit that.

And he was angry at himself for having underestimated the determination and resourcefulness of Colonel Shelby and his group.

There was a loud and heavy knocking, wood on wood, on the door of the sitting room, followed by a hoarse muffled cry. Recognizing his father's voice, Jonathan shouted an invitation to come in.

The heavy door swung in to reveal Jubal, standing in a half-darkened hallway wearing slippers and an old-fashioned nightshirt, and gripping his cane tightly in one hand. "Can't a man get a nap around here? What the hell is going on?"

"Dad! Come in but keep clear of the window!"

The old man's hands were trembling as he stumbled across the threshold, but his bushy eyebrows looked fierce, and his voice sounded ready for battle.

"Sons of bitches woke me up. What the hell is going on?" he repeated. The way he glared at Jonathan gave a momentary impression that he meant to hold his son personally responsible.

"We're doing our best not to get killed," Amanda informed her father-in-law, while Jonathan was still searching for words. "Come in and help us. But stay clear of the window."

Jubal stumbled in. After taking a hasty look up and down the hall and seeing no one, Jonathan slammed the door shut again and latched it, not knowing but that the house had already been invaded. The door wouldn't stop armed men for long, but they might rush on past it looking for some easier game. He had his global unit in hand now, and was rapidly punching in orders, trying to reach all of his security people,

and in the intervals of waiting get off an urgent call to the
Highway Patrol.

Then Jonathan Doors swore violently; somehow all the
channels available for regular global operation were being
jammed.

He tossed the unit to his father. "Here, Dad, see what you
can do. We've got to get through to the cops somehow."

"Jonathan!" Mandy screamed her warning. "Get away
from the window!"

He waved her back. "If I can't talk to anyone, I've got to
try to see."

The assault was almost overwhelming in its violence, as
any must be when carried out by attackers so well armed. But
so far, at least, there was no evidence that it had been intelli-
gently planned.

Hundreds of feet away from Casa Grande, a few feet
downhill from the plaza and to Jonathan's right as he looked
out, the watery surface of the outdoor pool, mirror-calm a
moment earlier, was shattered by the splash of a falling human
body, hurling the reflections of the remaining lights into dancing oblivion.

What little Jonathan could see of the fight, peering out
from one side of the window, included the sight of rapid muzzle flashes high on the flank of Casa Grande, assuring him that
the firing was not all one way. Doors felt a fierce elation that
some of his own people were managing to put up a pretty good
resistance, almost from the very start.

Closing his eyes and concentrating intently, he tried to
recall what weapons his security guards might have available.
He could definitely recall seeing only a couple of pistols.
Jonathan realized to his frustration that he really had very little idea how well his bodyguards and the wardens of his property were equipped. He felt sharp anger at himself for not
having seen to it that they were better prepared.

But who could have expected anything like this? Well,

anyone in his own position ought to have foreseen the possibility. It was only to be expected that the landing of alien spaceships would bring out every variety of fanatic that the earth possessed.

The few trained security people Doors had on hand were highly professional, but it was obvious from the volume of fire out there that they were greatly outnumbered, and this despite the fact that he had been able to move a few extra people here from elsewhere over the last couple of days. Thank God he had at least done that.

There was a brief interval of near-silence. One or two foolhardy souls in other rooms had just returned to the windows of Casa Grande and started to look out again, when they were driven back by more bursts of small-arms fire, coming in through half a dozen of the high windows of the big house. Bullets knocked chunks of cornice from ledges under the high balconies, broke iron railings, gouged armloads of imported stone out of the towering walls.

In another room, on the same level as that in which the Doors family were taking shelter, and frighteningly close, someone screamed in a high voice, making a sickening, ugly sound.

Doors crawled to the door leading out into the hall, stuck his head out, drew a full breath and bellowed at his people not to stick their necks out at the windows. Granted that those who were armed ought to make some effort to shoot back, there was no point in cooks and housekeepers getting their heads blown off.

Having delivered some stern orders to that effect, Jonathan promptly violated his own rule by scrambling back to the window and risking another quick peek. There had been a sudden pause in the shooting, while someone out in the darkness, armed with a bullhorn, treated whatever survivors remained in the big house to a rambling, semi-intelligible diatribe.

Most of this echoing outburst was unintelligible to Jonathan; he caught a few words about the racial purity of earthborn humanity, and how it was being endangered as never before. Whatever came after that was drowned out in a burst of return fire from the house. Still, he got the point of the lecture, not that there had been much doubt about it from the start.

"What was that all about?" Amanda queried in a fierce whisper.

"I think these guys have hidden all their womenfolk away in the hills, so the Taelons can't rape them."

"I see. That makes a lot of sense. About as much as the rest of what they're doing."

Jubal meanwhile had been making repeated efforts to contact the Highway Patrol; now he reported to his son that there seemed to be some kind of jamming or other interference, moving up and down all the usual communications frequencies.

That was hard to do when earth satellites were in the loop, with multiple-channel capacity, but it appeared that some of Shelby's friends or allies had found a way.

"Well, keep at it." Jonathan was trying hard to recall all he could of the physical communications system on the hill. The new fiber-optic lines were underground, but someone had torn a fistful of connectors from the side of the house, just above the place where they went down into the trench.

Before leaving the suite of rooms, he turned to Amanda again, and saw that her slender right hand now held a pistol, a graceful and pearl-handled thing, a personal weapon she had had for many years, for self-protection. Actually she was quite an effective shot.

He stared at the woman who after thirty years was still able to surprise him. "I didn't know you brought that! What made you bring it?"

"Just had a feeling, Johnny. Sometimes a person just has a feeling."

"How well I know it. Keep the gun with you, Mandy, just in case. Dad, you stay here too. You two look out for each other, will you? This door's a pretty good barrier." He put out a hand and thumped what felt like four inches of solid oak. "Better keep it shut and locked unless you know who's calling. I've got to go see about some other people."

"I'll do my best." Jubal, with his cane in hand, looked ready to fight, but the enemy was going to have to come to him. At well past eighty years of age, he was not about to undertake any feats of running or scrambling through the dark, in an effort to come to grips with them.

Both Jubal and Amanda also promised that they would keep trying to phone for help. Repeated attempts might be necessary. The communications system at San Simeon had been state-of-the-art—in 1936. A lot had been updated since then, of course, several times over, but there was nothing wired in place today that would serve as an intercom under these conditions.

Once more urging Amanda and Jubal to keep down, Jonathan prepared to leave the room to check up on his workers, to see who might have been killed or hurt, and who was having some success at fighting back.

He took back his global and clipped it on his belt—maybe there would be less interference in another room.

"Why should we keep down when you're sticking your neck out?" Amanda gasped after him in anguish.

Doors managed to ignore it. "Lock the door behind me. I'll give a trick knock"—he demonstrated on a tabletop—"when I come back."

On emerging into the hallway, Doors was struck by the fact that some of the interior lights of Casa Grande had already been shot out.

*   *   *

Doors supposed that the attackers had cut phone lines—
assuming they could find any, after the recent upgrading of
telecommunications gear. That was one of the first things he'd
ordered on becoming the new owner of San Simeon. The
Companions' own communication network, of course, worked
on an entirely different level from any human system from
whatever decade. They might be able to reach other Taelons,
in Los Angeles or San Francisco, and have them pass the word
along to human law enforcement there.

The only trouble with that hope, thought Jonathan
Doors, was that the Taelons at San Simeon seemed to be
totally concentrated on their own major problem. They
would be anxious to take off in their ship as soon as the Urod
was loaded aboard.

Over the years he had cultivated a nastily suspicious mind,
and now he toyed with the idea that the Taelons themselves
had somehow arranged for the militia attack; still, he couldn't
see how they were going to profit from it.

Dim forms were moving in the gloom. He held his breath
until he could recognize one of them.

In another suite of fantastically decorated rooms, a few
yards down the hall, Doors held a hasty, ragged conference
with a couple of his security people, and got the best estimate
available of the attackers' strength and positions.

They were crouched low in a hallway or entryway, out of
sight of any windows. The barrage outside had started up
again, with new ferocity.

Soon afterward, when Jonathan Doors once more found a van-
tage point from which to look down at the scene below, he
observed that the big cargo hatch on the shuttle was now

closed, the loading ramp withdrawn. The Urod and its transport device were nowhere to be seen, and he presumed they had been successfully taken aboard.

Jonathan's next glimpse outside showed him four or five of the attacking militia, running about in front of the Taelon ship. Even as Doors watched, one man wearing a black ski mask, stopped and sprayed the vessel with his automatic weapon at point-blank range—to no effect. A moment later some marksman in the big house dropped the masked man in his tracks. Doors let go a yell of savage triumph.

The three big machines the Taelon had used to immobilize and move their enemy were still approximately where Doors had seen them last, but it seemed that the Taelons had at least temporarily abandoned the blue dinosaurs, which had accomplished their important mission. One of them had now somehow been tipped over on its side. A hatch stood open, on the side that would have been uppermost when the machine stood upright. The operator's cab showed empty in the glow of one of the remaining lights.

As soon as Doors got back into the room where the old man and Amanda were still waiting, Jubal handed his son the global. "Got a caller for you, Johnny."

"Have you got the creature aboard your ship?" Doors demanded, as soon as a Taelon face showed up on the small screen. He wondered jealously if they had some way of forcing a clear signal through the jamming when they wanted to communicate.

"Fortunately that task has been completed. We are almost ready to depart." The Companion's voice was as unhurried as ever, though somewhat strained.

"Then you'd better lift off, get out of this firefight while you still can."

"One important matter remains to be accomplished,

Jonathan. It is essential to Amanda's welfare that she come with us."

"I think you'd better not wait on that. We can discuss her medical treatment later."

There was no answer. Jonathan was certain that they were ignoring his advice.

No human or Taelon had told him so, but he had no doubt that Va'lon and Namor, in a strong push for human co-operation, were even now making their way into Casa Grande. He could see, as if in his imagination or memory, an image of them walking, and wondered suddenly if it came from the Urod. The pair of Taelons would be looking for Amanda, insisting on her compliance.

Gently and patiently their voices nagged the listening humans, strongly implying that they were now delaying takeoff and taking chances with the Urod, solely for her benefit.

"We are entering the main house on the ground floor, Jonathan," the seemingly imperturbable voice informed him.

"Then you'd better turn around and get the hell out! Your ship looks safe, get on it. If you come in here, at least stay clear of the windows!"

Still they were coming on, as implacable as baseball umpires, as tax collectors.

"We wish to help Amanda," Namor told him sweetly, "and I have undertaken her treatment. She is my patient, and I am responsible for her welfare. Therefore we are coming to convey her to safety."

"All right, we'll wait for you upstairs." He cut off the communicator, shut it off as thoroughly as he could, and looked at his wife. Where were they going to hide?

She was standing straight now, and had tucked away the pistol somewhere out of sight, and disconnected the oxygen tank. For the moment Amanda looked twenty years younger.

"What're we going to do, Johnny? You'd better make the decision, you're the lad who knows what's going on."

He had to fight back an irrational urge to laugh. "That's the trouble, Mandy. I know just enough to make the decisions awfully hard."

TWENTY-THREE

Jonathan's global was vibrating again, and he flipped it open. A call for help, from a face that he recognized as one of his workers on the estate, though he could not immediately fit it to a name.

In moments when it was possible to see and hear the worker's outcries through the jamming, bits of hard information came through, enough for Doors to conclude that several people had been hit.

In a brief exchange Doors tried to find out which room the wounded people were in. That was difficult, but he thought he had it narrowed down to the right hallway.

With any luck at all it would take the Taelons a couple of minutes, at least, to find their way to where Amanda was taking shelter. Again Jonathan urged his wife and his father to keep their heads down, and defend themselves as best they could, while he dashed away to try to give assistance to another person for whom he felt responsibility.

"You stay put," he told his wife as he snatched up his father's sturdy cane and headed for the door. "I've got other people to look after."

"Never mind us, what about you?" his wife snapped back.

Just as he was leaving the room, Jubal, pulling one fist sharply away from the other, miming a drawing gesture, silently reminded his son about the concealed sword blade in the cane.

"S'all right, son. Go on with what you have to do. We'll be all right."

"Right. Hang in there, Dad." And that was all the time that Jonathan could spare.

As soon as Jonathan was gone, Jubal suffered an attack of faintness. He moved shakily to a chair and more or less fell into it.

Amanda hobbled to his side. "Are you all right, Dad?"

"Just dizzy. It'll pass."

Looking closely at the old man. Amanda was afraid that he was going to pass out. Jubal was sunken deeply into the big chair, some kind of antique rocker, imported at great cost from God knew where. Jubal sat there feebly rocking, his eyes looking into some distance beyond what Amanda could see. Suddenly his whole body looked smaller than before.

Now she was the one who needed to sit down. And where was her spare oxygen?

Making his way down the hall, Jonathan breathed in a faint smell of smoke, something other than the ubiquitous stink of burnt explosive from fired cartridges. The smoke wasn't thick or bad, and right now a serious fire seemed to Jonathan only a minor possibility. Anyone who tried to burn this building down would find that it was quite a job.

Having reached the branch of hallway that he thought he wanted, Doors began looking into room after room, cautiously seeking the one from which the call had come. He supposed the whole thing might be a cunning ambush, some trick to draw him out of hiding. But when one of his people cried for help . . .

Instead of an ambush, he found genuine disaster, two of his workers in one room, both sprawled on the floor, one still and the other moaning, There was a fair amount of blood. From the way the men were dressed, he judged they were both on the housekeeping staff.

Hasty examination showed that one was stone dead, with a head wound.

The living, breathing victim was oozing blood from a leg wound and in a fair amount of pain, but Jonathan thought the prognosis was quite good. No bones broken, no major blood vessels torn. The wound had probably been caused by a ricochet, or a chunk of antique European rock that had been blasted loose from a window casement. But obviously this man would be of no use running messages or scouting. In fact, there was probably no use trying to move him at all.

"I got hit, Boss." And the man muttered a string of obscenities, which seemed to be his preferred way of expressing pain.

"I can see that," Doors agreed. "Looks like you're through for the day, but you'll be all right. Let me see what I can do about this bleeding." Tearing, sometimes using his pocketknife to cut, he converted part of a sheet that had been covering furniture into pieces of handy size. In another minute, he quickly got a passable pressure bandage in place.

"Any guns in here?" Jonathan queried, looking hopefully about. But there was nothing better than a sword-cane, nothing at all in fact. These two unlucky gobs of cannon-fodder had not so much as a peashooter between them.

Bandaging completed, Doors tried his global again. The jamming still reigned supreme, and he barely restrained himself from hurling the device across the room.

After a few more words to his wounded employee—he hoped they were inspiring—Doors started back as quickly as possible to the room where he had left Amanda and his father.

Every time he went through a doorway, or even passed one, he took a tight grip on Jubal's cane, half-expecting to encounter invading militiamen. But still it seemed that none had found their way into the house, or at least they had not reached this level.

But, to Jonathan's amazement, during the few minutes he'd been absent two Companions had somehow found their way to the suite he shared with Amanda—it was as if the

Taelon pair had threaded their way through the maze of rooms and corridors and stairs with an exact knowledge of where to look for her, though Jonathan was reasonably sure that none of his interstellar visitors had entered this part of the big house before. Va'lon, like his compatriots, had been utterly absorbed in dealing with the Urod, and had not been in to see his patient.

And a new suspicion rose: Had they tagged her with some kind of tracer, so they were aware of her location at all times?

The snake again. It could well be something in the damned half-rubber snake.

When Jonathan burst into the room, Amanda was standing between two Taelons. Va'lon was on one side of her chair, Namor on the other, as if they had just helped her to her feet. And in that moment Jonathan had the impression, with no direct evidence to back it up, that they were on the point of marching her away like a prisoner between them.

Jubal had pushed himself up out of the rocking chair, and was making some ineffective protest, to which the visitors appeared to be listening with every show of courtesy.

Jonathan moved quickly to Amanda's side, in the process deliberately bumping Va'lon, who made no resistance or objection. But the Taelon moved away from her no farther than he had actually been pushed.

"Johnny, you're all blood!"

Doors looked down at himself, brushed at his shirt. "None of it's mine." He made no apology for the collision.

Amanda pulled free from Namor, who made no serious effort to restrain her. She clung to Jonathan, while he argued with the two visitors from beyond the stars. The Companions continued to be calmly insistent that Amanda must be transported to their waiting ship.

"Her condition urgently requires it," Namor insisted. His strong, pale fingers danced briefly around the special marker on her rubber snake, as if he might be adjusting something.

Doors wondered how effective a weapon a suddenly drawn

sword blade would be against two Taelons. He decided that the chance of changing their minds by that means was very small—so was the chance of disposing of them both. He was not entirely abandoning the option, and still held the cane in his hand, but he would only fall back on it as a last desperate resort.

Urgently he protested, "There are bandits out there."

"Bandits?" The Taelon seemed politely puzzled.

"I mean these lunatic attackers, whoever the hell they are. She can't go out there now." And Amanda added her own vigorous objections.

"A path of safety will be created as necessary," Va'lon promised, the last word being almost drowned out by a renewed sound of firing. He and his confederate stood there calmly, apparently unarmed in this almost undefended fortress, unfazed by the noise of death, spasmodically hammering and ricocheting nearby. They looked like men supremely confident of their authority whenever they chose to exert it, and Jonathan had to envy them their coolness.

In spite of the fact that one of them was wounded now. A bullet from that latest burst, or more likely a fragment of stone blasted out of the window embrasure, had scored on the right cheek of Va'lon, who ignored the injury.

Doors found the sight reassuring, evidence that they were not immune to physical harm. The trickle of blood looked gray, in the moments when he could see it at all in the window's half-light, compounded of flickering muzzle flashes and failing electricity.

"Better have that taken care of," Doors admonished. Neither Companion took notice.

"Jonathan, we are all intensely concerned about Amanda's welfare," the uninjured Taelon assured him.

"Of course, of course. My wife and I understand your position on that. It's just that we're upset." *And now, it might be time to try sudden capitulation.* Jonathan Doors, pretending now to be in full agreement with the Companions, insisted that he could and would assist his wife to the ship without help from anyone else.

"All right, we can't just argue all day. We'll go to your shuttle. Amanda gets aboard, but I stay here. Looks like I've got a war to fight." *Two wars, actually, and they're both crowding in on me at once.* And even as he spoke he secretly gave Mandy's arm a gentle squeeze, knowing that she would read the message properly.

"It *is* vitally important, Jonathan," Namor chided loftily.

"All right, I'll take her down on the elevator." He gave Amanda a look that said: *Trust me, play along for now.*

"That'll be easier for me—don't try carrying me down the stairs!" Amanda objected, picking up her cue immediately. The tone of her voice threatened panic.

Both of the Companions were trying to say something, offering orders or advice, but their words were drowned out by fresh battle noise. It sounded like the fighting was getting worse, if anything, and the occasional stray bullet came in a window.

Jonathan tossed the cane back to his father—Jubal fumbled the catch, but no one seemed to notice the heavy, metal-weighted thump of its landing on the parquet floor. Then Jonathan bent slightly and easily lifted his wife. His arms were strong, their strength augmented at this moment by adrenalin, and as always he was touched by the almost-weightless feel of her thin body. Amanda's eyes were locked on his, her arms around his neck, oxygen bottle resting on her stomach.

Namor was starting to speak again, but Doors did not wait to listen. Without pausing he strode out of the room, into a hallway darker than it had been a minute ago—there must have been some further partial failure of electricity, and now it was barely possible to see where you were going. But in any case he knew the way, and he went on, bearing Amanda down the dark hall in the direction of the elevator.

Over his shoulder he called back, "There's only room for two. We'll meet you downstairs, Namor, Va'lon."

"Very well, Jonathan. We will join you on the ground floor." The Taelon voice that came floating after him was musically, insanely calm, with bullets rattling on the walls again. Being in sight of a window meant you were likely to be sprayed with dust, riddled with dangerous flying fragments of lead and stone.

He almost had to grope to find the elevator, but then the tiny cage appeared just a little beyond the place where he had expected it to be. As soon as the two of them were inside and the door closed, Jonathan, squinting in near darkness, felt to locate the button for the top floor, and pushed it hard. Fortunately all electrical power had not yet been shot out.

Or could this surge have some other source? Jonathan knew a sudden insight, that some physical, probably electric power was being supplied somehow by his new ally, the Urod. How that might be done was beyond his comprehension, but by now he felt confident of being able to recognize the touch of that inhuman mind.

Beside him, Amanda seemed to be enduring a partial experience of the same vision. "Johnny, what was that? I thought I saw something—like a ghost. But it must have been my imagination."

"Your imagination's getting a boost from someone. A friend, I hope—no, I won't call him that. But maybe at least a temporary ally."

Aged machinery clanked and groaned and rumbled; Doors thanked God that the power had not yet been entirely cut off. There was some kind of emergency system, he seemed to recall, relatively modern, connected to lights in a few key places, and also to a couple of other items. He could hope the latter included the elevator.

Should I be thanking the Urod too? But taking a gracious attitude toward it would not be easy, knowing everything he did about its taste in human minds.

"What are we doing, Johnny?" Now Amanda sounded more like her old self.

"Taking some evasive action." He spoke with his lips close to her ear, so she could hear him above the primitive elevator noise, and the sounds of Armageddon from outside. "You're *not* going offworld with them. Least of all are you ever getting on the same ship with the Urod. You'd be better off dying here and now."

"That bad."

"That bad. But I don't want an open break with the Taelons yet, if we can possibly avoid it. Humanity can't afford that yet. Mandy, I'm going to set you down here somewhere, and pull this damned thing right off your arm—if I can. I think they may be able to use it to track your location. Getting rid of it may hurt, but I have some reason to believe it won't cause you serious damage. Anyway, it's got to be done."

She sucked in breath and wheezed it out. "If that's what it takes," she agreed, lifting her decorated arm slightly, and holding her voice steady with an effort.

He set Amanda on her feet, leaning her slender body back against the wall inside the little elevator. "I think it does. The whole future of the planet depends on how we . . . damn it, now what?"

The immediate problem was easy enough to see; the elevator had ground to a halt at the wrong place, and they were now stuck between floors. If only that would serve to keep the Taelons from getting at them—but it was not a hope he wanted to rely on.

Before even trying to get out of the elevator, he decided that he would forcibly disconnect Amanda from the Taelon device. He struggled to remember as many details as he could of what his father had told him about the problems and effects of unhooking Esther Summerson from her half-living snake.

At one point his wife cried out uncontrollably in the darkness.

"I'm sorry, Mandy."

"Do what you—ahh!—do what you have to do."

Jonathan did.

The crude operation caused Amanda some pain, but she survived, and suffered no serious injury. Her arm showed no sign of damage afterward—one more confirming parallel with Jubal's tale.

When the half-living thing came loose, it writhed in his grip, and on the floor of the cage when he had cast it down.

Amanda gasped in horror.

But then suddenly the elevator car lurched on. The little light inside the cage stayed off, but the cage itself jerked upward.

"What's happening, Johnny?"

"We're getting power from somewhere. I think we've got an ally. They call it re-adaptation."

At last the machine ground to a stop with its open gate overlapping a floor. Grunting as he squeezed his body through the tight space, Doors managed to boost his wife ahead of him, her oxygen bottle bumping along, and then climb out himself.

But just as they were ready to move off down another dark hall, there was once more a faint hum of power in the machinery, and the elevator lurched up to a stop at the proper level.

Probably the Urod yet again, Doors thought. Doing what it can to help us now, because it senses we are the enemies of its enemies. Whatever the explanation, he took advantage of the fact.

Leaving the small writhing bundle of Taelon gadgetry in the elevator, he tried to send the car back down to the ground floor. When he pushed the button he held his breath, fearing the cage would not move, but then it lurched again, and as he jumped out, began to descend the narrow shaft. He could only hope the Taelons would be innocently waiting down there for Amanda to be brought to them.

Meanwhile, it was time to be moving on. Amanda could still walk, with the support of her husband's arm. All he knew for certain was that they were somewhere on an upper floor. Not in a tower, but on the fourth or fifth level—if there was a fifth floor, he couldn't remember—looking for sanctuary. He hoped he would recognize it when it came in sight.

They had now entered one of the extensive regions within Casa Grande that Doors had never visited. There were not many windows and not much light. Some of the walls were painted, some papered, some were paneled. Practically all the lights were out now, and he could find his way only by the uncertain illumination washing in from outside. There were strangely angled corridors, odd corners that concealed only niches and not rooms, in one place a smashed skylight. The moonless night outside the shattered glass was clear, but here was a splash of water, and the sound of rain . . . no, not real rain on this clear night, but some indoor flow from broken plumbing. For a moment he had suspected that the Urod was playing tricks once more.

Soon Jonathan realized that at least one of the water storage tanks, high up above the rest of the house in the twin towers, must have been punctured by bullets. A steady flood of moderate size was in progress, ruining a prize assortment of fine woodwork and yet another ancient tapestry. The businessman that lived in Doors came to the surface long enough to wonder if the expensive insurance he had been forced to carry on the place would pay for damage due to acts of war and rebellion.

Flood or no flood, what they needed was a hiding place. Now Jonathan once more wished heartily that while negotiating the purchase of San Simeon, he had somehow found the time to go through the whole house at least once. But the total time he had spent here amounted to no more than a few days, and by far the largest part of the interior of Casa Grande was still a mystery to him—he knew there were more than a hundred rooms, but he had hardly been in ten of them as yet.

Of course, any Taelons who came looking for him and Amanda tonight ought to be even less familiar with the layout of the place—unless for some reason they had drawn up a floor plan in 1936, and kept it handy. He wouldn't be too surprised if they had—they were meticulous bastards when they set out to be.

A tremor went through the thin body at his side. "I can't walk much farther, Johnny."

Again he scooped up Amanda in his arms. Then, twice in the next minute, they had to stop again to adjust her oxygen tube, regulate the flow. Not much point in finding a hiding place, if she was going to choke to death in the process.

"Maybe, if we can just keep out of their sight long enough—they'll give up and jump in their ship and go." *And if they absolutely need a human mind as bait to control the Urod, they'll kidnap someone else. Not her.*

Her lungs were gasping but her mind was active. "Would it save—would it prevent a war, if I did go with them?"

"What gave you that idea? It wouldn't save anything good, or prevent anything bad. But I'm afraid it would be the end of you."

"You're going to have to tell me more than that, lover. A lot of details of this mess need to be filled in. How can I tell you what to do next, unless I know what's going on?"

"Gladly, as soon as we have a moment. No, I guess as soon as we have an hour would be more like it. It's a great story, and at first you won't believe a word of it."

"Where are we going, Johnny?"

"Looking for a niche, some kind of cozy hiding place. If we can lie low for a while, I think they'll leave without us. For them, right now, dealing with the Urod has to come before anything else."

Slowly and awkwardly Doors carried his wife from room to room within Casa Grande, where many of the windows, as they now discovered, were set so high in the high walls that it was all but impossible to see anything but sky when you looked out.

That was reassuring, in a way; it also ought to be impossible for those outside to see in, or to pour in bullets with any actual target in view. It was almost as if Hearst's master architect Julia Morgan had designed the big house as a fortress, to withstand this kind of an assault. In fact most of the rounds fired from outside had little effect except to destroy some of the world's oldest and most expensive ceilings. Whatever this gang of apes thought they were doing, their only actual accomplishment so far, other than a few murders, seemed to be vandalism on a world-class scale.

As if the deranged humans outside had been tuning in on Jonathan's thoughts, one of them now let loose with some kind of military rocket launcher: A loud *whoosh* followed almost instantly by a punishing, vicious bang, striking the house wall near the top and not many yards away. What precise target the rocketeer thought he was aiming at Doors did not know, but at least he had not missed the side of Casa Grande. The deafening blast had punched a hole in the thick solid wall big enough for a man to jump through, sending a cloud of dust and debris drifting down the hallway and through the several rooms that opened onto it.

But if the attacker's intent had been to bring the entire building, or any substantial portion of it, down in ruins, he was doomed to disappointment. Julia Morgan and her long-suffering but well-paid construction crews had planned and built the core of their structure with California earthquakes constantly in mind.

An old system of floodlights that had once brightened the entire exterior of Casa Grande at night was still in place, but no longer regularly turned on. Much of it had been modernized and incorporated into the security system, and patches of bright lighting had come on automatically when the militia attack burst in. Still the system had somehow been partially disabled by the attackers, and some among them seemed to be making an effort to shoot out all the lights that they could see. Fortunately their aim was not much better than their talent for tactical planning.

Jonathan wanted to use his global again, but hesitated, suddenly concerned that the Taelons might use the signal to locate him, despite the jamming.

And again he was suspicious: Were they, and not the feckless militia, responsible for the interference?

Abruptly they came upon another dead body, near a window. A small hole in the forehead, just above the open eyes.

"Who's that, Johnny?"

"One of my security men." He swore viciously under his breath, and looked around, eagerly at first, for a nonexistent gun. It looked like the man hadn't even been armed. But of course it was possible that his weapon had fallen out the window when he fell.

"I'm sorry," Amanda gasped, almost as if it had been her fault. "Oh, it's so terrible, all this."

Doors mumbled something. There was no way as yet of even estimating total casualties, but he could see that they were going to be high. That made two of his own dead now, that he knew of—no, three. But later there would be time for numbers.

Putting together what he had seen and what his security people had told him, he could estimate that so far the faceless, ski-masked enemy seemed to be worse off—the body count on their side was actually higher. But Jonathan could draw only minor satisfaction from the fact. He could see no Taelon casualties, and he assumed that if there had been any, they had been taken aboard the shuttle, where at least they would probably be safe from further damage.

Suddenly the sound of the intermittent firing had changed, as if most of it were no longer directed at the building, and he inched his way to a window that happened to be set low enough to let him peer out.

At the moment small-arms fire went drumming like hail on the blue glowing body of the big Taelon machine, doing no damage at all that Doors could see. Now the fanatic with the rocket launcher at his shoulder, standing no more than about thirty yards from the glowing blue shape, hit it with a lance of fire that could probably have taken out a medium tank. The surface of the Taclon craft sent it spraying away like cheap fireworks, doing no apparent harm.

Doors winced at this evidence of the enemy's technical superiority. In the days and years ahead he was going to have to fight them, really fight them, and it was going to be a terrible thing.

His global buzzed. Carson, one of the security people, wanting to have another conference.

TWENTY-FOUR

Amanda was still armed with her pistol and ready to use it when the chance arose. Leaving her in a room on what seemed to be the highest level of the house between the towers, Doors descended one flight to meet face-to-face with a couple of his surviving fighters. Giving up any idea of trying to be crafty in the use of his global, Jonathan turned it on again. There might be some risk, but the alternative would be an invitation to disaster. Without some good means of communication he would effectively be blind and deaf in this strange building, unable even to tell how many of his people still survived.

One of the survivors now with him asked, "Anybody got any idea who these donkeys are?" The lanky man jerked his head toward the nearest window, indicating the attackers.

"There's one possibility." Doors quickly outlined the story of his run-in on the road to San Simeon with Colonel Shelby and his gang. "I don't know if this is the same bunch. Companions landing everywhere must have brought a lot of creatures out of the woodwork."

The other survivor was shorter, almost chubby. "How many are out there now?"

The best guess they could come close to agreeing on was that probably about twenty to thirty men were involved in the assault.

"Hard to tell, when everybody can fire a thousand rounds a minute."

"The way it sounds, they must've each got off about that much already. Unless they're packin' in ammo on muleback, reckon the shootin's soon gonna be slowing down."

"Good point. Try to stay alive till then."

"That is a big part of my career plan."

Each surviving defender could claim at least one or two confirmed kills. They said the attackers' bodies were still lying where they had fallen.

"That put a little crimp in 'em, I'd say."

"Think they'll pull back?"

Doors didn't bother trying to answer that one. "Anybody got a gun I can borrow?"

The lanky man looked apologetic. "Sorry, Boss, I'm down to one."

The other man, who seemed to be known as Shorty, had a spare, but he was out of cartridges for it. "I'd let you have this one, Boss, but . . ."

"Absolutely not. You people keep your weapons. You're a lot more efficient with them than I would be." Now that he was with these men, some details about them were coming back to him; they were both veterans of the recent war in the Middle East.

The noise of fireworks surged up again, and now, to judge by the volume of automatic weapons fire, they might have been under attack by an army. All of the attackers Jonathan had seen so far were wearing ski masks and camouflage clothing, with combat boots.

"Are any of them in the house yet?"

"I think they have to be. There's several places on the ground floor where they can just walk in."

There was some discussion as to whether the enemy had entered the grounds by road, or across country and over or through the fences.

"I'd bet on fences. Cutting their way through wire would be part of the fun."

"But we didn't realize there'd been an intrusion until—"

Doors cut short the debate. "Time enough later to figure out what went wrong. What I want to know now is, why aren't we getting any help?"

People in the house had been trying for over an hour to make contact with the local police, and the Highway Patrol. The jamming had evidently been pretty successful.

He had underestimated Shelby and his colleagues once, and didn't want to do it again. "They might have been smart enough to create some distractions, too. Stage more road-blocks, or another raid somewhere else. Draw the cops away first."

Shorty had lost his own global, and was looking at Jonathan's. "Try channel 39 on that thing yet, Boss? You've got to switch it over manually."

"Here. Show me how."

Results were inconclusive. The lanky man still had his own unit to play around with. "Keep at it," Jonathan ordered, clipping his global back on his belt. It would be great to re-establish contact with other survivors among his crew; he assumed there were a substantial number, most of them just keeping quiet, keeping their heads down. "I'm going upstairs again to check on my wife."

Doors left his colleagues and started to climb. There was a window on these stairs, and his attention was caught by a narrow, vertical streak of fire, come and gone in an instant, shooting straight up the side of Casa Grande. He stared for a moment before realizing what he had just seen. Evidently at least one of the attackers had come equipped with the latest in scaling devices, small rocket-launched weights and claws to carry their assault lines all the way to the top of the twin spires.

"Well," he muttered to himself, "forget about their pulling back."

Forget, also, about revising upward his estimate of their intelligence. Firing a scaling line did not seem the easiest or most sensible way to invade a building whose doors were probably all standing open.

And now the man who had fired the scaling rocket, or someone else, was coming up the line, climbing with an automatic weapon of some kind slung over his back. Doors thought he had probably been waiting years for a chance like this—tonight fortune granted him not only a chance to use his toy, but to demonstrate his strength of arm as well. Yippee. *Come in reach of me tonight, you thug, and I will show you strength of arm.*

Jonathan looked in briefly on Amanda, and was almost immediately off again. "Got to try to see what's happening," he told his wife. "I'll be on this floor, probably in one of the rooms along this hallway." Quite possibly staying in one place would maximize his chances of personal survival, but he would be damned if he was going to sit passively while there was a chance he might accomplish something.

"Don't forget me." She wasn't taking the possibility seriously. "They seem to be really trying to set the place on fire."

"Not likely I'll forget you, lover. Anyway, I doubt very much the whole thing is going to burn."

Closing the door on Mandy, he went out again. No fire on this floor, not that Jonathan could see, though there was certainly a smell of smoke, waxing and waning. He knew there were automatic sprinkler systems throughout the building, and hoped some of them had come into play locally. Mainly he was relying on the fact that most of the furnishings had been treated for fire resistance, and the shell of the building was concrete and rebar.

The electric power was entirely knocked out now, and the high towers were almost entirely in darkness. Doors still wondered what the man who had gone climbing there might be up to.

Fire smoldering somewhere, smoke in the dark air, and a

fitful electric sparking. Occasional gunfire still, and the trickle
of running water.

*There was an abrupt surge of mental power from the expiring
Urod, a warning of fresh danger, a last desperate psychic thrash-
ing.* . . .

Doors did not see the man fall or jump, but heard the
impact close behind him. It was a heavy thump, and Doors
spun around, ready with his hands, wishing momentarily that
he had not left the sword-cane with Jubal.

But the man who had just landed on the balcony was not
going to attack anyone. He was crumpled on the terraced balcony, down and out, quite possibly dead but still twitching,

Running out on the terrace, bending over the broken
body, Doors couldn't tell at first whether the hooded invader
had been shot, or had simply lost his grip and fallen. He supposed that plummeting thirty feet or so onto hard flagstone
might well have much the same effect as a well-placed bullet.

Then Jonathan suddenly wondered if the Urod had somehow knocked the fellow loose from his high perch. It might
not have been difficult. A startling image in the mind at precisely the wrong moment. The last necessary handgrip fading
into unreality, even as an expectant hand reached out to grasp
it . . .

Doors quickly unslung the automatic weapon from the
victim's back, and dodged back again into the deeper shadows.
At last he would be able to shoot back! But the gun was of a
type he hadn't seen before and could not name.

Looking out from there, he spotted militia figures running
across the plaza, and was considering whether to try to shoot
the next one he saw, when there rose a more immediate danger, right in the house, on the same level.

Jonathan aimed from the hip and pressed the trigger.

Nothing happened. Hastily he retreated a step, seeking
the shelter of darkness.

Jonathan's intended victim had not seen him yet, and did
not aim or fire. In another moment he had moved away, out of

Jonathan's sight. If the invader kept going in that direction, Amanda should be safe from him.

Studying the unfamiliar weapon as best he could in the poor light, Doors couldn't be sure at first if there was some safety to be released. Then he realized that the fall had probably jammed the mechanism anyway. Or perhaps he owed the Urod one more debt of gratitude, for disabling the weapon when it was still in the enemy's hands.

Frustrated, Doors hurried back to the dead militiaman and searched the body, looking for some other weapon, maybe a holstered pistol, even a hunting knife, anything in the way of armament. He had one brief joyful moment when he came up with a pistol, but when he pulled out the magazine he found that it was empty. Not even a single round remained in the chamber.

Cursing, Jonathan realized that the attackers were probably all in the same boat with the defenders, on the verge of running out of ammunition—given the amount the invaders had expended in the early minutes of the battle, it could hardly be otherwise.

The global on Jonathan's belt was buzzing.

This time the face on the little screen was Jubal's, and he was jubilant at having got through at last.

"Got the Highway Patrol on for you, Johnny!"

Moments later, Doors was talking to a uniform.

"This is Jonathan Doors, at the Castle. We are under heavy attack here, and at least half a dozen people have been killed. Some of my people and I are still holding out in Casa Grande."

"We read you, sir. People have seen the fireworks, and we've had troopers trying to get to you for an hour now. They're being held up en route."

Jonathan went back to visit his wife in the nearby room where he had left her, and eagerly reported to Amanda his recent success in communication.

Having locked themselves in, they cautiously approached a window and looked out together. Amanda clutched his arm. "Look! Down there on the road!"

No doubt about it, there was a string of approaching headlights on the distant coastal road, and another, closer, on the long, winding drive ascending from the highway. They were coming closer at high speed.

Then, even as Doors watched, the distant flickering and flaring of small-arms fire. Headlights went out, or slewed sideways and stopped. It seemed the enemy had not yet used up all their ammunition.

And meanwhile, all this time, like background music of a particularly ugly style, running through his mind, Jonathan could still intermittently sense the struggling Urod.

His perception of it became somewhat clearer the more the contact was repeated and prolonged. A monstrous being trapped in the snares of its enemies, surrounded now by layers and meshes of metal, strange composite materials, and pure force, who even after being loaded on the ship, kept fighting to escape.

But the energies that gave the Urod its strange life were fading and failing, and Doors got the distinct impression that the creature's chances of breaking loose again were, at the moment, pitifully small. But it was still giving the Taelons as much as they could handle, distracting them, preventing them from watching the humans as closely as they might have otherwise.

The lanky security agent, Carson, called in again. No sir, he wasn't hit, nor was Shorty as far as he knew. But he, Carson, had a problem and needed some kind of help.

Doors went to see what was the matter.

He found Carson crouching in a closet, wondering if he was going mad. The combat veteran had put down his weapon and was clutching his head with both hands.

"God, Mr. Doors, what have they done, shot the house full of some kind of gas? I'm—I'm having visions—hearing things—"

"I doubt poison gas has anything to do with it. Probably not the militia at all, just some of the bad dreams that we were promised earlier. I can feel it too, if that's any comfort." *And how I can feel it.* "I guess the difference is, I've worked into it gradually, sort of, and I know what it is."

Carson looked marginally relieved. "But what can we do?"

"Hang in there and it'll go away." Doors tried to sound much more confident than he felt. "I close my eyes—just for a moment—and think of something else. Most of the time it works."

"What *is* the damned thing, Boss?"

"See me later and I'll tell you all I know, which isn't much." *And you will be a rich man, and so will all my other workers who have made it through this night with me. But we won't even talk about that now.*

The Urod's ongoing struggle was invisible to human eyes, but it was not without profound effect on human minds. Doors was sufficiently familiar with it that he thought he could chart the creature's progress toward oblivion. No doubt some of the other humans in the vicinity could do the same.

By now all the survivors of Casa Grande must know that staying awake was not always protection against bad dreams.

If the defenders were partially disabled by the mental effects produced, the attackers were no better off, also suffering the mental strains and delusions inflicted by the Urod. Doors saw a man run wildly across the plaza, spraying bullets into the air at nothing.

The Urod effect was probably the reason no coherent effort to occupy and search the building had yet begun.

Jonathan rejoined his wife. The room they were in contained some heavy furniture, a bureau and two massive chairs, and he began to tug and shift these pieces, creating a hiding place for Mandy, what he could hope would be a sanctuary. The fear and suspicion engendered by his father's story had gradually hardened into a practical certainty: What the dear Companions meant to do with his wife would mean her death, or possibly some fate that was genuinely worse than death—and now, at a time when anything that might happen to her could probably be blamed on the militia attack, it would be easier than ever for them to get away with it.

Jonathan had already torn her loose from their damned machine, and when a chance came he was going to get her away from here somehow, no matter what the risk. . . .

Danger loomed, worse than that from some fanatic's bullets. Two Taelons, Amanda's would-be kidnappers, were back in the building—if they had ever left it. Doors could hear their familiar, tireless, patient footsteps on the stairs.

The image of their approach came from the Urod—and Jonathan feared that he could expect no further help from his peculiar sometime ally—the Urod was now in the last stages of being finally, permanently, squelched.

Jonathan decided not to lock the door. If he left it open, maybe they could hide. Putting his lips against his wife's ear, he drew her back behind the heavy furniture, and whispered, "Not a sound. This time we won't be able to talk them out of it."

He could hear the Taelons coming down the hall, looking into one room after another. The first gray brightening of morning light, hazing the atmosphere outside the shattered windows, showed him the two tall figures, now actually entering the room. Va'lon's cheek was marked by a fresh scar.

298 GENE RODDENBERRY'S EARTH: FINAL CONFLICT

Doors pressed Amanda's slim form back behind the furniture, deeper into the shadows.

Va'lon's voice was clear and quiet, easy to understand despite the uproar. The fine tones of a great actor, maybe Richard Burton.

"Jonathan? Amanda? The way to our ship is open now, and it is safe."

Lying motionless, peering out between the bureau and a chair, Doors could see that one of them was carrying the same rubbery Siamese snake, or maybe its twin, that Jonathan had so recently and violently disconnected from Amanda's arm.

Jonathan pressed his wife more firmly than ever back into the niche where they were sheltering. Silently the pressure of his grip communicated: *Don't talk. Don't even breathe.*

Turning his eyes toward Amanda, he saw that she had her pistol drawn in her right hand.

In some distant portion of the great house alarms abruptly started ringing, buzzing, evidently powered by emergency batteries. Just a little late. He prayed that the sound would be enough to drown out Amanda's wheezing. Was Taelon hearing especially acute, more so than that of earthly humans? He had no way to know.

The sounds of fighting had largely died away, though there still came an occasional explosion of gunfire. There had been temporary lulls before, and probably this one was only temporary too.

The Taelons were still in the room. A clear and pleasant voice called out in cheerful tones. "Jonathan? Amanda? Come out! The way is clear, but we can wait no longer. The attacking humans will be here soon."

And the two tall, blue-clad forms fluted at each other in their own tongue. There was challenge and anger in the stance of their bodies and the tone of their voices.

But evidently they had decided not to search in every nook and cranny, but to move on to other rooms. One shook his head, and in a very human gesture probed his own ears with his fingers, as if trying to clear them. Suddenly Jonathan realized that the Urod was not yet vanquished altogether, the Taelon minds and senses were still suffering the effects of the long struggle.

Jonathan and Amanda remained in hiding until the Taelon pair had moved on. Despite the tones of calm and patience in the Companions' musical voices, Doors could see and hear that they were under a strain, and they were in a hurry.

Looking at Amanda's face, Jonathan saw that she was silently, grimly marveling at the decisions he was making, at the risks he was willing to take to keep her out of their control. He saw the urgent questions growing in her eyes. . . .

The two prowling Taelons were comparatively distant now, round several angles of hallway, and Jonathan thought that he could risk a whisper, barely audible.

"How're you doing, Mandy?"

Her response was no louder. "I think I feel better than I have any right to feel. Better this than . . ." She didn't finish. Instead she added, "I hope your dad's all right."

"I think he is. I talked to him on the global. . . . I think the visitors are going downstairs again."

Yes, the pair of Taelons were descending, he could hear the feet.

Moments after the two companions had moved on, the two humans heard heavier footsteps, and Jonathan knew they were made by the combat boots of the militia.

Then a few more gunshots hammered the early morning air, the first in some time, and frighteningly loud, sounding as if they came from just down the hallway. Someone was not yet entirely out of ammo. The only attackers with any cartridges left were those who had rationed their use early. The more dangerous among them, armed with at least half a brain apiece.

And now the sound of a single pair of combat boots, approaching.

Suddenly something was wrong with Mandy's oxygen, and she was gasping, loud enough to be heard well down the hall. Doors scrambled out from behind the furniture, and just managed to close the room's door and turn the latch, before he saw another pair of boots descending at the window, followed by camouflage pants. A man coming down a line. They must now be swarming over the house like ants.

The boots in the hall had stopped at the door. Jonathan pressed his body back against the wall, so he would be behind the door when it was broken open. And he waited.

TWENTY-FIVE

Sunrise could not be far away, and the lightening sky was hazing the atmosphere.

The smoldering treasures in distant portions of the house were flavoring the air with a rich campfire smell.

A blast of gunfire, louder than any yet, and a single human attacker, hooded and unidentifiable, came in through the door, having just shot the room's heavy oak door into splinters around the lock.

Whoever squandered bullets on this door might have reason to think the target he really wanted was behind it. Possibilities raced through Jonathan's brain. The gunman might be after Doors personally—a number of people usually were—and had seen him enter this room. Or, the shooter had just seen the two Taelons come out. And it was possible that the Urod, or the phantoms that the Urod evoked in human minds, had something to do with the attacker's choice.

Whether the simultaneous appearance of the man at the window was by accident or plan made little practical difference. If there was a plan it was not well executed, for the man in the doorway fired another wild burst as he came in, very nearly killing his colleague, who somehow escaped the bullets.

Jonathan, springing out from behind the door, hurled himself at the intruding gunman, and caught him from behind.

He heard the man's breath go out of him in an astonished *whuff* when they both hit the floor with Doors on top. He could hear himself moaning, screaming, a high, thin sound of pent-up rage, and he knew a savage satisfaction at having come solidly to grips with one of his enemies at last.

Doors was sitting astride his first victim and pounding the man's masked head on the floor, when the second one, now having kicked his way in through the window's broken glass, tried to aim his weapon, thought better of it with his colleague in the line of fire, and decided to kick Doors instead. The first swing of his boot almost missed, and Doors felt it go scraping up the side of his face, doing minor damage.

The man drew back his leg and tried again. On the second try Doors caught the booted foot in his two hands and twisted. The standing man made a strange sound and went down flat on his back.

Rage still coursed through Jonathan's muscles, multiplying strength. Abandoning the stunned body of his original victim, he launched himself at the second one.

The two rolled over and over, bumping into the heavy furniture behind which Amanda sheltered out of sight and tried to breathe. Small antique tables went crashing into splinters, and small objects that might have been priceless fragile ceramics joined the ruin.

All Jonathan had was his two hands and feet, and whatever other objects came within his reach. He put all of these to good use. The attackers were much younger than he, and there were two of them, but his fury more than made up the difference. He kicked his enemies, struck with knees and elbows.

Jonathan and the man who had entered by the door were both on their feet again, Doors driving his opponent back against the wall with savage blows. And when the man went down, Doors fell on him and beat some more.

And now Doors was once more standing upright, gripping in each hand the sturdy collar of a different camouflage suit.

With murderous glee he banged two hooded heads together. The sound pleased him so much that he tried it again.

Then he could relax his grip, let two heavy burdens fall to the floor.

In the struggle the hood had been torn from the head of his first victim, and Jonathan, looking down, saw Colonel Shelby's mustache.

The man who had come in at the window seemed to be beyond words. But Colonel Shelby was still conscious and he could still talk.

The colonel's body, his face, even his mustache looked smaller now. His voice was weak. "Was expecting... Taelons... in here. This room."

Doors let himself sit down at last. He sat down hard on the floor, but still found breath enough to call Shelby a filthy name.

The colonel seemed to be past caring about that. "Why... you attack me?"

Jonathan's voice grew louder. At the moment he did not care who heard him. "Why do you think, you bloody moron? You've been trying to shoot me to death for the past five hours."

"Saw... more Taelons come down. Land here. We saw their big machines."

The light in the room was growing incrementally brighter by the moment. From somewhere on the far side, behind the heavy furniture, Doors could hear the sound of Amanda's gasping breath, faint but reasonably steady—thank God, that with all the shooting she hadn't been hit, and he would go to her in a moment.

But there was one more item of business he needed to settle first.

It seemed likely that Shelby's mind was wandering inside his battered skull, for only now did he seem to realize the identity of his opponent. For some reason he found it deeply unsatisfactory. "Doors? You got free? Thought you might be hostage. We saw them bringing in . . . what looked like tanks. . . ."

"Is that what you thought they were? You've been right on only one thing, Shelby, and that wasn't it."

Shelby wasn't listening. He had started up a new litany of complaints about the Taelons. The real problem, causing all the others, was that they were just not human.

Doors tried to cut him short. "Yes, I know all that. I said you were right about one thing."

And not only were Shelby's alien opponents inhuman, they just weren't fighting fair. ". . . can't destroy them . . . we hit one ship with a rocket. . . ."

"Yeah, I know that too. I saw it. How does it feel, Colonel, to be an utter failure?" He jerked the man around, turning him roughly over, looking in his fatigue pockets, feeling at his belt. "Now, where's your global?"

"What?"

"Your communicator. How do you pass on orders to your men? You're going to order them to call off this damned attack."

Doors continued his rough search of Shelby, seeking some kind of communicator—it took him a moment to attribute the object he actually found to some spasmodic effort by the Urod.

The only item now hooked to Shelby's belt was a tiny miniature replica of a Urod statue, in dark heavy stone.

Shelby babbled on about it for a while. He and his men, watching from concealment before attacking, had seen the loading of the Urod, or part of the process, but it hadn't really meant much to them. Just more evidence that the place was swarming with aliens.

". . . one of those statues . . . probably priceless . . . by rights belonged to humanity . . ."

Doors interrupted. "Why the hell were you trying to kill us all?"

The colonel stirred. "I thought . . ."

"I doubt that, but it's possible. What do you think you thought?"

"Taelons . . . were probably holding you hostage."

Doors only looked at him.

Shelby was shaking his head. In the gradually growing light the bruises and swellings on his face were becoming visible, and he seemed to have lost two front teeth as well. Behind the damage he looked infinitely saddened. "Some of my people said . . . you were with the Taelons all along. I said, no. The Jonathan Doors I talked to wouldn't do that."

"You clowns haven't given me much choice."

Jonathan sat back on his heels, regarding his latest victim solemnly. *If, as now seems inevitable, I am really going to organize an underground war against the Taelons, many of those most eager to join me will be a lot like this man.* The prospect was not a pleasant one, but Doors could swallow it if he had to.

All gunfire had now ceased, but a faint sound of a different kind broke through his awareness. Amanda, still behind her barricade on the far side of the room, was trying to call his name. But her voice was so weak that he could barely hear it.

Scrambling quickly to her side, Doors saw that that burst of fire, when Shelby came barging in the door, had claimed a victim after all. There was a growing pool of blood.

"Mandy. *Mandy—!*"

Over the next half minute Jonathan Doors had to watch and listen while his wife gasped out her last rattling, dying breaths.

Amanda did her best to speak to him once more.

"You never did tell me what the Taelons . . . why . . ."

"Oh God. Oh God, Mandy, no I never did."

Jonathan was ready to tell her now, tell her all and everything, but her ears could no longer hear him, her eyes no longer see. He cradled Mandy helplessly, rocking her dead body back and forth. No need now for oxygen, no problems now with breathing. Her spirit no longer needed air, but she was gone from him. A pang, an agony of grief. But even at the worst moment, an undercurrent of something like relief: Better this, even this, than knowing she had been carried away to be used up in some experiment, or displayed as a specimen.

Everything was silent now, outside the house and inside, except for the distant, mad, useless continuation of alarms. He sat there, listening to them, while the California morning brightened beautifully around him, promising actual sunrise soon.

From the corner of his eye he caught a swift and silent movement of blue-white, well outside the window—the Taelon shuttle, lifting off. The removal of the Urod was at last being successfully accomplished.

Presently he realized that Shelby still breathed, was calling him by name.

Jonathan got to his feet and went back across the room, and stood there looking down at the colonel.

"Disappointed in you, Doors." Shelby was evidently profoundly disturbed at having to abandon his belief that Doors had somehow been held hostage by the Taelons. To think that would be much easier than admitting to himself that Doors had made an utter fool of him, back at the roadblock.

"Are you? Try this for disappointment," said Doors quietly, and lifted Shelby by the front of his combat fatigues, and banged his head with brutal force against the corner of the exquisitely designed stone fireplace. Again. And then once more.

Doors let the dead man drop from his bloody hands, and stood there swaying. Still his rage rose up and up.

I could have saved her, if we hadn't been forced to hide out from the Taelons. I could have saved her, kept her with me, and then next year, or the year after that, we earth-humans could have found a real cure for her disease . . .

Gladly will I portion out a good share of the blame to the mad-man who actually shot her. Doors glanced at the inert body beside the fireplace. *And he's paid for that. And I must bear some guilt myself.* He could feel that load already on his back, and he knew he would be carrying it for the rest of his life.

But the true blame, the main guilt, lies with the lying Taelons. With the dear Companions, their hands that look so pale and clean all soaked in secret, invisible blood.

Not that I will ever tell them that. No, I will never openly accuse sweet helpful Da'an and the others of anything at all.

Of course, had the Companions really been trying to help, I would have co-operated with them and they could have saved her.

Now the first lance of direct sunlight came striking in at the tall towers of Casa Grande, from over the inland hills. Now Doors could hear firm steady sirens in the distance. Soon law and order would have reestablished their claim along the California coast.

One of the first state troopers to come prowling, gun in hand, through the scorched and pock-marked halls of Casa Grande found him still sitting at Amanda's side, holding her hand. Some of the blood was Jonathan's, for his knuckles on both hands were badly torn. Jonathan's lips kept moving, as if he were saying something, over and over.

When the trooper had shaken him by the shoulder several times, Doors suddenly stood up.

With a vague sense of shock he realized that he had forgotten about his father for several minutes. At the thought of Jubal, something in him stirred to life again.

"Dad? Dad!"

But Jubal was not here, in the suite of rooms where Mandy and her murderers had died. Of course, they had left him back in the other room.

Jonathan went out of the room at a stumbling run, down

the shot-up hallway to that other room. He realized that it would even be a relief to find the old man dead. Better a bullet, better sudden heart failure, than . . .

The old man was not there, neither in spirit nor in body. And at once Jonathan felt certain, with a sudden new sinking of his heart, that Jubal had been taken aboard the Taelon ship.

Doors stood in the doorway looking, for once unable to think or plan.

He stood there for some time, seeing only the emptiness, before his eyes registered the fact that the wooden cane was lying on the parquet floor. An old man would have no need of a cane to help him walk, not if he had fainted. Not if an old man had somehow been put to sleep, and strong arms were carrying him away.

Jonathan saw that the sword had been drawn from the cane at last, but there was no blood on the blade, which had not been sheathed again. The cane lay in two parts on the fine floor, an elegant irrelevancy.

AFTERMATH

Final confirmation of Jonathan's worst fear did not come until some hours later. An ongoing, fruitless search of the Enchanted Hill, by police and mobilized National Guard, was suddenly called off when a message from the Companions informed the local authorities that Jubal's body was being brought back on a Taelon shuttle.

One of Jonathan's employees, following orders, woke him from an exhausted sleep to tell him that the final word had now come in regarding his father.

Jonathan roused himself somehow and stumbled from his bed to watch, as the shuttle landed peacefully right on the plaza in front of Casa Grande—there was no longer any need to worry about disturbing any nearby and nonhuman presence. The actual spot of landing was not far from the dried-up fountain where three dark stone statues still remained.

Presently Da'an emerged from the shuttle, politely evading questions from police—the media swarms were still being kept at bay—and advanced until he was standing directly in front of Jonathan Doors.

"I offer my deepest sympathy in your separation from Amanda, Jonathan."

"Thank you."

"And now, I regret, I bring news that will add to your burden of loss." Moments later, the Taelon representative to North America regretfully and formally informed Jonathan

Doors that his father had died of a heart attack, aboard a Taelon vessel, despite all that Taelon science had been able to do for him.

"I see." Jonathan's face and voice were wooden, as if with great fatigue. "How did he—?"

"How did he come to be aboard? There is a simple explanation. Va'lon and I discovered him wandering in one of the hallways of Casa Grande, in obvious distress. The fighting was then still in progress, and you were unavailable. . . ."

"Yes. I see."

"Also, we dared not delay the transportation of the Urod any longer. So in the circumstances the best thing we could do for Jubal was to bring him with us. . . ."

"Yes. I understand."

Jonathan asked that the body be brought off the shuttle as soon as possible, before the media vultures descended on the place in force. Their copters were wheeling in the air now, pushing the envelope of police restrictions, ignoring signaled warnings, edging and circling hungrily ever closer to the restricted airspace law enforcement had imposed over the compound.

When the cart with his father's body on it was rolled in a dignified progress down the ramp, Jonathan thought the vehicle probably looked much like that older one, that Jubal had called a gurney, and on which he had once wheeled Esther Summerson the movie star, trying to save her life.

Jubal was lying on his back, his body uncovered except for the nightshirt and slippers he had still been wearing when he died. His face in death looked peaceful. His hands, when Jonathan touched them, were cold and beginning to stiffen. Jonathan could detect no visible sign that any of his father's nightmares dating from 1936 had overtaken him at last. But then he supposed that the Companions were quite capable of molding any dead human face—or probably any live one, for that matter—into any expression they wanted it to wear, assuming they had any interest in the matter at all.

Doors had his father's remains brought into the house, where at least the vultures soon to be circling above would be unable to feast on the old man with their ever-hungry cameras.

Va'lon and Namor, neither of whom seemed to have gone on the ship carrying the Urod away, came to offer their personal condolences, and to convey the regrets of the entire Synod for the great personal loss that he had suffered in the deaths of his wife and his father.

Again they sought to reassure him that in the case of Jubal they had done everything medically possible.

"I'm sure you did," he readily agreed.

"We hope also that you will derive comfort from considering that Amanda and Jubal have moved on to the next level."

Doors thanked them graciously. His years of experience enabled him to do that. His voice sounded perfectly sincere when he thanked all the Taelons who had come to earth for all that they had done for humanity, and all they had tried to do.

The Companions were plainly relieved that he was taking his compound loss so well, and that he showed no tendency to hold them in any way responsible. "We hope you will soon feel well enough for an extended conversation, Jonathan. There are many things we have to talk about."

"There are indeed."

And as far as human science could tell, it was perfectly true that his father had died of a heart attack.

Before the new day was over, Jonathan had ordered a secret private autopsy. There was no sign of foul play. Just eighty-plus years of active life, and then a quick and peaceful, natural death—not a bad bargain to be made with fate. Not if that was all there really was to it.

But Jonathan could not believe it for a moment.

To be the chicken for the alligator's jaws . . .

Some people thought, and continued to think, that old Jubal had just died in Jonathan's arms, overcome by fear and shock in the course of the gun battle.

Standing over the body, before the autopsy, Doors marveled at how physically small his father suddenly seemed. And he made a solemn pledge to the dead: *I won't forget what you told me, Dad. Sorry I ever doubted you.*

Dr. Kimura came hobbling on crutches to offer her sympathy. She had been wounded in the leg early in the fighting, and had lain for hours in great pain, unable to reach her patient. Doors tried to reassure her, told her his appreciation of all that she had done.

Several of the nurses came by too. They had not been able to enter the estate until this morning. And after them, housekeeping people.

"We're so sorry, Chief. She was such a marvelous woman . . ."

"Yes. Yes, she was. Thank you."

Whoever survived among the security force came also to offer their condolences. And others from the staff of San Simeon, and from his personal staff.

Doors made a point that very day of visiting the badly wounded among his own people in a nearby hospital, of asking them if there was anything they needed, anything he could do. For one he arranged to pay off a house mortgage, for another to finance medical care for a relative.

By late afternoon, San Simeon was swarming with all kinds of law enforcement, police vehicles everywhere. Media helicopters were in the air, vultures as thick as butterflies right over the castle now, and for miles up and down the coast. Grief counselors, smelling blood and television coverage, were doubtless on their way from all around the nation. Doors and his security staff were being given worldwide credit for their heroic rearguard defense that had enabled several Taelons to escape assassination. So far no news regarding the Urod had leaked out.

And Jonathan Doors finally received a communication from his son, Joshua, who at the moment was en route to California from New York. Amanda's son was of course coming to her funeral. And it would be unnatural if he did not, under the circumstances, have at least a brief face-to-face meeting with his father.

The small image of Joshua's face on the little screen was hard for his father to read, as always. But if the image had been ten feet high, the father would have found it no easier.

Josh said, "I was trying to reach you last night, but somehow I couldn't get through."

This is my son, thought Jonathan Doors. *I truly wish that I had something honest and real to say to my son now.* He gave the matter thought, but the best he could come up with was, "There was a lot of communication failure here last night."

Josh perhaps picked up something in his voice; or maybe the lawyer was only being logical. "Dad, do you blame the Taelons for this?"

"Absolutely not." Jonathan glanced down briefly at the white knuckles of his own fist; he felt confident that nothing showed in his face or voice. Josh would not detect the lie. Jonathan had already answered the same question twenty times for the media.

Now he said, "The Companions were trying to help us out—but they had their own problems. Josh, there'll be a joint funeral service for your mother, and your grandfather, and for several of my people who were killed last night. I'm making the arrangements now."

He was gazing at the modest fountain and its little artificial pool, decorated by three harmless black basalt statues. He kept looking back, half-expecting that at any moment the fourth one might reappear. He didn't really expect that, but after all that had happened he couldn't rule it out. What would he do then? Probably try to make a deal with the Urod, somehow, against their common foe.

But that seemed a remote chance indeed.

"Son, the Companions did all they could to help her, and your grandfather too. And so did I, right up to the end. That's about all I can tell you at the moment."

Doors had on his polite and friendly mask; it was a kind of performance for which business, as conducted at the billionaire level, was excellent training.

On the surface, Jonathan Doors remained on good terms with the Companions, and in fact had taken a widely publicized position as one of their chief supporters. He had already agreed in principle to make a series of public appearances with Da'an.

But in fact Doors had now become the Companions' implacable enemy. In his private thoughts he was laying out plans for the underground organization he would create to fight them. It had already occurred to him that one important step in the process might be the counterfeiting of his own death.

And time passed.

The gun battle on the Enchanted Hill and its approaches, which for days dominated the news of the world on every continent, had left Jonathan Doors with not a shred of concrete evidence of Taelon wrongdoing to show the world. No use in making Jubal's story public when he had nothing to support it. Any attempt Jonathan might make now to denounce the Companions, to organize popular opinion against them, would doubtless bring out the fact that he had refused their offer to get Amanda out of Casa Grande, only moments before her death. What would his credibility be then?

Quite a few of Shelby's militia gang were dead, others under arrest. But about half of them had escaped, or fled before the police arrived in force, and those were still being hunted through the hills. *Maybe I will see some of them again,* thought Jonathan Doors. *Maybe some of those very men will be working for me, next time. Enlisted in my private, secret army, because that's what I'm going to need. I will use any tool that comes within my reach, to destroy the Taelon power. And I will provide those who follow me with infinitely better leadership than Shelby did.*

Doors considered that Shelby and his crew had been dead wrong, not only in their choice of tactics but in their strategy as well. In the early years of the twenty-first century, any straightforward warfare by earthly humans against an enemy as powerful and technically advanced as the Companions would be doomed to failure. The intruders, though they preferred subtlety and could usually afford to indulge their preference, were not only strong enough to defeat any armed counterattack that our backward race could put up; they were almost strong enough to ignore it.

The best con men in the universe, Jubal had called them. *Dad, how right you were.*

Open rebellion against the subtle conquerors of earth could not possibly succeed, not yet or for some years to come.

But there were other ways.

Jonathan Doors, his gaze following yet another departing Taelon shuttle up into the sky, thought: *They killed you, Mandy. They killed you, Dad. They've taken from me everyone who really mattered, destroyed the center of my life. And for all their crimes, I am going to make them pay.*

I will make them pay.

ABOUT THE AUTHOR

FRED SABERHAGEN is the author of over three dozen popular science-fiction and fantasy novels, including the *Swords* books and the *Berserker*® series. He lives in Albuquerque, New Mexico.